D1263867

Aldous Huxley

Unabridged and Unadapted From the Original Text

And With Fourteen Related Readings

E·V·E·R·B·I·N·D
ANTHOLOGIES
LODI, NEW JERSEY

Dedication

The Everbind Anthology series is dedicated to the memory of Mr. Mike Penn, founder of the Everbind/Marco Book Company, and to his forty years of perseverance, dedication to his customers, loyalty to his employees, and old-fashioned work ethic. When Mike began the company he was also a full-time teacher, but despite the many hours he devoted to his teaching and to building the company, he always found time for his family which was profoundly important to him. He will be greatly missed. –Stewart Penn

Acknowledgement

Carol Gladstone, Ph.D., Manhattanville College.
Consulting Editor for Related Readings.

Credits

Photograph of Aldous Huxley, circa 1925 by permission of Hulton Archive.
Brave New World by Aldous Huxley. Reprinted by permission of HarperCollins Publishers Inc. All rights reserved.
"The Politics of Stem Cell Research" by Jeffrey P. Kahn, Ph.D., M.P.H.
"Baby It's You! And You, and You..." © 2001 Time Inc. Reprinted by permission.
"Chapter 3 from Brave New World Revisited" by Aldous Huxley. Copyright © 1958 by Aldous Huxley.
Reprinted by permission of HarperCollins Publishers Inc.
"Subliminal Advertising" by Dr. John Leckenby.
"Current Issues About Drug Use" from www.theantidrug.com, and www.drugabuse.gov, retrieved May 7, 2006.
"Spring Break Study Brings 'Startling' Results" by Bharath M. Josiam, Ph.D., and George L. Smeaton, Ph.D., Stout Outlook.
"All Summer in a Day" by Ray Bradbury. Reprinted by permission of Don Congdon Associates, Inc. Copyright © 1954, renewed 1982 by Ray Bradbury.
"Relationships Can Be Lived on a Real Basis" from ON BECOMING A PERSON by Carl. R. Rogers. Copyright © 1961 by Carl R. Rogers, renewed 1989 by David E. Rogers and Natalie Rogers.
Reprinted by permission of Houghton Mifflin Company. All rights reserved.
"Harrison Bergeron" from WELCOME TO THE MONKEY HOUSE by Kurt Vonnegut, Jr., Copyright © 1961 by Kurt Vonnegut, Jr. Used by permission of Dell Publishing, a division of Random House, Inc.
Excerpt from ON DEATH AND DYING. Reprinted with the permission of Scribner, an imprint of Simon & Shuster Adult Publishing Group, fom ON DEATH AND DYING by Dr. Elisabeth Kübler-Ross. Copyright © 1969 by Elisabeth Kübler-Ross; copyright renewed © 1997 by Elisabeth Kübler-Ross.
"The Eye of the Beholder" Episode 42 from THE TWILIGHT ZONE by Rod Serling, November 11, 1960.
"Where Do Babies Come From?" Copyright © 2002 Sara Corbett. Distributed by The New York Times Special Features/Syndication Sales.
"The Packaged Soul?" from THE HIDDEN PERSUADERS by Vance Packard, © 1957. By permission of his estate.

Copyright

Library of Congress Control Number 2002110852
ISBN 0-9710756-9-7

Table of Contents

Aldous Huxley   **1894-1963**

Brave New World

by Aldous Huxley

Unabridged and Unadapted From the Original Text

Foreword

Chronic remorse, as all the moralists are agreed, is a most undesirable sentiment. If you have behaved badly, repent, make what amends you can and address yourself to the task of behaving better next time. On no account brood over your wrong-doing. Rolling in the muck is not the best way of getting clean.

Art also has its morality, and many of the rules of this morality are the same as, or at least analogous to, the rules of ordinary ethics. Remorse, for example, is as undesirable in relation to our bad art as it is in relation to our bad behaviour. The badness should be hunted out, acknowledged and, if possible, avoided in the future. To pore over the literary shortcomings of twenty years ago, to attempt to patch a faulty work into the perfection it missed at its first execution, to spend one's middle age in trying to mend the artistic sins committed and bequeathed by that different person who was oneself in youth — all this is surely vain and futile. And that is why this new *Brave New World* is the same as the old one. Its defects as a work of art are considerable; but in order to correct them I should have to rewrite the book — and in the process of rewriting, as an older, other person, I should probably get rid not only of some of the faults of the story, but also of such merits as it originally possessed. And so, resisting the temptation to wallow in artistic remorse, I prefer to leave both well and ill alone and to think about something else.

In the meantime, however, it seems worthwhile at least to mention the most serious defect in the story, which is this. The Savage is offered only two alternatives, an insane life in Utopia, or the life of a primitive in an Indian village, a life more human in some respects, but in others hardly less queer and abnormal. At the time the book was written this idea, that human beings are given free will in order to choose between insanity on the one hand and lunacy on the other, was one that I found amusing and regarded as quite possibly true. For the sake, however, of dramatic effect, the Savage is often permitted to speak more rationally than his upbringing among the practitioners of a religion that is half fertility cult and half *Penitente* ferocity would actually warrant. Even his acquaintance with Shakespeare would not in reality justify such utterances. And at the close, of course, he is made to retreat from sanity; his naive *Penitente*-ism reasserts its authority and he ends in maniacal self-torture and despairing suicide. "And so they died miserably ever after" — much to the reassurance of the amused, Pyrrhonic aesthete who was the author of the fable.

Today I feel no wish to demonstrate that sanity is impossible. On the contrary, though I remain no less sadly certain than in the past that sanity is a rather rare phenomenon, I am convinced that it can be achieved and would like to see more of it. For having said so in several recent books and, above all, for having compiled an anthology of what the sane have said about sanity and the means whereby it can be achieved, I have been told by an eminent academic critic that I am a sad symptom of the failure of an intellectual class in time of crisis. The implication being, I suppose, that the professor and his colleagues are hilarious symptoms of success. The benefactors of humanity deserve due honour and commemoration. Let us build a Pantheon for professors. It should be located among the ruins of one of the gutted cities of Europe or Japan, and over the entrance to the ossuary I would inscribe, in letters six or seven feet high, the simple words: SACRED TO THE MEMORY OF THE WORLD'S EDUCATORS: SI MONUMENTUM REQUIRIS CIRCUMSPICE.

But to return to the future . . . If I were now to rewrite the book, I would offer the Savage a third alternative. Between the utopian and the primitive horns of his dilemma would lie the possibility of sanity — a possibility already actualized, to some extent, in a community of exiles and refugees from the Brave New World, living within the borders of the Reservation. In this community economics would be decentralist and Henry-Georgian, politics Kropotkinesque cooperative. Science and technology would be used as though, like the Sabbath, they had been made for man, not (as at present and still more so in the Brave New World) as though man were to be adapted and enslaved to them. Religion would be the conscious and intelligent pursuit of man's Final End, the unitive knowledge of the immanent Tao or Logos, the transcendent Godhead or Brahman. And the prevailing philosophy of life would be a kind of Higher Utilitarianism, in which the Greatest Happiness principle would be secondary to the Final End principle — the first question to be asked and answered in every contingency of life being: "How will this thought or action contribute to, or interfere with, the achievement, by me and the greatest possible number of other individuals, of man's Final End?"

Brought up among the primitives, the Savage (in this hypothetical new version of the book) would not be transported to Utopia until he had had an opportunity of learning something at first hand about the nature of a society composed of freely co-operating individuals devoted to the pursuit of sanity. Thus altered, *Brave New World* would possess artistic and (if it is permissible to use so large a word in connection with a work of fiction) a philosophical completeness, which in its present form it evidently lacks.

But *Brave New World* is a book about the future and, whatever its artistic or philosophical qualities, a book about the future can interest us only if its prophecies look as though they might conceivably come true. From our present vantage point, fifteen years further down in the inclined plane of modern history, how plausible do its prognostications seem? What has happened in the painful interval to confirm or invalidate the forecasts of 1931?

One vast and obvious failure of foresight is immediately apparent. *Brave New World* contains no reference to nuclear fission. That it does not is actually rather odd, for the possibilities of atomic energy had been a popular topic of conversation for years before the book was written. My old friend, Robert Nichols, had even written a successful play about the subject, and I recall that I myself had casually mentioned it in a novel published in the late twenties. So it seems, as I say, very odd that the rockets and helicopters of the seventh century of Our Ford should not have been powered by disintegrating nuclei. The oversight may not be excusable; but at least it can be easily explained. The theme of *Brave New World* is not the advancement of science as such; it is the advancement of science as it affects human individuals. The triumphs of physics, chemistry and engineering are tacitly taken for granted. The only scientific advances to be specifically described are those involving the application to human beings of the results of future research in biology, physiology and psychology. It is only by means of the sciences of life that the quality of life can be radically changed. The sciences of matter can be applied in such a way that they will destroy life or make the living of it impossibly complex and uncomfortable; but, unless used as instruments by the biologists and psychologists, they can do nothing to modify the natural forms and expressions of life itself. The release of atomic energy marks a great revolution in human history, but not (unless we blow ourselves to bits and so put an end to history) the final and most searching revolution.

This really revolutionary revolution is to be achieved, not in the external world, but in the souls and flesh of human beings. Living as he did in a revolutionary period, the Marquis de Sade very naturally made use of this theory of revolutions in order to rationalize his peculiar brand of insanity. Robespierre had achieved the most superficial kind of revolution, the political. Going a little deeper, Babeuf had attempted the economic revolution. de Sade regarded himself as the apostle of the truly revolutionary revolution, beyond mere politics and economics — the revolution in individual men, women and children, whose bodies were henceforward to become the common sexual property of all and whose minds were to be purged of all the natural decencies, all the laboriously acquired inhibitions of traditional civilization. Between sadism and the really revolutionary revolution there is, of course, no necessary or inevitable connection. de Sade was a lunatic and the more or less conscious goal of his revolution was universal chaos and destruction. The people who govern the Brave New World may not be sane (in what may be called the absolute sense of the word); but they are not madmen, and their aim is not anarchy but social stability. It is in order to achieve stability that they carry out, by scientific means, the ultimate, personal, really revolutionary revolution.

But meanwhile we are in the first phase of what is perhaps the penultimate revolution. Its next phase may be atomic warfare, in which case we do not have to bother with prophecies about the future. But it is conceivable that we may have enough sense, if not to stop fighting altogether, at least to behave as rationally as did our eighteenth-century ancestors. The unimaginable horrors of the Thirty Years War actually taught men a lesson, and for more than a hundred years the politicians resisted the temptation to use their military resources to the limits of destructiveness or (in the majority of conflicts) to go on fighting until the enemy was totally annihilated. They were aggressors, of course, greedy for profit and glory; but they were also conservatives, determined at all costs to keep their world intact, as a going concern. For the last thirty years there have been no conservatives; there have been only nationalistic radicals of the right and nationalistic radicals of the left. The last conservative statesman was the fifth Marquess of Lansdowne; and when he wrote a letter to the *Times,* suggesting that the First World War should be concluded with a compromise, as most of the wars of the eighteenth century had been, the editor of that once conservative journal refused to print it. The nationalistic radicals had their way, with the consequences that we all know — Bolshevism, Fascism, inflation, depression, Hitler, the Second World War, the ruin of Europe and all but universal famine.

Assuming, then, that we are capable of learning as much from Hiroshima as our forefathers learned from Magdeburg, we may look forward to a period, not indeed of peace, but of limited and only partially ruinous warfare. During the period it may be assumed that nuclear energy will be harnessed to industrial uses. The result, pretty obviously, will be a series of economic and social changes unprecedented in rapidity and completeness. All the existing patterns of human life will be disrupted and new patterns will have to be improvised to conform with the nonhuman fact of atomic power. Procrustes in modern dress, the nuclear scientist will prepare the bed on which mankind must lie; and if mankind doesn't fit — well, that will be just too bad for mankind. There will have to be some stretching and a bit of amputation — the same sort of stretching and amputations as have been going on ever since applied science really got into its stride, only this time they will be a good deal more drastic than in the past. These far from painless operations will be directed by highly centralized totalitarian governments. Inevitably so; for the immediate future is likely to resemble the immediate past, and in the immediate past rapid technological changes, taking place in a mass-producing economy and among a population predominantly propertyless, have always tended to produce economic and social confusion. To deal with confusion, power has been centralized and government control increased. It is probable that all the world's governments will be more or less completely totalitarian even before the harnessing of atomic energy; that they will be totalitarian during and after the harnessing seems almost certain. Only a large-scale popular movement toward decentralization and self-help can arrest the present tendency toward statism. At present there is no sign that such a movement will take place.

There is, of course, no reason why the new totalitarianisms should resemble the old. Government by clubs and firing squads, by artificial famine, mass imprisonment and mass deportation, is not merely inhumane (nobody cares much about that nowadays), it is demonstrably inefficient and in an age of advanced technology, inefficiency is the sin against the

Holy Ghost. A really efficient totalitarian state would be one in which the all-powerful executive of political bosses and their army of managers control a population of slaves who do not have to be coerced, because they love their servitude. To make them love it is the task assigned, in present-day totalitarian states to ministries of propaganda, newspaper editors and schoolteachers. But their methods are still crude and unscientific. The old Jesuits' boast that, if they were given the schooling of the child, they could answer for the man's religious opinions, was a product of wishful thinking. And the modern pedagogue is probably rather less efficient at conditioning his pupils' reflexes than were the reverend fathers who educated Voltaire. The greatest triumphs of propaganda have been accomplished, not by doing something, but by refraining from doing. Great is truth, but still greater, from a practical point of view, is silence about truth. By simply not mentioning certain subjects, by lowering what Mr. Churchill calls an "iron curtain" between the masses and such facts or arguments as the local political bosses regard as undesirable, totalitarian propagandists have influenced opinion much more effectively than they could have done by the most eloquent denunciations, the most compelling of logical rebuttals. But silence is not enough. If persecution, liquidation and the other symptoms of social friction are to be avoided, the positive sides of propaganda must be made as effective as the negative. The most important Manhattan Projects of the future will be vast government-sponsored enquiries into what the politicians and the participating scientists will call "the problem of happiness" — in other words, the problem of making people love their servitude cannot possibly come into existence; for the sake of brevity, I assume that the all-powerful executive and its managers will succeed in solving the problem of permanent security. But security tends very quickly to be taken for granted. Its achievement is merely a superficial, external revolution. The love of servitude cannot be established except as the result of a deep, personal revolution in human minds and bodies. To bring about that revolution requires, among others, the following discoveries and inventions. First, a greatly improved technique of suggestion — through infant conditioning and, later, with the aid of drugs, such as scopolamine. Second, a fully developed science of human differences, enabling government managers to assign any given individual to his or her proper place in the social and economic hierarchy. (Round pegs in square holes tend to have dangerous thoughts about the social system and to infect others with their discontents.) Third (since reality, however utopian, is something from which people feel the need of taking pretty frequent holidays), a substitute of alcohol and the other narcotics, something at once less harmful and more pleasure-giving than gin or heroin. And fourth (but this would be a long-term project, which it would take generations of totalitarian control to bring to a successful conclusion), a fool-proof system of eugenics, designed to standardize the human product and so to facilitate the task of managers. In *Brave New World* this standardization of the human product has been pushed to fantastic, though not perhaps impossible, extremes. Technically and ideologically we are still a long way from bottled babies and Bokanovsky groups of semi-morons. But by A.F. 600, who knows what may not be happening? Meanwhile the other characteristic features of soma and hypnopaedia and the scientific caste system — are probably not more than three or four generations away. Nor does the sexual promiscuity of *Brave New World* seem so very distant. There are already certain American cities in which the number of divorces is equal to the number of marriages. In a few years, no doubt, marriage licenses will be sold like dog licenses, good for a period of twelve months, with no law against changing dogs or keeping more than one animal at a time. As political and economic freedom diminishes, sexual freedom tends compensatingly to increase. And the dictator (unless he needs cannon fodder and families with which to colonize empty or conquered territories) will do well to encourage that freedom. In conjunction with the freedom to daydream under the influence of dope and movies and the radio, it will help to reconcile his subjects to the servitude which is their fate.

All things considered it looks as though Utopia were far closer to us than anyone, only fifteen years ago, could have imagined. Then, I projected it six hundred years into the future. Today it seems quite possible that the horror may be upon us within a single century. That is, if we refrain from blowing ourselves to smithereens in the interval. Indeed, unless we choose to decentralize and to use applied science, not as the end to which human beings are to be made the means, but as the means to producing a race of free individuals, we have only two alternatives to choose from: either a number of national, militarized totalitarianisms, having as their root the terror of the atomic bomb and as their consequence the destruction of civilization (or, if the warfare is limited, the perpetuation of militarism); or else one supranational totalitarianism, called into existence by the social chaos resulting from rapid technological progress in general and the atomic revolution in particular, and developing, under the need for efficiency and stability, into the welfare-tyranny of Utopia. You pays your money and you takes your choice.

CHAPTER 1

A squat grey building of only thirty-four stories. Over the main entrance the words, CENTRAL LONDON HATCHERY AND CONDITIONING CENTRE, and, in a shield, the World State's motto, COMMUNITY, IDENTITY, STABILITY.

The enormous room on the ground floor faced towards the north. Cold for all the summer beyond the panes, for all the tropical heat of the room itself, a harsh thin light glared through the windows, hungrily seeking some draped lay figure, some pallid shape of academic goose-flesh, but finding only the glass and nickel and bleakly shining porcelain of a laboratory. Wintriness responded to wintriness. The overalls of the workers were white, their hands gloved with a pale corpse-coloured rubber. The light was frozen, dead, a ghost. Only from the yellow barrels of the microscopes did it borrow a certain rich and living substance, lying along the polished tubes like butter, streak after luscious streak in long recession down the work tables.

"And this," said the Director opening the door, "is the Fertilizing Room."

Bent over their instruments, three hundred Fertilizers were plunged, as the Director of Hatcheries and Conditioning entered the room, in the scarcely breathing silence, the absent-minded, soliloquizing hum or whistle, of absorbed concentration. A troop of newly arrived students, very young, pink and callow, followed nervously, rather abjectly, at the Director's heels. Each of them carried a notebook, in which, whenever the great man spoke, he desperately scribbled. Straight from the horse's mouth. It was a rare privilege. The D.H.C. for Central London always made a point of personally conducting his new students round the various departments.

"Just to give you a general idea," he would explain to them. For of course some sort of general idea they must have, if they were to do their work intelligently — though as little of one, if they were to be good and happy members of society, as possible. For particulars, as every one knows, make for virtue and happiness; generalities are intellectually necessary evils. Not philosophers but fretsawyers and stamp collectors compose the backbone of society.

"To-morrow," he would add, smiling at them with a slightly menacing geniality, "you'll be settling down to serious work. You won't have time for generalities. Meanwhile . . ."

Meanwhile, it was a privilege. Straight from the horse's mouth into the notebook. The boys scribbled like mad.

Tall and rather thin but upright, the Director advanced into the room. He had a long chin and big rather prominent teeth, just covered, when he was not talking, by his full, floridly curved lips. Old, young? Thirty? Fifty? Fifty-five? It was hard to say. And anyhow the question didn't arise; in this year of stability, A.F. 632, it didn't occur to you to ask it.

"I shall begin at the beginning," said the D.H.C. and the more zealous students recorded his intention in their notebooks: *Begin at the beginning.* "These," he waved his hand, "are the incubators." And opening an insulated door he showed them racks upon racks of numbered test-tubes. "The week's supply of ova. Kept," he explained, "at blood heat; whereas the male gametes," and here he opened another door, "they have to be kept at thirty-five instead of thirty-seven. Full blood heat sterilizes." Rams wrapped in theremogene beget no lambs.

Still leaning against the incubators he gave them, while the pencils scurried illegibly across the pages, a brief description of the modern fertilizing process; spoke first, of course, of its surgical introduction — "the operation undergone voluntarily for the good of Society, not to mention the fact that it carries a bonus amounting to six months' salary"; continued with some account of the technique for preserving the excised ovary alive and actively developing; passed on to a consideration of optimum temperature, salinity, viscosity; referred to the liquor in which the detached and ripened eggs were kept; and, leading his charges to the work tables, actually showed them how this liquor was drawn off from the test-tubes; how it was let out drop by drop onto the specially warmed slides of the microscopes; how the eggs which it contained were inspected for abnormalities, counted and transferred to a porous receptacle; how (and he now took them to watch the operation) this receptacle was immersed in a warm bouillon containing free-swimming spermatozoa — at a minimum concentration of one hundred thousand per cubic centimetre, he insisted; and how, after ten minutes, the container was lifted out of the liquor and its contents re-examined; how, if any of the eggs remained unfertilized, it was again immersed, and, if necessary, yet again; how the fertilized ova went back to the incubators; where the Alphas and Betas remained until definitely bottled; while the Gammas, Deltas and Epsilons were brought out again, after only thirty-six hours, to undergo Bokanovsky's Process.

"Bokanovsky's Process," repeated the Director, and the students underlined the words in their little notebooks.

One egg, one embryo, one adult — normality. But a bokanovskified egg will bud, will proliferate, will divide. From eight to ninety-six buds, and every bud will grow into a perfectly formed embryo, and every embryo into a full-sized adult. Making ninety-six human beings grow where only one grew before. Progress.

"Essentially," the D.H.C. concluded, "bokanovski-fication consists of a series of arrests of development. We check the normal growth and, paradoxically enough, the egg responds by budding."

Responds by budding. The pencils were busy.

He pointed. On a very slowly moving band a rack-full of test-tubes was entering a large metal box, another rack-full was emerging. Machinery faintly purred. It took eight minutes for the tubes to go through, he told them. Eight minutes of hard X-rays being about as much as an egg can stand. A few died; of the rest, the least susceptible divided into two; most put out four buds; some eight; all were returned to the incubators, where the buds began to develop; then, after two days, were suddenly chilled, chilled and checked. Two, four, eight, the buds in their turn budded; and having budded were dosed almost to death with alcohol; consequently burgeoned again and having budded — bud out of bud out of bud — were thereafter — further arrest being generally fatal — left to develop in peace. By which time the original egg was in a fair way to becoming anything from eight to ninety-six embryos — a prodigious improvement, you will agree, on nature. Identical twins — but not in piddling twos and threes as in the old viviparous days, when an egg would sometimes accidentally divide; actually by dozens, by scores at a time.

"Scores," the Director repeated and flung out his arms, as though he were distributing largesse. "Scores."

But one of the students was fool enough to ask where the advantage lay.

"My good boy!" The Director wheeled sharply round on him. "Can't you see? Can't you *see?*" He raised a hand; his expression was solemn. "Bokanovsky's Process is one of the major instruments of social stability!"

Major instruments of social stability.

Standard men and women; in uniform batches. The whole of a small factory staffed with the products of a single bokanovskified egg.

"Ninety-six identical twins working ninety-six identical machines!" The voice was almost tremulous with enthusiasm. "You really know where you are. For the first time in history." He quoted the planetary motto. "Community, Identity, Stability." Grand words. "If we could bokanovskify indefinitely the whole problem would be solved."

Solved by standard Gammas, unvarying Deltas, uniform Epsilons. Millions of identical twins. The principle of mass production at last applied to biology.

"But alas," the Director shook his head, "we can't bokanovskify indefinitely."

Ninety-six seemed to be the limit; seventy-two a good average. From the same ovary and with gametes of the same male to manufacture as many batches of identical twins as possible—that was the best (sadly a second best) that they could do. And even that was difficult.

"For in nature it takes thirty years for two hundred eggs to reach maturity. But our business is to stabilize the population at this moment, here and now. Dribbling out twins over a quarter of a century — what would be the use of that?"

Obviously, no use at all. But Podsnap's Technique had immensely accelerated the process of ripening. They could make sure of at least a hundred and fifty mature eggs within two years. Fertilize and bokanovskify — in other words, multiply by seventy-two — and you get an average of nearly eleven thousand brothers and sisters in a hundred and fifty batches of identical twins, all within two years of the same age.

"And in exceptional cases we can make one ovary yield us over fifteen thousand adult individuals."

Beckoning to a fair-haired, ruddy young man who happened to be passing at the moment. "Mr. Foster," he called. The ruddy young man approached. "Can you tell us the record for a single ovary, Mr. Foster?"

"Sixteen thousand and twelve in this Centre," Mr. Foster replied without hesitation. He spoke very quickly, had a vivacious blue eye, and took an evident pleasure in quoting figures. "Sixteen thousand and twelve; in one hundred and eighty-nine batches of identicals. But of course they've done much better," he rattled on, "in some of the tropical Centres. Singapore has often produced over sixteen thousand five hundred; and Mombasa has actually touched the seventeen thousand mark. But then they have unfair advantages. You should see the way a negro ovary responds to pituitary! It's quite astonishing, when you're used to working with European material. Still," he added, with a laugh (but the light of combat was in his eyes and the lift of his chin was challenging), "still, we mean to beat them if we can. I'm working on a wonderful Delta-Minus ovary at this moment. Only just eighteen months old. Over twelve thousand seven hundred children already, either decanted or in embryo. And still going strong. We'll beat them yet."

"That's the spirit I like!" cried the Director, and clapped Mr. Foster on the shoulder. "Come along with us, and give these boys the benefit of your expert knowledge."

Mr. Foster smiled modestly. "With pleasure." They went.

In the Bottling Room all was harmonious bustle and ordered activity. Flaps of fresh sow's peritoneum ready cut to the proper size came shooting up in little lifts from the Organ Store in the sub-basement. Whizz and then, click! the lift-hatches flew open; the bottle-liner had only to reach out a hand, take the flap, insert, smooth-down, and before the lined bottle had had time to travel out of reach along the endless band, whizz, click! another flap of peritoneum had shot up from the depths, ready to be slipped into yet another bottle, the next of that slow interminable procession on the band.

Next to the Liners stood the Matriculators. The procession advanced; one by one the eggs were transferred from their test-tubes to the larger containers; deftly the peritoneal lining was slit, the morula dropped into place, the saline solution poured in . . . and already the bottle had passed, and it was the turn of the labellers. Heredity, date of fertilization, membership of Bokanovsky Group — details were transferred from test-tube to bottle. No longer anonymous, but named, identified, the procession marched slowly on; on through an opening in the wall, slowly on into the Social Predestination Room.

"Eighty-eight cubic metres of card-index," said Mr. Foster with relish, as they entered.

"Containing all the relevant information," added the Director.

"Brought up to date every morning."

"And co-ordinated every afternoon."

"On the basis of which they make their calculations."

"So many individuals, of such and such quality," said Mr. Foster.

"Distributed in such and such quantities."

"The optimum Decanting Rate at any given moment."

"Unforeseen wastages promptly made good."

"Promptly," repeated Mr. Foster. "If you knew the amount of overtime I had to put in after the last Japanese earthquake!" He laughed goodhumouredly and shook his head.

"The Predestinators send in their figures to the Fertilizers."

"Who give them the embryos they ask for."

"And the bottles come in here to be predestined in detail."

"After which they are sent down to the Embryo Store."

"Where we now proceed ourselves."

And opening a door Mr. Foster led the way down a staircase into the basement.

The temperature was still tropical. They descended into a thickening twilight. Two doors and a passage with a double turn insured the cellar against any possible infiltration of the day.

"Embryos are like photograph film," said Mr. Foster waggishly, as he pushed open the second door. "They can only stand red light."

And in effect the sultry darkness into which the students now followed him was visible and crimson, like the darkness of closed eyes on a summer's afternoon. The bulging flanks of row on receding row and tier above tier of bottles glinted with innumerable rubies, and among the rubies moved the dim red spectres of men and women with purple eyes and all the symptoms of lupus. The hum and rattle of machinery faintly stirred the air.

"Give them a few figures, Mr. Foster," said the Director, who was tired of talking.

Mr. Foster was only too happy to give them a few figures.

Two hundred and twenty metres long, two hundred wide, ten high. He pointed upwards. Like chickens drinking, the students lifted their eyes towards the distant ceiling.

Three tiers of racks: ground floor level, first gallery, second gallery.

The spidery steel-work of gallery above gallery faded away in all directions into the dark. Near them three red ghosts were busily unloading demijohns from a moving staircase.

The escalator from the Social Predestination Room.

Each bottle could be placed on one of fifteen racks, each rack, though you couldn't see it, was a conveyor traveling at the rate of thirty-three and a third centimetres an hour. Two hundred and sixty-seven days at eight metres a day. Two thousand one hundred and thirty-six metres in all. One circuit of the cellar at ground level, one on the first gallery, half on the second, and on the two hundred and sixty-seventh morning, daylight in the Decanting Room. Independent existence — so called.

"But in the interval," Mr. Foster concluded, "we've managed to do a lot to them. Oh, a very great deal." His laugh was knowing and triumphant.

"That's the spirit I like," said the Director once more. "Let's walk around. You tell them everything, Mr. Foster."

Mr. Foster duly told them.

Told them of the growing embryo on its bed of peritoneum. Made them taste the rich blood surrogate on which it fed. Explained why it had to be stimulated with placentin and thyroxin. Told them of the *corpus luteum* extract. Showed them the jets through which at every twelfth metre from zero to 2040 it was automatically injected. Spoke of those gradually increasing doses of pituitary administered during the final ninety-six metres of their course. Described the artificial maternal circulation installed in every bottle at Metre 112; showed them the reservoir of blood-surrogate, the centrifugal pump that kept the liquid moving over the placenta and drove it through the synthetic lung and waste product filter. Referred to the embryo's troublesome tendency to anæmia, to the massive doses of hog's stomach extract and foetal foal's liver with which, in consequence, it had to be supplied.

Showed them the simple mechanism by means of which, during the last two metres out of every eight, all the embryos were simultaneously shaken into familiarity with movement. Hinted at the gravity of the so-called "trauma of decanting," and enumerated the precautions taken to minimize, by a suitable training of the bottled embryo, that dangerous shock. Told them of the test for sex carried out in the neighborhood of Metre 200. Explained the system of labelling — a T for the males, a circle for the females and for those who were destined to become freemartins a question mark, black on a white ground.

"For of course," said Mr. Foster, "in the vast majority of cases, fertility is merely a nuisance. One fertile ovary in twelve hundred — that would really be quite sufficient for our purposes. But we want to have a good choice. And of course one must always have an enormous margin of safety. So we allow as many as thirty per cent of the female embryos to develop normally. The others get a dose of male sex-hormone every twenty-four metres for the rest of the course. Result: they're decanted as freemartins — structurally quite normal (except," he had to admit, "that they *do* have the slightest tendency to grow beards), but sterile. Guaranteed sterile. Which brings us at last," continued Mr. Foster, "out of the realm of mere slavish imitation of nature into the much more interesting world of human invention."

He rubbed his hands. For of course, they didn't content themselves with merely hatching out embryos: any cow could do that.

"We also predestine and condition. We decant our babies as socialized human beings, as Alphas or Epsilons, as future sewage workers or future . . ." He was going to say "future World controllers," but correcting himself, said "future Directors of Hatcheries," instead.

The D.H.C. acknowledged the compliment with a smile.

They were passing Metre 320 on Rack 11. A young Beta-Minus mechanic was busy with screwdriver and spanner on the blood-surrogate pump of a passing bottle. The hum of the electric motor deepened by fractions of a tone as he turned the nuts. Down, down . . . A final twist, a glance at the revolution counter, and he was done. He moved two paces down the line and began the same process on the next pump.

"Reducing the number of revolutions per minute," Mr. Foster explained. "The surrogate goes round slower; therefore passes through the lung at longer intervals; therefore gives the embryo less oxygen. Nothing like oxygen-shortage for keeping an embryo below par." Again he rubbed his hands.

"But why do you want to keep the embryo below par?" asked an ingenuous student.

"Ass!" said the Director, breaking a long silence. "Hasn't it occurred to you that an Epsilon embryo must have an Epsilon environment as well as an Epsilon heredity?"

It evidently hadn't occurred to him. He was covered with confusion.

"The lower the caste," said Mr. Foster, "the shorter the oxygen." The first organ affected was the brain. After that the skeleton. At seventy per cent of normal oxygen you got dwarfs. At less than seventy eyeless monsters.

"Who are no use at all," concluded Mr. Foster.

Whereas (his voice became confidential and eager), if they could discover a technique for shortening the period of maturation what a triumph, what a benefaction to Society!

"Consider the horse."

They considered it.

Mature at six; the elephant at ten. While at thirteen a man is not yet sexually mature; and is only full-grown at twenty. Hence, of course, that fruit of delayed development, the human intelligence.

"But in Epsilons," said Mr. Foster very justly, "we don't need human intelligence."

Didn't need and didn't get it. But though the Epsilon mind was mature at ten, the Epsilon body was not fit to work till eighteen. Long years of superfluous and wasted immaturity. If the physical development could be speeded up till it was as quick, say, as a cow's, what an enormous saving to the Community!

"Enormous!" murmured the students. Mr. Foster's enthusiasm was infectious.

He became rather technical; spoke of the abnormal endocrine co-ordination which made men grow so slowly; postulated a germinal mutation to account for it. Could the effects of this germinal mutation be undone? Could the individual Epsilon embryo be made a revert, by a suitable technique, to the normality of dogs and cows? That was the problem. And it was all but solved.

Pilkington, at Mombasa, had produced individuals who were sexually mature at four and full-grown at six and a half. A scientific triumph. But socially useless. Six-year-old men and women were too stupid to do even Epsilon work. And the process was an all-or-nothing one; either you failed to modify at all, or else you modified the whole way. They were still trying to find the ideal compromise between adults of twenty and adults of six. So far without success. Mr. Foster sighed and shook his head.

Their wanderings through the crimson twilight had brought them to the neighborhood of Metre 170 on Rack 9. From this point onwards Rack 9 was enclosed and the bottles performed the remainder of their journey in a kind of tunnel, interrupted here and there by openings two or three metres wide.

"Heat conditioning," said Mr. Foster.

Hot tunnels alternated with cool tunnels. Coolness was wedded to discomfort in the form of hard X-rays. By the time they were decanted the embryos had a horror of cold. They were predestined to emigrate to the tropics, to be miner and acetate silk spinners and steel workers. Later on their minds would be made to endorse the judgment of their bodies. "We condition them to thrive on heat," concluded Mr. Foster. "Our colleagues upstairs will teach them to love it."

"And that," put in the Director sententiously, "that is the secret of happiness and virtue — liking what you've got to do. All conditioning aims at that: making people like their unescapable social destiny."

In a gap between two tunnels, a nurse was delicately probing with a long fine syringe into the gelatinous contents of a passing bottle. The students and their guides stood watching her for a few moments in silence.

"Well, Lenina," said Mr. Foster, when at last she withdrew the syringe and straightened herself up.

The girl turned with a start. One could see that, for all the lupus and the purple eyes, she was uncommonly pretty.

"Henry!" Her smile flashed redly at him — a row of coral teeth.

"Charming, charming," murmured the Director and, giving her two or three little pats, received in exchange a rather deferential smile for himself.

"What are you giving them?" asked Mr. Foster, making his tone very professional.

"Oh, the usual typhoid and sleeping sickness."

"Tropical workers start being inoculated at Metre 150," Mr. Foster explained to the students. "The embryos still have gills. We immunize the fish against the future man's diseases." Then, turning back to Lenina, "Ten to five on the roof this afternoon," he said, "as usual."

"Charming," said the Director once more, and, with a final pat, moved away after the others.

On Rack 10 rows of next generation's chemical workers were being trained in the toleration of lead, caustic soda, tar, chlorine. The first of a batch of two hundred and fifty embryonic rocket-plane engineers was just passing the eleven hundred metre mark on Rack 3. A special mechanism kept their containers in constant rotation. "To improve their sense of balance," Mr. Foster explained. "Doing repairs on the outside of a rocket in mid-air is a ticklish job. We slacken off the circulation when they're right way up, so that they're half starved, and double the flow of surrogate when they're upside down. They learn to associate topsy-turvydom with well-being; in fact, they're only truly happy when they're standing on their heads.

"And now," Mr. Foster went on, "I'd like to show you some very interesting conditioning for Alpha Plus Intellectuals. We have a big batch of them on Rack 5. First Gallery level," he called to two boys who had started to go down to the ground floor.

"They're round about Metre 900," he explained. "You can't really do any useful intellectual conditioning till the foetuses have lost their tails. Follow me."

But the Director had looked at his watch. "Ten to three," he said. "No time for the intellectual embryos, I'm afraid. We must go up to the Nurseries before the children have finished their afternoon sleep."

Mr. Foster was disappointed. "At least one glance at the Decanting Room," he pleaded.

"Very well then." The Director smiled indulgently. "Just one glance."

CHAPTER 2

Mr. Foster was left in the Decanting Room. The D.H.C. and his students stepped into the nearest lift and were carried up to the fifth floor.

INFANT NURSERIES. NEO-PAVLOVIAN CONDITIONING ROOMS, announced the notice board.

The Director opened a door. They were in a large bare room, very bright and sunny; for the whole of the southern wall was a single window. Half a dozen nurses, trousered and jacketed in the regulation white viscose-linen uniform, their hair aseptically hidden under white caps, were engaged in setting out bowls of roses in a long row across the floor. Big bowls, packed tight with blossom. Thousands of petals, ripe-blown and silkily smooth, like the cheeks of innumerable little cherubs, but of cherubs, in that bright light, not exclusively pink and Aryan, but also luminously Chinese, also Mexican, also apoplectic with too much blowing of celestial trumpets, also pale as death, pale with the posthumous whiteness of marble.

The nurses stiffened to attention as the D.H.C. came in.

"Set out the books," he said curtly.

In silence the nurses obeyed his command. Between the rose bowls the books were duly set out — a row of nursery quartos opened invitingly each at some gaily coloured image of beast or fish or bird.

"Now bring in the children."

They hurried out of the room and returned in a minute or two, each pushing a kind of tall dumb-waiter laden, on all its four wire-netted shelves, with eight-month-old babies, all exactly alike (a Bokanovsky Group, it was evident) and all (since their caste was Delta) dressed in khaki.

"Put them down on the floor."

The infants were unloaded.

"Now turn them so that they can see the flowers and books."

Turned, the babies at once fell silent, then began to crawl towards those clusters of sleek colours, those shapes so gay and brilliant on the white pages. As they approached, the sun came out of a momentary eclipse behind a cloud. The roses flamed up as though with a sudden passion from within; a new and profound significance seemed to suffuse the shining pages of the books. From the ranks of the crawling babies came little squeals of excitement, gurgles and twitterings of pleasure.

The Director rubbed his hands. "Excellent!" he said. "It might almost have been done on purpose."

The swiftest crawlers were already at their goal. Small hands reached out uncertainly, touched, grasped, unpetaling the transfigured roses, crumpling the illuminated pages of the books. The Director waited until all were happily busy. Then, "Watch carefully," he said. And, lifting his hand, he gave the signal.

The Head Nurse, who was standing by a switchboard at the other end of the room, pressed down a little lever.

There was a violent explosion. Shriller and ever shriller, a siren shrieked. Alarm bells maddeningly sounded.

The children started, screamed; their faces were distorted with terror.

"And now," the Director shouted (for the noise was deafening), "now we proceed to rub in the lesson with a mild electric shock."

He waved his hand again, and the Head Nurse pressed a second lever. The screaming of the babies suddenly changed its tone. There was something desperate, almost insane, about the sharp spasmodic yelps to which they now gave utterance. Their little bodies twitched and stiffened; their limbs moved jerkily as if to the tug of unseen wires.

"We can electrify that whole strip of floor," bawled the Director in explanation. "But that's enough," he signalled to the nurse.

The explosions ceased, the bells stopped ringing, the shriek of the siren died down from tone to tone into silence. The stiffly twitching bodies relaxed, and what had become the sob and yelp of infant maniacs broadened out once more into a normal howl of ordinary terror.

"Offer them the flowers and the books again."

The nurses obeyed; but at the approach of the roses, at the mere sight of those gaily-coloured images of pussy and cock-a-doodle-doo and baa-baa black sheep, the infants shrank away in horror, the volume of their howling suddenly increased.

"Observe," said the Director triumphantly, "observe."

Books and loud noises, flowers and electric shocks — already in the infant mind these couples were compromisingly linked; and after two hundred repetitions of the same or a similar lesson would be wedded indissolubly. What man has joined, nature is powerless to put asunder.

"They'll grow up with what the psychologists used to call an 'instinctive' hatred of books and flowers.

Reflexes unalterably conditioned. They'll be safe from books and botany all their lives." The Director turned to his nurses. "Take them away again."

Still yelling, the khaki babies were loaded on to their dumb-waiters and wheeled out, leaving behind them the smell of sour milk and a most welcome silence.

One of the students held up his hand; and though he could see quite well why you couldn't have lower-cast people wasting the Community's time over books, and that there was always the risk of their reading something which might undesirably decondition one of their reflexes, yet . . . well, he couldn't understand about the flowers. Why go to the trouble of making it psychologically impossible for Deltas to like flowers?

Patiently the D.H.C. explained. If the children were made to scream at the sight of a rose, that was on grounds of high economic policy. Not so very long ago (a century or thereabouts), Gammas, Deltas, even Epsilons, had been conditioned to like flowers — flowers in particular and wild nature in general. The idea was to make them want to be going out into the country at every available opportunity, and so compel them to consume transport.

"And didn't they consume transport?" asked the student.

"Quite a lot," the D.H.C. replied. "But nothing else."

Primroses and landscapes, he pointed out, have one grave defect: they are gratuitous. A love of nature keeps no factories busy. It was decided to abolish the love of nature, at any rate among the lower classes; to abolish the love of nature, but not the tendency to consume transport. For of course it was essential that they should keep on going to the country, even though they hated it. The problem was to find an economically sounder reason for consuming transport than a mere affection for primroses and landscapes. It was duly found.

"We condition the masses to hate the country," concluded the Director. "But simultaneously we condition them to love all country sports. At the same time, we see to it that all country sports shall entail the use of elaborate apparatus. So that they consume manufactured articles as well as transport. Hence those electric shocks."

"I see," said the student, and was silent, lost in admiration.

There was a silence; then, clearing his throat, "Once upon a time," the Director began, "while our Ford was still on earth, there was a little boy called Reuben Rabinovitch. Reuben was the child of Polish-speaking parents." The Director interrupted himself. "You know what Polish is, I suppose?"

"A dead language."

"Like French and German," added another student, officiously showing off his learning.

"And 'parent'?" questioned the D.H.C.

There was an uneasy silence. Several of the boys blushed. They had not yet learned to draw the significant but often very fine distinction between smut and pure science. One, at last, had the courage to raise a hand.

"Human beings used to be . . ." he hesitated; the blood rushed to his cheeks. "Well, they used to be viviparous."

"Quite right." The Director nodded approvingly.

"And when the babies were decanted . . ."

" 'Born,' " came the correction.

"Well, then they were the parents — I mean, not the babies, of course; the other ones." The poor boy was overwhelmed with confusion.

"In brief," the Director summed up, "the parents were the father and the mother." The smut that was really science fell with a crash into the boys' eye-avoiding silence. "Mother," he repeated loudly rubbing in the science; and, leaning back in his chair, "These," he said gravely, "are unpleasant facts; I know it. But then most historical facts *are* unpleasant."

He returned to Little Reuben — to Little Reuben, in whose room, one evening, by an oversight, his father and mother (crash, crash!) happened to leave the radio turned on.

("For you must remember that in those days of gross viviparous reproduction, children were always brought up by their parents and not in State Conditioning Centres.")

While the child was asleep, a broadcast programme from London suddenly started to come through; and the next morning, to the astonishment of his crash and crash (the more daring of the boys ventured to grin at one another), Little Reuben woke up repeating word for word a long lecture by that curious old writer ("one of the very few whose works have been permitted to come down to us"), George Bernard Shaw, who was speaking, according to a well-authenticated tradition, about his own genius. To Little Reuben's wink and snigger, this lecture was, of course, perfectly incomprehensible and, imagining that their child had suddenly gone mad, they sent for a doctor. He, fortunately, understood English, recognized the discourse as that which Shaw had broadcasted the previous evening, realized the significance of what had happened, and sent a letter to the medical press about it.

"The principle of sleep-teaching, or hypnopædia, had been discovered." The D.H.C. made an impressive pause.

The principle had been discovered; but many, many years were to elapse before that principle was usefully applied.

"The case of Little Reuben occurred only twenty-three years after Our Ford's first T-Model was put on the market." (Here the Director made a sign of the T on his stomach and all the students reverently followed suit.) "And yet . . ."

Furiously the students scribbled. *"Hypnopædia, first used officially in A.F. 214. Why not before? Two reasons. (a) . . ."*

"These early experimenters," the D.H.C. was saying, "were on the wrong track. They thought that hypnopædia could be made an instrument of intellectual education . . ."

(A small boy asleep on his right side, the right arm stuck out, the right hand hanging limp over the edge of the bed. Through a round grating in the side of a box a voice speaks softly.

"The Nile is the longest river in Africa and the second in length of all the rivers of the globe. Although falling short of the length of the Mississippi-Missouri, the Nile is at the head of all rivers as regards the length of its basin, which extends through 35 degrees of latitude . . ."

At breakfast the next morning, "Tommy," some one says, "do you know which is the longest river in Africa?" A shaking of the head. "But don't you remember something that begins: The Nile is the . . ."

"The - Nile - is - the - longest - river - in - Africa - and - the - second - in - length - of - all - the - rivers - of - the - globe . . ." The words come rushing out.

"Although - falling - short - of . . ."

"Well now, which is the longest river in Africa?"

The eyes are blank. "I don't know."

"But the Nile, Tommy."

"The - Nile - is - the - longest - river - in - Africa - and - second . . ."

"Then which river is the longest, Tommy?"

Tommy burst into tears. "I don't know," he howls.)

That howl, the Director made it plain, discouraged the earliest investigators. The experiments were abandoned. No further attempt was made to teach children the length of the Nile in their sleep. Quite rightly. You can't learn a science unless you know what it's all about.

"Whereas, if they'd only started on *moral* education," said the Director, leading the way towards the door. The students followed him, desperately scribbling as they walked and all the way up in the lift. "Moral education, which ought never, in any circumstances, to be rational."

"Silence, silence," whispered a loud speaker as they stepped out at the fourteenth floor, and "Silence, silence," the trumpet mouths indefatigably repeated at intervals down every corridor. The students and even the Director himself rose automatically to the tips of their toes. They were Alphas, of course, but even Alphas have been well conditioned. "Silence, silence." All the air of the fourteenth floor was sibilant with the categorical imperative.

Fifty yards of tiptoeing brought them to a door which the Director cautiously opened. They stepped over the threshold into the twilight of a shuttered dormitory. Eighty cots stood in a row against the wall. There was a sound of light regular breathing and a continuous murmur, as of very faint voices remotely whispering.

A nurse rose as they entered and came to attention before the Director.

"What's the lesson this afternoon?" he asked.

"We had Elementary Sex for the first forty minutes," she answered. "But now it's switched over to Elementary Class Consciousness."

The Director walked slowly down the long line of cots. Rosy and relaxed with sleep, eighty little boys and girls lay softly breathing. There was a whisper under every pillow. The D.H.C. halted and, bending over one of the little beds, listened attentively.

"Elementary Class Consciousness, did you say? Let's have it repeated a little louder by the trumpet."

At the end of the room a loud speaker projected from the wall. The Director walked up to it and pressed a switch.

" . . . all wear green," said a soft but very distinct voice, beginning in the middle of a sentence, "and Delta Children wear khaki. Oh no, I don't want to play with Delta children. And Epsilons are still worse. They're too stupid to be able to read or write. Besides they wear black, which is such a beastly colour. I'm *so* glad I'm a Beta."

There was a pause; then the voice began again.

"Alpha children wear grey. They work much harder than we do, because they're so frightfully clever. I'm really awfuly glad I'm a Beta, because I don't work so hard. And then we are much better than the Gammas and Deltas. Gammas are stupid. They all wear green, and Delta children wear khaki. Oh no, I *don't* want to play with Delta children. And Epsilons are still worse. They're too stupid to be able . . ."

The Director pushed back the switch. The voice

was silent. Only its thin ghost continued to mutter from beneath the eighty pillows.

"They'll have that repeated forty or fifty times more before they wake; then again on Thursday, and again on Saturday. A hundred and twenty times three times a week for thirty months. After which they go on to a more advanced lesson."

Roses and electric shocks, the khaki of Deltas and a whiff of asafœtida — wedded indissolubly before the child can speak. But wordless conditioning is crude and wholesale; cannot bring home the finer distinctions, cannot inculcate the more complex courses of behaviour. For that there must be words, but words without reason. In brief, hypnopædia.

"The greatest moralizing and socializing force of all time."

The students took it down in their little books. Straight from the horse's mouth.

Once more the Director touched the switch.

". . . so frightfully clever," the soft, insinuating, indefatigable voice was saying, "I'm really awfully glad I'm a Beta, because . . ."

Not so much like drops of water, though water, it is true, can wear holes in the hardest granite; rather, drops of liquid sealing-wax, drops that adhere, incrust, incorporate themselves with what they fall on, till finally the rock is all one scarlet blob.

"Till at last the child's mind *is* these suggestions, and the sum of the suggestions *is* the child's mind. And not the child's mind only. The adult's mind too — all his life long. The mind that judges and desires and decides — made up of these suggestions. But all these suggestions are *our* suggestions!" — The Director almost shouted in his triumph. "Suggestions from the State." He banged the nearest table. "It therefore follows . . ."

A noise made him turn round.

"Oh, Ford!" he said in another tone, "I've gone and woken the children."

CHAPTER 3

Outside, in the garden, it was playtime. Naked in the warm June sunshine, six or seven hundred little boys and girls were running with shrill yells over the lawns, or playing ball games, or squatting silently in twos and threes among the flowering shrubs. The roses were in bloom, two nightingales soliloquized in the boskage, a cuckoo was just going out of tune among the lime trees. The air was drowsy with the murmur of bees and helicopters.

The Director and his students stood for a short time watching a game of Centrifugal Bumble-puppy. Twenty children were grouped in a circle round a chrome steel tower. A ball thrown up so as to land on the platform at the top of the tower rolled down into the interior, fell on a rapidly revolving disk, was hurled through one or other of the numerous apertures pierced in the cylindrical casing, and had to be caught.

"Strange," mused the Director, as they turned away, "strange to think that even in Our Ford's day most games were played without more apparatus than a ball or two and a few sticks and perhaps a bit of netting. Imagine the folly of allowing people to play elaborate games which do nothing whatever to increase consumption. It's madness. Nowadays the Controllers won't approve of any new game unless it can be shown that it requires at least as much apparatus as the most complicated of existing games." He interrupted himself.

"That's a charming little group," he said, pointing.

In a little grassy bay between tall clumps of Mediterranean heather, two children, a little boy of about seven and a little girl who might have been a year older, were playing, very gravely and with all the focussed attention of scientists intent on a labour of discovery, a rudimentary sexual game.

"Charming, charming!" the D.H.C. repeated sentimentally.

"Charming," the boys politely agreed. But their smile was rather patronizing. They had put aside similar childish amusements too recently to be able to watch them now without a touch of contempt. Charming? but it was just a pair of kids fooling about; that was all. Just kids.

"I always think," the Director was continuing in the same rather maudlin tone, when he was interrupted by a loud boo-hooing.

From a neighbouring shrubbery emerged a nurse, leading by the hand a small boy, who howled as he went. An anxious-looking little girl trotted at her heels.

"What's the matter?" asked the Director.

The nurse shrugged her shoulders. "Nothing much," she answered. "It's just that this little boy seems rather reluctant to join in the ordinary erotic play. I'd noticed it once or twice before. And now again to-day. He started yelling just now . . ."

"Honestly," put in the anxious-looking little girl, "I didn't mean to hurt him or anything. Honestly."

"Of course you didn't, dear," said the nurse reassuringly. "And so," she went on, turning back to the Director, "I'm taking him in to see the Assistant Superintendent of Psychology. Just to see if anything's at all abnormal."

"Quite right," said the Director. "Take him in. You stay here, little girl," he added, as the nurse moved away with her still howling charge. "What's your name?"

"Polly Trotsky."

"And a very good name too," said the Director. "Run away now and see if you can find some other little boy to play with."

The child scampered off into the bushes and was lost to sight.

"Exquisite little creature!" said the Director, looking after her. Then, turning to his students, "What I'm going to tell you now," he said, "may sound incredible. But then, when you're not accustomed to history, most facts about the past *do* sound incredible."

He let out the amazing truth. For a very long period before the time of Our Ford, and even for some generations afterwards, erotic play between children had been regarded as abnormal (there was a roar of laughter); and not only abnormal, actually immoral (no!): and had therefore been rigorously suppressed.

A look of astonished incredulity appeared on the faces of his listeners. Poor little kids not allowed to amuse themselves? They could not believe it.

"Even adolescents," the D.H.C. was saying, "even adolescents like yourselves . . ."

"Not possible!"

"Barring a little surreptitious auto-erotism and homosexuality — absolutely nothing."

"*Nothing?*"

"In most cases, till they were over twenty years old."

"Twenty years old?" echoed the students in a chorus of loud disbelief.

"Twenty," the Director repeated. "I told you that you'd find it incredible."

"But what happened?" they asked. "What were the results?"

"The results were terrible." A deep resonant voice broke startlingly into the dialogue.

They looked around. On the fringe of the little group stood a stranger — a man of middle height, black-haired, with a hooked nose, full red lips, eyes very piercing and dark. "Terrible," he repeated.

The D.H.C. had at that moment sat down on one of the steel and rubber benches conveniently scattered through the gardens; but at the sight of the stranger, he sprang to his feet and darted forward, his hand outstretched, smiling with all his teeth, effusive.

"Controller! What an unexpected pleasure! Boys, what are you thinking of? This is the Controller; this is his fordship, Mustapha Mond."

In the four thousand rooms of the Centre the four thousand electric clocks simultaneously struck four. Discarnate voices called from the trumpet mouths.

"Main Day-shift off duty. Second Day-shift take over. Main Day-shift off . . ."

In the lift, on their way up to the changing rooms, Henry Foster and the Assistant Director of Predestination rather pointedly turned their backs on Bernard Marx from the Psychology Bureau: averted themselves from that unsavoury reputation.

The faint hum and rattle of machinery still stirred the crimson air in the Embryo Store. Shifts might come and go, one lupus-coloured face give place to another; majestically and for ever the conveyors crept forward with their load of future men and women.

Lenina Crowne walked briskly towards the door.

His fordship Mustapha Mond! The eyes of the saluting students almost popped out of their heads. Mustapha Mond! The Resident Controller for Western Europe! One of the Ten World Controllers. One of the Ten . . . and he sat down on the bench with the D.H.C., he was going to stay, to stay, yes, and actually talk to them . . . straight from the horse's mouth. Straight from the mouth of Ford himself.

Two shrimp-brown children emerged from a neighbouring shrubbery, stared at them for a moment with large, astonished eyes, then returned to their amusements among the leaves.

"You all remember," said the Controller, in his strong deep voice, "you all remember, I suppose, that beautiful and inspired saying of Our Ford's: History is bunk. History," he repeated slowly, "is bunk."

He waved his hand; and it was as though, with an invisible feather whisk, he had brushed away a little dust, and the dust was Harappa, was Ur of the Chaldees; some spider-webs, and they were Thebes and Babylon and Cnossos and Mycenae. Whisk. Whisk — and where was Odysseus, where was Job, where were Jupiter and Gotama and Jesus? Whisk — and those specks of antique dirt called Athens and Rome, Jerusalem and the Middle Kingdom — all were gone. Whisk — the place where Italy had been was empty. Whisk, the cathedrals; whisk, whisk, King Lear and the Thoughts of Pascal. Whisk, Passion; whisk, Requiem; whisk, Symphony; whisk . . .

"Going to the Feelies this evening, Henry?" enquired the Assistant Predestinator. "I hear the new one at the Alhambra is first-rate. There's a love scene on a bearskin rug; they say it's marvellous. Every hair of the bear reproduced. The most amazing tactual effects."

"That's why you're taught no history," the Controller was saying. "But now the time has come . . ."

The D.H.C. looked at him nervously. There were those strange rumours of old forbidden books hidden in a safe in the Controller's study. Bibles, poetry — Ford knew what.

Mustapha Mond intercepted his anxious glance and the corners of his red lips twitched ironically.

"It's all right, Director," he said in a tone of faint derision, "I won't corrupt them."

The D.H.C. was overwhelmed with confusion.

Those who feel themselves despised do well to look despising. The smile on Bernard Marx's face was contemptuous. Every hair on the bear indeed!

"I shall make a point of going," said Henry Foster.

《《

Mustapha Mond leaned forward, shook a finger at them. "Just try to realize it," he said, and his voice sent a strange thrill quivering along their diaphragms. "Try to realize what it was like to have a viviparous mother."

That smutty word again. But none of them dreamed, this time, of smiling.

"Try to imagine what 'living with one's family' meant."

They tried; but obviously without the smallest success.

"And do you know what a 'home' was?"

They shook their heads.

From her dim crimson cellar Lenina Crowne shot up seventeen stories, turned to the right as she stepped out of the lift, walked down a long corridor and, opening the door marked GIRLS' DRESSING-ROOM, plunged into a deafening chaos of arms and bosoms and underclothing. Torrents of hot water were splashing into or gurgling out of a hundred baths. Rumbling and hissing, eighty vibro-vacuum massage machines were simultaneously kneading and sucking the firm and sunburnt flesh of eighty superb female specimens. Every one was talking at the top of her voice. A Synthetic Music machine was warbling out a super-cornet solo.

"Hullo, Fanny," said Lenina to the young woman who had the pegs and locker next to hers.

Fanny worked in the Bottling Room, and her surname was also Crowne. But as the two thousand million inhabitants of the planet had only ten thousand names between them, the coincidence was not particularly surprising.

Lenina pulled at her zippers — downwards on the jacket, downwards with a double-handed gesture at the two that held trousers, downwards again to loosen her undergarment. Still wearing her shoes and stockings, she walked off towards the bathrooms.

Home, home — a few small rooms, stiflingly over-inhabited by a man, by a periodically teeming woman, by a rabble of boys and girls of all ages. No air, no space; an understerilized prison; darkness, disease, and smells.

(The Controller's evocation was so vivid that one of the boys, more sensitive than the rest, turned pale at the mere description and was on the point of being sick.)

Lenina got out of the bath, toweled herself dry, took hold of a long flexible tube plugged into the wall, presented the nozzle to her breast, as though she meant to commit suicide, pressed down the trigger. A blast of warmed air dusted her with the finest talcum powder. Eight different scents and eau-de-Cologne were laid on in little taps over the wash-basin. She turned on the third from the left, dabbed herself with chypre and, carrying her shoes and stockings in her hand, went out to see if one of the vibro-vacuum machines were free.

And home was as squalid psychically as physically. Psychically, it was a rabbit hole, a midden, hot with the frictions of tightly packed life, reeking with emotion. What suffocating intimacies, what dangerous, insane, obscene relationships between the members of the family group! Maniacally, the mother brooded over her children (her children) . . . brooded over them like a cat over its kittens; but a cat that could talk, a cat that could say, "My baby, my baby," over and over again. "My baby, and oh, oh, at my breast, the little hands, the hunger, and that unspeakable agonizing pleasure! Till at last my baby sleeps, my baby sleeps with a bubble of white milk at the corner of his mouth. My little baby sleeps . . ."

"Yes," said Mustapha Mond, nodding his head, "you may well shudder."

"Who are you going out with to-night?" Lenina asked, returning from the vibro-vac like a pearl illuminated from within, pinkly glowing.

"Nobody."

Lenina raised her eyebrows in astonishment.

"I've been feeling rather out of sorts lately," Fanny explained. "Dr. Wells advised me to have a Pregnancy Substitute."

"But, my dear, you're only nineteen. The first Pregnancy Substitute isn't compulsory till twenty-one."

"I know, dear. But some people are better if they begin earlier. Dr. Wells told me that brunettes with wide pelvises, like me, ought to have their first Pregnancy Substitute at seventeen. So I'm really two years late, not two years early." She opened the door of her locker and pointed to the row of boxes and labelled phials on the upper shelf.

"SYRUP OF CORPUS LUTEUM," Lenina read the names aloud. "OVARIN, GUARANTEED FRESH: NOT TO BE USED AFTER AUGUST 1ST, A.F. 632. MAMMARY GLAND EXTRACT: TO BE TAKEN THREE TIMES DAILY, BEFORE MEALS, WITH A LITTLE WATER. PLACENTIN: 5cc TO BE INJECTED INTRAVENALLY EVERY THIRD DAY . . . Ugh!" Lenina shuddered. "How I loathe intravenals, don't you?"

"Yes. But when they do one good . . ." Fanny was a particularly sensible girl.

Our Ford — or Our Freud, as, for some inscrutable reason, he chose to call himself whenever he spoke of psychological matters — Our Freud had been the first to reveal the appalling dangers of family life. The world was full of fathers — was therefore full of misery; full of mothers — therefore of every kind of perversion from sadism to chastity; full of brothers, sisters, uncles, aunts — full of madness and suicide.

"And yet, among the savages of Samoa, in certain islands off the coast of New Guinea . . ."

The tropical sunshine lay like warm honey on the naked bodies of children tumbling promiscuously among the hibiscus blossoms. Home was in any one of twenty palm-thatched houses. In the Trobriands conception was the work of ancestral ghosts; nobody had ever heard of a father.

"Extremes," said the Controller, "meet. For the good reason that they were made to meet."

"Dr. Wells says that a three months' Pregnancy Substitute now will make all the difference to my health for the next three or four years."

"Well, I hope he's right," said Lenina. "But, Fanny, do you really mean to say that for the next three months you're not supposed to . . ."

"Oh no, dear. Only for a week or two, that's all. I shall spend the evening at the Club playing Musical Bridge. I suppose you're going out?"

Lenina nodded.

"Who with?"

"Henry Foster."

"Again?" Fanny's kind, rather moon-like face took on an incongruous expression of pained and disapproving astonishment. "Do you mean to tell me you're *still* going out with Henry Foster?"

Mothers and fathers, brothers and sisters. But there were also husbands, wives, lovers. There were also monogamy and romance.

"Though you probably don't know what those are," said Mustapha Mond.

They shook their heads.

Family, monogamy, romance. Everywhere exclusiveness, a narrow channelling of impulse and energy.

"But every one belongs to every one else," he concluded, citing the hypnopædic proverb.

The students nodded, emphatically agreeing with a statement which upwards of sixty-two thousand repetitions in the dark had made them accept, not merely as true, but as axiomatic, self-evident, utterly indisputable.

"But after all," Lenina was protesting, "it's only about four months now since I've been having Henry."

"*Only* four months! I like that. And what's more," Fanny went on, pointing an accusing finger, "there's been nobody else except Henry all that time. Has there?"

Lenina blushed scarlet; but her eyes, the tone of her voice remained defiant. "No, there hasn't been any one else," she answered almost truculently. "And I jolly well don't see why there should have been."

"Oh, she jolly well doesn't see why there should have been," Fanny repeated, as though to an invisible listener behind Lenina's left shoulder. Then, with a sudden change of tone, "But seriously," she said, "I really do think you ought to be careful. It's such horribly bad form to go on and on like this with one man. At forty, or thirty-five, it wouldn't be so bad. But at *your* age, Lenina! No, it really won't do. And you know how strongly the D.H.C. objects to anything intense or long-drawn. Four months of Henry Foster, without having another man — why, he'd be furious if he knew . . ."

"Think of water under pressure in a pipe." They thought of it. "I pierce it once," said the Controller. "What a jet!"

He pierced it twenty times. There were twenty piddling little fountains.

"My baby. My baby . . . !"

"Mother!" The madness is infectious.

"My love, my one and only, precious, precious . . ."

Mother, monogamy, romance. High spurts the fountain; fierce and foamy the wild jet. The urge has but a single outlet. My love, my baby. No wonder these poor pre-moderns were mad and wicked and miserable. Their world didn't allow them to take things easily, didn't allow them to be sane, virtuous, happy. What with mothers and lovers, what with the prohibitions they were not conditioned to obey, what with the temptations and the lonely remorses, what with all the diseases and the endless isolating pain, what with the uncertainties and the poverty — they were forced to feel strongly. And feeling strongly (and strongly, what was more, in solitude, in hopelessly individual isolation), how could they be stable?

《《

"Of course there's no need to give him up. Have somebody else from time to time, that's all. He has other girls, doesn't he?"

Lenina admitted it.

"Of course he does. Trust Henry Foster to be the perfect gentleman — always correct. And then there's the Director to think of. You know what a stickler . . ."

Nodding, "He patted me on the behind this afternoon," said Lenina.

"There, you see!" Fanny was triumphant. "That shows what *he* stands for. The strictest conventionality."

"Stability," said the Controller, "stability. No civilization without social stability. No social stability without individual stability." His voice was a trumpet. Listening they felt larger, warmer.

The machine turns, turns and must keep on turning — for ever. It is death if it stands still. A thousand millions scrabbled the crust of the earth. The wheels began to turn. In a hundred and fifty years there were two thousand millions. Stop all the wheels. In a hundred and fifty weeks there are once more only a thousand millions; a thousand thousand thousand men and women have starved to death.

Wheels must turn steadily, but cannot turn untended. There must be men to tend them, men as steady as the wheels upon their axles, sane men, obedient men, stable in contentment.

Crying: My baby, my mother, my only, only love groaning: My sin, my terrible God; screaming with pain, muttering with fever, bemoaning old age and poverty — how can they tend the wheels? And if they cannot tend the wheels . . . The corpses of a thousand thousand thousand men and women would be hard to bury or burn.

"And after all," Fanny's tone was coaxing, "it's not as though there were anything painful or disagreeable about having one or two men besides Henry. And seeing that you *ought* to be a little more promiscuous. . ."

"Stability," insisted the Controller, "stability. The primal and the ultimate need. Stability. Hence all this."

With a wave of his hand he indicated the gardens, the huge building of the Conditioning Centre, the naked children furtive in the undergrowth or running across the lawns.

Lenina shook her head. "Somehow," she mused, "I hadn't been feeling very keen on promiscuity lately. There are times when one doesn't. Haven't you found that too, Fanny?"

Fanny nodded her sympathy and understanding. "But one's got to make the effort," she said, sententiously, "one's got to play the game. After all, every one belongs to every one else."

"Yes, every one belongs to every one else," Lenina repeated slowly and, sighing, was silent for a moment; then, taking Fanny's hand, gave it a little squeeze. "You're quite right, Fanny. As usual. I'll make the effort."

Impulse arrested spills over, and the flood is feeling, the flood is passion, the flood is even madness: it depends on the force of the current, the height and strength of the barrier. The unchecked stream flows smoothly down its appointed channels into a calm well-being. The embryo is hungry; day in, day out, the blood-surrogate pump unceasingly turns its eight hundred revolutions a minute. The decanted infant howls; at once a nurse appears with a bottle of external secretion. Feeling lurks in that interval of time between desire and its consummation. Shorten that interval, break down all those old unnecessary barriers.

"Fortunate boys!" said the Controller. "No pains have been spared to make your lives emotionally easy — to preserve you, so far as that is possible, from having emotions at all."

"Ford's in his flivver," murmured the D.H.C. "All's well with the world."

"Lenina Crowne?" said Henry Foster, echoing the Assistant Predestinator's question as he zipped up his trousers. "Oh, she's a splendid girl. Wonderfully pneumatic. I'm surprised you haven't had her."

"I can't think how it is I haven't," said the Assistant Predestinator. "I certainly will. At the first opportunity."

From his place on the opposite side of the changing-room aisle, Bernard Marx overheard what they were saying and turned pale.

"And to tell the truth," said Lenina, "I'm beginning to get just a tiny bit bored with nothing but Henry every day." She pulled on her left stocking. "Do you know Bernard Marx?" she asked in a tone whose excessive casualness was evidently forced.

Fanny looked startled. "You don't mean to say . . .?"

"Why not? Bernard's an Alpha Plus. Besides, he asked me to go to one of the Savage Reservations with him. I've always wanted to see a Savage Reservation."

"But his reputation?"

"What do I care about his reputation?"

"They say he doesn't like Obstacle Golf."

"They say, they say," mocked Lenina.

"And then he spends most of his time by himself — *alone*." There was horror in Fanny's voice.

"Well, he won't be alone when he's with me. And anyhow, why are people so beastly to him? I think he's rather sweet." She smiled to herself; how absurdly shy he had been! Frightened almost — as though she were a World Controller and he a Gamma-Minus machine minder.

"Consider your own lives," said Mustapha Mond. "Has any of you ever encountered an insurmountable obstacle?"

The question was answered by a negative silence.

"Has any of you been compelled to live through a long time-interval between the consciousness of a desire and its fufilment?"

"Well," began one of the boys, and hesitated.

"Speak up," said the D.H.C. "Don't keep his fordship waiting."

"I once had to wait nearly four weeks before a girl I wanted would let me have her."

"And you felt a strong emotion in consequence?"

"Horrible!"

"Horrible; precisely," said the Controller. "Our ancestors were so stupid and short-sighted that when the first reformers came along and offered to deliver them from those horrible emotions, they wouldn't have anything to do with them."

"Talking about her as though she were a bit of meat." Bernard ground his teeth. "Have her here, have her there. Like mutton. Degrading her to so much mutton. She said she'd think it over, she said she'd give me an answer this week. Oh, Ford, Ford, Ford." He would have liked to go up to them and hit them in the face — hard, again and again.

"Yes, I really do advise you to try her," Henry Foster was saying.

"Take Ectogenesis. Pfitzner and Kawaguchi had got the whole technique worked out. But would the Governments look at it? No. There was something called Christianity. Women were forced to go on being viviparous."

"He's so ugly!" said Fanny.

"But I rather like his looks."

"And then so *small*." Fanny made a grimace; small-ness was so horribly and typically low-caste.

"I think that's rather sweet," said Lenina. "One feels one would like to pet him. You know. Like a cat."

Fanny was shocked. "They say somebody made a mistake when he was still in the bottle — thought he was a Gamma and put alcohol into his blood-surrogate. That's why he's so stunted."

"What nonsense!" Lenina was indignant.

"Sleep teaching was actually prohibited in England. There was something called liberalism. Parliament, if you know what that was, passed a law against it. The records survive. Speeches about liberty of the subject. Liberty to be inefficient and miserable. Freedom to be a round peg in a square hole."

《《

"But, my dear chap, you're welcome, I assure you. You're welcome." Henry Foster patted the Assistant Predestinator on the shoulder. "Every one belongs to every one else, after all."

One hundred repetitions three nights a week for four years, thought Bernard Marx, who was a specialist on hypnopædia. Sixty-two thousand four hundred repetitions make one truth. Idiots!

"Or the Caste System. Constantly proposed, constantly rejected. There was something called democracy. As though men were more than physico-chemically equal."

"Well, all I can say is that I'm going to accept his invitation."

Bernard hated them, hated them. But they were two, they were large, they were strong.

"Then the Nine Years' War began in A.F. 141."

"Not even if it *were* true about the alcohol in his blood-surrogate."

"Phosgene, chloropicrin, ethyl iodoacetate, diphenyl-cyanarsine, trichlormethyl, chloroformate, dichlo-rethyl sulphide. Not to mention hydrocyanic acid."

"Which I simply don't believe," Lenina concluded.

"The noise of fourteen thousand aeroplanes advancing in open order. But in the Kurfurstendamm and the Eighth Arrondissement, the explosion of the anthrax bombs is hardly louder than the popping of a paper bag."

"Because I *do* want to see a Savage Reservation."

$Ch_8C_6H_2(NO_2)_8$ + $Hg(CNO)_2$ = well, what? An enormous hole in the ground, a pile of masonry, some bits of flesh and mucus, a foot, with the boot still on it, flying through the air and landing, flop, in the middle of the geraniums — the scarlet ones; such a splendid show that summer!

"You're hopeless, Lenina, I give you up."

"The Russian technique for infecting water supplies was particularly ingenious."

Back turned to back, Fanny and Lenina continued their changing in silence.

"The Nine Years' War, the great Economic Collapse. There was a choice between World Control and destruction. Between stability and . . ."

"Fanny Crowne's a nice girl too," said the Assistant Predestinator.

In the nurseries, the Elementary Class Consciousness lesson was over, the voices were adapting future demand to future industrial supply. "I do love flying," they whispered, "I do love flying, I do love having new clothes, I do love . . ."

« «

"Liberalism, of course, was dead of anthrax, but all the same you couldn't do things by force."

"Not nearly so pneumatic as Lenina. Oh, not nearly."

"But old clothes are beastly," continued the untiring whisper. "We always throw away old clothes. Ending is better than mending, ending is better than mending, ending is better . . ."

"Government's an affair of sitting, not hitting. You rule with the brains and the buttocks, never with the fists. For example, there was the conscription of consumption."

"There, I'm ready," said Lenina, but Fanny remained speechless and averted. "Let's make peace, Fanny darling."

"Every man, woman and child compelled to consume so much a year. In the interests of industry. The sole result . . ."

"Ending is better than mending. The more stitches, the less riches; the more stitches . . ."

"One of these days," said Fanny, with dismal emphasis, "you'll get into trouble."

"Conscientious objection on an enormous scale. Anything not to consume. Back to nature."

"I do love flying. I do love flying."

《《《《《《《《《《《《《《《《《《《《《《《《《《《《《《《《《《《《《《《

"Back to culture. Yes, actually to culture. You can't consume much if you sit still and read books."

"Do I look all right?" Lenina asked. Her jacket was made of bottle green acetate cloth with green viscose fur at the cuffs and collar.

"Eight hundred Simple Lifers were mowed down by machine guns at Golders Green."

"Ending is better than mending, ending is better than mending."

Green corduroy shorts and white viscose-woollen stockings turned down below the knee.

"Then came the famous British Museum Massacre. Two thousand culture fans gassed with dichlorethyl sulphide."

A green-and-white jockey cap shaded Lenina's eyes; her shoes were bright green and highly polished.

"In the end," said Mustapha Mond, "the Controllers realized that force was no good. The slower but infinitely surer methods of ectogenesis, neo-Pavlovian conditioning and hypnopædia . . ."

And round her waist she wore a silver-mounted green morocco-surrogate cartridge belt, bulging (for Lenina was not a freemartin) with the regulation supply of contraceptives.

《《《

"The discoveries of Pfitzner and Kawaguchi were at last made use of. An intensive propaganda against viviparous reproduction . . ."

"Perfect!" cried Fanny enthusiastically. She could never resist Lenina's charm for long. "And what a perfectly *sweet* Malthusian belt!"

"Accompanied by a campaign against the Past; by the closing of museums, the blowing up of historical monuments (luckily most of them had already been destroyed during the Nine Years' War); by the suppression of all books published before A.F. 150."

"I simply must get one like it," said Fanny.

"There were some things called the pyramids, for example."

"My old black-patent bandolier . . ."

"And a man called Shakespeare. You've never heard of them of course."

"It's an absolute disgrace — that bandolier of mine."

"Such are the advantages of a really scientific education."

"The more stitches the less riches; the more stitches the less . . ."

《《

"The introduction of Our Ford's first T-Model . . ."

"I've had it nearly three months."

"Chosen as the opening date of the new era."

"Ending is better than mending; ending is better . . . "

"There was a thing, as I've said before, called Christianity."

"Ending is better than mending."

"The ethics and philosophy of under-consumption. . ."

"I love new clothes, I love new clothes, I love . . ."

"So essential when there was under-production; but in an age of machines and the fixation of nitrogen — positively a crime against society."

"Henry Foster gave it me."

"All crosses had their tops cut and became T's. There was also a thing called God."

"It's real morocco-surrogate."

"We have the World State now. And Ford's Day celebrations, and Community Sings, and Solidarity Services."

《《

"Ford, how I hate them!" Bernard Marx was thinking.

"There was a thing called Heaven; but all the same they used to drink enormous quantities of alcohol."

"Like meat, like so much meat."

"There was a thing called the soul and a thing called immortality."

"Do ask Henry where he got it."

"But they used to take morphia and cocaine."

"And what makes it worse, she thinks of herself as meat."

"Two thousand pharmacologists and bio-chemists were subsidized in A.F. 178."

"He does look glum," said the Assistant Predestinator, pointing at Bernard Marx.

"Six years later it was being produced commercially. The perfect drug."

"Let's bait him."

"Euphoric, narcotic, pleasantly hallucinant."

«««««««««««««««««««««««««««««««««««««««

"Glum, Marx, glum." The clap on the shoulder made him start, look up. It was that brute Henry Foster. "What you need is a gramme of *soma*."

"All the advantages of Christianity and alcohol; none of their defects."

"Ford, I should like to kill him!" But all he did was to say, "No, thank you," and fend off the proffered tube of tablets.

"Take a holiday from reality whenever you like, and come back without so much as a headache or a mythology."

"Take it," insisted Henry Foster, "take it."

"Stability was practically assured."

"One cubic centimetre cures ten gloomy sentiments," said the Assistant Predestinator, citing a piece of homely hypnopædic wisdom.

"It only remained to conquer old age."

"Damn you, damn you!" shouted Bernard Marx.

"Hoity-toity."

"Gonadal hormones, transfusion of young blood, magnesium salts . . ."

《《《

"And do remember that a gramme is better than a damn." They went out, laughing.

"All the physiological stigmata of old age have been abolished. And along with them, of course . . ."

"Don't forget to ask him about that Malthusian belt," said Fanny.

"Along with them all the old man's mental peculiarities. Characters remain constant throughout a whole lifetime."

". . . two rounds of Obstacle Golf to get through before dark. I must fly."

"Work, play — at sixty our powers and tastes are what they were at seventeen. Old men in the bad old days used to renounce, retire, take to religion, spend their time reading, thinking — *thinking!*"

"Idiots, swine!" Bernard Marx was saying to himself, as he walked down the corridor to the lift.

"Now — such is progress — the old men work, the old men copulate, the old men have no time, no leisure from pleasure, not a moment to sit down and think — or if ever by some unlucky chance such a crevice of time should yawn in the solid substance of their distractions, there is always *soma*, delicious *soma*, half a gramme for a half-holiday, a gramme for a week-end, two grammes for a trip to the gorgeous East, three for a dark eternity on the moon; returning whence they find themselves on the other side of the crevice, safe on the solid ground of daily labour and distraction, scampering from feely to feely, from girl to pneumatic girl, from Electromagnetic Golf course to . . ."

"Go away, little girl," shouted the D.H.C. angrily. "Go away, little boy! Can't you see that his fordship's busy? Go and do your erotic play somewhere else."

"Suffer little children," said the Controller.

Slowly, majestically, with a faint humming of machinery, the Conveyors moved forward, thirty-three centimetres an hour. In the red darkness glinted innumerable rubies.

CHAPTER 4

Part 1

The lift was crowded with men from the Alpha Changing Rooms, and Lenina's entry was greeted by many friendly nods and smiles. She was a popular girl and, at one time or another, had spent a night with almost all of them.

They were dear boys, she thought, as she returned their salutations. Charming boys! Still, she did wish that George Edzel's ears weren't quite so big (perhaps he'd been given just a spot too much parathyroid at Metre 328?). And looking at Benito Hoover, she couldn't help remembering that he was really *too* hairy when he took his clothes off.

Turning, with eyes a little saddened by the recollection of Benito's curly blackness, she saw in a corner the small thin body, the melancholy face of Bernard Marx.

"Bernard!" she stepped up to him. "I was looking for you." Her voice rang clear above the hum of the mounting lift. The others looked round curiously. "I wanted to talk to you about our New Mexico plan." Out of the tail of her eye she could see Benito Hoover gaping with astonishment. The gape annoyed her. "Surprised I shouldn't be begging to go with *him* again!" she said to herself. Then aloud, and more warmly than ever, "I'd simply *love* to come with you for a week in July," she went on. (Anyhow, she was publicly proving her unfaithfulness to Henry. Fanny ought to be pleased, even though it was Bernard.) "That is," Lenina gave him her most deliciously significant smile, "if you still want to have me."

Bernard's pale face flushed. "What on earth for?" she wondered, astonished, but at the same time touched by this strange tribute to her power.

"Hadn't we better talk about it somewhere else?" he stammered, looking horribly uncomfortable.

"As though I'd been saying something shocking," thought Lenina. "He couldn't look more upset if I'd made a dirty joke — asked him who his mother was, or something like that."

"I mean, with all these people about . . ." He was choked with confusion.

Lenina's laugh was frank and wholly unmalicious. "How funny you are!" she said; and she quite genuinely did think him funny. "You'll give me at least a week's warning, won't you," she went on in another tone. "I suppose we take the Blue Pacific Rocket? Does it start from the Charing-T Tower? Or is it from Hampstead?"

Before Bernard could answer, the lift came to a standstill.

"Roof!" called a creaking voice.

The liftman was a small simian creature, dressed in the black tunic of an Epsilon-Minus Semi-Moron.

"Roof!"

He flung open the gates. The warm glory of afternoon sunlight made him start and blink his eyes. "Oh, roof!" he repeated in a voice of rapture. He was as though suddenly and joyfully awakened from a dark annihilating stupor. "Roof!"

He smiled up with a kind of doggily expectant adoration into the faces of his passengers. Talking and laughing together, they stepped out into the light. The liftman looked after them.

"Roof?" he said once more, questioningly.

Then a bell rang, and from the ceiling of the lift

a loud speaker began, very softly and yet very imperiously, to issue its commands.

"Go down," it said, "go down. Floor Eighteen. Go down, go down. Floor Eighteen. Go down, go . . ."

The liftman slammed the gates, touched a button and instantly dropped back into the droning twilight of the well, the twilight of his own habitual stupor.

It was warm and bright on the roof. The summer afternoon was drowsy with the hum of passing helicopters; and the deeper drone of the rocket-planes hastening, invisible, through the bright sky five or six miles overhead was like a caress on the soft air. Bernard Marx drew a deep breath. He looked up into the sky and round the blue horizon and finally down into Lenina's face.

"Isn't it beautiful!" His voice trembled a little.

She smiled at him with an expression of the most sympathetic understanding. "Simply perfect for Obstacle Golf," she answered rapturously. "And now I must fly, Bernard. Henry gets cross if I keep him waiting. Let me know in good time about the date." And waving her hand she ran away across the wide flat roof towards the hangars. Bernard stood watching the retreating twinkle of the white stockings, the sunburnt knees vivaciously bending and unbending again, again, and the softer rolling of those well-fitted corduroy shorts beneath the bottle green jacket. His face wore an expression of pain.

"I should say she was pretty," said a loud and cheery voice just behind him.

Bernard started and looked around. The chubby red face of Benito Hoover was beaming down at him — beaming with manifest cordiality. Benito was notoriously good-natured. People said of him that he could have got through life without ever touching *soma*. The malice and bad tempers from which other people had to take holidays never afflicted him. Reality for Benito was always sunny.

"Pneumatic too. And how!" Then, in another tone: "But, I say," he went on, "you do look glum! What you need is a gramme of *soma*." Diving into his right-hand trouser-pocket, Benito produced a phial. "One cubic centimetre cures ten gloomy . . . But, I say!"

Bernard had suddenly turned and rushed away.

Benito stared after him. "What can be the matter with the fellow?" he wondered, and, shaking his head, decided that the story about the alcohol having been put into the poor chap's blood-surrogate must be true. "Touched his brain, I suppose."

He put away the *soma* bottle, and taking out a packet of sex-hormone chewing-gum, stuffed a plug into his cheek and walked slowly away towards the hangars, ruminating.

Henry Foster had had his machine wheeled out of its lock-up and, when Lenina arrived, was already seated in the cockpit, waiting.

"Four minutes late," was all his comment, as she climbed in beside him. He started the engines and threw the helicopter screws into gear. The machine shot vertically into the air. Henry accelerated; the humming of the propeller shrilled from hornet to wasp, from wasp to mosquito; the speedometer showed that they were rising at the best part of two kilometres a minute. London diminished beneath them. The huge table-topped buildings were no more, in a few seconds, than a bed of geometrical mushrooms sprouting from the green of park and garden. In the midst of them, thin-stalked, a taller, slenderer fungus, the Charing-T Tower lifted towards the sky a disk of shining concrete.

Like the vague torsos of fabulous athletes, huge fleshy clouds lolled on the blue air above their heads. Out of one of them suddenly dropped a small scarlet insect, buzzing as it fell.

"There's the Red Rocket," said Henry, "just come in from New York." Looking at his watch. "Seven minutes behind time," he added, and shook his head. "These Atlantic services — they're really scandalously unpunctual."

He took his foot off the accelerator. The humming of the screws overhead dropped an octave and a half, back through wasp and hornet to bumble bee, to cockchafer, to stag-beetle. The upward rush of the machine slackened off; a moment later they were hanging motionless in the air. Henry pushed at a lever; there was a click. Slowly at first, then faster and faster, till it was a circular mist before their eyes, the propeller in front of them began to revolve. The wind of a horizontal speed whistled ever more shrilly in the stays. Henry kept his eye on the revolution-counter; when the needle touched the twelve hundred mark, he threw the helicopter screws out of gear. The machine had enough forward momentum to be able to fly on its planes.

Lenina looked down through the window in the floor between her feet. They were flying over the six kilometre zone of park-land that separated Central London from its first ring of satellite suburbs. The green was maggoty with fore-shortened life. Forests of Centrifugal Bumble-puppy towers gleamed between the trees. Near Shepherd's Bush two thousand Beta-Minus mixed doubles were playing Riemann-surface tennis. A double row of Escalator Fives Courts lined the main road from Notting Hill to Willesden. In the Ealing stadium a Delta gymnastic display and community sing was in progress.

"What a hideous colour khaki is," remarked Lenina, voicing the hypnopædic prejudices of her caste.

The buildings of the Hounslow Feely Studio covered seven and a half hectares. Near them a black and khaki army of labourers was busy revitrifying the surface of the Great West Road. One of the huge travelling crucibles was being tapped as they flew over. The molten stone poured out in a stream of dazzling incandescence across the road, the asbestos rollers came and went; at the tail of an insulated watering cart the steam rose in white clouds.

At Brentford the Television Corporation's factory was like a small town.

"They must be changing the shift," said Lenina.

Like aphides and ants, the leaf-green Gamma girls, the black Semi-Morons swarmed round the entrances, or stood in queues to take their places in the mono-rail tram-cars. Mulberry-coloured Beta-Minuses came and went among the crowd. The roof of the main building was alive with the alighting and departure of helicopters.

"My word," said Lenina, "I'm glad I'm not a Gamma."

Ten minutes later they were at Stoke Poges and had started their first round of Obstacle Golf.

CHAPTER 4

Part 2

With eyes for the most part downcast and, if ever they lighted on a fellow creature, at once and furtively averted, Bernard hastened across the roof. He was like a man pursued, but pursued by enemies he does not wish to see, lest they should seem more hostile even than he had supposed, and he himself be made to feel guiltier and even more helplessly alone.

"That horrible Benito Hoover!" And yet the man had meant well enough. Which only made it, in a way, much worse. Those who meant well behaved in the same way as those who meant badly. Even Lenina was making him suffer. He remembered those weeks of timid indecision, during which he had looked and longed and despaired of ever having the courage to ask her. Dared he face the risk of being humiliated by a contemptuous refusal? But if she were to say yes, what rapture! Well, now she had said it and he was still wretched — wretched that she should have thought it such a perfect afternoon for Obstacle Golf, that she should have trotted away to join Henry Foster, that she should have found him funny for not wanting to talk of their most private affairs in public. Wretched, in a word, because she had behaved as any healthy and virtuous English girl ought to behave and not in some other, abnormal, extraordinary way.

He opened the door of his lock-up and called to a lounging couple of Delta-Minus attendants to come and push his machine out on to the roof. The hangars were staffed by a single Bokanovsky Group, and the men were twins, identically small, black and hideous. Bernard gave his orders in the sharp, rather arrogant and even offensive tone of one who does not feel himself too secure in his superiority. To have dealings with members of the lower castes was always, for Bernard, a most distressing experience. For whatever the cause (and the current gossip about the alcohol in his blood-surrogate may very likely — for accidents will happen — have been true) Bernard's physique was hardly better than that of the average Gamma. He stood eight centimetres short of the standard Alpha height and was slender in proportion. Contact with members of the lower castes always reminded him painfully of this physical inadequacy. "I am I, and wish I wasn't"; his self-consciousness was acute and stressing. Each time he found himself looking on the level, instead of downward, into a Delta's face, he felt humiliated. Would the creature treat him with the respect due to his caste? The question haunted him. Not without reason. For Gammas, Deltas and Epsilons had been to some extent conditioned to associate corporeal mass with social superiority. Indeed, a faint hypnopædic prejudice in favour of size was universal. Hence the laughter of the women to whom he made proposals, the practical joking of his equals among the men. The mockery made him feel an outsider; and feeling an outsider he behaved like one, which increased the prejudice against him and intensified the contempt and hostility aroused by his physical defects. Which in turn increased his sense of being alien and alone. A chronic fear of being slighted made him avoid his equals, made him stand, where his inferiors were concerned, self-consciously on his dignity. How bitterly he envied men like Henry Foster and Benito Hoover! Men who never had to shout at an Epsilon to get an order obeyed; men who took their position for granted; men who moved through the caste system as a fish through water — so utterly at home as to be unaware either of themselves or of the beneficent and comfortable element in which they had their being.

Slackly, it seemed to him, and with reluctance, the twin attendants wheeled his plane out on the roof.

"Hurry up!" said Bernard irritably. One of them glanced at him. Was that a kind of bestial derision that he detected in those blank grey eyes? "Hurry up!" he shouted more loudly, and there was an ugly rasp in his voice.

He climbed into the plane and, a minute later, was flying southwards, towards the river.

The various Bureaux of Propaganda and the College of Emotional Engineering were housed in a single sixty-story building in Fleet Street. In the basement and on the low floors were the presses and offices of the three great London newspapers — *The Hourly Radio,* an upper-caste sheet, the pale green *Gamma Gazette,* and, on khaki paper and in words exclusively of one syllable, *The Delta Mirror.* Then came the Bureaux of Propaganda by Television, by Feeling Picture, and by Synthetic Voice and Music respectively — twenty-two floors of them. Above were the search laboratories and the padded rooms in which Sound-Track Writers and Synthetic Composers did their delicate work. The top eighteen floors were occupied by the College of Emotional Engineering.

Bernard landed on the roof of Propaganda House and stepped out.

"Ring down to Mr. Helmholtz Watson," he ordered the Gamma-Plus porter, "and tell him that Mr. Bernard Marx is waiting for him on the roof."

He sat down and lit a cigarette.

Helmholtz Watson was writing when the message came down.

"Tell him I'm coming at once," he said and hung up the receiver. Then, turning to his secretary, "I'll leave you to put my things away," he went on in the same official and impersonal tone; and, ignoring her lustrous smile, got up and walked briskly to the door.

He was a powerfully built man, deep-chested, broad-shouldered, massive, and yet quick in his movements, springy and agile. The round strong pillar of his neck supported a beautifully shaped head. His hair was dark and curly, his features strongly marked. In a forcible emphatic way, he was handsome and looked, as his secretary was never tired of repeating, every centimetre an Alpha Plus. By profession he was a lecturer at the College of Emotional Engineering (Department of Writing) and in the intervals of his educational activities, a working Emotional Engineer. He wrote regularly for *The Hourly Radio,* composed feely scenarios, and had the happiest knack for slogans and hypnopædic rhymes.

"Able," was the verdict of his superiors. "Perhaps, (and they would shake their heads, would significantly lower their voices) a little *too* able."

Yes, a little too able; they were right. A mental excess had produced in Helmholtz Watson effects very similar to those which, in Bernard Marx, were the result of a physical defect. Too little bone and brawn had isolated Bernard from his fellow men, and the sense of this apartness, being, by all the current standards, a mental excess, became in its turn a cause of wider separation. That which had made Helmholtz so uncomfortably aware of being himself and all alone was too much ability. What the two men shared was the knowledge that they were individuals. But whereas the physically defective Bernard had suffered all his life from the consciousness of being separate, it was only quite recently that, grown aware of his mental excess,

Helmholtz Watson had also become aware of his difference from the people who surrounded him. This Escalator-Squash champion, this indefatigable lover (it was said that he had had six hundred and forty different girls in under four years), this admirable committee man and best mixer had realized quite suddenly that sport, women, communal activities were only, so far as he was concerned, second bests. Really, and at the bottom, he was interested in something else. But in what? In what? That was the problem which Bernard had come to discuss with him — or rather, since it was always Helmholtz who did all the talking, to listen to his friend discussing, yet once more.

Three charming girls from the Bureaux of Propaganda by Synthetic Voice waylaid him as he stepped out of the lift.

"Oh, Helmholtz, darling, *do* come and have a picnic supper with us on Exmoor." They clung round him imploringly.

He shook his head, he pushed his way through them. "No, no."

"We're not inviting any other man."

But Helmholtz remained unshaken even by this delightful promise. "No," he repeated, "I'm busy." And he held resolutely on his course. The girls trailed after him. It was not till he had actually climbed into Bernard's plane and slammed the door that they gave up pursuit. Not without reproaches.

"These women!" he said, as the machine rose into the air. "These women!" And he shook his head, he frowned. "Too awful," Bernard hypocritically agreed, wishing, as he spoke the words, that he could have as many girls as Helmholtz did, and with as little trouble. He was seized with a sudden urgent need to boast. "I'm taking Lenina Crowne to New Mexico with me," he said in a tone as casual as he could make it.

"Are you?" said Helmholtz, with a total absence of interest. Then after a little pause, "This last week or two," he went on, "I've been cutting all my committees and all my girls. You can't imagine what a hullabaloo they've been making about it at the College. Still, it's been worth it, I think. The effects . . ." He hesitated. "Well, they're odd, they're very odd."

A physical shortcoming could produce a kind of mental excess. The process, it seemed, was reversible. Mental excess could produce, for its own purposes, the voluntary blindness and deafness of deliberate solitude, the artificial impotence of asceticism.

The rest of the short flight was accomplished in silence. When they had arrived and were comfortably stretched out on the pneumatic sofas in Bernard's room, Helmholtz began again.

Speaking very slowly, "Did you ever feel," he asked, "as though you had something inside you that was only waiting for you to give it a chance to come out? Some sort of extra power that you aren't using — you know, like all the water that goes down the falls instead of through the turbines?" He looked at Bernard questioningly.

"You mean all the emotions one might be feeling if things were different?"

Helmholtz shook his head. "Not quite. I'm thinking of a queer feeling I sometimes get, a feeling that I've got something important to say and the power to say it — only I don't know what it is, and I can't make any use of the power. If there was some different way of writing . . . Or else something else to write about . . ." He was silent; then, "You see," he went on at last, "I'm pretty good at inventing phrases — you know, the sort of words that suddenly make you jump, almost as though you'd sat on a pin, they seem so new and exciting even though they're about something hypnopædically obvious. But that doesn't seem enough. It's not enough for the phrases to be good; what you make with them ought to be good too."

"But your things are good, Helmholtz."

"Oh, as far as they go." Helmholtz shrugged his shoulders. "But they go such a little way. They aren't important enough, somehow. I feel I could do something much more important. Yes, and more intense, more violent. But what? What is there more important to say? And how can one be violent about the sort of things one's expected to write about? Words can be like X-rays, if you use them properly — they'll go through anything. You read and you're pierced. That's one of the things I try to teach my students — how to write piercingly. But what on earth's the good of being pierced by an article about a Community Sing, or the latest improvement in scent organs? Besides, can you make words really piercing — you know, like the very hardest X-rays — when you're writing about that sort of thing? Can you say something about nothing? That's what it finally boils down to. I try and I try . . ."

"Hush!" said Bernard suddenly, and lifted a warning finger; they listened. "I believe there's somebody at the door," he whispered.

Helmholtz got up, tiptoed across the room, and with a sharp quick movement flung the door wide open. There was, of course, nobody there.

"I'm sorry," said Bernard, feeling and looking uncomfortably foolish. "I suppose I've got things on my nerves a bit. When people are suspicious with you, you start being suspicious with them."

He passed his hand across his eyes, he sighed, his voice became plaintive. He was justifying himself.

"If you knew what I'd had to put up with recently," he said almost tearfully — and the uprush of his self-pity was like a fountain suddenly released. "If you only knew!"

Helmholtz Watson listened with a certain sense of discomfort. "Poor little Bernard!" he said to himself. But at the same time he felt rather ashamed for his friend. He wished Bernard would show a little more pride.

By eight o'clock the light was failing. The loud speaker in the tower of the Stoke Poges Club House began, in a more than human tenor, to announce the closing of the courses. Lenina and Henry abandoned their game and walked back towards the Club. From the grounds of the Internal and External Secretion Trust came the lowing of those thousands of cattle which provided, with their hormones and their milk, the raw materials for the great factory at Farnham Royal.

An incessant buzzing of helicopters filled the twilight. Every two and a half minutes a bell and the screech of whistles announced the departure of one of the light monorail trains which carried the lower caste golfers back from their separate course to the metropolis.

Lenina and Henry climbed into their machine and started off. At eight hundred feet Henry slowed down the helicopter screws, and they hung for a minute or two poised above the fading landscape. The forest of Burnham Beeches stretched like a great pool of darkness towards the bright shore of the western sky. Crimson at the horizon, the last of the sunset faded, through orange, upwards into yellow and a pale watery green. Northwards, beyond and above the trees, the Internal and External Secretions factory glared with a fierce electric brilliance from every window of its twenty stories. Beneath them lay the buildings of the Golf Club — the huge Lower Caste barracks and, on the other side of a dividing wall, the smaller houses reserved for Alpha and Beta members. The approaches to the monorail station were black with the ant-like pullulation of lower-caste activity. From under the glass vault a lighted train shot out into the open. Following its southeasterly course across the dark plain their eyes were drawn to the majestic buildings of the Slough Crematorium. For the safety of night-flying planes, its four tall chimneys were flood-lighted and tipped with crimson danger signals. It was a landmark.

"Why do the smoke-stacks have those things like balconies around them?" enquired Lenina.

"Phosphorus recovery," explained Henry telegraph-ically. "On their way up the chimney the gases go through four separate treatments. P_2O_5 used to go right out of circulation every time they cremated some one. Now they recover over ninety-eight per cent of it. More than a kilo and a half per adult corpse. Which makes the best part of four hundred tons of phos-phorus every year from England alone." Henry spoke with a happy pride, rejoicing whole-heartedly in the achievement, as though it had been his own. "Fine to think we can go on being socially useful even after we're dead. Making plants grow."

Lenina, meanwhile, had turned her eyes away and was looking perpendicularly downwards at the mono-rail station. "Fine," she agreed. "But queer that Alphas and Betas won't make any more plants grow than those nasty little Gammas and Deltas and Epsilons down there."

"All men are physico-chemically equal," said Henry sententiously. "Besides, even Epsilons perform indispensable services."

"Even an Epsilon . . ." Lenina suddenly remem-bered an occasion when, as a little girl at school, she had woken up in the middle of the night and become aware, for the first time, of the whispering that had haunted all her sleeps. She saw again the beam of moonlight, the row of small white beds; heard once more the soft, soft voice that said (the words were there, unforgotten, unforgettable after so many night-long repetitions): "Every one works for every one else. We can't do without any one. Even Epsilons are useful. We couldn't do without Epsilons. Every one works for every one else. We can't do without any one . . ." Lenina remembered her first shock of fear and surprise; her speculations through half a wakeful hour; and then, under the influence of those endless repetitions, the gradual soothing of her mind, the soothing, the smoothing, the stealthy creeping of sleep. . . ."

"I suppose Epsilons don't really mind being Epsilons," she said aloud.

"Of course they don't. How can they? They don't know what it's like being anything else. We'd mind, of course. But then we've been differently conditioned. Besides, we start with a different heredity."

"I'm glad I'm not an Epsilon," said Lenina, with conviction.

"And if you were an Epsilon," said Henry, "your conditioning would have made you no less thankful that you weren't a Beta or an Alpha." He put his forward propeller into gear and headed the machine towards London. Behind them, in the west, the crimson and orange were almost faded; a dark bank of cloud had crept into the zenith. As they flew over the crematorium, the plane shot upwards on the column of hot air rising from the chimneys, only to fall as suddenly when it passed into the descending chill beyond.

"What a marvellous switchback!" Lenina laughed delightedly.

But Henry's tone was almost, for a moment, melancholy. "Do you know what that switchback was?" he said. "It was some human being finally and definitely disappearing. Going up in a squirt of hot gas. It would be curious to know who it was — a man or a woman, an Alpha or an Epsilon. . . ." He sighed. Then, in a resolutely cheerful voice, "Anyhow," he concluded, "there's one thing we can be certain of; whoever he may have been, he was happy when he was alive. Everybody's happy now."

"Yes, everybody's happy now," echoed Lenina. They had heard the words repeated a hundred and fifty times every night for twelve years.

Landing on the roof of Henry's forty-story apartment house in Westminster, they went straight down to the dining-hall. There, in a loud and cheerful company, they ate an excellent meal. *Soma* was served with the coffee. Lenina took two half-gramme tablets and Henry three. At twenty past nine they walked across the street to the newly opened Westminster Abbey Cabaret. It was a night almost without clouds, moonless and starry; but of this on the whole depressing fact Lenina and Henry were fortunately unaware. The electric sky-signs effectively shut off the outer darkness. "CALVIN STOPES AND HIS SIXTEEN SEXOPHONISTS." From the façade of the new Abbey the giant letters invitingly glared. "LONDON'S FINEST SCENT AND COLOUR ORGAN. ALL THE LATEST SYNTHETIC MUSIC."

They entered. The air seemed hot and somehow breathless with the scent of ambergris and sandalwood. On the domed ceiling of the hall, the colour organ had momentarily painted a tropical sunset. The Sixteen Sexophonists were playing an old favourite: "There ain't no Bottle in all the world like that dear little Bottle of mine." Four hundred couples were five-stepping round the polished floor. Lenina and Henry were soon the four hundred and first. The sexophones wailed like melodious cats under the moon, moaned in the alto and tenor registers as though the little death were upon them. Rich with a wealth of harmonics, their tremulous chorus mounted towards a climax, louder and ever louder — until at last, with a wave of his hand, the conductor let loose the final shattering note of ether-music and blew the sixteen merely human blowers clean out of existence. Thunder in A flat major. And then, in all but silence, in all but darkness, there followed a gradual deturgescence, a *diminuendo* sliding gradually, through quarter tones, down, down to a faintly whispered dominant chord that lingered on (while the five-four rhythms still pulsed below) charging the darkened seconds with an intense expectancy. And at last expectancy was fulfilled. There was a sudden explosive sunrise, and simultaneously, the Sixteen burst into song:

"*Bottle of mine, it's you I've always wanted!*

Bottle of mine, why was I ever decanted?

Skies are blue inside of you,

The weather's always fine;

For

There ain't no Bottle in all the world

Like that dear little Bottle of mine."

Five-stepping with the other four hundred round and round Westminster Abbey, Lenina and Henry were yet dancing in another world — the warm, the richly coloured, the infinitely friendly world of *soma*-holiday. How kind, how good-looking, how delightfully amusing every one was! "Bottle of mine, it's you I've always wanted . . ." But Lenina and Henry had what they wanted . . . They were inside, here and now — safely inside with the fine weather, the perennially blue sky. And when, exhausted, the Sixteen had laid by their sexophones and the Synthetic Music apparatus was producing the very latest in slow Malthusian Blues, they might have been twin embryos gently rocking together on the waves of a bottled ocean of blood-surrogate.

"Good-night, dear friends. Good-night, dear friends." The loud speakers veiled their commands in a genial and musical politeness. — "Good-night, dear friends . . ."

Obediently, with all the others, Lenina and Henry left the building. The depressing stars had travelled quite some way across the heavens. But though the separating screen of the sky-signs had now to a great extent dissolved, the two young people still retained their happy ignorance of the night.

Swallowing half an hour before closing time, that second dose of *soma* had raised a quite impenetrable wall between the actual universe and their minds. Bottled, they crossed the street; bottled, they took the lift up to Henry's room on the twenty-eighth floor. And yet, bottled as she was, and in spite of that second gramme of *soma*, Lenina did not forget to take all the contraceptive precautions prescribed by the regulations. Years of intensive hypnopædia and, from twelve to seventeen, Malthusian drill three times a week had made the taking of these precautions almost as automatic and inevitable as blinking.

"Oh, and that reminds me," she said, as she came back from the bathroom, "Fanny Crowne wants to know where you found that lovely green morocco-surrogate cartridge belt you gave me."

CHAPTER 5
Part 2

Alternate Thursdays were Bernard's Solidarity Service days. After an early dinner at the Aphroditæum (to which Helmholtz had recently been elected under Rule Two) he took leave of his friend and, hailing a taxi on the roof, told the man to fly to the Fordson Community Singery. The machine rose a couple of hundred metres, then headed eastwards, and as it turned, there before Bernard's eyes, gigantically beautiful, was the Singery. Flood-lighted, its three hundred and twenty metres of white Carrara-surrogate gleamed with a snowy incandescence over Ludgate Hill; at each of the four corners of its helicopter platform an immense T shone crimson against the night, and from the mouths of twenty-four vast golden trumpets rumbled a solemn synthetic music.

"Damn, I'm late," Bernard said to himself as he first caught sight of Big Henry, the Singery clock. And sure enough, as he was paying off his cab, Big Henry sounded the hour. "Ford," sang out an immense bass voice from all the golden trumpets. "Ford, Ford, Ford . . ." Nine times. Bernard ran for the lift.

The great auditorium for Ford's Day celebrations and other massed Community Sings was at the bottom of the building. Above it, a hundred to each floor, were the seven thousand rooms used by Solidarity Groups for their fortnight services. Bernard dropped down to floor thirty-three, hurried along the corridor, stood hesitating for a moment outside Room 3210, then, having wound himself up, opened the door and walked in.

Thank Ford! he was not the last. Three chairs of the twelve arranged round the circular table were still unoccupied. He slipped into the nearest of them as inconspicuously as he could and prepared to frown at the yet later comers whenever they should arrive.

Turning towards him, "What were you playing this afternoon?" the girl on his left enquired. "Obstacle, or Electro-magnetic?"

Bernard looked at her (Ford! it was Morgana Rothschild) and blushingly had to admit that he had been playing neither. Morgana stared at him with astonishment. There was an awkward silence.

Then pointedly she turned away and addressed herself to the more sporting man on her left.

"A good beginning for a Solidarity Service," thought Bernard miserably, and foresaw for himself yet another failure to achieve atonement. If only he had given himself time to look around instead of scuttling for the nearest chair! He could have sat between Fifi Bradlaugh and Joanna Diesel. Instead of which he had gone and blindly planted himself next to Morgana. *Morgana!* Ford! Those black eyebrows of hers — that eyebrow, rather — for they met above the nose. Ford! And on his right was Clara Deterding. True, Clara's eyebrows didn't meet. But she was really *too* pneumatic. Whereas Fifi and Joanna were absolutely right. Plump, blonde, not too large . . . And it was that great lout, Tom Kawaguchi, who now took the seat between them.

The last arrival was Sarojini Engels.

"You're late," said the President of the Group severely. "Don't let it happen again."

Sarojini apologized and slid into her place between Jim Bokanovsky and Herbert Bakunin. The group was now complete, the solidarity circle perfect and without flaw. Man, woman, man, in a ring of endless alternation round the table. Twelve of them ready to be made one, waiting to come together, to be fused, to lose their twelve separate identities in a larger being.

The President stood up, made the sign of the T and, switching on the synthetic music, let loose the soft indefatigable beating of drums and a choir of instruments — near-wind and super-string — that plangently repeated and repeated the brief and unescapably haunting melody of the first Solidarity Hymn. Again, again — and it was not the ear that heard the pulsing rhythm, it was the midriff; the wail and clang of those recurring harmonies haunted, not the mind, but the yearning bowels of compassion.

The President made another sign of the T and sat down. The service had begun. The dedicated *soma* tablets were placed in the centre of the table. The loving cup of strawberry ice-cream *soma* was passed from hand to hand and, with the formula, "I drink to my annihilation," twelve times quaffed. Then to the accompaniment of the synthetic orchestra the First Solidarity Hymn was sung.

"*Ford, we are twelve; oh, make us one,*

Like drops within the Social River,

Oh, make us now together run

As swiftly as they shining Flivver.

Twelve yearning stanzas. And then the loving cup was passed a second time. "I drink to the Greater Being" was now the formula. All drank. Tirelessly the music played. The drums beat. The crying and clashing of the harmonies were an obsession in the melted bowels. The Second Solidarity Hymn was sung.

"*Come, Greater Being, Social Friend,*

Annihilating Twelve-in-One!

> We long to die, for when we end,
>> Our larger life has but begun."

Again twelve stanzas. By this time the *soma* had begun to work. Eyes shone, cheeks were flushed, the inner light of universal benevolence broke out on every face in happy, friendly smiles. Even Bernard felt himself a little melted. When Morgana Rothschild turned and beamed at him, he did his best to beam back. But the eyebrow, that black two-in-one — alas, it was still there; he couldn't ignore it, couldn't, however hard he tried. The melting hadn't gone far enough. Perhaps if he had been sitting between Fifi and Joanna . . . For the third time the loving cup went round; "I drink to the imminence of His Coming," said Morgana Rothschild, whose turn it happened to be to initiate the circular rite. Her tone was loud, exultant. She drank and passed the cup to Bernard. "I drink to the imminence of His Coming," he repeated, with a sincere attempt to feel that the Coming was imminent; but the eyebrow continued to haunt him, and the Coming, so far as he was concerned, was horribly remote. He drank and handed the cup to Clara Deterding. "It'll be a failure again," he said to himself. "I know it will." But he went on doing his best to beam.

The loving cup had made its circuit. Lifting his hand, the President gave a signal; the chorus broke out into the third Solidarity Hymn.

> "Feel how the Greater Being comes!
>> Rejoice and, in rejoicings, die!
> Melt in the music of the drums!
>> For I am you and you are I."

As verse succeeded verse the voices thrilled with an ever intenser excitement. The sense of the Coming's imminence was like an electric tension in the air. The President switched off the music and, with the final note of the final stanza, there was absolute silence — the silence of stretched expectancy, quivering and creeping with a galvanic life. The President reached out his hand; and suddenly a Voice, a deep strong Voice, more musical than any merely human voice, richer, warmer, more vibrant with love and yearning and compassion, a wonderful, mysterious, supernatural Voice spoke from above their heads. Very slowly, "Oh, Ford, Ford, Ford," it said diminishingly and on a descending scale. A sensation of warmth radiated thrillingly out from the solar plexus to every extremity of the bodies of those who listened; tears came into their eyes; their hearts, their bowels seemed to move within them, as though with an independent life. "Ford!" they were melting, "Ford!" dissolved, dissolved. Then, in another tone, suddenly, startlingly. "Listen!" trumpeted the voice. "Listen!" They listened. After a pause, sunk to a whisper, but a whisper, somehow, more penetrating than the loudest cry. "The feet of the Greater Being," it went on, and repeated the words: "The feet of the Greater Being." The whisper almost expired. "The feet of the Greater Being are on the stairs." And once more there was silence; and the expectancy, momentarily relaxed, was stretched again, tauter, tauter, almost to the tearing point. The feet of the Greater Being — oh, they heard them, they heard them, coming softly down the stairs, coming nearer and nearer down the invisible stairs. The feet of the Greater Being. And suddenly the tearing point was reached. Her eyes staring, her lips parted. Morgana Rothschild sprang to her feet.

"I hear him," she cried. "I hear him."

"He's coming," shouted Sarojini Engels.

"Yes, he's coming, I hear him." Fifi Bradlaugh and Tom Kawaguchi rose simultaneously to their feet.

"Oh, oh, oh!" Joanna inarticulately testified.

"He's coming!" yelled Jim Bokanovsky.

The President leaned forward and, with a touch, released a delirium of cymbals and blown brass, a fever of tom-tomming.

"Oh, he's coming!" screamed Clara Deterding. "Aie!" and it was as though she were having her throat cut.

Feeling that it was time for him to do something, Bernard also jumped up and shouted: "I hear him; He's coming." But it wasn't true. He heard nothing and, for him, nobody was coming. Nobody — in spite of the music, in spite of the mounting excitement. But he waved his arms, he shouted with the best of them; and when the others began to jig and stamp and shuffle, he also jigged and shuffled.

Round they went, a circular procession of dancers, each with hands on the hips of the dancer preceding, round and round, shouting in unison, stamping to the rhythm of the music with their feet, beating it, beating it out with hands on the buttocks in front; twelve pairs of hands beating as one; as one, twelve buttocks slabbily resounding. Twelve as one, twelve as one. "I hear Him, I hear Him coming." The music quickened; faster beat the feet, faster, faster fell the rhythmic hands. And all at once a great synthetic bass boomed out the words which announced the approaching atonement and final consummation of solidarity, the coming of the Twelve-in-One, the incarnation of the Greater Being. "Orgy-porgy," it sang, while the tom-toms continued to beat their feverish tattoo:

"Orgy-porgy, Ford and fun,
Kiss the girls and make them One.

Boys at one with girls at peace;

Orgy-porgy gives release."

"Orgy-porgy," the dancers caught up the liturgical refrain, "Orgy-porgy, Ford and fun, kiss the girls . . ." And as they sang, the lights began slowly to fade — to fade and at the same time to grow warmer, richer, redder, until at last they were dancing in the crimson twilight of an Embryo Store. "Orgy-porgy . . ." In their blood-coloured and foetal darkness the dancers continued for a while to circulate, to beat and beat out the indefatigable rhythm. "Orgy-porgy . . ." Then the circle wavered, broke, fell in partial dis-integration on the ring of couches which surrounded — circle enclosing circle — the table and its planetary chairs. "Orgy-porgy . . ." Tenderly the deep Voice crooned and cooed; in the red twilight it was as though some enormous negro dove were hovering benevolently over the now prone or supine dancers.

They were standing on the roof; Big Henry had just sung eleven. The night was calm and warm.

"Wasn't it wonderful?" said Fifi Bradlaugh. "Wasn't it simply wonderful?" She looked at Bernard with an expression of rapture, but of rapture in which there was no trace of agitation or excitement — for to be excited is still to be unsatisfied. Hers was the calm ecstasy of achieved consummation, the peace, not of mere vacant satiety and nothingness, but of balanced life, of energies at rest and in equilibrium. A rich and living peace. For the Solidarity Service had given as well as taken, drawn off only to replenish. She was full, she was made perfect, she was still more than merely herself. "Didn't you think it was wonderful?" she insisted, looking into Bernard's face with those supernaturally shining eyes.

"Yes, I thought it was wonderful," he lied and looked away; the sight of her transfigured face was at once an accusation and an ironical reminder of his own separateness. He was as miserably isolated now as he had been when the service began — more isolated by reason of his unreplenished emptiness, his dead satiety. Separate and unatoned, while the others were being fused into the Greater Being; alone even in Morgana's embrace — much more alone, indeed, more hopelessly himself than he had ever been in his life before. He had emerged from that crimson twilight into the common electric glare with a self-consciousness intensified to the pitch of agony. He was utterly miserable, and perhaps (her shining eyes accused him), perhaps it was his own fault. "Quite wonderful," he repeated; but the only thing he could think of was Morgana's eyebrow.

CHAPTER 6

Part 1

Odd, odd, *odd*, was Lenina's verdict on Bernard Marx. So odd, indeed, that in the course of the succeeding weeks she had wondered more than once whether she shouldn't change her mind about the New Mexico holiday, and go instead to the North Pole with Benito Hoover. The trouble was that she knew the North Pole, had been there with George Edzel only last summer, and what was more, found it pretty grim. Nothing to do, and the hotel too hopelessly old-fashioned — no television laid on in the bedrooms, no scent organ, only the most putrid synthetic music, and not more than twenty-five Escalator-Squash Courts for over two hundred guests. No, decidedly she couldn't face the North Pole again. Added to which, she had only been to America once before. And even then, how inadequately! A cheap week-end in New York — had it been with Jean-Jacques Habibullah or Bokanovsky Jones? She couldn't remember. Anyhow, it was of absolutely no importance. The prospect of flying West again, and for a whole week, was very inviting. Moreover, for at least three days of that week they would be in the Savage Reservation. Not more than half a dozen people in the whole Centre had ever been inside a Savage Reservation. As an Alpha-Plus psychologist, Bernard was one of the few men she knew entitled to a permit. For Lenina, the opportunity was unique. And yet, so unique also was Bernard's oddness that she had hesitated to take it, had actually thought of risking the Pole again with funny old Benito. At least Benito was normal. Whereas Bernard

• • •

"Alcohol in his blood-surrogate," was Fanny's explanation of every eccentricity. But Henry, with whom, one evening when they were in bed together, Lenina had rather anxiously discussed her new lover, Henry had compared poor Bernard to a rhinoceros.

"You can't teach a rhinoceros tricks," he had explained in his brief and vigorous style. "Some men are almost rhinoceroses; they don't respond properly to conditioning. Poor Devils! Bernard's one of them. Luckily for him, he's pretty good at his job. Otherwise the Director would never have kept him. However," he added consolingly, "I think he's pretty harmless."

Pretty harmless, perhaps; but also pretty disquieting. That mania, to start with, for doing things in private. Which meant, in practice, not doing anything at all. For what was there that one *could* do in private. (Apart, of course, from going to bed: but one couldn't do that all the time.) Yes, what *was* there? Precious little. The first afternoon they went out together was particularly fine. Lenina had suggested a swim at Toquay Country Club followed by dinner at the Oxford Union. But Bernard thought there would be too much of a crowd. Then what about a round of Electro-magnetic Golf at St. Andrew's? But again, no: Bernard considered that Electro-magnetic Golf was a waste of time.

"Then what's time for?" asked Lenina in some astonishment.

Apparently, for going on walks in the Lake District; for that was what he now proposed. Land on the top of Skiddaw and walk for a couple of hours in the heather. "Alone with you, Lenina."

"But, Bernard, we shall be alone all night."

Bernard blushed and looked away. "I meant, alone for talking," he mumbled.

"Talking? But what about?" Walking and talking —

that seemed a very odd way of spending an afternoon.

In the end she persuaded him, much against his will, to fly over to Amsterdam to see the Semi-Demi-Finals of the Women's Heavyweight Wrestling Championship.

"In a crowd," he grumbled. "As usual." He remained obstinately gloomy the whole afternoon; wouldn't talk to Lenina's friends (of whom they met dozens in the ice-cream *soma* bar between the wrestling bouts); and in spite of his misery absolutely refused to take the half-gramme raspberry sundae which she pressed upon him. "I'd rather be myself," he said. "Myself and nasty. Not somebody else, however jolly."

"A gramme in time saves nine," said Lenina, producing a bright treasure of sleep-taught wisdom.

Bernard pushed away the proffered glass impatiently.

"Now, don't lose your temper," she said. "Remember one cubic centimetre cures ten gloomy sentiments."

"Oh, for Ford's sake, be quiet!" he shouted.

Lenina shrugged her shoulders. "A gramme is always better than a damn," she concluded with dignity, and drank the sundae herself.

On their way back across the Channel, Bernard insisted on stopping his propeller and hovering on his helicopter screws within a hundred feet of the waves. The weather had taken a change for the worse; a south-westerly wind had sprung up, the sky was cloudy.

"Look," he commanded.

"But it's horrible," said Lenina, shrinking back from the window. She was appalled by the rushing emptiness of the night, by the black foam-flecked water heaving beneath them, by the pale face of the moon, so haggard and distracted among the hastening clouds. "Let's turn on the radio. Quick!" She reached for the dialling knob on the dashboard and turned it at random.

". . . skies are blue inside of you," sang sixteen tremoloing falsettos, "the weather's always . . ."

Then a hiccough and silence. Bernard had switched off the current.

"I want to look at the sea in peace," he said. "One can't even look with that beastly noise going on."

"But it's lovely. And I don't want to look."

"But I do," he insisted. "It makes me feel as though . . ." he hesitated, searching for words with which to express himself, "as though I were more *me*, if you see what I mean. More on my own, not so completely a part of something else. Not just a cell in the social body. Doesn't it make you feel like that, Lenina?"

But Lenina was crying. "It's horrible, it's horrible," she kept repeating. "And how can you talk like that about not wanting to be a part of the social body? After all, every one works for every one else. We can't do without any one. Even Epsilons . . ."

"Yes, I know," said Bernard derisively. "'Even Epsilons are useful'! So am I. And I damned well wish I weren't!"

Lenina was shocked by his blasphemy. "Bernard!" She protested in a voice of amazed distress. "How can you?"

In a different key, "How can I?" he repeated meditatively. "No, the real problem is: How is it that I can't, or rather — because, after all, I know quite well why I can't — what would it be like if I could, if I were free — not enslaved by my conditioning."

"But, Bernard, you're saying the most awful things."

"Don't you wish you were free, Lenina?"

"I don't know what you mean. I am free. Free to have the most wonderful time. Everybody's happy nowadays."

He laughed, "Yes, 'Everybody's happy nowadays.' We begin giving the children that at five. But wouldn't you like to be free to be happy in some other way, Lenina? In your own way, for example; not in everybody else's way."

"I don't know what you mean," she repeated. Then, turning to him, "Oh, do let's go back, Bernard," she besought; "I do so hate it here."

"Don't you like being with me?"

"But of course, Bernard. It's this horrible place."

"I thought we'd be more . . . more *together* here — with nothing but the sea and moon. More together than in that crowd, or even in my rooms. Don't you understand that?"

"I don't understand anything," she said with decision, determined to preserve her incomprehension intact. "Nothing. Least of all," she continued in another tone "why you don't take *soma* when you have these dreadful ideas of yours. You'd forget all about them. And instead of feeling miserable, you'd be jolly. *So* jolly," she repeated and smiled, — for all the puzzled anxiety in her eyes — with what was meant to be an inviting and voluptuous cajolery.

He looked at her in silence, his face unresponsive and very grave — looked at her intently. After a few seconds Lenina's eyes flinched away; she uttered a nervous little laugh, tried to think of something to say and couldn't. The silence prolonged itself.

When Bernard spoke at last, it was in a small tired voice. "All right then," he said, "we'll go back." And stepping hard on the accelerator, he sent the machine rocketing up into the sky. At four thousand he started his propeller. They flew in silence for a minute or two. Then, suddenly, Bernard began to laugh. Rather oddly, Lenina thought, but still, it was laughter.

"Feeling better?" she ventured to ask.

For answer, he lifted one hand from the controls and, slipping his arm around her, began to fondle her breasts.

"Thank Ford," she said to herself, "he's all right again."

Half an hour later they were back in his rooms. Bernard swallowed four tablets of *soma* at a gulp, turned on the radio and television and began to undress.

"Well," Lenina enquired, with significant archness when they met next afternoon on the roof, "did you think it was fun yesterday?"

Bernard nodded. They climbed into the plane. A little jolt, and they were off.

"Every one says I'm awfully pneumatic," said Lenina reflectively, patting her own legs.

"Awfully." But there was an expression of pain in Bernard's eyes. "Like meat," he was thinking.

She looked up with a certain anxiety. "But you don't think I'm *too* plump, do you?"

He shook his head. Like so much meat.

"You think I'm all right." Another nod. "In every way?"

"Perfect," he said aloud. And inwardly. "She thinks of herself that way. She doesn't mind being meat."

Lenina smiled triumphantly. But her satisfaction was premature.

"All the same," he went on, after a little pause, "I still rather wish it had all ended differently."

"Differently?" Were there other endings?

"I didn't want it to end with our going to bed," he specified.

Lenina was astonished.

"Not at once, not the first day."

"But then what . . . ?"

He began to talk a lot of incomprehensible and dangerous nonsense. Lenina did her best to stop the ears of her mind; but every now and then a phrase would insist on becoming audible. ". . . to try the effect of arresting my impulses," she heard him say. The words seemed to touch a spring in her mind.

"Never put off till to-morrow the fun you can have to-day," she said gravely.

"Two hundred repetitions, twice a week from fourteen to sixteen and a half," was all his comment. The mad bad talk rambled on. "I want to know what passion is," she heard him saying. "I want to feel something strongly."

"When the individual feels, the community reels," Lenina pronounced.

"Well, why shouldn't it reel a bit?"

"Bernard!"

But Bernard remained unabashed.

"Adults intellectually and during working hours," he went on. "Infants where feeling and desire are concerned."

"Our Ford loved infants."

Ignoring the interruption. "It suddenly struck me the other day," continued Bernard, "that it might be possible to be an adult all the time."

"I don't understand." Lenina's tone was firm.

"I know you don't. And that's why we went to bed together yesterday — like infants — instead of being adults and waiting."

"But it was fun," Lenina insisted. "Wasn't it?"

"Oh, the greatest fun," he answered, but in a voice so mournful, with an expression so profoundly miserable, that Lenina felt all her triumph suddenly evaporate. Perhaps he had found her too plump, after all.

"I told you so," was all that Fanny said, when Lenina came and made her confidences. "It's the alcohol they put in his surrogate."

"All the same," Lenina insisted. "I do like him. He has such awfully nice hands. And the way he moves his shoulders—that's very attractive." She sighed. "But I wish he weren't so odd."

Halting for a moment outside the door of the Director's room, Bernard drew a deep breath and squared his shoulders, bracing himself to meet the dislike and disapproval which he was certain of finding within. He knocked and entered.

"A permit for you to initial, Director," he said as airily as possible, and laid the paper on the writing-table.

The Director glanced at him sourly. But the stamp of the World Controller's Office was at the head of the paper and the signature of Mustapha Mond, bold and black, across the bottom. Everything was perfectly in order. The Director had no choice. He pencilled his initials — two small pale letters abject at the feet of Mustapha Mond — and was about to return the paper without a word of comment or genial Ford-speed, when his eye was caught by something written in the body of the permit.

"For the New Mexican Reservation?" he said, and his tone, the face he lifted to Bernard, expressed a kind of agitated astonishment.

Surprised by his surprise, Bernard nodded. There was a silence.

The Director leaned back in his chair, frowning. "How long ago was it?" he said, speaking more to himself than to Bernard. "Twenty years, I suppose. Nearer twenty-five. I must have been your age . . ." He sighed and shook his head.

Bernard felt extremely uncomfortable. A man so conventional, so scrupulously correct as the Director

— and to commit so gross a solecism! It made him want to hide his face, to run out of the room. Not that he himself saw anything intrinsically objectionable in people talking about the remote past; that was one of those hypnopædic prejudices he had (so he imagined) completely got rid of. What made him feel shy was the knowledge that the Director disapproved — disapproved and yet had been betrayed into doing the forbidden thing. Under what inward compulsion? Through his discomfort Bernard eagerly listened.

"I had the same idea as you," the Director was saying. "Wanted to have a look at the savages. Got a permit for New Mexico and went there for my summer holiday. With the girl I was having at the moment. She was a Beta-Minus, and I think" (he shut his eyes), "I think she had yellow hair. Anyhow she was pneumatic, particularly pneumatic; I remember that. Well, we went there, and we looked at the savages, and we rode about on horses and all that. And then — it was almost the last day of my leave — then . . . well, she got lost. We'd gone riding up one of those revolting mountains, and it was horribly hot and oppressive, and after lunch we went to sleep. Or at least I did. She must have gone for a walk, alone. At any rate, when I woke up, she wasn't there. And the most frightful thunderstorm I've ever seen was just bursting on us. And it poured and roared and flashed; and the horses broke loose and ran away; and I fell down, trying to catch them, and hurt my knee, so that I could hardly walk. Still, I searched and I shouted and I searched. But there was no sign of her. Then I thought she must have gone back to the rest-house by herself. So I crawled down into the valley by the way we had come. My knee was agonizingly painful, and I'd lost my *soma*. It took me hours. I didn't get back to the rest-house till after midnight. And she wasn't there; she wasn't there," the Director repeated.

There was a silence. "Well," he resumed at last, "the next day there was a search. But we couldn't find her. She must have fallen into a gully somewhere; or been eaten by a mountain lion. Ford knows. Anyhow it was horrible. It upset me very much at the time. More than it ought to have done, I dare say. Because, after all, it's the sort of accident that might have happened to any one; and, of course, the social body persists although the component cells may change." But this sleep-taught consolation did not seem to be very effective. Shaking his head, "I actually dream about it sometimes," the Director went on in a low voice. "Dream of being woken up by that peal of thunder and finding her gone; dream of searching and searching for her under the trees." He lapsed into the silence of reminiscence.

"You must have had a terrible shock," said Bernard, almost enviously.

At the sound of his voice the Director started into a guilty realization of where he was; shot a glance at Bernard, and averting his eyes, blushed darkly; looked at him again with sudden suspicion and, angrily on his dignity, "Don't imagine," he said, "that I'd had any indecorous relation with the girl. Nothing emotional, nothing long-drawn. It was all perfectly healthy and normal." He handed Bernard the permit. "I really don't know why I bored you with this trivial anecdote." Furious with himself for having given away a discreditable secret, he vented his rage on Bernard. The look in his eyes was now frankly malignant. "And I should like to take this opportunity, Mr. Marx," he went on, "of saying that I'm not at all pleased with the reports I receive of your behaviour outside working hours. You may say that this is not my business. But it is. I have the good name of the Centre to think of. My workers must be above suspicion, particularly those of the highest castes. Alphas are so conditioned that they do not *have* to be infantile in their emotional behaviour. But that is all the more reason for their making a special effort to conform. It is their duty to be infantile, even against their inclination. And so, Mr. Marx, I give you fair warning." The Director's voice vibrated with an indignation that had now become wholly righteous and impersonal — was the expression of the disapproval of Society itself. "If ever I hear again of any lapse from a proper standard of infantile decorum, I shall ask for your transference to a Sub-Centre — preferably to Iceland. Good morning." And swivelling round in his chair, he picked up his pen and began to write.

"That'll teach him," he said to himself. But he was mistaken. For Bernard left the room with a swagger, exulting, as he banged the door behind him, in the thought that he stood alone, embattled against the order of things; elated by the intoxicating conscious-ness of his individual significance and importance. Even the thought of persecution left him undismayed, was rather tonic than depressing. He felt strong enough to meet and overcome affliction, strong enough to face even Iceland. And this confidence was the greater for his not for a moment really believing that he would be called upon to face anything at all. People simply weren't transferred for things like that. Iceland was just a threat. A most stimulating and life-giving threat. Walking along the corridor, he actually whistled.

Heroic was the account he gave that evening of his interview with the D.H.C. "Whereupon," it con-cluded, "I simply told him to go to the Bottomless Past and marched out of the room. And that was that." He looked at Helmholtz Watson expectantly, awaiting his due reward of sympathy, encouragement, admiration. But no word came. Helmholtz sat silent, staring at the floor.

He liked Bernard; he was grateful to him for being the only man of his acquaintance with whom he could talk about the subjects he felt to be important. Nevertheless, there were things in Bernard which he hated. This boasting, for example. And the outbursts of an abject self-pity with which it alternated. And his deplorable habit of being bold after the event, and full, in absence, of the most extraordinary presence of mind. He hated these things — just because he liked Bernard. The seconds passed. Helmholtz continued to stare at the floor. And suddenly Bernard blushed and turned away.

Part 3

The journey was quite uneventful. The Blue Pacific Rocket was two and a half minutes early at New Orleans, lost four minutes in a tornado over Texas, but flew into a favourable air current at Longitude 95 West, and was able to land at Santa Fé less than forty seconds behind schedule time.

"Forty seconds on a six and a half hour flight. Not so bad," Lenina conceded.

They slept that night at Santa Fé. The hotel was excellent — incomparably better, for example, than that horrible Aurora Bora Palace in which Lenina had suffered so much the previous summer. Liquid air, television, vibro-vacuum massage, radio, boiling caffeine solution, hot contraceptives, and eight different kinds of scent were laid on in every bedroom. The synthetic music plant was working as they entered the hall and left nothing to be desired. A notice in the lift announced that there were sixty Escalator-Squash-Racket Courts in the hotel, and that Obstacle and Electro-magnetic Golf could both be played in the park.

"But it sounds simply too lovely," cried Lenina. "I almost wish we could stay here. Sixty Escalator-Squash Courts . . ."

"There won't be any in the Reservation," Bernard warned her. "And no scent, no television, no hot water even. If you feel you can't stand it, stay here till I come back."

Lenina was quite offended. "Of course I can stand it. I only said it was lovely here because . . . well, because progress *is* lovely, isn't it?"

"Five hundred repetitions once a week from thirteen to seventeen," said Bernard wearily, as though to himself.

"What did you say?"

"I said that progress was lovely. That's why you mustn't come to the Reservation unless you really want to."

"But I do want to."

"Very well, then," said Bernard; and it was almost a threat.

Their permit required the signature of the Warden of the Reservation, at whose office next morning they duly presented themselves. An Epsilon-Plus negro porter took in Bernard's card, and they were admitted almost immediately.

The Warden was a blond and brachycephalic Alpha-Minus, short, red, moon-faced, and broad-shouldered, with a loud booming voice, very well adapted to the utterance of hypnopædic wisdom. He was a mine of irrelevant information and unasked-for good advice. Once started, he went on and on — boomingly.

". . . five hundred and sixty thousand square kilometres, divided into four distinct Sub-Reservations, each surrounded by a high-tension wire fence."

At this moment, and for no apparent reason, Bernard suddenly remembered that he had left the Eau de Cologne tap in his bathroom wide open and running.

". . . supplied with current from the Grand Canyon hydro-electric station."

"Cost me a fortune by the time I get back." With his mind's eye, Bernard saw the needle on the scent meter creeping round and round, antlike, indefatigable. "Quickly telephone to Helmholtz Watson."

". . . upwards of five thousand kilometres of fencing at sixty thousand volts."

"You don't say so," said Lenina politely, not knowing in the least what the Warden had said, but taking her cue from his dramatic pause. When the Warden started booming, she had inconspicuously swallowed half a gramme of *soma*, with the result that she could now sit, serenely not listening, thinking of nothing at all, but with her large blue eyes fixed on the Warden's face in an expression of rapt attention.

"To touch the fence is instant death," pronounced the Warden solemnly. "There is no escape from a Savage Reservation."

The word "escape" was suggestive. "Perhaps," said Bernard, half rising, "we ought to think of going." The little black needle was scurrying, an insect, nibbling through time, eating into his money.

"No escape," repeated the Warden, waving him back into his chair; and as the permit was not yet countersigned Bernard had no choice but to obey. "Those who are born in the Reservation — and remember, my dear young lady," he added, leering obscenely at Lenina, and speaking in an improper whisper, "remember that, in the Reservation, children still *are* born, yes, actually born, revolting as that may seem ..." (He hoped that this reference to a shameful subject would make Lenina blush; but she only smiled with simulated intelligence and said, "You don't say so!" Disappointed, the Warden began again.) "Those, I repeat, who are born in the Reservation are destined to die there."

Destined to die . . . A decilitre of Eau de Cologne every minute. Six litres an hour. "Perhaps," Bernard tried again, "we ought . . ."

Leaning forward, the Warden tapped the table with his forefinger. "You ask me how many people live in the Reservation. And I reply" — triumphantly — "I reply that we do not know. We can only guess."

"You don't say so."

"My dear young lady, I do say so."

Six times twenty-four — no, it would be nearer six times thirty-six. Bernard was pale and trembling with impatience. But inexorably the booming continued.

". . . about sixty thousand Indians and half-breeds . . . absolute savages . . . our inspectors occasionally visit . . . otherwise, no communication whatever with the civilized world . . . still preserve their repulsive habits and customs . . . marriage, if you know what that is, my dear young lady; families . . . no conditioning . . . monstrous superstitions . . . Christianity and totemism and ancestor worship . . . extinct languages, such as Zuñi and Spanish and Athapascan . . . pumas, porcupines and other ferocious animals. . . infectious diseases . . . priests . . . venomous lizards . . ."

"You don't say so?"

They got away at last. Bernard dashed to the telephone. Quick, quick; but it took him nearly three minutes to get on to Helmholtz Watson. "We might be among the savages already," he complained. "Damned incompetence!"

"Have a gramme," suggested Lenina.

He refused, preferring his anger. And at last, thank Ford, he was through and, yes, it was Helmholtz; Helmholtz, to whom he explained what had happened, and who promised to go round at once, at once, and turn off the tap, yes, at once, but took this opportunity to tell him what the D.H.C. had said, in public, yesterday evening . . .

"What? He's looking out for some one to take my place?" Bernard's voice was agonized. "So it's actually decided? Did he mention Iceland? You say he did? Ford! Iceland . . ." He hung up the receiver and turned back to Lenina. His face was pale, his expression utterly dejected.

"What's the matter?" she asked.

"The matter?" He dropped heavily into a chair. "I'm going to be sent to Iceland."

Often in the past he had wondered what it would be like to be subjected (*soma*-less and with nothing but his own inward resources to rely on) to some great trial, some pain, some persecution; he had even longed for affliction. As recently as a week ago, in the Director's office, he had imagined himself courageously resisting, stoically accepting suffering without a word. The Director's threats had actually elated him, made him feel larger than life. But that, as he now realized, was because he had not taken the threats quite seriously, he had not believed that, when it came to the point, the D.H.C. would ever do anything. Now that it looked as though the threats were really to be fulfilled, Bernard was appalled. Of that imagined stoicism, that theoretical courage, not a trace was left.

He raged against himself — what a fool! — against the Director — how unfair not to give him that other chance, that other chance which, he now had no doubt at all, he had always intended to take. And Iceland, Iceland . . .

Lenina shook her head. "Was and will make me ill," she quoted, "I take a gramme and only am."

In the end she persuaded him to swallow four tablets of *soma*. Five minutes later roots and fruits were abolished; the flower of the present rosily blossomed. A message from the porter announced that, at the Warden's orders, a Reservation Guard had come round with a plane and was waiting on the roof of the hotel.

They went up at once. An octoroon in Gamma-green uniform saluted and proceeded to recite the morning's programme.

A bird's-eye view of ten or a dozen of the principal pueblos, then a landing for lunch in the valley of Malpais. The rest-house was comfortable there, and up at the pueblo the savages would probably be celebrating their summer festival. It would be the best place to spend the night.

They took their seats in the plane and set off. Ten minutes later they were crossing the frontier that separated civilization from savagery. Uphill and down, across the deserts of salt or sand, through forests, into the violet depth of canyons, over crag and peak and table-topped mesa, the fence marched on and on, irresistibly the straight line, the geometrical symbol of triumphant human purpose. And at its foot, here and there, a mosaic of white bones, a still un-rotted carcase dark on the tawny ground marked the place where deer or steer, puma or porcupine or coyote, or the greedy turkey buzzards drawn down by the whiff of carrion and fulminated as though by a poetic justice, had come too close to the destroying wires.

"They never learn," said the green-uniformed pilot, pointing down at the skeletons on the ground below them. "And they never will learn," he added and laughed, as though he had somehow scored a personal triumph over the electrocuted animals.

Bernard also laughed; after two grammes of *soma* the joke seemed, for some reason, good. Laughed and then, almost immediately, dropped off to sleep, and sleeping was carried over Taos and Tesuque; over Nambe and Picuris and Pojoaque, over Sia and Cochiti, over Laguna and Acoma and the Enchanted Mesa, over Zuñi and Cibola and Ojo Caliente, and woke at last to find the machine standing on the ground, Lenina carrying the suit-cases into a small square house, and the Gamma-green octoroon talking incomprehensibly with a young Indian.

"Malpais," explained the pilot, as Bernard stepped out. "This is the rest-house. And there's a dance this afternoon at the pueblo. He'll take you there." He pointed to the sullen young savage. "Funny, I expect." He grinned. "Everything they do is funny." And with that he climbed into the plane and started up the engines. "Back to-morrow. And remember," he added reassuringly to Lenina, "they're perfectly tame; savages won't do you any harm. They've got enough experience of gas bombs to know that they mustn't play any tricks." Still laughing, he threw the helicopter screws into gear, accelerated, and was gone.

CHAPTER 7

The mesa was like a ship becalmed in a strait of lion-coloured dust. The channel wound between precipitous banks, and slanting from one wall to the other across the valley ran a streak of green — the river and its fields. On the prow of that stone ship in the centre of the strait, and seemingly a part of it, a shaped and geometrical outcrop of the naked rock, stood the pueblo of Malpais. Block above block, each story smaller than the one below, the tall houses rose like stepped and amputated pyramids into the blue sky. At their feet lay a straggle of low buildings, a criss-cross of walls; and on three sides the precipices fell sheer into the plain. A few columns of smoke mounted perpendicularly into the windless air and were lost.

"Queer," said Lenina. "Very queer." It was her ordinary word of condemnation. "I don't like it. And I don't like that man." She pointed to the Indian guide who had been appointed to take them up to the pueblo. Her feeling was evidently reciprocated; the very back of the man, as he walked along before them, was hostile, sullenly contemptuous.

"Besides," she lowered her voice, "he smells."

Bernard did not attempt to deny it. They walked on.

Suddenly it was as though the whole air had come alive and were pulsing, pulsing with the indefatigable movement of blood. Up there, in Malpais, the drums were being beaten. Their feet fell in with the rhythm of that mysterious heart; they quickened their pace. Their path led them to the foot of the precipice. The sides of the great mesa ship towered over them, three hundred feet to the gunwale.

"I wish we could have brought the plane," said Lenina, looking up resentfully at the blank impending rock-face. "I hate walking. And you feel so small when you're on the ground at the bottom of a hill."

They walked along for some way in the shadow of the mesa, rounded a projection, and there, in a water-worn ravine, was the way up the companion ladder. They climbed. It was a very steep path that zigzagged from side to side of the gully. Sometimes the pulsing of the drums was all but inaudible, at others they seemed to be beating only just round the corner.

When they were half-way up, an eagle flew past so close to them that the wind of his wings blew chill on their faces. In a crevice of the rock lay a pile of bones. It was all oppressively queer, and the Indian smelt stronger and stronger. They emerged at last from the ravine into the full sunlight. The top of the mesa was a flat deck of stone.

"Like the Charing-T Tower," was Lenina's comment. But she was not allowed to enjoy her discovery of this reassuring resemblance for long. A padding of soft feet made them turn round. Naked from throat to navel, their dark brown bodies painted with white lines ("like asphalt tennis courts," Lenina was later to explain), their faces inhuman with daubings of scarlet, black and ochre, two Indians came running along the path. Their black hair was braided with fox fur and red flannel. Cloaks of turkey feathers fluttered from their shoulders; huge feather diadems exploded gaudily round their heads. With every step they took came the clink and rattle of their silver bracelets, their heavy necklaces of bone and turquoise beads. They came on without a word, running quietly in their deerskin moccasins. One of them was holding a feather brush; the other carried, in either hand, what looked at a distance like three or four pieces of thick rope. One of the ropes writhed uneasily, and suddenly Lenina saw that they were snakes.

The men came nearer and nearer; their dark eyes looked at her, but without giving any sign of recognition, any smallest sign that they had seen her or were aware of her existence. The writhing snake hung limp again with the rest. The men passed.

"I don't like it," said Lenina. "I don't like it."

She liked even less what awaited her at the entrance to the pueblo, where their guide had left them while he went inside for instructions. The dirt, to start with, the piles of rubbish, the dust, the dogs, the flies. Her face wrinkled up into a grimace of disgust. She held her handkerchief to her nose.

"But how can they live like this?" she broke out in a voice of indignant incredulity. (It wasn't possible.)

Bernard shrugged his shoulders philosophically. "Anyhow," he said, "they've been doing it for the last five or six thousand years. So I suppose they must be used to it by now."

"But cleanliness is next to fordliness," she insisted.

"Yes, and civilization is sterilization," Bernard went on, concluding on a tone of irony the second hypnopædic lesson in elementary hygiene. "But these people have never heard of Our Ford, and they aren't civilized. So there's no point in . . ."

"Oh!" She gripped his arm. "Look."

An almost naked Indian was very slowly climbing down the ladder from the first-floor terrace of a neighboring house — rung after rung, with the tremulous caution of extreme old age. His face was profoundly wrinkled and black, like a mask of obsidian. The toothless mouth had fallen in. At the corners of the lips, and on each side of the chin, a few long bristles gleamed almost white against the dark skin. The long unbraided hair hung down in grey wisps round his face. His body was bent and emaciated to the bone, almost flesh-less. Very slowly he came down, pausing at each rung before he ventured another step.

"What's the matter with him?" whispered Lenina. Her eyes were wide with horror and amazement.

"He's old, that's all," Bernard answered as carelessly as he could. He too was startled; but he made an effort to seem unmoved.

"Old?" she repeated. "But the Director's old; lots of people are old; they're not like that."

"That's because we don't allow them to be like that. We preserve them from diseases. We keep their internal secretions artificially balanced at a youthful equilibrium. We don't permit their magnesium-calcium ratio to fall below what it was at thirty. We give them transfusion of young blood. We keep their metabolism permanently stimulated. So, of course, they don't look like that. Partly," he added, "because most of them die long before they reach this old creature's age. Youth almost unimpaired till sixty, and then, crack! the end."

But Lenina was not listening. She was watching the old man. Slowly, slowly he came down. His feet touched the ground. He turned. In their deep-sunken orbits his eyes were still extraordinarily bright. They looked at her for a long moment expressionlessly, without surprise, as though she had not been there at all. Then slowly, with bent back the old man hobbled past them and was gone.

"But it's terrible," Lenina whispered. "It's awful. We ought not to have come here." She felt in her pocket for her *soma* — only to discover that, by some unprece-dented oversight, she had left the bottle down at the rest-house. Bernard's pockets were also empty.

Lenina was left to face the horrors of Malpais un-aided. They came crowding in on her thick and fast. The spectacle of two young women giving breast to their babies made her blush and turn away her face. She had never seen anything so indecent in her life. And what made it worse was that, instead of tact-fully ignoring it, Bernard proceeded to make open comments on this revoltingly viviparous scene. Ashamed, now that the effects of the *soma* had worn off, of the weakness he had displayed that morning in the hotel, he went out of his way to show himself strong and unorthodox.

"What a wonderfully intimate relationship," he said, deliberately outrageous. "And what an intensity of feeling it must generate! I often think one may have missed something in not having had a mother. And perhaps you've missed something in not *being* a mother, Lenina. Imagine yourself sitting there with a little baby of your own. . . ."

"Bernard! How can you?" The passage of an old woman with ophthalmia and a disease of the skin distracted her from her indignation.

"Let's go away," she begged. "I don't like it."

But at this moment their guide came back and, beckoning them to follow, led the way down the narrow street between the houses. They rounded a corner. A dead dog was lying on a rubbish heap; a woman with a goitre was looking for lice in the hair of a small girl. Their guide halted at the foot of a ladder, raised his hand perpendicularly, then darted it horizontally forward. They did what he mutely commanded — climbed the ladder and walked through the doorway, to which it gave access, into a long narrow room, rather dark and smelling of smoke and cooked grease and long-worn, long-unwashed clothes. At the further end of the room was another doorway, through which came a shaft of sunlight and the noise, very loud and close, of the drums.

They stepped across the threshold and found themselves on a wide terrace. Below them, shut in by the tall houses, was the village square, crowded with Indians. Bright blankets, and feathers in black hair, and the glint of turquoise, and dark skins shining with heat. Lenina put her handkerchief to her nose again. In the open space at the centre of the square were two circular platforms of masonry and trampled clay — the roofs, it was evident, of underground chambers; for in the centre of each platform was an open hatchway, with a ladder emerging from the lower darkness. A sound of subterranean flute playing came up and was almost lost in the steady remorseless persistence of the drums.

Lenina liked the drums. Shutting her eyes she abandoned herself to their soft repeated thunder, allowed it to invade her consciousness more and more completely, till at last there was nothing left in the world but that one deep pulse of sound. It reminded her reassuringly of the synthetic noises made at Solidarity Services and Ford's Day celebrations. "Orgy-porgy," she whispered to herself. These drums beat out just the same rhythms.

There was a sudden startling burst of singing — hundreds of male voices crying out fiercely in harsh metallic unison. A few long notes and silence, the thunderous silence of the drums; then shrill, in a neighing treble, the women's answer. Then again the drums; and once more the men's deep savage affirmation of their manhood.

Queer—yes. The place was queer, so was the music, so were the clothes and the goitres and the skin diseases and the old people. But the performance itself — there seemed to be nothing specially queer about that.

"It reminds me of a lower-caste Community Sing," she told Bernard.

But a little later it was reminding her a good deal less of that innocuous function. For suddenly there had swarmed up from those round chambers underground a ghastly troop of monsters. Hideously masked or painted out of all semblance of humanity, they had tramped out a strange limping dance round the square; round and again round, singing as they went, round and round — each time a little faster; and the drums had changed and quickened their rhythm, so that it became like the pulsing of fever in the ears; and the crowd had begun to sing with the dancers, louder and louder; and first one woman had shrieked, and then another and another, as though they were being killed; and then suddenly the leader of the dancers broke out of the line, ran to a big wooden chest which was standing at one end of the square, raised the lid and pulled out a pair of black snakes. A great yell went up from the crowd, and all the other dancers ran towards him with out-stretched hands. He tossed the snakes to the first-comers, then dipped back into the chest for more. More and more, black snakes and brown and mottled — he flung them out. And then the dance began again on a different rhythm. Round and round they went with their snakes, snakily, with a soft undulating movement at the knees and hips. Round and round. Then the leader gave a signal, and one after another, all the snakes were flung down in the middle of the square; an old man came up from underground and sprinkled them with corn meal, and from the other hatchway came a woman and sprinkled them with water from a black jar. Then the old man lifted his hand and, startlingly, terrifyingly, there was absolute silence. The drums stopped beating, life seemed to have come to an end. The old man pointed towards the two hatchways that gave entrance to the lower world. And slowly, raised by invisible hands from below, there emerged from the one a painted image of an eagle, from the other that of a man, naked, and nailed to a cross. They hung there, seemingly self-sustained, as though watching. The old man clapped his hands. Naked but for a white cotton breech-cloth, a boy of about eighteen stepped out of the crowd and stood before him, his hands crossed over his chest, his head bowed. The old man made the sign of the cross over him and turned away. Slowly, the boy began to walk round the writhing heap of snakes. He had completed the first circuit and was half-way through the second when, from among the dancers, a tall man wearing the mask of a coyote and holding in his hand a whip of plaited leather, advanced towards him. The boy moved on as though unaware of the other's existence. The coyote-man raised his whip, there was a long moment of expectancy, then a swift movement, the whistle of the lash and its loud flat-sounding impact on the flesh. The boy's body quivered; but he made no sound, he walked on at the same slow, steady pace. The coyote struck again, again; and at every blow at first a gasp, and then a deep groan went up from the crowd. The boy walked. Twice, thrice, four times round he went. The blood was streaming. Five times round, six times round. Suddenly Lenina covered her face with her hands and began to sob. "Oh, stop them, stop them!" she implored. But the whip fell and fell inexorably. Seven times round. Then all at once the boy staggered and, still without a sound, pitched forward on to his face. Bending over him, the old man touched his back with a long white feather, held it up for a moment, crimson, for the people to see, then shook it thrice over the snakes. A few drops fell, and suddenly the drums broke out again into a panic of hurrying notes; there was a great shout. The dancers rushed forward, picked up the snakes and ran out of the square.

Men, women, children, all the crowd ran after them. A minute later the square was empty, only the boy remained, prone where he had fallen, quite still. Three old women came out of one of the houses, and with some difficulty lifted him and carried him in. The eagle and the man on the cross kept guard for a little while over the empty pueblo; then, as though they had seen enough, sank slowly down through their hatchways, out of sight, into the nether world.

Lenina was still sobbing. "Too awful," she kept repeating, and all Bernard's consolations were in vain. "Too awful! That blood!" She shuddered. "Oh, I wish I had my *soma*."

There was the sound of feet in the inner room.

Lenina did not move, but sat with her face in her hands, unseeing, apart. Only Bernard turned round.

The dress of the young man who now stepped out on to the terrace was Indian; but his plaited hair was straw-coloured, his eyes a pale blue, and his skin a white skin, bronzed.

"Hullo. Good-morrow," said the stranger, in fault-less but peculiar English. "You're civilized, aren't you? You come from the Other Place, outside the Reservation?"

"Who on earth . . . ?" Bernard began in astonish-ment.

The young man sighed and shook his head. "A most unhappy gentleman." And, pointing to the blood-stains in the centre of the square, "Do you see that damned spot?" he asked in a voice that trembled with emotion.

"A gramme is better than a damn," said Lenina mechanically from behind her hands. "I wish I had my *soma*!"

"*I* ought to have been there," the young man went

on. "Why wouldn't they let me be the sacrifice? I'd have gone round ten times twelve, fifteen. Palowhtiwa only got as far as seven. They could have had twice as much blood from me. The multitudinous seas incarnadine." He flung out his arms in a lavish gesture; then, despairingly, let them fall again. "But they wouldn't let me. They disliked me for my complexion. It's always been like that. Always." Tears stood in the young man's eyes; he was ashamed and turned away.

Astonishment made Lenina forget the deprivation of *soma*. She uncovered her face and, for the first time, looked at the stranger. "Do you mean to say that you *wanted* to be hit with that whip?"

Still averted from her, the young man made a sign of affirmation. "For the sake of the pueblo — to make the rain come and the corn grow. And to please Pookong and Jesus. And then to show that I can bear pain without crying out. Yes," and his voice suddenly took on a new resonance, he turned with a proud squaring of the shoulders, a proud, defiant lifting of the chin "to show that I'm a man . . . Oh!" He gave a gasp and was silent, gaping. He had seen, for the first time in his life, the face of a girl whose cheeks were not the colour of chocolate or dogskin, whose hair was auburn and permanently waved, and whose expression (amazing novelty!) was one of benevolent interest. Lenina was smiling at him; such a nice-looking boy, she was thinking, and a really beautiful body. The blood rushed up into the young man's face; he dropped his eyes, raised them again for a moment only to find her still smiling at him, and was so much overcome that he had to turn away and pretend to be looking very hard at something on the other side of the square.

Bernard's questions made a diversion. Who? How? When? From where? Keeping his eyes fixed on Bernard's face (for so passionately did he long to see

Lenina smiling that he simply dared not look at her), the young man tried to explain himself. Linda and he — Linda was his mother (the word made Lenina look uncomfortable) — were strangers in the Reservation. Linda had come from the Other Place long ago, before he was born, with a man who was his father. (Bernard pricked up his ears.) She had gone walking alone in those mountains over there to the North, had fallen down a steep place and hurt her head. ("Go on, go on," said Bernard excitedly.) Some hunters from Malpais had found her and brought her to the pueblo. As for the man who was his father, Linda had never seen him again. His name was Tomakin. (Yes, "Thomas" was the D.H.C.'s first name.) He must have flown away, back to the Other Place, away without her — a bad, unkind, unnatural man.

"And so I was born in Malpais," he concluded. "In Malpais." And he shook his head.

The squalor of that little house on the outskirts of the pueblo!

A space of dust and rubbish separated it from the village. Two famine-stricken dogs were nosing obscenely in the garbage at its door. Inside, when they entered, the twilight stank and was loud with flies.

"Linda!" the young man called.

From the inner room a rather hoarse female voice said, "Coming."

They waited. In bowls on the floor were the remains of a meal, perhaps of several meals.

The door opened. A very stout blonde squaw stepped across the threshold and stood looking at the strangers, staring incredulously, her mouth open. Lenina noticed with disgust that two of the front teeth were missing. And the colour of the ones that remained . . . She shuddered. It was worse than the old man. So fat. And all the lines in her face, the flabbiness, the wrinkles. And the sagging cheeks, with those purplish blotches. And the red veins on her nose, the bloodshot eyes. And that neck — that neck; and the blanket she wore over her head — ragged and filthy. And under the brown sack-shaped tunic those enormous breasts, the bulge of the stomach, the hips. Oh, much worse than the old man, much worse! And suddenly the creature burst out in a torrent of speech, rushed at her with outstretched arms and — Ford! Ford! it was too revolting, in another moment she'd be sick — pressed her against the bulge, the bosom, and began to kiss her. Ford! to *kiss*, slobberingly, and smelt too horrible, obviously never had a bath, and simply reeked of that beastly stuff that was put into Delta and Epsilon bottles (no, it wasn't true about Bernard), positively stank of alcohol. She broke away as quickly as she could.

A blubbered and distorted face confronted her; the creature was crying.

"Oh, my dear, my dear." The torrent of words flowed sobbingly. "If you knew how glad — after all these years! A civilized face. Yes, and civilized clothes. Because I thought I should never see a piece of real acetate silk again." She fingered the sleeve of Lenina's shirt. The nails were black. "And those adorable viscose velveteen shorts! Do you know, dear, I've still got my old clothes, the ones I came in, put away in a box. I'll show them to you afterwards. Though, of course, the acetate has all gone into holes. But such a lovely white bandolier — though I must say your green morocco is even lovelier. Not that it did *me* much good, that bandolier." Her tears began to flow again. "I suppose John told you. What I had to suffer — and not a gramme of *soma* to be had. Only a drink of *mescal* every now and then, when Popé used to bring it. Popé is a boy I used to know. But it makes you feel so bad afterwards, the *mescal* does, and you're sick with the *peyotl;* besides it always made that awful feeling of being ashamed much worse the next day. And I *was* so ashamed. Just think of it: me, a Beta — having a baby: put yourself in my place." (The mere suggestion made Lenina shudder.) "Though it wasn't my fault, I swear; because I still don't know how it happened, seeing that I did all the Malthusian Drill — you know, by numbers, One, two, three, four, always, I swear it; but all the same it happened, and of course there wasn't anything like an Abortion Centre here. Is it still down in Chelsea, by the way?" she asked. Lenina nodded. "And still floodlighted on Tuesdays and Fridays?" Lenina nodded again. "That lovely pink glass tower!" Poor Linda lifted her face and with closed eyes ecstatically contemplated the bright remembered image. "And the river at night," she whispered. Great tears oozed slowly out from behind her tight-shut eyelids. "And flying back in the evening from Stoke Poges. And then a hot bath and vibro-vacuum massage . . . But there." She drew a deep breath, shook her head, opened her eyes again, sniffed once or twice, then blew her nose on her fingers and wiped them on the skirt of her tunic. "Oh, I'm so sorry," she said in response to Lenina's involuntary grimace of disgust. "I oughtn't to have done that. I'm sorry. But what are you to do when there aren't any handkerchiefs? I remember how it used to upset me, all that dirt, and nothing being aseptic. I had an awful cut on my head when they first brought me here. You can't imagine what they used to put on it. Filth, just filth. 'Civilization is Sterilization,' I used to say to them. And 'Streptocock-Gee to Banbury-T, to see a fine bathroom and W.C.' as though they were children. But of course they didn't understand. How should they? And in the end I suppose I got used to it. And anyhow, how *can* you keep things clean when there isn't hot water laid on? And look at these clothes. This beastly wool isn't like acetate. It lasts and lasts. And you're supposed to mend it if it gets torn. But I'm a Beta; I worked in the Fertilizing Room; nobody ever taught me to do anything like that. It wasn't my business. Besides, it never used to be right to mend clothes. Throw them away when they've got holes in them and buy new. 'The more stitches, the less riches.' Isn't that right? Mending's anti-social. But it's all different here. It's like living with lunatics. Everything they do is mad." She looked round; saw John and Bernard had left them and were walking up and down in the dust and garbage outside the house; but, none the less confidentially lowering her voice, and leaning, while Lenina stiffened and shrank, so close that the blown reek of embryo-poison stirred the hair on her cheek. "For instance," she hoarsely whispered, "take the way they have one another here. Mad, I tell you, absolutely mad. Everybody belongs to every one else — don't they? don't they?" she insisted, tugging at Lenina's sleeve. Lenina nodded her averted head, let out the breath she had been holding and managed to draw another one, relatively untainted. "Well, here," the other went on, "nobody's supposed to belong to more than one person. And if you have people in the ordinary way, the others think you're wicked and anti-social. They hate and despise you. Once a lot of women came and made a scene because their men came to see me. Well, why not? And then they rushed at me . . . No, it was too awful. I can't tell you about it." Linda covered her face with her hands and shuddered. "They're so hateful, the women here. Mad, mad and cruel. And of course they don't know anything about Malthusian Drill, or bottles, or decanting, or anything of that sort. So they're having children all the time — like dogs. It's too revolting. And to think that I . . . Oh, Ford, Ford, Ford! And yet John *was* a great comfort to me. I don't know what I should have done without him. Even though he did get so upset whenever a man . . . Quite as a tiny boy, even. Once (but that was when he was bigger) he tried to kill poor Waihusiwa — or was it Popé? — just because I used to have them sometimes. Because I never *could* make him understand that that was what civilized people ought to do. Being mad's infectious, I believe. Anyhow, John seems to have caught it from the Indians. Because, of course, he was with them a lot. Even though they always were so beastly to him and wouldn't let him do all the things the other boys did. Which was a good thing in a way, because it made it easier for me to condition him a little. Though you've no idea how difficult that is. There's so much one doesn't know; it wasn't my business to know. I mean, when a child asks you how a helicopter works or who made the world — well, what are you to answer if you're a Beta and have always worked in the Fertilizing Room? What *are* you to answer?"

CHAPTER 8

Outside, in the dust and among the garbage (there were four dogs now), Bernard and John were walking slowly up and down.

"So hard for me to realize," Bernard was saying, "to reconstruct. As though we were living on different planets, in different centuries. A mother, and all this dirt, and gods, and old age, and disease . . ." He shook his head. "It's almost inconceivable. I shall never understand, unless you explain."

"Explain what?"

"This." He indicated the pueblo. "That." And it was the little house outside the village. "Everything. All your life."

"But what is there to say?"

"From the beginning. As far back as you can remember."

"As far back as I can remember." John frowned. There was a long silence.

It was very hot. They had eaten a lot of tortillas and sweet corn. Linda said, "Come and lie down, Baby." They lay down together in the big bed. "Sing," and Linda sang. Sang "Streptocock-Gee to Banbury-T" and "Bye Baby Banting, soon you'll need decanting." Her voice got fainter and fainter . . .

There was a loud noise, and he woke with a start. A man was saying something to Linda, and Linda was laughing. She had pulled the blanket up to her chin, but the man pulled it down again. His hair was like two black ropes, and round his arm was a lovely silver bracelet with blue stones in it. He liked the bracelet;

but all the same, he was frightened; he hid his face against Linda's body. Linda put her hand on him and he felt safer. In those other words he did not understand so well, she said to the man, "Not with John here." The man looked at him, then again at Linda, and said a few words in a soft voice. Linda said, "No." But the man bent over the bed towards him and his face was huge, terrible; the black ropes of hair touched the blanket. "No," Linda said again, and he felt her hand squeezing him more tightly. "No, no!" But the man took hold of one of his arms, and it hurt. He screamed. The man put up his other hand and lifted him up. Linda was still holding him, still saying, "No, no." The man said something short and angry, and suddenly her hands were gone. "Linda, Linda." He kicked and wriggled; but the man carried him across to the door, opened it, put him down on the floor in the middle of the other room, and went away, shutting the door behind him. He got up, he ran to the door. Standing on tiptoe he could just reach the big wooden latch. He lifted it and pushed; but the door wouldn't open. "Linda," he shouted. She didn't answer.

He remembered a huge room, rather dark; and there were big wooden things with strings fastened to them, and lots of women standing round them — making blankets, Linda said. Linda told him to sit in the corner with the other children, while she went and helped the women. He played with the little boys for a long time. Suddenly people started talking very loud, and there were the women pushing Linda away, and Linda was crying. She went to the door and he ran after her. He asked her why they were angry. "Because I broke something," she said. And then she got angry too. "How should I know how to do their beastly weaving?" she said. "Beastly savages." He asked her what savages were. When they got back to their house, Popé was waiting at the door, and he came in with them. He had a big gourd full of stuff that looked like water; only it wasn't water, but something with a bad smell that burnt your mouth and made you cough. Linda drank some and Popé drank some, and then Linda laughed a lot and talked very loud; and then she and Popé went into the other room. When Popé went away, he went into the room. Linda was in bed and so fast asleep that he couldn't wake her.

Popé used to come often. He said the stuff in the gourd was called *mescal*; but Linda said it ought to be called *soma*; only it made you feel ill afterwards. He hated Popé. He hated them all — all the men who came to see Linda. One afternoon, when he had been playing with the other children — it was cold, he remembered, and there was snow on the mountains — he came back to the house and heard angry voices in the bedroom. They were women's voices, and they said words he didn't understand, but he knew they were dreadful words. Then suddenly, crash! something was upset; he heard people moving about quickly, and there was another crash and then a noise like hitting a mule, only not so bony; then Linda screamed. "Oh, don't, don't, don't!" she said. He ran in. There were three women in dark blankets. Linda was on the bed. One of the women was holding her wrists. Another was lying across her legs, so that she couldn't kick. The third was hitting her with a whip. Once, twice, three times; and each time Linda screamed. Crying, he tugged at the fringe of the woman's blanket. "Please, please." With her free hand she held him away. The whip came down again, and again Linda screamed. He caught hold of the woman's enormous brown hand between his own and bit it with all his might. She cried out, wrenched her hand free, and gave him such a push that he fell down. While he was lying on the ground she hit him three times with the whip. It hurt more than anything he had ever felt

— like fire. The whip whistled again, fell. But this time it was Linda who screamed.

"But why did they want to hurt you, Linda?" he asked that night. He was crying, because the red marks of the whip on his back still hurt so terribly. But he was also crying because people were so beastly and unfair, and because he was only a little boy and couldn't do anything against them. Linda was crying too. She was grown up, but she wasn't big enough to fight against three of them. It wasn't fair for her either. "Why did they want to hurt you, Linda?"

"I don't know. How should I know?" It was difficult to hear what she said, because she was lying on her stomach and her face was in the pillow. "They say those men are *their* men," she went on; and she did not seem to be talking to him at all; she seemed to be talking with some one inside herself. A long talk which he didn't understand; and in the end she started crying louder than ever.

"Oh, don't cry, Linda. Don't cry."

He pressed himself against her. He put his arm round her neck. Linda cried out. "Oh, be careful. My shoulder! Oh!" and she pushed him away, hard. His head banged against the wall. "Little idiot!" she shouted; and then, suddenly, she began to slap him. Slap, slap . . .

"Linda," he cried out. "Oh, mother, don't!"

"I'm not your mother. I won't be your mother."

"But, Linda . . . Oh!" She slapped him on the cheek.

"Turned into a savage," she shouted. "Having young ones like an animal . . . If it hadn't been for you, I might have gone to the Inspector, I might have got away. But not with a baby. That would have been too shameful."

He saw that she was going to hit him again, and lifted his arm to guard his face. "Oh, don't, Linda, please don't."

"Little beast!" She pulled down his arm; his face was uncovered.

"Don't, Linda." He shut his eyes, expecting the blow.

But she didn't hit him. After a little time, he opened his eyes again and saw that she was looking at him. He tried to smile at her. Suddenly she put her arms round him and kissed him again and again.

Sometimes, for several days, Linda didn't get up at all. She lay in bed and was sad. Or else she drank the stuff that Popé brought and laughed a great deal and went to sleep. Sometimes she was sick. Often she forgot to wash him, and there was nothing to eat except cold tortillas. He remembered the first time she found those little animals in his hair, how she screamed and screamed.

The happiest times were when she told him about the Other Place. "And you really can go flying, whenever you like?"

"Whenever you like." And she would tell him about the lovely music that came out of a box, and all the nice games you could play, and the delicious things to eat and drink, and the light that came when you pressed a little thing in the wall, and the pictures that you could hear and feel and smell, as well as see, and another box for making nice smells, and the pink and green and blue and silver houses as high as mountains, and everybody happy and no one ever sad or angry, and every one belonging to every one else, and the boxes where you could see and hear what was happening at the other side of the world, and babies in lovely clean bottles — everything so clean, and no nasty smells, no dirt at all — and people never lonely, but living together and being so jolly and happy, like the summer dances here in Malpais, but much happier, and the happiness being there every day, every day. . . . He listened by the hour. And sometimes, when he and the other children were tired with too much playing, one of the old men of the pueblo would talk to them, in those other words, of the great Transformer of the World, and of the long fight between Right Hand and Left Hand, between Wet and Dry; of Awonawilona, who made a great fog by thinking in the night, and then made the whole world out of the fog; of Earth Mother and Sky Father; of Ahaiyuta and Marsailema, the twins of War and Chance; of Jesus and Pookong; of Mary and Etsanatlehi, the woman who makes herself young again; of the Black Stone at Laguna and the Great Eagle and Our Lady of Acoma. Strange stories, all the more wonderful to him for being told in the other words and so not fully understood. Lying in bed, he would think of Heaven and London and Our Lady of Acoma and the rows and rows of babies in clean bottles and Jesus flying up and Linda flying up and the great Director of World Hatcheries and Awonawilona.

« «

Lots of men came to see Linda. The boys began to point their fingers at him. In the strange other words they said that Linda was bad; they called her names he did not understand, but that he knew were bad names. One day they sang a song about her, again and again. He threw stones at them. They threw back; a sharp stone cut his cheek. The blood wouldn't stop; he was covered with blood.

Linda taught him to read. With a piece of charcoal she drew pictures on the wall — an animal sitting down, a baby inside a bottle; then she wrote letters. THE CAT IS ON THE MAT. THE TOT IS IN THE POT. He learned quickly and easily. When he knew how to read all the words she wrote on the wall, Linda opened her big wooden box and pulled out from under those funny little red trousers she never wore a thin little book. He had often seen it before. "When you're bigger," she had said, "you can read it." Well, now he was big enough. He was proud. "I'm afraid you won't find it very exciting," she said. "But it's the only thing I have." She sighed. "If only you could see the lovely reading machines we used to have in London!" He began reading. *The Chemical and Bacteriological Conditioning of the Embryo. Practical Instructions for Beta Embryo-Store Workers.* It took him a quarter of an hour to read the title alone. He threw the book on the floor. "Beastly, beastly book!" he said, and began to cry.

The boys still sang their horrible song about Linda. Sometimes, too, they laughed at him for being so ragged. When he tore his clothes, Linda did not know how to mend them. In the Other Place, she told him, people threw away clothes with holes in them and got new ones. "Rags, rags!" the boys used to shout at him. "But I can read," said to himself, "and they can't. They don't even know what reading is." It was fairly easy, if he thought hard enough about the reading, to pretend that he didn't mind when they made fun of him. He asked Linda to give him the book again.

The more the boys pointed and sang, the harder he read. Soon he could read all the words quite well. Even the longest. But what did they mean? He asked Linda; but even when she could answer it didn't seem to make it very clear. And generally she couldn't answer at all.

"What are chemicals?" he would ask.

"Oh, stuff like magnesium salts, and alcohol for keeping the Deltas and Epsilons small and backward, and calcium carbonate for bones, and all that sort of thing."

"But how do you make chemicals, Linda? Where do they come from?"

"Well, I don't know. You get them out of bottles. And when the bottles are empty, you send up to the Chemical Store for more. It's the Chemical Store people who make them, I suppose. Or else they send to the factory for them. I don't know. I never did any chemistry. My job was always with the embryos."

It was the same with everything else he asked about. Linda never seemed to know. The old men of the pueblo had much more definite answers.

"The seed of men and all creatures, the seed of the sun and the seed of earth and the seed of the sky — Awonawilona made them all out of the Fog of Increase. Now the world has four wombs; and he laid the seeds in the lowest of the four wombs. And gradually the seeds began to grow . . ."

«««««««««««««««««««««««««««««««««««««««

One day (John calculated later that it must have been soon after his twelfth birthday) he came home and found a book that he had never seen before lying on the floor in the bedroom. It was a thick book and looked very old. The binding had been eaten by mice; some of its pages were loose and crumpled. He picked it up, looked at the title-page: the book was called *The Complete Works of William Shakespeare*.

Linda was lying on the bed, sipping that horrible stinking *mescal* out of a cup. "Popé brought it," she said. Her voice was thick and hoarse like somebody else's voice. "It was lying in one of the chests of the

Antelope Kiva. It's supposed to have been there for hundreds of years. I expect it's true, because I looked at it, and it seemed to be full of nonsense. Uncivilized. Still, it'll be good enough for you to practice your reading on." She took a last sip, set the cup down on the floor beside the bed, turned over on her side, hiccoughed once or twice and went to sleep.

He opened the book at random.

Nay, but to live

In the rank sweat of an enseamed bed,

Stew'd in corruption, honeying and making love

Over the nasty sty . . .

The strange words rolled through his mind; rumbled, like the drums at the summer dances, if the drums could have spoken; like the men singing the Corn Song, beautiful, beautiful, so that you cried; like old Mitsima saying magic over his feathers and his carved sticks and his bits of bone and stone — *kiathla tsilu silokwe silokwe silokwe. Kiai silu silu, tsithl* — but better than Mitsima's magic, because it meant more, because it talked to *him*, talked wonderfully and only half-understandably, a terrible beautiful magic, about Linda; about Linda lying there snoring, with the empty cup on the floor beside the bed; about Linda and Popé, Linda and Popé.

He hated Popé more and more. A man can smile and smile and be a villain. Remorseless, treacherous, lecherous, kindless villain. What did the words exactly mean? He only half knew. But their magic was strong and went on rumbling in his head, and somehow it was as though he had never really hated Popé before; never really hated him because he had never been able to say how much he hated him. But now he had these words, these words like drums and singing and magic. These words and the strange, strange story out of which they were taken (he couldn't make head or tail of it, but it was wonderful, wonderful all the same) — they gave him a reason for hating Popé; and they made his hatred more real; they even made Popé himself more real.

One day, when he came in from playing, the door of the inner room was open, and he saw them lying together on the bed, asleep — white Linda and Popé almost black beside her, with one arm under her shoulders and the other dark hand on her breast, and one of the plaits of his long hair lying across her throat, like a black snake trying to strangle her. Popé's gourd and a cup were standing on the floor near the bed. Linda was snoring.

His heart seemed to have disappeared and left a hole. He was empty. Empty, and cold, and rather sick, and giddy. He leaned against the wall to steady himself. Remorseless, treacherous, lecherous . . . Like drums, like the men singing for the corn, like magic, the words repeated and repeated themselves in his head. From being cold he was suddenly hot. His cheeks burnt with the rush of blood, the room swam and darkened before his eyes. He ground his teeth. "I'll kill him, I'll kill him, I'll kill him," he kept saying. And suddenly there were more words.

When he is drunk asleep, or in his rage

Or in the incestuous pleasure of his bed . . .

The magic was on his side, the magic explained and gave orders. He stepped back in the outer room. "When he is drunk asleep . . ." The knife for the meat was lying on the floor near the fireplace. He picked it up and tiptoed to the door again. "When he is drunk asleep, drunk asleep . . ." He ran across the room and stabbed — oh, the blood! — stabbed again, as Popé heaved out of his sleep, lifted his hand to stab once more, but found his wrist caught, held and — oh, oh!

— twisted. He couldn't move, he was trapped, and there were Popé's small black eyes, very close, staring into his own. He looked away. There were two cuts on Popé's left shoulder. "Oh, look at the blood!" Linda was crying. "Look at the blood!" She had never been able to bear the sight of blood. Popé lifted his other hand — to strike him, he thought. He stiffened to receive the blow. But the hand only took him under the chin and turned his face, so that he had to look again into Popé's eyes. For a long time, for hours and hours. And suddenly — he couldn't help it — he began to cry. Popé burst out laughing. "Go," he said, in the other Indian words. "Go, my brave Ahaiyuta." He ran out into the other room to hide his tears.

"You are fifteen," said old Mitsima, in the Indian words. "Now I may teach you to work the clay."

Squatting by the river, they worked together.

"First of all," said Mitsima, taking a lump of the wetted clay between his hands, "we make a little moon." The old man squeezed the lump into a disk, then bent up the edges; the moon became a shallow cup.

Slowly and unskilfully he imitated the old man's delicate gestures.

"A moon, a cup, and now a snake." Mitsima rolled out another piece of clay into a long flexible cylinder, hooped it into a circle and pressed it on to the rim of the cup. "Then another snake. And another. And another." Round by round, Mitsima built up the sides of the pot; it was narrow, it bulged, it narrowed again towards the neck. Mitsima squeezed and patted, stroked and scraped; and there at last it stood, in shape the familiar water pot of Malpais, but creamy white instead of black, and still soft to the touch. The crooked parody of Mitsima's, his own stood beside it. Looking at the two pots, he had to laugh.

"But the next one will be better," he said, and began to moisten another piece of clay.

To fashion, to give form, to feel his fingers gaining in skill and power — this gave him an extraordinary pleasure. "A, B, C, Vitamin D," he sang to himself as he worked. "The fat's in the liver, the cod's in the sea." And Mitsima also sang a song about killing a bear. They worked all day, and all day he was filled with an intense, absorbing happiness.

"Next winter," said old Mitsima, "I will teach you to make the bow."

He stood for a long time outside the house, and at last the ceremonies within were finished. The door opened; they came out. Kothlu came first, his right hand outstretched and tightly closed, as though over some precious jewel. Her clenched hand similarly out-stretched, Kiakimé followed. They walked in silence, and in silence, behind them, came the brothers and sisters and cousins and all the troop of old people.

They walked out of the pueblo, across the mesa. At the edge of the cliff they halted, facing the early morning sun. Kothlu opened his hand. A pinch of corn meal lay white on the palm; he breathed on it, murmured a few words, then threw it, a handful of white dust, towards the sun. Kiakimé did the same. Then Kiakimé's father stepped forward, and holding up a feathered prayer stick, made a long prayer, then threw the stick after the corn meal.

"It is finished," said old Mitsima in a loud voice. "They are married."

"Well," said Linda, as they turned away, "all I can say is, it does seem a lot of fuss to make about so little.

In civilized countries, when a boy wants to have a girl, he just . . . But where *are* you going, John?"

He paid no attention to her calling, but ran on, away, away, anywhere to be by himself.

It is finished. Old Mitsima's words repeated themselves in his mind. Finished, finished . . . In silence and from a long way off, but violently, desperately, hopelessly, he had loved Kiakimé. And now it was finished. He was sixteen.

At the full moon, in the Antelope Kiva, secrets would be told, secrets would be done and borne. They would go down, boys, into the kiva and come out again, men. The boys were all afraid and at the same time impatient. And at last it was the day. The sun went down, the moon rose. He went with the others. Men were standing, dark, at the entrance to the kiva; the ladder went down into the red lighted depths. Already the leading boys had begun to climb down. Suddenly, one of the men stepped forward, caught him by the arm, and pulled him out of the ranks. He broke free and dodged back into his place among the others. This time the man struck him, pulled his hair. "Not for you, white-hair!" "Not for the son of the she-dog," said one of the other men. The boys laughed. "Go!" And as he still hovered on the fringes of the group, "Go!" the men shouted again. One of them bent down, took a stone, threw it. "Go, go, go!" There was a shower of stones. Bleeding, he ran away into the darkness. From the red-lit kiva came the noise of singing. The last of the boys had climbed down the ladder. He was all alone.

All alone, outside the pueblo, on the bare plain of the mesa. The rock was like bleached bones in the moonlight. Down in the valley, the coyotes were howling at the moon. The bruises hurt him, the cuts were still bleeding; but it was not for pain that he sobbed; it was because he was all alone, because he had been driven out, alone, into this skeleton world of rocks and moonlight. At the edge of the precipice he sat down. The moon was behind him; he looked down into the black shadow of the mesa, into the black shadow of death. He had only to take one step, one little jump. . . . He held out his right hand in the moonlight. From the cut on his wrist the blood was still oozing. Every few seconds a drop fell, dark, almost colourless in the dead light. Drop, drop, drop. To-morrow and to-morrow and to-morrow . . .

He had discovered Time and Death and God.

«««««««««««««««««««««««««««««««««««««

"Alone, always alone," the young man was saying.

The words awoke a plaintive echo in Bernard's mind. Alone, alone . . . "So am I," he said, on a gush of confidingness. "Terribly alone."

"Are you?" John looked surprised. "I thought that in the Other Place . . . I mean, Linda always said that nobody was ever alone there."

Bernard blushed uncomfortably. "You see," he said, mumbling and with averted eyes, "I'm rather different from most people, I suppose. If one happens to be decanted different . . ."

"Yes, that's just it." The young man nodded. "If one's different, one's bound to be lonely. They're beast-ly to one. Do you know, they shut me out of absolute-ly everything? When the other boys were sent out to spend the night on the mountains — you know, when you have to dream which your sacred animal is — they wouldn't let me go with the others; they wouldn't tell me any of the secrets. I did it by myself, though," he added. "Didn't eat anything for five days and then went out one night alone into those mountains there." He pointed.

Patronizingly, Bernard smiled. "And did you dream of anything?" he asked.

The other nodded. "But I mustn't tell you what." He was silent for a little; then, in a low voice, "Once," he went on, "I did something that none of the others did: I stood against a rock in the middle of the day, in summer, with my arms out, like Jesus on the Cross."

"What on earth for?"

"I wanted to know what it was like being crucified. Hanging there in the sun . . ."

"But why?"

"Why? Well . . ." He hesitated. "Because I felt I ought to. If Jesus could stand it. And then, if one has done something wrong . . . Besides, I was unhappy; that was another reason."

"It seems a funny way of curing your unhappiness," said Bernard. But on second thoughts he decided that there was, after all, some sense in it. Better than taking *soma* . . .

"I fainted after a time," said the young man."Fell down on my face. Do you see the mark where I cut myself?" He lifted the thick yellow hair from his forehead. The scar showed, pale and puckered, on his right temple.

Bernard looked, and then quickly, with a little shudder, averted his eyes. His conditioning had made him not so much pitiful as profoundly squeamish. The mere suggestion of illness or wounds was to him not only horrifying, but even repulsive and rather disgusting. Like dirt, or deformity, or old age. Hastily he changed the subject.

"I wonder if you'd like to come back to London with us?" he asked, making the first move in a campaign whose strategy he had been secretly elaborating ever since, in the little house, he had realized who the "father" of this young savage must be. "Would you like that?"

The young man's face lit up. "Do you really mean it?"

"Of course; if I can get permission, that is."

"Linda too?"

"Well . . ." He hesitated doubtfully. That revolting creature! No, it was impossible. Unless, unless . . . It suddenly occurred to Bernard that her very revolting-ness might prove an enormous asset. "But of course!" he cried, making up for his first hesitations with an excess of noisy cordiality.

The young man drew a deep breath. "To think it should be coming true — what I've dreamt of all my life. Do you remember what Miranda says?"

"Who's Miranda?"

But the young man had evidently not heard the question. "O wonder!" he was saying; and his eyes shone, his face was brightly flushed. "How many good-ly creatures are there here! How beauteous mankind is!" The flush suddenly deepened; he was thinking of Lenina, of an angel in bottle-green viscose, lustrous with youth and skin food, plump, benevolently smil-ing. His voice faltered. "O brave new world," he began, then suddenly interrupted himself; the blood had left his cheeks; he was as pale as paper. "Are you married to her?" he asked.

"Am I what?"

"Married. You know — for ever. They say 'for ever' in the Indian words; it can't be broken."

"Ford, no!" Bernard couldn't help laughing.

John also laughed, but for another reason — laughed for pure joy.

"O brave new world," he repeated. "O brave new world that has such people in it. Let's start at once."

"You have a most peculiar way of talking sometimes," said Bernard, staring at the young man in perplexed astonishment. "And, anyhow, hadn't you better wait till you actually see the new world?"

CHAPTER 9

Lenina felt herself entitled, after this day of queerness and horror, to a complete and absolute holiday. As soon as they got back to the rest-house, she swallowed six half-gramme tablets of *soma*, lay down on her bed, and within ten minutes had embarked for lunar eternity. It would be eighteen hours at the least before she was in time again.

Bernard meanwhile lay pensive and wide-eyed in the dark. It was long after midnight before he fell asleep. Long after midnight; but his insomnia had not been fruitless; he had a plan.

Punctually, on the following morning, at ten o'clock, the green-uniformed octoroon stepped out of his helicopter. Bernard was waiting for him among the agaves.

"Miss Crowne's gone on *soma*-holiday," he explained. "Can hardly be back before five. Which leaves us seven hours."

He could fly to Santa Fé, do all the business he had to do, and be in Malpais again long before she woke up.

"She'll be quite safe here by herself?"

"Safe as helicopters," the octoroon assured him.

They climbed into the machine and started off at once. At ten thirty-four they landed on the roof of the Santa Fé Post Office; at ten thirty-seven Bernard had got through to the World Controller's Office in Whitehall; at ten thirty-seven he was speaking to his fordship's fourth personal secretary; at ten forty-four he was repeating his story to the first secretary, and at ten forty-seven and a half it was the deep, resonant voice of Mustapha Mond himself that sounded in his ears.

"I ventured to think," stammered Bernard, "that your fordship might find the matter of sufficient scientific interest . . ."

"Yes, I do find it of sufficient scientific interest," said the deep voice. "Bring these two individuals back to London with you."

"Your fordship is aware that I shall need a special permit . . ."

"The necessary orders," said Mustapha Mond, "are being sent to the Warden of the Reservation at this moment. You will proceed at once to the Warden's Office. Good-morning, Mr. Marx."

There was silence. Bernard hung up the receiver and hurried up to the roof.

"Warden's Office," he said to the Gamma-green octoroon.

At ten fifty-four Bernard was shaking hands with the Warden.

"Delighted, Mr. Marx, delighted." His boom was deferential. "We have just received special orders . . ."

"I know," said Bernard, interrupting him. "I was talking to his fordship on the phone a moment ago." His bored tone implied that he was in the habit of talking to his fordship every day of the week. He dropped into a chair. "If you'll kindly take all the necessary steps as soon as possible. As soon as possible," he emphatically repeated. He was thoroughly enjoying himself.

At eleven three he had all the necessary papers in his pocket.

"So long," he said patronizingly to the Warden,

who had accompanied him as far as the lift gates. "So long."

He walked across to the hotel, had a bath, a vibro-vac massage, and an electrolytic shave, listened in to the morning's news, looked in for half an hour on the televisor, ate a leisured luncheon, and at half-past two flew back with the octoroon to Malpais.

The young man stood outside the rest-house.

"Bernard," he called. "Bernard!" There was no answer.

Noiseless on his deerksin moccasins, he ran up the steps and tried the door. The door was locked.

They were gone! Gone! It was the most terrible thing that had ever happened to him. She had asked him to come and see them, and now they were gone. He sat down on the steps and cried.

Half an hour later it occurred to him to look through the window. The first thing he saw was a green suit-case, with the initials L.C. painted on the lid. Joy flared up like fire within him. He picked up a stone. The smashed glass tinkled on the floor. A moment later he was inside the room. He opened the green suit-case; and all at once he was breathing Lenina's perfume, filling his lungs with her essential being. His heart beat wildly; for a moment he was almost faint. Then, bending over the precious box, he touched, he lifted into the light, he examined. The zippers on Lenina's spare pair of viscose velveteen shorts were at first a puzzle, then solved, a delight. Zip, and then zip; zip, and then zip; he was enchanted. Her green slippers were the most beautiful things he had ever seen. He unfolded a pair of zippicamiknicks, blushed, put them hastily away again; but kissed a perfumed acetate handkerchief and wound a scarf round his neck.

Opening a box, he spilt a cloud of scented powder. His hands were floury with the stuff. He wiped them on his chest, on his shoulders, on his bare arms. Delicious perfume! He shut his eyes; he rubbed his cheek against his own powdered arm. Touch of smooth skin against his face, scent in his nostrils of musky dust — her real presence. "Lenina," he whispered. "Lenina!"

A noise made him start, made him guiltily turn. He crammed up his thieveries into the suit-case and shut the lid; then listened again, looked. Not a sign of life, not a sound. And yet he had certainly heard something — something like a sigh, something like the creak of a board. He tiptoed to the door and, cautiously opening it, found himself looking on to a broad landing. On the opposite side of the landing was another door, ajar. He stepped out, pushed, peeped.

There, on a low bed, the sheet flung back, dressed in a pair of pink one-piece zippyjamas, lay Lenina, fast asleep and so beautiful in the midst of her curls, so touchingly childish with her pink toes and her grave sleeping face, so trustful in the helplessness of her limp hands and melted limbs, that the tears came to his eyes.

With an infinity of quite unnecessary precautions — for nothing short of a pistol shot could have called Lenina back from her *soma*-holiday before the appointed time — he entered the room, he knelt on the floor beside the bed. He gazed, he clasped his hands, his lips moved. "Her eyes," he murmured,

> "*Her eyes, her hair, her cheek, her gait, her voice;*
> *Handlest in thy discourse O! that her hand,*
> *In whose comparison all whites are ink*
> *Writing their own reproach; to whose soft seizure*
> *The cygnet's down is harsh . . .*"

A fly buzzed round her; he waved it away. "Flies," he remembered,

> "On the white wonder of dear Juliet's hand, may seize
> And steal immortal blessing from her lips,
> Who, even in pure and vestal modesty,
> Still blush, as thinking their own kisses sin."

Very slowly, with the hesitating gesture of one who reaches forward to stroke a shy and possibly rather dangerous bird, he put out his hand. It hung there trembling, within an inch of those limp fingers, on the verge of contact. Did he dare? Dare to profane with his unworthiest hand that . . . No, he didn't. The bird was too dangerous. His hand dropped back. How beautiful she was! How beautiful!

Then suddenly he found himself reflecting that he had only to take hold of the zipper at her neck and give one long, strong pull . . . He shut his eyes, he shook his head with the gesture of a dog shaking its ears as it emerges from the water. Detestable thought! He was ashamed of himself. Pure and vestal modesty . . .

There was a humming in the air. Another fly trying to steal immortal blessings? A wasp? He looked, saw nothing. The humming grew louder and louder, localized itself as being outside the shuttered windows. The plane! In a panic, he scrambled to his feet and ran into the other room, vaulted through the open window, and hurrying along the path between the tall agaves was in time to receive Bernard Marx as he climbed out of the helicopter.

CHAPTER 10

The hands of all the four thousand electric clocks in all the Bloomsbury Centre's four thousand rooms marked twenty-seven minutes past two. "This hive of industry," as the Director was fond of calling it, was in the full buzz of work. Every one was busy, everything in ordered motion. Under the microscopes, their long tails furiously lashing, spermatozoa were burrowing head first into eggs; and, fertilized, the eggs were expanding, dividing, or if bokanovskified, budding and breaking up into whole populations of separate embryos. From the Social Predestination Room the escalators went rumbling down into the basement, and there, in the crimson darkness, stewingly warm on their cushion of peritoneum and gorged with blood-surrogate and hormones, the foetuses grew and grew or, poisoned, languished into a stunted Epsilon-hood. With a faint hum and rattle the moving racks crawled imperceptibly through the weeks and the recapitulated aeons to where, in the Decanting Room, the newly-unbottled babes uttered their first yell of horror and amazement.

The dynamos purred in the sub-basement, the lifts rushed up and down. On all the eleven floors of Nurseries it was feeding time. From eighteen hundred bottles eighteen hundred carefully labelled infants were simultaneously sucking down their pint of pasteurized external secretion.

Above them, in ten successive layers of dormitory, the little boys and girls who were still young enough to need an afternoon sleep were as busy as every one else, though they did not know it, listening unconsciously to hypnopædic lessons in hygiene and sociability, in class-consciousness and the toddler's love-life. Above these again were the play-rooms where, the weather having turned to rain, nine hundred older children were amusing themselves with bricks and clay modelling, hunt-the-zipper, and erotic play.

Buzz, buzz! the hive was humming, busily, joyfully. Blithe was the singing of the young girls over their test-tubes, the Predestinators whistled as they worked, and in the Decanting Room what glorious jokes were cracked above the empty bottles! But the Director's face, as he entered the Fertilizing Room with Henry Foster, was grave, wooden with severity.

"A public example," he was saying. "In this room, because it contains more high-caste workers than any other in the Centre. I have told him to meet me here at half-past two."

"He does his work very well," put in Henry, with hypocritical generosity.

"I know. But that's all the more reason for severity. His intellectual eminence carries with it corresponding moral responsibilities. The greater a man's talents, the greater his power to lead astray. It is better that one should suffer than that many should be corrupted. Consider the matter dispassionately, Mr. Foster, and you will see that no offence is so heinous as unortho-doxy of behaviour. Murder kills only the individual — and, after all, what is an individual?" With a sweeping gesture he indicated the rows of microscopes, the test-tubes, the incubators. "We can make a new one with the greatest ease — as many as we like. Unorthodoxy threatens more than the life of a mere individual; it strikes at Society itself. Yes, at Society itself," he repeated. "Ah, but here he comes."

Bernard had entered the room and was advancing between the rows of fertilizers towards them. A veneer of jaunty self-confidence thinly concealed his nervousness. The voice in which he said, "Good-morning, Director," was absurdly too loud; that in which, correcting his mistake, he said, "You asked me to come and speak to you here," ridiculously soft, a squeak.

"Yes, Mr. Marx," said the Director portentously. "I did ask you to come to me here. You returned from your holiday last night, I understand."

"Yes," Bernard answered.

"Yes-s," repeated the Director, lingering, a serpent, on the "s." Then, suddenly raising his voice, "Ladies and gentlemen," he trumpeted, "ladies and gentlemen."

The singing of the girls over their test-tubes, the preoccupied whistling of the Microscopists, suddenly ceased. There was a profound silence; every one looked round.

"Ladies and gentlemen," the Director repeated once more, "excuse me for thus interrupting your labours. A painful duty constrains me. The security and stability of Society are in danger. Yes, in danger, ladies and gentlemen. This man," he pointed accusingly at Bernard, "this man who stands before you here, this Alpha-Plus to whom so much has been given, and from whom, in consequence, so much must be expected, this colleague of yours — or should I anticipate and say this ex-colleague? — has grossly betrayed the trust imposed in him. By his heretical views on sport and *soma*, by the scandalous unorthodoxy of his sexlife, by his refusal to obey the teachings of Our Ford and behave out of office hours, 'even as a little infant,' " (here the Director made the sign of the T), "he has proved himself an enemy of Society, a subverter, ladies and gentlemen, of all Order and Stability, a conspirator against Civilization itself. For this reason I propose to dismiss him, to dismiss him with ignominy from the post he has held in this Centre; I propose forthwith to apply for his transference to a Subcentre of the lowest order and, that his punishment may serve the best interest of Society, as far as possible removed from any important Centre of population. In Iceland he will have small opportunity to lead others astray by his unfordly example." The Director paused; then, folding his arms, he turned impressively to Bernard. "Marx," he said, "can you show any reason why I should not now execute the judgment passed upon you?"

"Yes, I can," Bernard answered in a very loud voice.

Somewhat taken aback, but still majestically, "Then show it," said the Director.

"Certainly. But it's in the passage. One moment." Bernard hurried to the door and threw it open. "Come in," he commanded, and the reason came in and showed itself.

There was a gasp, a murmur of astonishment and horror; a young girl screamed; standing on a chair to get a better view some one upset two test-tubes full of spermatozoa. Bloated, sagging, and among those firm youthful bodies, those undistorted faces, a strange and terrifying monster of middle-agedness, Linda advanced into the room, coquettishly smiling her broken and discoloured smile, and rolling as she walked, with what was meant to be a voluptuous undulation, her enormous haunches. Bernard walked beside her.

"There he is," he said, pointing at the Director.

"Did you think I didn't recognize him?" Linda asked indignantly; then, turning to the Director, "Of course I knew you; Tomakin, I should have known you anywhere, among a thousand. But perhaps you've forgotten me. Don't you remember? Don't you remember, Tomakin? Your Linda." She stood looking at him, her head on one side, still smiling, but with a smile that became progressively, in face of the Director's expression of petrified disgust, less and less self-confident, that wavered and finally went out. "Don't you remember, Tomakin?" she repeated in a voice that trembled. Her eyes were anxious, agonized. The blotched and sagging face twisted grotesquely into the grimace of extreme grief. "Tomakin!" She held out her arms. Some one began to titter.

"What's the meaning," began the Director, "of this monstrous . . ."

"Tomakin!" She ran forward, her blanket trailing behind her, threw her arms round his neck, hid her face on his chest.

A howl of laughter went up irrepressibly.

". . . this monstrous practical joke," the Director shouted.

Red in the face, he tried to disengage himself from her embrace. Desperately she clung. "But I'm Linda, I'm Linda." The laughter drowned her voice. "You made me have a baby," she screamed above the uproar. There was a sudden and appalling hush; eyes floated uncomfortably, not knowing where to look. The Director went suddenly pale, stopped struggling and stood, his hands on her wrists, staring down at her, horrified. "Yes, a baby — and I was its mother." She flung the obscenity like a challenge into the outraged silence; then, suddenly breaking away from him, ashamed, ashamed, covered her face with her hands, sobbing. "It wasn't my fault, Tomakin. Because I always did my drill, didn't I? Didn't I? Always . . . I don't know how . . . If you knew how awful, Tomakin . . . But he was a comfort to me, all the same." Turning towards the door, "John!" she called. "John!"

He came in at once, paused for a moment just inside the door, looked round, then soft on his moccasined feet strode quickly across the room, fell on his knees in front of the Director, and said in a clear voice: "My father!"

The word (for "father" was not so much obscene as — with its connotation of something at one remove from the loathsomeness and moral obliquity of child-bearing — merely gross, a scatological rather than a pornographic impropriety); the comically smutty word relieved what had become a quite intolerable tension. Laughter broke out, enormous, almost hysterical, peal after peal, as though it would never stop. My father — and it was the Director! My *father!* Oh Ford, oh Ford! That was really too good. The whooping and the roaring renewed themselves, faces seemed on the point of disintegration, tears were streaming. Six more test-tubes of spermatozoa were upset. My *father!*

Pale, wild-eyed, the Director glared about him in an agony of bewildered humiliation.

My *father!* The laughter, which had shown signs of dying away, broke out again more loudly than ever. He put his hands over his ears and rushed out of the room.

CHAPTER 11

After the scene in the Fertilizing Room, all upper-caste London was wild to see this delicious creature who had fallen on his knees before the Director of Hatcheries and Conditioning — or rather the ex-Director, for the poor man had resigned immediately afterwards and never set foot inside the Centre again — had flopped down and called him (the joke was almost too good to be true!) "my father." Linda, on the contrary, cut no ice; nobody had the smallest desire to see Linda. To say one was a mother — that was past a joke: it was an obscenity. Moreover, she wasn't a real savage, had been hatched out of a bottle and conditioned like any one else: so couldn't have really quaint ideas. Finally — and this was by far the strongest reason for people's not wanting to see poor Linda — there was her appearance. Fat; having lost her youth; with bad teeth, and a blotched complexion, and that figure (Ford!) — you simply couldn't look at her without feeling sick, yes, positively sick. So the best people were quite determined *not* to see Linda. And Linda, for her part, had no desire to see them. The return to civilization was for her the return to *soma*, was the possibility of lying in bed and taking holiday after holiday, without ever having to come back to a headache or a fit of vomiting, without ever being made to feel as you always felt after *peyotl*, as though you'd done something so shamefully anti-social that you could never hold up your head again. *Soma* played none of these unpleasant tricks. The holiday it gave was perfect and, if the morning after was disagreeable, it was so, not intrinsically, but only by comparison with the joys of the holiday. The remedy was to make the holiday continuous. Greedily she clamoured for ever larger, ever more frequent doses. Dr. Shaw at first demurred; then let her have what she wanted. She took as much as twenty grammes a day.

"Which will finish her off in a month or two," the doctor confided to Bernard. "One day the respiratory centre will be paralyzed. No more breathing. Finished. And a good thing too. If we could rejuvenate, of course it would be different. But we can't."

Surprisingly, as every one thought (for on *soma*-holiday Linda was most conveniently out of the way), John raised objections.

"But aren't you shortening her life by giving her so much?"

"In one sense, yes," Dr. Shaw admitted. "But in another we're actually lengthening it." The young man stared, uncomprehending. "*Soma* may make you lose a few years in time," the doctor went on. "But think of the enormous, immeasurable durations it can give you out of time. Every *soma*-holiday is a bit of what our ancestors used to call eternity."

John began to understand. "Eternity was in our lips and eyes," he murmured.

"Eh?"

"Nothing."

"Of course," Dr. Shaw went on, "you can't allow people to go popping off into eternity if they've got any serious work to do. But as she hasn't got any serious work . . ."

"All the same," John persisted, "I don't believe it's right."

The doctor shrugged his shoulders. "Well, of course, if you prefer to have her screaming mad all the time . . ."

In the end John was forced to give in. Linda got her *soma*. Thenceforward she remained in her little room on the thirty-seventh floor of Bernard's apartment house, in bed, with the radio and television always on, and the patchouli tap just dripping, and the *soma* tablets within reach of her hand — there she remained; and yet wasn't there at all, was all the time away, infinitely far away, on holiday; on holiday in some other world, where the music of the radio was a labyrinth of sonorous colours, a sliding, palpitating labyrinth, that led (by what beautifully inevitable windings) to a bright centre of absolute conviction; where the dancing images of the television box were the performers in some indescribably delicious all-singing feely; where the dripping patchouli was more than scent — was the sun, was a million sexophones, was Popé making love, only much more so, incomparably more, and without end.

"No, we can't rejuvenate. But I'm very glad," Dr. Shaw had concluded, "to have had this opportunity to see an example of senility in a human being. Thank you so much for calling me in." He shook Bernard warmly by the hand.

It was John, then, they were all after. And as it was only through Bernard, his accredited guardian, that John could be seen, Bernard now found himself, for the first time in his life, treated not merely normally, but as a person of outstanding importance. There was no more talk of the alcohol in his blood-surrogate, no gibes at his personal appearance. Henry Foster went out of his way to be friendly; Benito Hoover made him a present of six packets of sexhormone chewing-gum; the Assistant Predestinator came out and cadged almost abjectly for an invitation to one of Bernard's evening parties. As for the women, Bernard had only to hint at the possibility of an invitation, and he could have whichever of them he liked.

"Bernard's asked me to meet the Savage next Wednesday," Fanny announced triumphantly.

"I'm so glad," said Lenina. "And now you must admit that you were wrong about Bernard. Don't you think he's really rather sweet?"

Fanny nodded. "And I must say," she said, "I was quite agreeably surprised."

The Chief Bottler, the Director of Predestination, three Deputy Assistant Fertilizer-Generals, the Professor of Feelies in the College of Emotional Engineering, the Dean of the Westminster Community Singery, the Supervisor of Bokanovskification — the list of Bernard's notabilities was interminable.

"And I had six girls last week," he confided to Helmholtz Watson. "One on Monday, two on Tuesday, two more on Friday, and one on Saturday. And if I'd had the time or the inclination, there were at least a dozen more who were only too anxious . . ."

Helmholtz listened to his boastings in a silence so gloomily disapproving that Bernard was offended.

"You're envious," he said.

Helmholtz shook his head. "I'm rather sad, that's all," he answered.

Bernard went off in a huff. Never, he told himself, never would he speak to Helmholtz again.

The days passed. Success went fizzily to Bernard's head, and in the process completely reconciled him (as any good intoxicant should do) to a world which, up till then, he had found very unsatisfactory. In so far as it recognized him as important, the order of things was good. But, reconciled by his success, he yet refused to forego the privilege of criticizing this order. For the act of criticizing heightened his sense of importance, made him feel larger. Moreover, he did genuinely believe that there were things to criticize.

(At the same time, he genuinely liked being a success and having all the girls he wanted.) Before those who now, for the sake of the Savage, paid their court to him, Bernard would parade a carping unorthodoxy. He was politely listened to. But behind his back people shook their heads. "That young man will come to a bad end," they said, prophesying the more confidently in that they themselves would in due course personally see to it that the end was bad. "He won't find another Savage to help him out a second time," they said. Meanwhile, however, there was the first Savage; they were polite. And because they were polite, Bernard felt positively gigantic — gigantic and at the same time light with elation, lighter than air.

"Lighter than air," said Bernard, pointing upwards.

Like a pearl in the sky, high, high above them, the Weather Department's captive balloon shone rosily in the sunshine.

". . . the said Savage," so ran Bernard's instructions, "to be shown civilized life in all its aspects. . . ."

He was being shown a bird's-eye view of it at present, a bird's-eye view from the platform of the Charing-T Tower. The Station Master and the Resident Meteorologist were acting as guides. But it was Bernard who did most of the talking. Intoxicated, he was behaving as though, at the very least, he were a visiting World Controller. Lighter than air.

The Bombay Green Rocket dropped out of the sky. The passengers alighted. Eight identical Dravidian twins in khaki looked out of the eight portholes of the cabin — the stewards.

"Twelve hundred and fifty kilometres an hour," said the Station Master impressively. "What do you think of that, Mr. Savage?"

John thought it very nice. "Still," he said, "Ariel could put a girdle round the earth in forty minutes."

"The Savage," wrote Bernard in his report to Mustapha Mond, "shows surprisingly little astonishment at, or awe of, civilized inventions. This is partly due, no doubt, to the fact that he has heard them talked about by the woman Linda, his m——."

(Mustapha Mond frowned. "Does the fool think I'm too squeamish to see the word written out at full length?")

"Partly on his interest being focussed on what he calls 'the soul,' which he persists in regarding as an entity independent of the physical environment, whereas, as I tried to point out to him . . ."

The Controller skipped the next sentences and was just about to turn the page in search of something more interestingly concrete, when his eye was caught by a series of quite extraordinary phrases. ". . . though I must admit," he read, "that I agree with the Savage in finding civilized infantility too easy or, as he puts it, not expensive enough; and I would like to take this opportunity of drawing your fordship's attention to. . ."

Mustapha Mond's anger gave place almost at once to mirth. The idea of this creature solemnly lecturing him — *him* — about the social order was really too grotesque. The man must have gone mad. "I ought to give him a lesson," he said to himself; then threw back his head and laughed aloud. For the moment, at any rate, the lesson would not be given.

It was a small factory of lighting-sets for helicopters, a branch of the Electrical Equipment Corporation. They were met on the roof itself (for that circular letter of recommendation from the Controller was magical in its effects) by the Chief Technician and the Human

Element Manager. They walked downstairs into the factory.

"Each process," explained the Human Element Manager, "is carried out, so far as possible, by a single Bokanovsky Group."

And, in effect, eighty-three almost noseless black brachycephalic Deltas were cold-pressing. The fifty-six four-spindle chucking and turning machines were being manipulated by fifty-six aquiline and ginger Gammas. One hundred and seven heat-conditioned Epsilon Senegalese were working in the foundry. Thirty-three Delta females, long-headed, sandy, with narrow pelvises, and all within 20 millimetres of 1 metre 69 centimetres tall, were cutting screws. In the assembling room, the dynamos were being put together by two sets of Gamma-Plus dwarfs. The two low work-tables faced one another; between them crawled the conveyor with its load of separate parts; forty-seven blonde heads were confronted by forty-seven brown ones. Forty-seven snubs by forty-seven hooks; forty-seven receding by forty-seven prognathous chins. The completed mechanisms were inspected by eighteen identical curly auburn girls in Gamma green, packed in crates by thirty-four short-legged, left-handed male Delta-Minuses, and loaded into the waiting trucks and lorries by sixty-three blue-eyed, flaxen and freckled Epsilon Semi-Morons.

"O brave new world . . ." By some malice of his memory the Savage found himself repeating Miranda's words. "O brave new world that has such people in it."

"And I assure you," the Human Element Manager concluded, as they left the factory, "we hardly ever have any trouble with our workers. We always find . . ."

But the Savage had suddenly broken away from his companions and was violently retching, behind a clump of laurels, as though the solid earth had been a helicopter in an air pocket.

"The Savage," wrote Bernard, "refuses to take *soma*, and seems much distressed because the woman Linda, his m——, remains permanently on holiday. It is worthy of note that, in spite of his m——'s senility and the extreme repulsiveness of her appearance, the Savage frequently goes to see her and appears to be much attached to her — an interesting example of the way in which early conditioning can be made to modify and even run counter to natural impulses (in this case, the impulse to recoil from an unpleasant object)."

At Eton they alighted on the roof of Upper School. On the opposite side of School Yard, the fifty-two stories of Lupton's Tower gleamed white in the sunshine. College on their left and, on their right, the School Community Singery reared their venerable piles of ferro-concrete and vita-glass. In the centre of the quadrangle stood the quaint old chrome-steel statue of Our Ford.

Dr. Gaffney, the Provost, and Miss Keate, the Head Mistress, received them as they stepped out of the plane.

"Do you have many twins here?" the Savage asked rather apprehensively, as they set out on their tour of inspection.

"Oh, no," the Provost answered. "Eton is reserved exclusively for upper-caste boys and girls. One egg, one adult. It makes education more difficult of course. But as they'll be called upon to take responsibilities and deal with unexpected emergencies, it can't be helped." He sighed.

Bernard, meanwhile, had taken a strong fancy to Miss Keate. "If you're free any Monday, Wednesday, or Friday evening," he was saying. Jerking his thumb towards the Savage, "He's curious, you know," Bernard added. "Quaint."

Miss Keate smiled (and her smile was really charming, he thought); said Thank you; would be delighted to come to one of his parties. The Provost opened a door.

Five minutes in that Alpha Double Plus classroom left John a trifle bewildered.

"What *is* elementary relativity?" he whispered to Bernard. Bernard tried to explain, then thought better of it and suggested that they should go to some other classroom.

From behind a door in the corridor leading to the Beta-Minus geography room, a ringing soprano voice called, "One, two, three, four," and then, with a weary impatience, "As you were."

"Malthusian Drill," explained the Head Mistress. "Most of our girls are freemartins, of course. I'm a freemartin myself." She smiled at Bernard. "But we have about eight hundred unsterilized ones who need constant drilling."

In the Beta-Minus geography room John learnt that "a savage reservation is a place which, owing to unfavourable climatic or geological conditions, or poverty of natural resources, has not been worth the expense of civilizing." A click; the room was darkened; and suddenly, on the screen above the Master's head, there were the *Penitentes* of Acoma prostrating themselves before Our Lady, and wailing as John had heard them wail, confessing their sins before Jesus on the Cross, before the eagle image of Pookong. The young Etonians fairly shouted with laughter. Still wailing, the *Penitentes* rose to their feet, stripped off their upper garments and, with knotted whips, began to beat themselves, blow after blow. Redoubled, the laughter drowned even the amplified record of their groans.

"But why do they laugh?" asked the Savage in a pained bewilderment.

"Why?" The Provost turned towards him a still broadly grinning face. "Why? But because it's so extraordinarily funny."

In the cinematographic twilight, Bernard risked a gesture which, in the past, even total darkness would hardly have emboldened him to make. Strong in his new importance, he put his arm around the Head Mistress's waist. It yielded, willowily. He was just about to snatch a kiss or two and perhaps a gentle pinch, when the shutters clicked open again.

"Perhaps we had better go on," said Miss Keate, and moved towards the door.

"And this," said the Provost a moment later, "is Hypnopædic Control Room."

Hundreds of synthetic music boxes, one for each dormitory, stood ranged in shelves round three sides of the room; pigeon-holed on the fourth were the paper sound-track rolls on which the various hypnopædic lessons were printed.

"You slip the roll in here," explained Bernard, interrupting Dr. Gaffney, "press down this switch . . ."

"No, that one," corrected the Provost, annoyed.

"That one, then. The roll unwinds. The selenium cells transform the light impulses into sound waves, and . . ."

"And there you are," Dr. Gaffney concluded.

"Do they read Shakespeare?" asked the Savage as they walked, on their way to the Bio-chemical Laboratories, past the School Library.

"Certainly not," said the Head Mistress, blushing.

"Our library," said Dr. Gaffney, "contains only books of reference. If our young people need distraction, they can get it at the feelies. We don't encourage them to indulge in any solitary amusements."

Five bus-loads of boys and girls, singing or in a silent embracement, rolled past them over the vitrified highway.

"Just returned," explained Dr. Gaffney, while Bernard, whispering, made an appointment with the Head Mistress for that very evening, "from the Slough Crematorium. Death conditioning begins at eighteen months. Every tot spends two mornings a week in a Hospital for the Dying. All the best toys are kept there, and they get chocolate cream on death days. They learn to take dying as a matter of course."

"Like any other physiological process," put in the Head Mistress professionally.

Eight o'clock at the Savoy. It was all arranged.

On their way back to London they stopped at the Television Corporation's factory at Brentford.

"Do you mind waiting here a moment while I go and telephone?" asked Bernard.

The Savage waited and watched. The Main Day-Shift was just going off duty. Crowds of lower-caste workers were queued up in front of the mono-rail station — seven or eight hundred Gamma, Delta and Epsilon men and women, with not more than a dozen faces and statures between them. To each of them, with his or her ticket, the booking clerk pushed over a little cardboard pillbox. The long caterpillar of men and women moved slowly forward.

"What's in those" (remembering *The Merchant of Venice*) "those caskets?" the Savage enquired when Bernard had rejoined him.

"The day's *soma* ration," Bernard answered rather indistinctly; for he was masticating a piece of Benito Hoover's chewing-gum. "They get it after their work's over. Four half-gramme tablets. Six on Saturdays."

He took John's arm affectionately and they walked back towards the helicopter.

« «

Lenina came singing into the Changing Room.

"You seem very pleased with yourself," said Fanny.

"I *am* pleased," she answered. Zip! "Bernard rang up half an hour ago." Zip, zip! She stepped out of her shorts. "He has an unexpected engagement." Zip! "Asked me if I'd take the Savage to the feelies this evening. I must fly." She hurried away towards the bathroom.

"She's a lucky girl," Fanny said to herself as she watched Lenina go.

There was no envy in the comment; good-natured Fanny was merely stating a fact. Lenina *was* lucky; lucky in having shared with Bernard a generous portion of the Savage's immense celebrity, lucky in reflecting from her insignificant person the moment's supremely fashionable glory. Had not the Secretary of the Young Women's Fordian Association asked her to give a lecture about her experiences? Had she not been invited to the Annual Dinner of the Aphroditeum Club? Had she not already appeared in the Feelytone News — visibly, audibly and tactually appeared to countless millions all over the planet?

Hardly less flattering had been the attentions paid her by conspicuous individuals. The Resident World Controller's Second Secretary had asked her to dinner and breakfast. She had spent one week-end with the Ford Chief-Justice, and another with the Arch-Community-Songster of Canterbury. The President of the Internal and External Secretions Corporation was perpetually on the phone, and she had been to Deauville with the Deputy-Governor of the Bank of Europe.

"It's wonderful, of course. And yet in a way," she had confessed to Fanny, "I feel as though I were getting something on false pretences. Because, of course, the first thing they all want to know is what it's like to make love to a Savage. And I have to say I don't know." She shook her head. "Most of the men don't believe me, of course. But it's true. I wish it weren't," she added sadly and sighed. "He's terribly good-looking; don't you think so?"

"But doesn't he like you?" asked Fanny.

"Sometimes I think he does and sometimes I think he doesn't. He always does his best to avoid me; goes out of the room when I come in; won't touch me; won't even look at me. But sometimes if I turn round suddenly, I catch him staring; and then — well, you know how men look when they like you."

Yes, Fanny knew.

"I can't make it out," said Lenina.

She couldn't make it out; and not only was be-wildered; was also rather upset.

"Because, you see, Fanny, I like him."

Liked him more and more. Well, now there'd be a real chance, she thought, as she scented herself after her bath. Dab, dab, dab — a real chance. Her high spirits overflowed in a song.

"Hug me till you drug me, honey;
Kiss me till I'm in a coma;
Hug me, honey, snuggly bunny;
Love's as good as soma."

The scent organ was playing a delightfully refreshing Herbal Capriccio — rippling arpeggios of thyme and lavender, of rosemary, basil, myrtle, tarragon; a series of daring modulations through the spice keys into ambergris; and a slow return through sandalwood, camphor, cedar and new-mown hay (with occasional subtle touches of discord — a whiff of kidney pudding, the faintest suspicion of pig's dung) back to the simple aromatics with which the piece began. The final blast of thyme died away; there was a round of applause; the lights went up. In the synthetic music machine the sound-track roll began to unwind. It was a trio for hyper-violin, super-cello and oboe-surrogate that now filled the air with its agreeable languor. Thirty or forty bars — and then, against this instrumental background, a much more than human voice began to warble; now throaty, now from the head, now hollow as a flute, now charged with yearning harmonics, it effortlessly passed from Gaspard's Forster's low record on the very frontiers of musical tone to a trilled bat-note high above the highest C to which (in 1770, at the ducal opera of Parma, and to the astonishment of Mozart) Lucrezia Ajugari, alone of all the singers in history, once piercingly gave utterance.

Sunk in their pneumatic stalls, Lenina and the Savage sniffed and listened. It was now the turn also for eyes and skin.

The house lights went down; fiery letters stood out solid and as though self-supported in the darkness. THREE WEEKS IN A HELICOPTER. AN ALL-SUPER-SINGING, SYNTHETIC-TALKING, COLOURED,

STEREOSCOPIC FEELY. WITH SYNCHRONIZED SCENT-ORGAN ACCOMPANIMENT.

"Take hold of those metal knobs on the arms of your chair," whispered Lenina. "Otherwise you won't get any of the feely effects."

The Savage did as he was told.

Those fiery letters, meanwhile, had disappeared; there were ten seconds of complete darkness; then suddenly, dazzling and incomparably more solid-looking than they would have seemed in actual flesh and blood, far more real than reality, there stood the stereoscopic images, locked in one another's arms, of a gigantic negro and a golden-haired young brachy-cephalic Beta-Plus female.

The Savage started. That sensation on his lips! He lifted a hand to his mouth; the titillation ceased; let his hand fall back on the metal knob; it began again. The scent organ, meanwhile, breathed pure musk. Expiringly, a sound-track super-dove cooed "Oo-ooh"; and vibrating only thirty-two times a second, a deeper than African bass made answer: "Aa-aah." "Ooh-ah! Ooh-ah!" the stereoscopic lips came together again, and once more the facial erogenous zones of the six thousand spectators in the Alhambra tingled with almost intolerable galvanic pleasure. "Ooh . . ."

The plot of the film was extremely simple. A few minutes after the first Oohs and Aahs (a duet having been sung and a little love made on that famous bearskin, every hair of which — the Assistant Predestinator was perfectly right — could be separately and distinctly felt), the negro had a helicopter accident, fell on his head. Thump! what a twinge through the forehead! A chorus of *ow's* and *aie's* went up from the audience.

The concussion knocked all the negro's conditioning into a cocked hat. He developed for the Beta blonde an exclusive and maniacal passion. She protested. He persisted. There were struggles, pursuits, an assault on a rival, finally a sensational kidnapping. The Beta blonde was ravished away into the sky and kept there, hovering, for three weeks in a wildly antisocial tête-à-tête with the black madman. Finally, after a whole series of adventures and much aerial acrobacy three handsome young Alphas succeeded in rescuing her. The negro was packed off to an Adult Reconditioning Centre and the film ended happily and decorously, with the Beta blonde becoming the mistress of all her three rescuers. They interrupted themselves for a moment to sing a synthetic quartet, with full super-orchestral accompaniment and gardenias on the scent organ. Then the bearskin made a final appearance and, amid a blare of sexophones, the last stereoscopic kiss faded into darkness, the last electric titillation died on the lips like a dying moth that quivers, quivers, ever more feebly, ever more faintly, and at last is quite, quite still.

But for Lenina the moth did not completely die. Even after the lights had gone up, while they were shuffling slowly along with the crowd towards the lifts, its ghost still fluttered against her lips, still traced fine shuddering roads of anxiety and pleasure across her skin. Her cheeks were flushed. She caught hold of the Savage's arm and pressed it, limp, against her side. He looked down at her for a moment, pale, pained, desiring, and ashamed of his desire. He was not worthy, not . . . Their eyes for a moment met. What treasures hers promised! A queen's ransom of temperament. Hastily he looked away, disengaged his imprisoned arm. He was obscurely terrified lest she should cease to be something he could feel himself unworthy of.

"I don't think you ought to see things like that," he said, making haste to transfer from Lenina herself to the surrounding circumstances the blame for any past or possible future lapse from perfection.

"Things like what, John?"

"Like this horrible film."

"Horrible?" Lenina was genuinely astonished. "But I thought it was lovely."

"It was base," he said indignantly, "it was ignoble."

She shook her head. "I don't know what you mean." Why was he so queer? Why did he go out of his way to spoil things?

In the taxicopter he hardly even looked at her. Bound by strong vows that had never been pronounced, obedient to laws that had long since ceased to run, he sat averted and in silence. Sometimes, as though a finger had plucked at some taut, almost breaking string, his whole body would shake with a sudden nervous start.

The taxicopter landed on the roof of Lenina's apartment house. "At last," she thought exultantly as she stepped out of the cab. At last — even though he *had* been so queer just now. Standing under a lamp, she peered into her hand mirror. At last. Yes, her nose was a bit shiny. She shook the loose powder from her puff. While he was paying off the taxi — there would just be time. She rubbed at the shininess, thinking: "He's terribly good-looking. No need for him to be shy like Bernard. And yet . . . Any other man would have done it long ago. Well, now at last." That fragment of a face in the little round mirror suddenly smiled at her.

"Good-night," said a strangled voice behind her. Lenina wheeled round. He was standing in the doorway of the cab, his eyes fixed, staring; had evidently been staring all this time while she was powdering her nose, waiting — but what for? or hesitating, trying to make up his mind, and all the time thinking, thinking — she could not imagine what extraordinary thoughts. "Good-night, Lenina," he repeated, and made a strange grimacing attempt to smile.

"But, John . . . I thought you were . . . I mean, aren't you? . . ."

He shut the door and bent forward to say something to the driver. The cab shot up into the air.

Looking down through the window in the floor, the Savage could see Lenina's upturned face, pale in the bluish light of the lamps. The mouth was open, she was calling. Her foreshortened figure rushed away from him; the diminishing square of the roof seemed to be falling through the darkness.

Five minutes later he was back in his room. From its hiding-place he took out his mouse-nibbled volume, turned with religious care its stained and crumbled pages, and began to read *Othello*. Othello, he remembered, was like the hero of *Three Weeks in a Helicopter* — a black man.

Drying her eyes, Lenina walked across the roof to the lift. On her way down to the twenty-seventh floor she pulled out her *soma* bottle. One gramme, she decided, would not be enough; hers had been more than a one-gramme affliction. But if she took two grammes, she ran the risk of not waking up in time to-morrow morning. She compromised and, into her cupped left palm, shook out three half-gramme tablets.

CHAPTER *12*

Bernard had to shout through the locked door; the Savage would not open.

"But everybody's there, waiting for you."

"Let them wait," came back the muffled voice through the door.

"But you know quite well, John" (how difficult it is to sound persuasive at the top of one's voice!) "I asked them on purpose to meet you."

"You ought to have asked *me* first whether I wanted to meet *them*."

"But you always came before, John."

"That's precisely why I don't want to come again."

"Just to please me," Bernard bellowingly wheedled. "Won't you come to please me?"

"No."

"Do you seriously mean it?"

"Yes."

Despairingly, "But what shall I do?" Bernard wailed.

"Go to hell!" bawled the exasperated voice from within.

"But the Arch-Community-Songster of Canterbury is there to-night." Bernard was almost in tears.

"*Ai yaa tákwa!*" It was only in Zuñi that the Savage could adequately express what he felt about the Arch-Community-Songster. "*Háni!*" he added as an after-thought; and then (with what derisive ferocity!): "*Sons éso tse-ná.*" And he spat on the ground, as Popé might have done.

In the end Bernard had to slink back, diminished, to his rooms and inform the impatient assembly that the Savage would not be appearing that evening. The news was received with indignation. The men were furious at having been tricked into behaving politely to this insignificant fellow with the unsavoury reputation and the heretical opinions. The higher their position in the hierarchy, the deeper their resentment.

"To play such a joke on me," the Arch-Songster kept repeating, "on *me!*"

As for the women, they indignantly felt that they had been had on false pretences — had by a wretched little man who had had alcohol poured into his bottle by mistake — by a creature with a Gamma-Minus physique. It was an outrage, and they said so, more and more loudly. The Head Mistress of Eton was particularly scathing.

Lenina alone said nothing. Pale, her blue eyes clouded with an unwonted melancholy, she sat in a corner, cut off from those who surrounded her by an emotion which they did not share. She had come to the party filled with a strange feeling of anxious exultation. "In a few minutes," she had said to herself, as she entered the room, "I shall be seeing him, talking to him, telling him" (for she had come with her mind made up) "that I like him — more than anybody I've ever known. And then perhaps he'll say . . ."

What would he say? The blood had rushed to her cheeks.

"Why was he so strange the other night, after the feelies? So queer. And yet I'm absolutely sure he really does rather like me. I'm sure . . ."

It was at this moment that Bernard had made his announcement; the Savage wasn't coming to the party.

Lenina suddenly felt all the sensations normally experienced at the beginning of a Violent Passion Surrogate treatment — a sense of dreadful emptiness, a breathless apprehension, a nausea. Her heart seemed to stop beating.

"Perhaps it's because he doesn't like me," she said to herself. And at once this possibility became an established certainty: John had refused to come because he didn't like her. He didn't like her. . . .

"It really is a bit *too* thick," the Head Mistress of Eton was saying to the Director of Crematoria and Phosphorus Reclamation. "When I think that I actually . . ."

"Yes," came the voice of Fanny Crowne, "it's absolutely true about the alcohol. Some one I know knew some one who was working in the Embryo Store at the time. She said to my friend, and my friend said to me . . ."

"Too bad, too bad," said Henry Foster, sympathizing with the Arch-Community-Songster. "It may interest you to know that our ex-Director was on the point of transferring him to Iceland."

Pierced by every word that was spoken, the tight balloon of Bernard's happy self-confidence was leaking from a thousand wounds. Pale, distraught, abject and agitated, he moved among his guests, stammering incoherent apologies, assuring them that next time the Savage would certainly be there, begging them to sit down and take a carotene sandwich, a slice of vitamin A *pâté*, a glass of champagne-surrogate. They duly ate, but ignored him; drank and were either rude to his face or talked to one another about him, loudly and offensively, as though he had not been there.

"And now, my friends," said the Arch-Community-Songster of Canterbury, in that beautiful ringing voice with which he led the proceedings at Ford's Day

Celebrations, "Now, my friends, I think perhaps the time has come . . ." He rose, put down his glass, brushed from his purple viscose waistcoat the crumbs of a considerable collation, and walked towards the door.

Bernard darted forward to intercept him.

"Must you really, Arch-Songster? . . . It's very early still. I'd hoped you would . . ."

Yes, what hadn't he hoped, when Lenina confidentially told him that the Arch-Community-Songster would accept an invitation if it were sent. "He's really rather sweet, you know." And she had shown Bernard the little golden zipper-fastening in the form of a T which the Arch-Songster had given her as a memento of the week-end she had spent at Lambeth. *To meet the Arch-Community-Songster of Canterbury and Mr. Savage.* Bernard had proclaimed his triumph on every invitation card. But the Savage had chosen this evening of all evenings to lock himself up in his room, to shout "*Háni!*" and even (it was lucky that Bernard didn't understand Zuñi) "*Sons éso tse-ná!*" What should have been the crowning moment of Bernard's whole career had turned out to be the moment of his greatest humiliation.

"I'd so much hoped . . ." he stammeringly repeated, looking up at the great dignitary with pleading and distracted eyes.

"My young friend," said the Arch-Community-Songster in a tone of loud and solemn severity; there was a general silence. "Let me give you a word of advice." He wagged his finger at Bernard. "Before it's too late. A word of good advice." (His voice became sepulchral.) "Mend your ways, my young friend, mend your ways." He made the sign of the T over him and turned away. "Lenina, my dear," he called in another tone. "Come with me."

Obediently, but unsmiling and (wholly insensible of the honour done to her) without elation, Lenina walked after him, out of the room. The other guests followed at a respectful interval. The last of them slammed the door. Bernard was all alone.

Punctured, utterly deflated, he dropped into a chair and, covering his face with his hands, began to weep. A few minutes later, however, he thought better of it and took four tablets of *soma*.

Upstairs in his room the Savage was reading *Romeo and Juliet.*

Lenina and the Arch-Community-Songster stepped out on to the roof of Lambeth Palace. "Hurry up, my young friend — I mean, Lenina," called the Arch-Songster impatiently from the lift gates. Lenina, who had lingered for a moment to look at the moon, dropped her eyes and came hurrying across the roof to rejoin him.

"A New Theory of Biology" was the title of the paper which Mustapha Mond had just finished reading. He sat for some time, meditatively frowning, then picked up his pen and wrote across the title-page: "The author's mathematical treatment of the conception of purpose is novel and highly ingenious, but heretical and, so far as the present social order is concerned, dangerous and potentially subversive. *Not to be published.*" He underlined the words. "The author will be kept under supervision. His transference to the Marine Biological Station of St. Helena may become necessary." A pity, he thought, as he signed his name. It was a masterly piece of work. But once you began admitting explanations in terms of purpose — well, you didn't know what the result might be. It was the sort of idea that might easily decondition the more unsettled minds among the higher castes — make them lose their faith in happiness as the Sovereign Good and take to believing, instead, that the goal was somewhere beyond, somewhere outside the present human sphere, that the purpose of life was not the maintenance of well-being, but some intensification and refining of consciousness, some enlargement of knowledge. Which was, the Controller reflected, quite possibly true. But not, in the present circumstance, admissible. He picked up his pen again, and under the words "*Not to be published*" drew a second line, thicker and blacker than the first; then sighed, "What fun it would be," he thought, "if one didn't have to think about happiness!"

《《

With closed eyes, his face shining with rapture, John was softly declaiming to vacancy:

"*Oh! she doth teach the torches to burn bright.*

It seems she hangs upon the cheek of night,

Like a rich jewel in an Ethiop's ear;

Beauty too rich for use, for earth too dear . . ."

The golden T lay shining on Lenina's bosom. Sportively, the Arch-Community-Songster caught hold of it, sportively he pulled, pulled. "I think," said Lenina suddenly, breaking a long silence, "I'd better take a couple of grammes of *soma.*"

Bernard, by this time, was fast asleep and smiling at the private paradise of his dreams. Smiling, smiling. But inexorably, every thirty seconds, the minute hand of the electric clock above his bed jumped forward with an almost imperceptible click. Click, click, click, click . . . And it was morning. Bernard was back among the miseries of space and time. It was in the lowest spirits that he taxied across to his work at the Conditioning Centre. The intoxication of success had evaporated; he was soberly his old self; and by contrast with the temporary balloon of these last weeks, the old self seemed unprecedentedly heavier than the surrounding atmosphere.

To this deflated Bernard the Savage showed himself unexpectedly sympathetic.

"You're more like what you were at Malpais," he said, when Bernard had told him his plaintive story. "Do you remember when we first talked together? Outside the little house. You're like what you were then."

"Because I'm unhappy again; that's why."

"Well, I'd rather be unhappy than have the sort of false, lying happiness you were having here."

"I like that," said Bernard bitterly. "When it's you who were the cause of it all. Refusing to come to my party and so turning them all against me!" He knew that what he was saying was absurd in its injustice; he admitted inwardly, and at last even aloud, the truth of all that the Savage now said about the worthlessness of friends who could be turned upon so slight a provocation into persecuting enemies. But in spite of this knowledge and these admissions, in spite of the fact that his friend's support and sympathy were now his only comfort, Bernard continued perversely to nourish, along with his quite genuine affection, a secret grievance against the Savage, to meditate a campaign of small revenges to be wreaked upon him. Nourishing a grievance against the Arch-Community-Songster was useless; there was no possibility of being revenged on the Chief Bottler or the Assistant Predestinator. As a victim, the Savage possessed, for Bernard, this enormous superiority over the others:

that he was accessible. One of the principal functions of a friend is to suffer (in a milder and symbolic form) the punishments that we should like, but are unable, to inflict upon our enemies.

Bernard's other victim-friend was Helmholtz. When, discomfited, he came and asked once more for the friendship which, in his prosperity, he had not thought it worth his while to preserve. Helmholtz gave it; and gave it without a reproach, without a comment, as though he had forgotten that there had ever been a quarrel. Touched, Bernard felt himself at the same time humiliated by this magnanimity — a magnanimity the more extraordinary and therefore the more humiliating in that it owed nothing to *soma* and everything to Helmholtz's character. It was the Helmholtz of daily life who forgot and forgave, not the Helmholtz of a half-gramme holiday. Bernard was duly grateful (it was an enormous comfort to have his friend again) and also duly resentful (it would be pleasure to take some revenge on Helmholtz for his generosity).

At their first meeting after the estrangement, Bernard poured out the tale of his miseries and accepted consolation. It was not till some days later that he learned, to his surprise and with a twinge of shame, that he was not the only one who had been in trouble. Helmholtz had also come into conflict with Authority.

"It was over some rhymes," he explained. "I was giving my usual course of Advanced Emotional Engineering for Third Year Students. Twelve lectures, of which the seventh is about rhymes. 'On the Use of Rhymes in Moral Propaganda and Advertisement,' to be precise. I always illustrate my lecture with a lot of technical examples. This time I thought I'd give them one I'd just written myself. Pure madness, of course; but I couldn't resist it." He laughed. "I was curious to see what their reactions would be.

Besides," he added more gravely, "I wanted to do a bit of propaganda; I was trying to engineer them into feeling as I'd felt when I wrote the rhymes. Ford!" He laughed again. "What an outcry there was! The Principal had me up and threatened to hand me the immediate sack. I'm a marked man."

"But what were your rhymes?" Bernard asked.

"They were about being alone."

Bernard's eyebrows went up.

"I'll recite them to you, if you like." And Helmholtz began:

> "Yesterday's committee,
> Sticks, but a broken drum,
> Midnight in the City,
> Flutes in a vacuum,
> Shut lips, sleeping faces,
> Every stopped machine,
> The dumb and littered places
> Where crowds have been: . . .
> All silences rejoice,
> Weep (loudly or low),
> Speak — but with the voice
> Of whom, I do not know.
> Absence, say, of Susan's,
> Absence of Egeria's
> Arms and respective bosoms,
> Lips and, ah, posteriors,
> Slowly form a presence;
> Whose? and, I ask, of what
> So absurd an essence,
> That something, which is not,

Nevertheless should populate
Empty night more solidly
Than that with which we copulate,
Why should it seem so squalidly?

Well, I gave them that as an example, and they reported me to the Principal."

"I'm not surprised," said Bernard. "It's flatly against all their sleep-teaching. Remember, they've had at least a quarter of a million warnings against solitude."

"I know. But I thought I'd like to see what the effect would be."

"Well, you've seen now."

Helmholtz only laughed. "I feel," he said, after a silence, "as though I were just beginning to have something to write about. As though I were beginning to be able to use that power I feel I've got inside me — that extra, latent power. Something seems to be coming to me." In spite of all his troubles, he seemed, Bernard thought, profoundly happy.

Helmholtz and the Savage took to one another at once. So cordially indeed that Bernard felt a sharp pang of jealousy. In all these weeks he had never come to so close an intimacy with the Savage as Helmholtz immediately achieved. Watching them, listening to their talk, he found himself sometimes resentfully wishing that he had never brought them together. He was ashamed of his jealousy and alternately made efforts of will and took *soma* to keep himself from feeling it. But the efforts were not very successful; and between the *soma*-holidays there were, of necessity, intervals. The odious sentiment kept on returning.

At his third meeting with the Savage, Helmholtz recited his rhymes on Solitude.

"What do you think of them?" he asked when he had done.

The Savage shook his head. "Listen to *this*," was his answer; and unlocking the drawer in which he kept his mouse-eaten book, he opened and read:

> *"Let the bird of loudest lay*
>
> *On the sole Arabian tree,*
>
> *Herald sad and trumpet be . . ."*

Helmholtz listened with a growing excitement. At "sole Arabian tree" he started; at "thou shrieking harbinger" he smiled with sudden pleasure; at "every fowl of tyrant wing" the blood rushed up into his cheeks; but at "defunctive music" he turned pale and trembled with an unprecedented emotion. The Savage read on:

> *"Property was thus appall'd,*
>
> *That the self was not the same;*
>
> *Single nature's double name*
>
> *Neither two nor one was call'd*
>
> *Reason in itself confounded*
>
> *Saw division grow together . . ."*

"Orgy-porgy!" said Bernard, interrupting the reading with a loud, unpleasant laugh. "It's just a Solidarity Service hymn." He was revenging himself on his two friends for liking one another more than they liked him.

In the course of their next two or three meetings he frequently repeated this little act of vengeance. It was simple and, since both Helmholtz and the Savage were dreadfully pained by the shattering and defilement of a favourite poetic crystal, extremely effective. In the end, Helmholtz threatened to kick him out of the room if he dared to interrupt again. And yet, strangely enough, the next interruption, the most disgraceful of all, came from Helmholtz himself.

The Savage was reading *Romeo and Juliet* aloud — reading (for all the time he was seeing himself as Romeo and Lenina as Juliet) with an intense and quivering passion. Helmholtz had listened to the scene of the lovers' first meeting with a puzzled interest. The scene in the orchard had delighted him with its poetry; but the sentiments expressed had made him smile. Getting into such a state about having a girl — it seemed rather ridiculous. But, taken detail by verbal detail, what a superb piece of emotional engineering! "That old fellow," he said, "he makes our best propaganda technicians look absolutely silly." The Savage smiled triumphantly and resumed his reading. All went tolerably well until, in the last scene of the third act, Capulet and Lady Capulet began to bully Juliet to marry Paris. Helmholtz had been restless throughout the entire scene; but when, pathetically mimed by the Savage, Juliet cried out:

"*Is there no pity sitting in the clouds,*

That sees into the bottom of my grief?

O sweet my mother, cast me not away:

Delay this marriage for a month, a week;

Or, if you do not, make the bridal bed

In that dim monument where Tybalt lies ..."

when Juliet said this, Helmholtz broke out in an explosion of uncontrollable guffawing.

The mother and father (grotesque obscenity) forcing the daughter to have some one she didn't want! And the idiotic girl not saying that she was having some one else whom (for the moment, at any rate) she preferred! In its smutty absurdity the situation was irresistibly comical. He had managed, with a heroic effort, to hold down the mounting pressure of his hilarity; but "sweet mother" (in the Savage's tremulous tone of anguish) and the reference to Tybalt lying dead, but evidently uncremated and wasting his phosphorus on a dim monument, were too much for him. He laughed and laughed till the tears streamed down his face — quenchlessly laughed while, pale with a sense of outrage, the Savage looked at him over the top of his book and then, as the laughter still continued, closed it indignantly, got up and, with the gesture of one who removes his pearl from before swine, locked it away in its drawer.

"And yet," said Helmholtz when, having recovered breath enough to apologize, he had mollified the Savage into listening to his explanations, "I know quite well that one needs ridiculous, mad situations like that; one can't write really well about anything else. Why was that old fellow such a marvellous propaganda technician? Because he had so many insane, excruciating things to get excited about. You've got to be hurt and upset; otherwise you can't think of the really good, penetrating, X-rayish phrases. But fathers and mothers!" He shook his head. "You can't expect me to keep a straight face about fathers and mothers. And who's going to get excited about a boy having a girl or not having her?" (The Savage winced; but Helmholtz, who was staring pensively at the floor, saw nothing.) "No," he concluded, with a sigh, "it won't do. We need some other kind of madness and violence. But what? What? Where can one find it?" He was silent; then, shaking his head, "I don't know," he said at last, "I don't know."

CHAPTER 13

Henry Foster loomed up through the twilight of the Embryo Store.

"Like to come to a feely this evening?"

Lenina shook her head without speaking.

"Going out with some one else?" It interested him to know which of his friends was being had by which other. "Is it Benito?" he questioned.

She shook her head again.

Henry detected the weariness in those purple eyes, the pallor beneath that glaze of lupus, the sadness at the corners of the unsmiling crimson mouth. "You're not feeling ill, are you?" he asked, a trifle anxiously, afraid that she might be suffering from one of the few remaining infectious diseases.

Yet once more Lenina shook her head.

"Anyhow, you ought to go and see the doctor," said Henry. "A doctor a day keeps the jim-jams away," he added heartily, driving home his hypnopædic adage with a clap on the shoulder. "Perhaps you need a Pregnancy Substitute," he suggested. "Or else an extra-strong V.P.S. treatment. Sometimes, you know, the standard passion surrogate isn't quite . . ."

"Oh, for Ford's sake," said Lenina, breaking her stubborn silence, "shut up!" And she turned back to her neglected embryos.

A V.P.S. treatment indeed! She would have laughed, if she hadn't been on the point of crying. As though she hadn't got enough V.P. of her own! She sighed profoundly as she refilled her syringe. "John," she murmured to herself, "John . . ." Then "My Ford," she wondered, "have I given this one its sleeping sickness injection, or haven't I?" She simply couldn't remember. In the end, she decided not to run the risk of letting it have a second dose, and moved down the line to the next bottle.

Twenty-two years, eight months, and four days from that moment, a promising young Alpha-Minus administrator at Mwanza-Mwanza was to die of trypanosomiasis — the first case for over half a century. Sighing, Lenina went on with her work.

An hour later, in the Changing Room, Fanny was energetically protesting. "But it's absurd to let yourself get into a state like this. Simply absurd," she repeated. "And what about? A man — *one* man."

"But he's the one I want."

"As though there weren't millions of other men in the world."

"But I don't want them."

"How can you know till you've tried?"

"I have tried."

"But how many?" asked Fanny, shrugging her shoulders contemptuously. "One, two?"

"Dozens. But," shaking her head, "it wasn't any good," she added.

"Well, you must persevere," said Fanny sententiously. But it was obvious that her confidence in her own prescriptions had been shaken. "Nothing can be achieved without perseverance."

"But meanwhile . . ."

"Don't think of him."

"I can't help it."

"Take *soma*, then."

"I do."

"Well, go on."

"But in the intervals I still like him. I shall always like him."

"Well, if that's the case," said Fanny, with decision, "why don't you just go and take him. Whether he wants it or no."

"But if you knew how terribly *queer* he was!"

"All the more reason for taking a firm line."

"It's all very well to *say* that."

"Don't stand any nonsense. Act." Fanny's voice was a trumpet; she might have been a Y.W.F.A. lecturer giving an evening talk to adolescent Beta-Minuses. "Yes, act — at once. Do it now."

"I'd be scared," said Lenina

"Well, you've only got to take half a gramme of *soma* first. And now I'm going to have my bath." She marched off, trailing her towel.

The bell rang, and the Savage, who was impatiently hoping that Helmholtz would come that afternoon (for having at last made up his mind to talk to Helmholtz about Lenina, he could not bear to postpone his confidences a moment longer), jumped up and ran to the door.

"I had a premonition it was you, Helmholtz," he shouted as he opened.

On the threshold, in a white acetate-satin sailor suit, and with a round white cap rakishly tilted over her left ear, stood Lenina.

"Oh!" said the Savage, as though some one had struck him a heavy blow.

Half a gramme had been enough to make Lenina forget her fears and her embarrassments. "Hullo, John," she said, smiling, and walked past him into the room. Automatically he closed the door and followed her. Lenina sat down. There was a long silence.

"You don't seem very glad to see me, John," she said at last.

"Not glad?" The Savage looked at her reproachfully; then suddenly fell on his knees before her and, taking Lenina's hand, reverently kissed it. "Not glad? Oh, if you only knew," he whispered and, venturing to raise his eyes to her face, "Admired Lenina," he went on, "indeed the top of admiration, worth what's dearest in the world." She smiled at him with a luscious tenderness. "Oh, you so perfect" (she was leaning towards him with parted lips), "so perfect and so peerless are created" (nearer and nearer) "of every creature's best." Still nearer. The Savage suddenly scrambled to his feet. "That's why," he said speaking with averted face, "I wanted to *do* something first . . . I mean, to show I was worthy of you. Not that I could ever really be that. But at any rate to show I wasn't absolutely *unworthy*. I wanted to do *something*."

"Why should you think it necessary . . ." Lenina began, but left the sentence unfinished. There was a note of irritation in her voice. When one has leant forward, nearer and nearer, with parted lips — only to find oneself, quite suddenly, as a clumsy oaf scrambles to his feet, leaning towards nothing at all — well, there is a reason, even with half a gramme of *soma* circulating in one's blood-stream, a genuine reason for annoyance.

"At Malpais," the Savage was incoherently mumbling, "you had to bring her the skin of a mountain lion — I mean, when you wanted to marry some one. Or else a wolf."

"There aren't any lions in England," Lenina almost snapped.

"And even if there were," the Savage added, with sudden contemptuous resentment, "people would kill them out of helicopters, I suppose, with poison gas or something. I wouldn't do *that*, Lenina." He squared his shoulders, he ventured to look at her and was met with a stare of annoyed incomprehension. Confused, "I'll do anything," he went on, more and more incoherently. "Anything you tell me. There be some sports are painful — you know. But their labour delight in them sets off. That's what I feel. I mean I'd sweep the floor if you wanted."

"But we've got vacuum cleaners here," said Lenina in bewilderment. "It isn't necessary."

"No, of course it isn't *necessary*. But some kinds of baseness are nobly undergone. I'd like to undergo something nobly. Don't you see?"

"But if there *are* vacuum cleaners . . ."

"That's not the point."

"And Epsilon Semi-Morons to work them," — she went on, "well, really, *why*?"

"Why? But for you, for *you*. Just to show that I . . ."

"And what on earth vacuum cleaners have got to do with lions . . ."

"To show how much . . ."

"Or lions with being glad to see *me* . . ." She was getting more and more exasperated.

"How much I love you, Lenina," he brought out almost desperately.

An emblem of the inner tide of startled elation, the blood rushed up into Lenina's cheeks. "Do you mean it, John?"

"But I hadn't meant to say so," cried the Savage, clasping his hands in a kind of agony. "Not until . . . Listen, Lenina; in Malpais people get married."

"Get what?" The irritation had begun to creep back into her voice. What was he talking about now?

"For always. They make a promise to live together for always."

"What a horrible idea!" Lenina was genuinely shocked.

"Outliving beauty's outward with a mind that doth renew swifter than blood decays."

"*What?*"

"It's like that in Shakespeare too. 'If thou dost break her virgin knot before all sanctimonious ceremonies may with full and holy rite . . .' "

"For Ford's sake, John, talk sense. I can't understand a word you say. First it's vacuum cleaners; then it's knots. You're driving me crazy." She jumped up and, as though afraid that he might run away from her physically, as well as with his mind, caught him by the wrist. "Answer me this question: do you really like me, or don't you?"

There was a moment's silence; then, in a very low voice, "I love you more than anything in the world," he said.

"Then why on earth didn't you say so?" she cried, and so intense was her exasperation that she drove her sharp nails into the skin of his wrist. "Instead of drivelling away about knots and vacuum cleaners and lions, and making me miserable for weeks and weeks."

She released his hand and flung it angrily away from her.

"If I didn't like you so much," she said, "I'd be furious with you."

And suddenly her arms were round his neck; he felt her lips soft against his own. So deliciously soft, so warm and electric that inevitably he found himself thinking of the embraces in *Three Weeks in a Helicopter.* Ooh! ooh! the stereoscopic blonde and aah! the more than real blackamoor. Horror, horror, horror . . . he fired to disengage himself; but Lenina tightened her embrace.

"Why didn't you say so?" she whispered, drawing back her face to look at him. Her eyes were tenderly reproachful.

"The murkiest den, the most opportune place" (the voice of conscience thundered poetically), "the strongest suggestion our worser genius can, shall never melt mine honour into lust. Never, never!" he resolved.

"You silly boy!" she was saying. "I wanted you so much. And if you wanted me too, why didn't you? . . ."

"But, Lenina . . ." he began protesting; and as she immediately untwined her arms, as she stepped away from him, he thought, for a moment, that she had taken his unspoken hint. But when she unbuckled her white patent cartridge belt and hung it carefully over the back of a chair, he began to suspect that he had been mistaken.

"Lenina!" he repeated apprehensively.

She put her hand to her neck and gave a long vertical pull; her white sailor's blouse was ripped to the hem; suspicion condensed into a too, too solid certainty. "Lenina, what *are* you doing?"

Zip, zip! Her answer was wordless. She stepped out of her bell-bottomed trousers. Her zippicamiknicks were a pale shell pink. The Arch-Community-Songster's golden T dangled at her breast.

"For those milk paps that through the window bars bore at men's eyes. . . ." The singing, thundering, magical words made her seem doubly dangerous, doubly alluring. Soft, soft, but how piercing! boring and drilling into reason, tunnelling through resolution. "The strongest oaths are straw to the fire i' the blood. Be more abstemious, or else . . ."

Zip! The rounded pinkness fell apart like a neatly divided apple. A wriggle of the arms, a lifting first of the right foot, then the left: the zippicami-knicks were lying lifeless and as though deflated on the floor.

Still wearing her shoes and socks, and her rakishly tilted round white cap, she advanced towards him. "Darling. *Darling!* If only you'd said so before!" She held out her arms.

But instead of also saying "Darling!" and holding out *his* arms, the Savage retreated in terror, flapping his hands at her as though he were trying to scare away some intruding and dangerous animal. Four back-wards steps, and he was brought to bay against the wall.

"Sweet!" said Lenina and, laying her hands on his shoulders, pressed herself against him. "Put your arms round me," she commanded. "Hug me till you drug me, honey." She too had poetry at her command, knew words that sang and were spells and beat drums. "Kiss me"; she closed her eyes, she let her voice sink to a sleepy murmur, "kiss me till I'm in a coma. Hug me, honey, snuggly . . ."

The Savage caught her by the wrists, tore her hands from his shoulders, thrust her roughly away at arm's length.

"Ow, you're hurting me, you're . . . oh!" She was suddenly silent. Terror had made her forget the pain.

Opening her eyes, she had seen his face — no, not *his* face, a ferocious stranger's, pale, distorted, twitching with some insane, inexplicable fury. Aghast, "But what is it, John?" she whispered. He did not answer, but only stared into her face with those mad eyes. The hands that held her wrists were trembling. He breathed deeply and irregularly. Faint almost to imperceptibility, but appalling, she suddenly heard the grinding of his teeth. "What is it?" she almost screamed.

And as though awakened by her cry he caught her by the shoulders and shook her. "Whore!" he shouted. "Whore! Impudent strumpet!"

"Oh, don't, do-on't," she protested in a voice made grotesquely tremulous by his shaking.

"Whore!"

"Ple-ease."

"Damned whore!"

"A gra-amme is be-etter . . ." she began.

The Savage pushed her away with such force that she staggered and fell. "Go," he shouted, standing over her menacingly, "get out of my sight or I'll kill you." He clenched his fists.

Lenina raised her arm to cover her face. "No, please don't, John . . ."

"Hurry up. Quick!"

One arm still raised, and following his every movement with a terrified eye, she scrambled to her feet and still crouching, still covering her head, made a dash for the bathroom.

The noise of that prodigious slap by which her departure was accelerated was like a pistol shot.

"Ow!" Lenina bounded forward.

Safely locked into the bathroom, she had leisure to take stock of her injuries. Standing with her back to the mirror, she twisted her head. Looking over her left shoulder she could see the imprint of an open hand standing out distinct and crimson on the pearly flesh. Gingerly she rubbed the wounded spot.

Outside, in the other room, the Savage was striding up and down, marching, marching to the drums and music of magical words "The wren goes to't and the small gilded fly does lecher in my sight." Maddeningly they rumbled in his ears. "The fitchew nor the soiled horse goes to't with a more riotous appetite. Down from the waist they are Centaurs, though women all above. But to the girdle do the gods inherit. Beneath is all the fiend's. There's hell, there's darkness, there is the sulphurous pit, burning, scalding, stench, consumption; fie, fie, fie, pah, pah! Give me an ounce of civet, good apothecary, to sweeten my imagination."

"John!" ventured a small ingratiating voice from the bathroom. "John!"

"O thou weed, who are so lovely fair and smell'st so sweet that the sense aches at thee. Was this most goodly book made to write 'whore' upon? Heaven stops the nose at it . . ."

But her perfume still hung about him, his jacket was white with the powder that had scented her velvety body. "Impudent strumpet, impudent strumpet, impudent strumpet." The inexorable rhythm beat itself out. "Impudent . . ."

"John, do you think I might have my clothes?"

He picked up the bell-bottomed trousers, the blouse, the zippicamiknicks.

"Open!" he ordered, kicking the door.

"No, I won't." The voice was frightened and defiant.

"Well, how do you expect me to give them to you?"

"Push them through the ventilator over the door."

He did what she suggested and returned to his uneasy pacing of the room. "Impudent strumpet, impudent strumpet. The devil Luxury with his fat rump and potato finger . . ."

"John."

He would not answer. "Fat rump and potato finger."

"John."

"What is it?" he asked gruffly.

"I wonder if you'd mind giving me my Malthusian belt."

Lenina sat, listening to the footsteps in the other room, wondering, as she listened, how long he was likely to go tramping up and down like that; whether she would have to wait until he left the flat; or if it would be safe, after allowing his madness a reasonable time to subside, to open the bathroom door and make a dash for it.

She was interrupted in the midst of these uneasy speculations by the sound of the telephone bell ringing in the other room. Abruptly the tramping ceased. She heard the voice of the Savage parleying with silence.

"Hullo."

. . . . .

"Yes."

. . . . .

"If I do not usurp myself, I am."

. . . . .

"Yes, didn't you hear me say so? Mr. Savage speaking."

. . . . .

"What? Who's ill? Of course it interests me."

. . . . .

"But is it serious? Is she really bad? I'll go at once . . ."

. . . . .

"Not in her rooms any more? Where has she been taken?"

. . . . .

"Oh, my God! What's the address?"

. . . . .

"Three Park Lane — is that it? Three? Thanks."

Lenina heard the click of the replaced receiver, then hurrying steps. A door slammed. There was silence. Was he really gone?

With an infinity of precautions she opened the door a quarter of an inch; peeped through the crack; was encouraged by the view of emptiness; opened a little further, and put her whole head out; finally tiptoed into the room; stood for a few seconds with strongly beating heart, listening, listening; then darted to the front door, opened, slipped through, slammed, ran. It was not till she was in the lift and actually dropping down the well that she began to feel herself secure.

CHAPTER 14

The Park Lane Hospital for the Dying was a sixty-story tower of primrose tiles. As the Savage stepped out of his taxicopter a convoy of gaily-coloured aerial hearses rose whirring from the roof and darted away across the Park, westwards, bound for the Slough Crematorium. At the lift gates the presiding porter gave him the information he required, and he dropped down to Ward 81 (a Galloping Senility ward, the porter explained) on the seventeenth floor.

It was a large room bright with sunshine and yellow paint, and containing twenty beds, all occupied. Linda was dying in company — in company and with all the modern conveniences. The air was continuously alive with gay synthetic melodies. At the foot of every bed, confronting its moribund occupant, was a television box. Television was left on, a running tap, from morning till night. Every quarter of an hour the prevailing perfume of the room was automatically changed. "We try," explained the nurse, who had taken charge of the Savage at the door, "we try to create a thoroughly pleasant atmosphere here, something between a first-class hotel and a feely-palace, if you take my meaning."

"Where is she?" asked the Savage, ignoring these polite explanations.

The nurse was offended. "You *are* in a hurry," she said.

"Is there any hope?" he asked.

"You mean, of her not dying?" (He nodded.) "No, of course there isn't. When somebody's sent here, there's no . . ." Startled by the expression of distress on his pale face, she suddenly broke off. "Why, whatever is the matter?" she asked. She was not accustomed to this kind of thing in visitors. (Not that there were many visitors anyhow: or any reason why there should be many visitors.) "You're not feeling ill, are you?"

He shook his head. "She's my mother," he said in a scarcely audible voice.

The nurse glanced at him with startled, horrified eyes; then quickly looked away. From throat to temple she was all one hot blush.

"Take me to her," said the Savage, making an effort to speak in an ordinary tone.

Still blushing, she led the way down the ward. Faces still fresh and unwithered (for senility galloped so hard that it had no time to age the cheeks, only the heart and brain) turned as they passed. Their progress was followed by the blank, incurious eyes of second infancy. The Savage shuddered as he looked.

Linda was lying in the last of the long row of beds, next to the wall. Propped up on pillows, she was watching the Semi-finals of the South American Riemann-Surface Tennis Championship, which were being played in silent and diminished reproduction on the screen of the television box at the foot of the bed. Hither and thither across their square of illuminated glass the little figures noiselessly darted, like fish in an aquarium — the silent but agitated inhabitants of another world.

Linda looked on, vaguely and uncomprehendingly smiling. Her pale, bloated face wore an expression of imbecile happiness. Every now and then her eyelids closed, and for a few seconds she seemed to be dozing. Then with a little start she would wake up again — wake up to the aquarium antics of the Tennis

Champions, to the Super-Vox-Wurlitzeriana rendering of "Hug me till you drug me, honey," to the warm draught of verbena that came blowing through the ventilator above her head — would wake to these things, or rather to a dream of which these things, transformed and embellished by the *soma* in her blood, were the marvellous constituents, and smile once more her broken and discoloured smile of infantile contentment.

"Well, I must go," said the nurse. "I've got my batch of children coming. Besides, there's Number 3." She pointed up the ward. "Might go off any minute now. Well, make yourself comfortable." She walked briskly away.

The Savage sat down beside the bed.

"Linda," he whispered, taking her hand.

At the sound of her name, she turned. Her vague eyes brightened with recognition. She squeezed his hand, she smiled, her lips moved; then quite suddenly her head fell forward. She was asleep. He sat watching her — seeking through the tired flesh, seeking and finding that young, bright face which had stooped over his childhood in Malpais, remembering (and he closed his eyes) her voice, her movements, all the events of their life together. "Streptocock-Gee to Banbury T . . ." How beautiful her singing had been! And those childish rhymes, how magically strange and mysterious!

A, B, C, vitamin D:

The fat's in the liver, the cod's in the sea.

He felt the hot tears welling up behind his eyelids as he recalled the words and Linda's voice as she repeated them. And then the reading lessons: The tot is in the pot, the cat is on the mat; and the Elementary Instructions for Beta Workers in the

Embryo Store. And long evenings by the fire or, in summertime, on the roof of the little house, when she told him those stories about the Other Place, outside the Reservation: that beautiful, beautiful Other Place, whose memory, as of a heaven, a paradise of goodness and loveliness, he still kept whole and intact, undefiled by contact with the reality of this real London, these actual civilized men and women.

A sudden noise of shrill voices made him open his eyes and, after hastily brushing away the tears, look round. What seemed an interminable stream of identical eight-year-old male twins was pouring into the room. Twin after twin, twin after twin, they came — a nightmare. Their faces, their repeated face — for there was only one between the lot of them — puggishly stared, all nostrils and pale goggling eyes. Their uniform was khaki. All their mouths hung open. Squealing and chattering they entered. In a moment, it seemed, the ward was maggoty with them. They swarmed between the beds, clambered over, crawled under, peeped into the television boxes, made faces at the patients.

Linda astonished and rather alarmed them. A group stood clustered at the foot of her bed, staring with the frightened and stupid curiosity of animals suddenly confronted by the unknown.

"Oh, look, look!" They spoke in low, scared voices. "Whatever is the matter with her? Why is she so fat?"

They had never seen a face like hers before — had never seen a face that was not youthful and taut-skinned, a body that had ceased to be slim and upright. All these moribund sexagenarians had the appearance of childish girls. At forty-four, Linda seemed, by contrast, a monster of flaccid and distorted senility.

"Isn't she awful?" came the whispered comments. "Look at her teeth!"

Suddenly from under the bed a pug-faced twin popped up between John's chair and the wall, and began peering into Linda's sleeping face.

"I say . . ." he began; but the sentence ended prematurely in a squeal. The Savage had seized him by the collar, lifted him clear over the chair and, with a smart box on the ears, sent him howling away.

His yells brought the Head Nurse hurrying to the rescue.

"What have you been doing to him?" she demanded fiercely. "I won't have you striking the children."

"Well then, keep them away from this bed." The Savage's voice was trembling with indignation. "What are these filthy little brats doing here at all? It's disgraceful!"

"Disgraceful? But what do you mean? They're being death-conditioned. And I tell you," she warned him truculently, "if I have any more of your interference with their conditioning, I'll send for the porters and have you thrown out."

The Savage rose to his feet and took a couple of steps towards her. His movements and the expression on his face were so menacing that the nurse fell back in terror. With a great effort he checked himself and, without speaking, turned away and sat down again by the bed.

Reassured, but with a dignity that was a trifle shrill and uncertain, "I've warned you," said the nurse, "so mind." Still, she led the too inquisitive twins away and made them join in the game of hunt-the-zipper, which had been organized by one of her colleagues at the other end of the room.

"Run along now and have your cup of caffeine solution, dear," she said to the other nurse. The exercise of authority restored her confidence, made her feel better. "Now children!' she called.

Linda had stirred uneasily, had opened her eyes for a moment, looked vaguely around, and then once more dropped off to sleep. Sitting beside her, the Savage tried hard to recapture his mood of a few minutes before. "A, B, C, vitamin D," he repeated to himself, as though the words were a spell that would restore the dead past to life. But the spell was ineffective. Obstinately the beautiful memories refused to rise; there was only a hateful resurrection of jealousies and uglinesses and miseries. Popé with the blood trickling down from his cut shoulder; and Linda hideously asleep, and the flies buzzing round the spilt *mescal* on the floor beside the bed; and the boys calling those names as she passed. . . . Ah, no, no! He shut his eyes, he shook his head in strenuous denial of these memories. "A, B, C, vitamin D . . ." He tried to think of those times when he sat on her knees and she put her arms about him and sang, over and over again, rocking him, rocking him to sleep. "A, B, C, vitamin D, vitamin D, vitamin D . . ."

The Super-Vox-Wurlitzeriana had risen to a sobbing crescendo; and suddenly the verbena gave place, in the scent-circulating system, to an intense patchouli. Linda stirred, woke up, stared for a few seconds bewilderedly at the Semi-finalists, then, lifting her face, sniffed once or twice at the newly perfumed air and suddenly smiled — a smile of childish ecstasy.

"Popé!" she murmured, and closed her eyes. "Oh, I do so like it, I do . . ." She sighed and let herself sink back into the pillows.

"But, Linda!" The Savage spoke imploringly, "Don't you know me?" He had tried so hard, had done his very best; why wouldn't she allow him to forget?

He squeezed her limp hand almost with violence, as though he would force her to come back from this dream of ignoble pleasures, from these base and hateful memories — back into the present, back into reality; the appalling present, the awful reality — but sublime, but significant, but desperately important precisely because of the imminence of that which made them so fearful. "Don't you know me, Linda?"

He felt the faint answering pressure of her hand. The tears started into his eyes. He bent over her and kissed her.

Her lips moved. "Popé!" she whispered again, and it was as though he had had a pailful of ordure thrown in his face.

Anger suddenly boiled up in him. Balked for the second time, the passion of his grief had found another outlet, was transformed into a passion of agonized rage.

"But I'm John!" he shouted. "I'm John!" And in his furious misery he actually caught her by the shoulder and shook her.

Linda's eyes fluttered open; she saw him, knew him — "John!" — but situated the real face, the real and violent hands, in an imaginary world — among the inward and private equivalents of patchouli and the Super-Wurlitzer, among the transfigured memories and the strangely transposed sensations that constituted the universe of her dream. She knew him for John, her son, but fancied him an intruder into that paradisal Malpais where she had been spending her *soma*-holiday with Popé. He was angry because she liked Popé, he was shaking her because Popé was there in the bed — as though there were something wrong, as though all civilized people didn't do the same. "Every one belongs to every . . ." Her voice suddenly died into an almost inaudible breathless croaking. Her mouth fell open:

she made a desperate effort to fill her lungs with air. But it was as though she had forgotten how to breathe. She tried to cry out — but no sound came; only the terror of her staring eyes revealed what she was suffering. Her hands went to her throat, then clawed at the air — the air she could no longer breathe, the air that, for her, had ceased to exist.

The Savage was on his feet, bent over her. "What is it, Linda? What is it?" His voice was imploring; it was as though he were begging to be reassured.

The look she gave him was charged with an unspeakable terror — with terror and, it seemed to him, reproach. She tried to raise herself in bed, but fell back on to the pillows. Her face was horribly distorted, her lips blue.

The Savage turned and ran up the ward.

"Quick, quick!" he shouted. "Quick!"

Standing in the centre of a ring of zipper-hunting twins, the Head Nurse looked round. The first moment's astonishment gave place almost instantly to disapproval. "Don't shout! Think of the little ones," she said, frowning. "You might decondition . . . But what are you doing?" He had broken through the ring. "Be careful!" A child was yelling.

"Quick, quick!" He caught her by the sleeve, dragged her after him. "Quick! Something's happened. I've killed her."

By the time they were back at the end of the ward Linda was dead.

The Savage stood for a moment in frozen silence, then fell on his knees beside the bed and, covering his face with his hands, sobbed uncontrollably.

The nurse stood irresolute, looking now at the kneeling figure by the bed (the scandalous exhibition!) and now (poor children!) at the twins who had stopped their hunting of the zipper and were staring from the other end of the ward, staring with all their eyes and nostrils at the shocking scene that was being enacted round Bed 20. Should she speak to him? try to bring him back to a sense of decency? remind him of where he was? of what fatal mischief he might do to these poor innocents? Undoing all their wholesome death-conditioning with this disgusting outcry — as though death were something terrible, as though any one mattered as much as all that! It might give them the most disastrous ideas about the subject, might upset them into reacting in the entirely wrong, the utterly anti-social way.

She stepped forward, she touched him on the shoulder. "Can't you behave?" she said in a low, angry voice. But, looking around, she saw that half a dozen twins were already on their feet and advancing down the ward. The circle was disintegrating. In another moment . . . No, the risk was too great; the whole Group might be put back six or seven months in its conditioning. She hurried back towards her menaced charges.

"Now, who wants a chocolate éclair?" she asked in a loud, cheerful tone.

"Me!" yelled the entire Bokanovsky Group in chorus. Bed 20 was completely forgotten.

"Oh, God, God, God . . ." the Savage kept repeating to himself. In the chaos of grief and remorse that filled his mind it was the one articulate word. "God!" he whispered it aloud. "God . . ."

"Whatever is he saying?" said a voice, very near, distinct and shrill through the warblings of the Super-Wurlitzer.

The Savage violently started and, uncovering his face, looked round. Five khaki twins, each with the stump of a long éclair in his right hand, and their identical faces variously smeared with liquid chocolate, were standing in a row, puggily goggling at him.

They met his eyes and simultaneously grinned. One of them pointed with his éclair butt.

"Is she dead?" he asked.

The Savage stared at them for a moment in silence. Then in silence he rose to his feet, in silence slowly walked towards the door.

"Is she dead?" repeated the inquisitive twin trotting at his side.

The Savage looked down at him and still without speaking pushed him away. The twin fell on the floor and at once began to howl. The Savage did not even look round.

CHAPTER 15

The menial staff of the Park Lane Hospital for the Dying consisted of one hundred and sixty-two Deltas divided into two Bokanovsky Groups of eighty-four red-headed female and seventy-eight dark dolychocephalic male twins, respectively. At six, when their working day was over, the two Groups assembled in the vestibule of the Hospital and were served by the Deputy Sub-Bursar with their *soma* ration.

From the lift the Savage stepped out into the midst of them. But his mind was elsewhere — with death, with his grief, and his remorse; mechanically, without consciousness of what he was doing, he began to shoulder his way through the crowd.

"Who are you pushing? Where do you think you're going?"

High, low, from a multitude of separate throats, only two voices squeaked or growled. Repeated indefinitely, as though by a train of mirrors, two faces, one a hairless and freckled moon haloed in orange, the other a thin, beaked bird-mask, stubbly with two days' beard, turned angrily towards him. Their words and, in his ribs, the sharp nudging of elbows, broke through his unawareness. He woke once more to external reality, looked round him, knew what he saw — knew it, with a sinking sense of horror and disgust, for the recurrent delirium of his days and nights, the nightmare of swarming indistinguishable sameness. Twins, twins. . . . Like maggots they had swarmed defilingly over the mystery of Linda's death. Maggots again, but larger, full grown, they now crawled across his grief and his repentance. He halted and, with bewildered and horrified eyes, stared round him at the khaki mob, in the midst of which, overtopping it by a full head, he stood. "How many goodly creatures are there here!" The singing words mocked him derisively. "How beauteous mankind is! O brave new world . . ."

"*Soma* distribution!" shouted a loud voice. "In good order, please. Hurry up there."

A door had been opened, a table and chair carried into the vestibule. The voice was that of a jaunty young Alpha, who had entered carrying a black iron cash-box. A murmur of satisfaction went up from the expectant twins. They forgot all about the Savage. Their attention was now focussed on the black cash-box, which the young man had placed on the table, and was now in process of unlocking. The lid was lifted.

"Oo-oh!" said all the hundred and sixty-two simultaneously, as though they were looking at fireworks.

The young man took out a handful of tiny pill-boxes. "Now," he said peremptorily, "step forward, please. One at a time, and no shoving."

One at a time, with no shoving, the twins stepped forward. First two males, then a female, then another male, then three females, then . . .

The Savage stood looking on. "O brave new world, O brave new world . . ." In his mind the singing words seemed to change their tone. They had mocked him through his misery and remorse, mocked him with how hideous a note of cynical derision! Fiendishly laughing, they had insisted on the low squalor, the nauseous ugliness of the nightmare. Now, suddenly, they trumpeted a call to arms. "O brave new world!" Miranda was proclaiming the possibility of loveliness, the possibility of transforming even the nightmare into something fine and noble. "O brave new world!" It was a challenge, a command.

"No shoving there now!" shouted the Deputy Sub-Bursar in a fury. He slammed down the lid of his cash-box. "I shall stop the distribution unless I have good behaviour."

The Deltas muttered, jostled one another a little, and then were still. The threat had been effective. Deprivation of *soma* — appalling thought!

"That's better," said the young man, and reopened his cash-box.

Linda had been a slave, Linda had died; others should live in freedom, and the world be made beautiful. A reparation, a duty. And suddenly it was luminously clear to the Savage what he must do; it was as though a shutter had been opened, a curtain drawn back.

"Now," said the Deputy Sub-Bursar.

Another khaki female stepped forward.

"Stop!" called the Savage in a loud and ringing voice. "Stop!"

He pushed his way to the table; the Deltas stared at him with astonishment.

"Ford!" said the Deputy Sub-Bursar, below his breath. "It's the Savage." He felt scared.

"Listen, I beg of you," cried the Savage earnestly. "Lend me your ears . . ." He had never spoken in public before, and found it very difficult to express what he wanted to say. "Don't take that horrible stuff. It's poison, it's poison."

"I say, Mr. Savage," said the Deputy Sub-Bursar, smiling propitiatingly. "Would you mind letting me . . ."

"Poison to soul as well as body."

"Yes, but let me get on with my distribution, won't you? There's a good fellow." With the cautious tenderness of one who strokes a notoriously vicious animal, he patted the Savage's arm. "Just let me . . ."

"Never!" cried the Savage.

"But look here, old man . . ."

"Throw it all away, that horrible poison."

The words "Throw it all away" pierced through the enfolding layers of incomprehension to the quick of the Delta's consciousness. An angry murmur went up from the crowd.

"I come to bring you freedom," said the Savage, turning back towards the twins. "I come . . ."

The Deputy Sub-Bursar heard no more; he had slipped out of the vestibule and was looking up a number in the telephone book.

"Not in his own rooms," Bernard summed up. "Not in mine, not in yours. Not at the Aphroditæum; not at the Centre or the College. Where can he have got to?"

Helmholtz shrugged his shoulders. They had come back from their work expecting to find the Savage waiting for them at one or other of the usual meeting-places, and there was no sign of the fellow. Which was annoying, as they had meant to nip across to Biarritz in Helmholtz's four-seater sporticopter. They'd be late for dinner if he didn't come soon.

"We'll give him five more minutes," said Helmholtz. "If he doesn't turn up by then, we'll . . ."

The ringing of the telephone bell interrupted him. He picked up the receiver. "Hullo. Speaking." Then, after a long interval of listening, "Ford in Flivver!" he swore. "I'll come at once."

"What is it?" Bernard asked.

"A fellow I know at the Park Lane Hospital," said

Helmholtz. "The Savage is there. Seems to have gone mad. Anyhow, it's urgent. Will you come with me?"

Together they hurried along the corridor to the lifts.

"But do you like being slaves?" the Savage was saying as they entered the Hospital. His face was flushed, his eyes bright with ardour and indignation. "Do you like being babies? Yes, babies. Mewling and puking," he added, exasperated by their bestial stupidity into throwing insults at those he had come to save. The insults bounced off their carapace of thick stupidity; they stared at him with a blank expression of dull and sullen resentment in their eyes. "Yes, puking!" he fairly shouted. Grief and remorse, compassion and duty — all were forgotten now and, as it were, absorbed into an intense overpowering hatred of these less than human monsters. "Don't you want to be free and men? Don't you even understand what manhood and freedom are?" Rage was making him fluent; the words came easily, in a rush. "Don't you?" he repeated, but got no answer to his question. "Very well then," he went on grimly. "I'll teach you; I'll *make* you be free whether you want to or not." And pushing open a window that looked on to the inner court of the Hospital, he began to throw the little pill-boxes of *soma* tablets in handfuls out into the area.

For a moment the khaki mob was silent, petrified, at the spectacle of this wanton sacrilege, with amazement and horror.

"He's mad," whispered Bernard, staring with wide open eyes. "They'll kill him. They'll . . ." A great shout suddenly went up from the mob; a wave of movement drove it menacingly towards the Savage. "Ford help him!" said Bernard, and averted his eyes.

"Ford helps those who help themselves." And with a laugh, actually a laugh of exultation, Helmholtz Watson pushed his way through the crowd.

"Free, free!" the Savage shouted, and with one hand continued to throw the *soma* into the area while, with the other, he punched the indistinguishable faces of his assailants. "Free!" And suddenly there was Helmholtz at his side — "Good old Helmholtz!" — also punching — "Men at last!" — and in the interval also throwing the poison out by handfuls through the open window. "Yes, men! men!" and there was no more poison left. He picked up the cash-box and showed them its black emptiness. "You're free!"

Howling, the Deltas charged with a redoubled fury.

Hesitant on the fringes of the battle. "They're done for," said Bernard and, urged by a sudden impulse, ran forward to help them; then thought better of it and halted; then, ashamed, stepped forward again; then again thought better of it, and was standing in an agony of humiliated indecision — thinking that *they* might be killed if he didn't help them, and that *he* might be killed if he did — when (Ford be praised!), goggle-eyed and swine-snouted in their gas-masks, in ran the police.

Bernard dashed to meet them. He waved his arms; and it was action, he was doing something. He shouted "Help!" several times, more and more loudly so as to give himself the illusion of helping. "Help! *Help!* HELP!"

The policemen pushed him out of the way and got on with their work. Three men with spraying machines buckled to their shoulders pumped thick clouds of *soma* vapour into the air. Two more were busy round the portable Synthetic Music Box. Carrying water pistols charged with a powerful anæsthetic, four others had pushed their way into the crowd and were methodically laying out, squirt by squirt, the more ferocious of the fighters.

"Quick, quick!" yelled Bernard. "They'll be killed if you don't hurry. They'll . . . Oh!" Annoyed by his chatter, one of the policemen had given him a shot from his water pistol. Bernard stood for a second or two wambling unsteadily on legs that seemed to have lost their bones, their tendons, their muscles, to have become mere sticks of jelly, and at last not even jelly—water: he tumbled in a heap on the floor.

Suddenly, from out of the Synthetic Music Box a Voice began to speak. The Voice of Reason, the Voice of Good Feeling. The sound-track roll was unwinding itself in Synthetic Anti-Riot Speech Number Two (Medium Strength). Straight from the depths of a non-existent heart, "My friends, my friends!" said the Voice so pathetically, with a note of such infinitely tender reproach that, behind their gas masks, even the policemen's eyes were momentarily dimmed with tears, "what is the meaning of this? Why aren't you all being happy and good together? Happy and good," the Voice repeated. "At peace, at peace." It trembled, sank into a whisper and momentarily expired. "Oh, I do want you to be happy," it began, with a yearning earnestness. "I do so want you to be good! Please, please be good and . . ."

Two minutes later the Voice and the *soma* vapour had produced their effect. In tears, the Deltas were kissing and hugging one another — half a dozen twins at a time in a comprehensive embrace. Even Helmholtz and the Savage were almost crying. A fresh supply of pill-boxes was brought in from the Bursary; a new distribution was hastily made and, to the sound of the Voice's richly affectionate, baritone valedictions, the twins dispersed, blubbering as though their hearts would break. "Good-bye, my dearest, dearest friends,

Ford keep you! Good-bye, my dearest, dearest friends, Ford keep you. Good-bye my dearest, dearest . . ."

When the last of the Deltas had gone the policeman switched off the current. The angelic Voice fell silent.

"Will you come quietly?" asked the Sergeant, "or must we anæsthetize?" He pointed his water pistol menacingly.

"Oh, we'll come quietly," the Savage answered, dabbing alternately a cut lip, a scratched neck, and a bitten left hand.

Still keeping his handkerchief to his bleeding nose Helmholtz nodded in confirmation.

Awake and having recovered the use of his legs, Bernard had chosen this moment to move as inconspicuously as he could towards the door.

"Hi, you there," called the Sergeant, and a swine-masked policeman hurried across the room and laid a hand on the young man's shoulder.

Bernard turned with an expression of indignant innocence. Escaping? He hadn't dreamed of such a thing. "Though what on earth you want *me* for," he said to the Sergeant, "I really can't imagine."

"You're a friend of the prisoner's, aren't you?"

"Well . . ." said Bernard, and hesitated. No, he really couldn't deny it. "Why shouldn't I be?" he asked.

"Come on then," said the Sergeant, and led the way towards the door and the waiting police car.

CHAPTER 16

The room into which the three were ushered was the Controller's study.

"His fordship will be down in a moment." The Gamma butler left them to themselves.

Helmholtz laughed aloud.

"It's more like a caffeine-solution party than a trial," he said, and let himself fall into the most luxurious of the pneumatic arm-chairs. "Cheer up, Bernard," he added, catching sight of his friend's green unhappy face. But Bernard would not be cheered; without answering, without even looking at Helmholtz, he went and sat down on the most uncomfortable chair in the room, carefully chosen in the obscure hope of somehow deprecating the wrath of the higher powers.

The Savage meanwhile wandered restlessly round the room, peering with a vague superficial inquisitiveness at the books in the shelves, at the sound-track rolls and reading machine bobbins in their numbered pigeon-holes. On the table under the window lay a massive volume bound in limp black leather-surrogate, and stamped with large golden T's. He picked it up and opened it. MY LIFE AND WORK, BY OUR FORD. The book had been published at Detroit by the Society for the Propagation of Fordian Knowledge. Idly he turned the pages, read a sentence here, a paragraph there, and had just come to the conclusion that the book didn't interest him, when the door opened, and the Resident World Controller for Western Europe walked briskly into the room.

Mustapha Mond shook hands with all three of them; but it was to the Savage that he addressed himself. "So you don't much like civilization, Mr. Savage," he said.

The Savage looked at him. He had been prepared to lie, to bluster, to remain sullenly unresponsive; but, reassured by the good-humoured intelligence of the Controller's face, he decided to tell the truth, straightforwardly. "No." He shook his head.

Bernard started and looked horrified. What would the Controller think? To be labelled as the friend of a man who said that he didn't like civilization — said it openly and, of all people, to the Controller — it was terrible. "But, John," he began. A look from Mustapha Mond reduced him to an abject silence.

"Of course," the Savage went on to admit, "there are some very nice things. All that music in the air, for instance . . ."

"Sometimes a thousand twangling instruments will hum about my ears and sometimes voices."

The Savage's face lit up with a sudden pleasure. "Have you read it too?" he asked. "I thought nobody knew about that book here, in England."

"Almost nobody. I'm one of the very few. It's prohibited, you see. But as I make the laws here, I can also break them. With impunity, Mr. Marx," he added, turning to Bernard. "Which I'm afraid you *can't* do."

Bernard sank into a yet more hopeless misery.

"But why is it prohibited?" asked the Savage. In the excitement of meeting a man who had read Shakespeare he had momentarily forgotten everything else.

The Controller shrugged his shoulders. "Because it's old; that's the chief reason. We haven't any use for old things here."

"Even when they're beautiful?"

"Particularly when they're beautiful. Beauty's attractive, and we don't want people to be attracted by old things. We want them to like the new ones."

"But the new ones are so stupid and horrible. Those plays, where there's nothing but helicopters flying about and you *feel* the people kissing." He made a grimace. "Goats and monkeys!" Only in Othello's words could he find an adequate vehicle for his contempt and hatred.

"Nice tame animals, anyhow," the Controller murmured parenthetically.

"Why don't you let them see *Othello* instead?"

"I've told you; it's old. Besides, they couldn't understand it."

Yes, that was true. He remembered how Helmholtz had laughed at *Romeo and Juliet*. "Well then," he said, after a pause, "something new that's like *Othello,* and that they could understand."

"That's what we've all been wanting to write," said Helmholtz, breaking a long silence.

"And it's what you never will write," said the Controller. "Because, if it were really like *Othello* nobody could understand it, however new it might be. And if it were new, it couldn't possibly be like *Othello.*"

"Why not?"

"Yes, why not?" Helmholtz repeated. He too was forgetting the unpleasant realities of the situation. Green with anxiety and apprehension, only Bernard remembered them; the others ignored him. "Why not?"

"Because our world is not the same as Othello's world. You can't make flivvers without steel — and you can't make tragedies without social instability. The world's stable now. People are happy; they get what they want, and they never want what they can't get. They're well off; they're safe; they're never ill; they're not afraid of death; they're blissfully ignorant of passion and old age; they're plagued with no mothers or fathers; they've got no wives, or children, or lovers to feel strongly about; they're so conditioned that they practically can't help behaving as they ought to behave. And if anything should go wrong, there's *soma*. Which you go and chuck out of the window in the name of liberty, Mr. Savage. *Liberty!*" He laughed. "Expecting Deltas to know what liberty is! And now expecting them to understand *Othello!* My good boy!"

The Savage was silent for a little. "All the same," he insisted obstinately, "*Othello's* good, *Othello's* better than those feelies."

"Of course it is," the Controller agreed. "But that's the price we have to pay for stability. You've got to choose between happiness and what people used to call high art. We've sacrificed the high art. We have the feelies and the scent organ instead."

"But they don't mean anything."

"They mean themselves; they mean a lot of agreeable sensations to the audience."

"But they're . . . they're told by an idiot."

The Controller laughed. "You're not being very polite to your friend, Mr. Watson. One of our most distinguished Emotional Engineers . . ."

"But he's right," said Helmholtz gloomily. "Because it is idiotic. Writing when there's nothing to say . . ."

"Precisely. But that requires the most enormous ingenuity. You're making flivvers out of the absolute minimum of steel — works of art out of practically nothing but pure sensation."

The Savage shook his head. "It all seems to me quite horrible."

"Of course it does. Actual happiness always looks pretty squalid in comparison with the over-compensations for misery. And, of course, stability isn't nearly so spectacular as instability. And being contented has none of the glamour of a good fight against misfortune, none of the picturesqueness of a struggle with temptation, or a fatal overthrow by passion or doubt. Happiness is never grand."

"I suppose not," said the Savage after a silence. "But need it be quite so bad as those twins?" He passed his hand over his eyes as though he were trying to wipe away the remembered image of those long rows of identical midgets at the assembling tables, those queued-up twin-herds at the entrance to the Brentford monorail station, those human maggots swarming round Linda's bed of death, the endlessly repeated face of his assailants. He looked at his bandaged left hand and shuddered. "Horrible!"

"But how useful! I see you don't like our Bokanovsky Groups; but, I assure you, they're the foundation on which everything else is built. They're the gyroscope that stabilizes the rocket plane of state on its unswerving course." The deep voice thrillingly vibrated; the gesticulating hand implied all space and the onrush of the irresistible machine. Mustapha Mond's oratory was almost up to synthetic standards.

"I was wondering," said the Savage, "why you had them at all — seeing that you can get whatever you want out of those bottles. Why don't you make ever-body an Alpha Double Plus while you're about it?"

Mustapha Mond laughed. "Because we have no wish to have our throats cut," he answered. "We believe in happiness and stability. A society of Alphas couldn't fail to be unstable and miserable. Imagine a factory staffed by Alphas — that is to say by separate and unrelated individuals of good heredity and conditioned so as to be capable (within limits) of making a free choice and assuming responsibilities. Imagine it!" he repeated.

The Savage tried to imagine it, not very successfully.

"It's an absurdity. An Alpha-decanted, Alpha-conditioned man would go mad if he had to do Epsilon Semi-Moron work — go mad, or start smashing things up. Alphas can be completely socialized — but only on condition that you make them do Alpha work. Only an Epsilon can be expected to make Epsilon sacrifices, for the good reason that for him they aren't sacrifices; they're the line of least resistance. His conditioning has laid down rails along which he's got to run. He can't help himself; he's foredoomed. Even after decanting, he's still inside a bottle — an invisible bottle of infantile and embryonic fixations. Each one of us, of course," the Controller meditatively continued, "goes through life inside a bottle. But if we happen to be Alphas, our bottles are, relatively speaking, enormous. We should suffer acutely if we were confined in a narrower space. You cannot pour upper-caste champagne-surrogate into lower-caste bottles. It's obvious theoretically. But it has also been proved in actual practice. The result of the Cyprus experiment was convincing."

"What was that?" asked the Savage.

Mustapha Mond smiled. "Well, you can call it an experiment in rebottling if you like. It began in A.F. 473. The Controllers had the island of Cyprus cleared of all its existing inhabitants and re-colonized with a specially prepared batch of twenty-two thousand Alphas. All agricultural and industrial equipment was handed over to them and they were left to manage their own affairs. The result exactly fulfilled all the theoretical predictions. The land wasn't properly worked; there were strikes in all the factories; the laws were set at naught, orders disobeyed; all the people detailed for a spell of low-grade work were perpetually intriguing for high-grade jobs, and all the people with high-grade jobs were counter-intriguing at all costs to stay where they were. Within six years they were having a first-class civil war. When nineteen out of the twenty-two thousand had been killed, the survivors unanimously petitioned the World Controllers to resume the government of the island. Which they did. And that was the end of the only society of Alphas that the world has ever seen."

The Savage sighed, profoundly.

"The optimum population," said Mustapha Mond, "is modelled on the iceberg — eight-ninths below the water line, one-ninth above."

"And they're happy below the water line?"

"Happier than above it. Happier than your friend here, for example." He pointed.

"In spite of that awful work?"

"Awful? *They* don't find it so. On the contrary, they like it. It's light, it's childishly simple. No strain on the mind or the muscles. Seven and a half hours of mild, unexhausting labour, and then the *soma* ration and games and unrestricted copulation and the feelies. What more can they ask for? True," he added, "they might ask for shorter hours. And of course we could give them shorter hours. Technically, it would be perfectly simple to reduce all lower-caste working hours to three or four a day. But would they be any the happier for that? No, they wouldn't. The experiment was tried, more than a century and a half ago. The whole of Ireland was put on to the four-hour day.

What was the result? Unrest and a large increase in the consumption of *soma*; that was all. Those three and a half hours of extra leisure were so far from being a source of happiness, that people felt constrained to take a holiday from them. The Inventions Office is stuffed with plans for labour-saving processes. Thousands of them." Mustapha Mond made a lavish gesture. " And why don't we put them into execution? For the sake of the labourers; it would be sheer cruelty to afflict them with excessive leisure. It's the same with agriculture. We could synthesize every morsel of food, if we wanted to. But we don't. We prefer to keep a third of the population on the land. For their own sakes — because it takes *longer* to get food out of the land than out of a factory. Besides, we have our stability to think of. We don't want to change. Every change is a menace to stability. That's another reason why we're so chary of applying new inventions. Every discovery in pure science is potentially subversive; even science must sometimes be treated as a possible enemy. Yes, even science."

Science? The Savage frowned. He knew the word. But what it exactly signified he could not say. Shakespeare and the old men of the pueblo had never mentioned science, and from Linda he had only gathered the vaguest hints: science was something you made helicopters with, something that caused you to laugh at the Corn Dances, something that prevented you from being wrinkled and losing your teeth. He made a desperate effort to take the Controller's meaning.

"Yes," Mustapha Mond was saying, "that's another item in the cost of stability. It isn't only art that's incompatible with happiness; it's also science. Science is dangerous; we have to keep it most carefully chained and muzzled."

"What?" said Helmholtz, in astonishment. "But we're always saying that science is everything. It's a hypnopædic platitude."

"Three times a week between thirteen and seventeen," put in Bernard.

"And all the science propaganda we do at the College . . ."

"Yes; but what sort of science?" asked Mustapha Mond sarcastically. "You've had no scientific training, so you can't judge. I was a pretty good physicist in my time. Too good — good enough to realize that all our science is just a cookery book, with an orthodox theory of cooking that nobody's allowed to question, and a list of recipes that mustn't be added to except by special permission from the head cook. I'm the head cook now. But I was an inquisitive young scullion once. I started doing a bit of cooking on my own. Unorthodox cooking, illicit cooking. A bit of real science, in fact." He was silent.

"What happened?" asked Helmholtz Watson.

The Controller sighed. "Very nearly what's going to happen to you young men. I was on the point of being sent to an island."

The words galvanized Bernard into violent and unseemly activity. "Send *me* to an island?" He jumped up, ran across the room, and stood gesticulating in front of the Controller. "You can't send *me*. I haven't done anything. It was the others. I swear it was the others." He pointed accusingly to Helmholtz and the Savage. "Oh, please don't send me to Iceland. I promise I'll do what I ought to do. Give me another chance. Please give me another chance." The tears began to flow. "I tell you, it's their fault," he sobbed. "And not to Iceland. Oh please, your fordship, please . . ." And in a paroxysm of abjection he threw himself on his knees before the Controller. Mustapha Mond tried to make him get up; but Bernard persisted in his grovelling; the stream of words poured out inexhaustibly. In the end the Controller had to ring for his fourth secretary.

"Bring three men," he ordered, "and take Mr. Marx into a bedroom. Give him a good *soma* vaporization and then put him to bed and leave him."

The fourth secretary went out and returned with three green-uniformed twin footmen. Still shouting and sobbing, Bernard was carried out.

"One would think he was going to have his throat cut," said the Controller, as the door closed. "Whereas, if he had the smallest sense, he'd understand that his punishment is really a reward. He's being sent to an island. That's to say, he's being sent to a place where he'll meet the most interesting set of men and women to be found anywhere in the world. All the people who, for one reason or another, have got too self-consciously individual to fit into community-life. All the people who aren't satisfied with orthodoxy, who've got independent ideas of their own. Every one, in a word, who's any one. I almost envy you, Mr. Watson."

Helmholtz laughed. "Then why aren't you on an island yourself?"

"Because, finally, I preferred this," the Controller answered. "I was given the choice: to be sent to an island, where I could have got on with my pure science, or to be taken on to the Controllers' Council with the prospect of succeeding in due course to an actual Controllership. I chose this and let the science go." After a little silence, "Sometimes," he added, "I rather regret the science. Happiness is a hard master — particularly other people's happiness. A much harder master, if one isn't conditioned to accept it unquestioningly, than truth." He sighed, fell silent again, then continued in a brisker tone, "Well, duty's duty. One can't consult one's own preference. I'm interested in truth, I like science. But truth's a menace, science is a public danger. As dangerous as it's been beneficent. It has given us the stablest equilibrium in history. China's was hopelessly insecure by comparison; even the primitive matriarchies weren't steadier than we are. Thanks, I repeat, to science. But we can't allow science to undo its own good work. That's why we so carefully limit the scope of its researches — that's why I almost got sent to an island. We don't allow it to deal with any but the most immediate problems of the moment. All other enquiries are most sedulously discouraged. It's curious," he went on after a little pause, "to read what people in the time of Our Ford used to write about scientific progress. They seemed to have imagined that it could be allowed to go on indefinitely, regardless of everything else. Knowledge was the highest good, truth the supreme value; all the rest was secondary and subordinate. True, ideas were beginning to change even then. Our Ford himself did a great deal to shift the emphasis from truth and beauty to comfort and happiness. Mass production demanded the shift. Universal happiness keeps the wheels steadily turning; truth and beauty can't. And, of course, whenever the masses seized political power, then it was happiness rather than truth and beauty that mattered. Still, in spite of everything, unrestricted scientific research was still permitted. People still went on talking about truth and beauty as though they were the sovereign goods. Right up to the time of the Nine Years' War. *That* made them change their tune all right. What's the point of truth or beauty or knowledge when the anthrax bombs are popping all around you? That was when science first began to be controlled — after the Nine Years' War. People were ready to have even their appetites controlled then. Anything for a quiet life. We've gone on controlling ever since. It hasn't been very good for truth, of course. But it's been very good for happiness. One can't have something for nothing. Happiness has got to be paid for. You're paying for it, Mr. Watson — paying because you happen to be too much interested in beauty. I was too much interested in truth; I paid too."

"But *you* didn't go to an island," said the Savage, breaking a long silence.

The Controller smiled. "That's how I paid. By choosing to serve happiness. Other people's — not mine. It's lucky," he added, after a pause, "that there are such a lot of islands in the world. I don't know what we should do without them. Put you all in the lethal chamber, I suppose. By the way, Mr. Watson, would you like a tropical climate? The Marquesas, for example; or Samoa? Or something rather more bracing?"

Helmholtz rose from his pneumatic chair. "I should like a thoroughly bad climate," he answered. "I believe one would write better if the climate were bad. If there were a lot of wind and storms, for example . . ."

The Controller nodded his approbation. "I like your spirit, Mr. Watson. I like it very much indeed. As much as I officially disapprove of it." He smiled. "What about the Falkland Islands?"

"Yes, I think that will do," Helmholtz answered. "And now, if you don't mind, I'll go and see how poor Bernard's getting on."

CHAPTER 17

"Art, science — you seem to have paid a fairly high price for your happiness," said the Savage, when they were alone. "Anything else?"

"Well, religion, of course," replied the Controller. "There used to be something called God — before the Nine Years' War. But I was forgetting; you know all about God, I suppose."

"Well . . ." The Savage hesitated. He would have liked to say something about solitude, about night, about the mesa lying pale under the moon, about the precipice, the plunge into shadowy darkness, about death. He would have liked to speak; but there were no words. Not even in Shakespeare.

The Controller, meanwhile, had crossed to the other side of the room and was unlocking a large safe set into the wall between the bookshelves. The heavy door swung open. Rummaging in the darkness within, "It's a subject," he said, "that has always had a great interest for me." He pulled out a thick black volume. "You've never read this, for example."

The Savage took it. "*The Holy Bible, containing the Old and New Testaments,*" he read aloud from the title-page.

"Nor this." It was a small book and had lost its cover.

"*The Imitation of Christ.*"

"Nor this." He handed out another volume.

"*The Varieties of Religious Experience.* By William James."

"And I've got plenty more," Mustapha Mond continued, resuming his seat. "A whole collection of pornographic old books. God in the safe and Ford on the shelves." He pointed with a laugh to his avowed library — to the shelves of books, the rack full of reading-machine bobbins and sound-track rolls.

"But if you know about God, why don't you tell them?" asked the Savage indignantly. "Why don't you give them these books about God?"

"For the same reason as we don't give them *Othello*: they're old; they're about God hundreds of years ago. Not about God now."

"But God doesn't change."

"Men do, though."

"What difference does that make?"

"All the difference in the world," said Mustapha Mond. He got up again and walked to the safe. "There was a man called Cardinal Newman," he said. "A cardinal," he exclaimed parenthetically, "was a kind of Arch-Community-Songster."

"'I Pandulph, of fair Milan, cardinal.' I've read about them in Shakespeare."

"Of course you have. Well, as I was saying, there was a man called Cardinal Newman. Ah, here's the book." He pulled it out. "And while I'm about it I'll take this one too. It's by a man called Maine de Biran. He was a philosopher, if you know what that was."

"A man who dreams of fewer things than there are in heaven and earth," said the Savage promptly.

"Quite so. I'll read you one of the things he *did* dream of in a moment. Meanwhile, listen to what this old Arch-Community-Songster said." He opened the book at the place marked by a slip of paper and began to read. " 'We are not our own any more than what we possess is our own. We did not make ourselves, we cannot be supreme over ourselves. We are not our own masters. We are God's property. Is it not our happiness thus to view the matter? Is it any happiness or any comfort, to consider that we *are* our own? It may be thought so by the young and prosperous. These may think it a great thing to have everything, as they suppose, their own way — to depend on no one — to have to think of nothing out of sight, to be without the irksomeness of continual acknowledgment, continual prayer, continual reference of what they do to the will of another. But as time goes on, they, as all men, will find that independence was not made for man — that it is an unnatural state — will do for a while, but will not carry us on safely to the end . . .' " Mustapha Mond paused, put down the first book and, picking up the other, turned over the pages. "Take this, for example," he said, and in his deep voice once more began to read: " 'A man grows old; he feels in himself that radical sense of weakness, of listlessness, of discomfort, which accompanies the advance of age; and, feeling thus, imagines himself merely sick, lulling his fears with the notion that this distressing condition is due to some particular cause, from which, as from an illness, he hopes to recover. Vain imaginings! That sickness is old age; and a horrible disease it is. They say that it is the fear of death and of what comes after death that makes men turn to religion as they advance in years. But my own experience has given me the conviction that, quite apart from any such terrors or imaginings, the religious sentiment tends to develop as we grow older; to develop because, as the passions grow calm, as the fancy and sensibilities are less excited and less excitable, our reason becomes less troubled in its working, less obscured by the images, desires and distractions, in which it used to be absorbed; whereupon God emerges as from behind a cloud; our soul feels, sees, turns towards the source of all light; turns naturally and inevitably; for now that all that gave to the world of sensations its life and charms has begun to leak away from us, now that phenomenal existence is no more bolstered up by impressions from within or from without, we feel the need to lean on something that abides, something that will never play us false — a reality, an absolute and everlasting truth. Yes, we inevitably turn to God; for this religious sentiment is of its nature so pure, so delightful to the soul that experiences it, that it makes up to us for all our other losses.' " Mustapha Mond shut the book and leaned back in his chair. "One of the numerous things in heaven and earth that these philosophers didn't dream about was this" (he waved his hand), "us, the modern world. 'You can only be independent of God while you've got youth and pros-perity; independence won't take you safely to the end.' Well, we've now got youth and prosperity right up to the end. What follows? Evidently, that we can be independent of God. 'The religious sentiment will compensate us for all our losses.' But there aren't any losses for us to compensate; religious sentiment is superfluous. And why should we go hunting for a substitute for youthful desires, when youthful desires never fail? A substitute for distractions, when we go on enjoying all the old fooleries to the very last? What need have we of repose when our minds and bodies continue to delight in activity? of consolation, when we have *soma*? of something immovable, when there is the social order?"

"Then you think there is no God?"

"No, I think there quite probably is one."

"Then why? . . ."

Mustapha Mond checked him. "But he manifests himself in different ways to different men. In premodern times he manifested himself as the being that's described in these books. Now . . ."

"How does he manifest himself now?" asked the Savage.

"Well, he manifests himself as an absence; as though he weren't there at all."

"That's your fault."

"Call it the fault of civilization. God isn't compatible with machinery and scientific medicine and universal happiness. You must make your choice. Our civilization has chosen machinery and medicine and happiness. That's why I have to keep these books locked up in the safe. They're smut. People would be shocked if . . ."

The Savage interrupted him. "But isn't it *natural* to feel there's a God?"

"You might as well ask if it's natural to do up one's trousers with zippers," said the Controller sarcastically. "You remind me of another of those old fellows called Bradley. He defined philosophy as the finding of bad reason for what one believes by instinct. As if one believed anything by instinct! One believes things because one has been conditioned to believe them. Finding bad reasons for what one believes for other bad reasons — that's philosophy. People believe in God because they've been conditioned to believe in God."

"But all the same," insisted the Savage, "it is natural to believe in God when you're alone — quite alone, in the night, thinking about death . . ."

"But people never are alone now," said Mustapha Mond. "We make them hate solitude; and we arrange their lives so that it's almost impossible for them ever to have it."

The Savage nodded gloomily. At Malpais he had suffered because they had shut him out from the communal activities of the pueblo, in civilized London he was suffering because he could never escape from those communal activities, never be quietly alone.

"Do you remember that bit in *King Lear*?" said the Savage at last. "'The gods are just and of our pleasant vices make instruments to plague us; the dark and vicious place where thee he got cost him his eyes,' and Edmund answers — you remember, he's wounded, he's dying — 'Thou hast spoken right; 'tis true. The wheel has come full circle; I am here.' What about that now? Doesn't there seem to be a God managing things, punishing, rewarding?"

"Well, does there?" questioned the Controller in his turn. "You can indulge in any number of pleasant vices with a freemartin and run no risks of having your eyes put out by your son's mistress. 'The wheel has come full circle; I am here.' But where would Edmund be nowadays? Sitting in a pneumatic chair, with his arm round a girl's waist, sucking away at his sex-hormone chewing-gum and looking at the feelies. The gods are just. No doubt. But their code of law is dictated, in the last resort, by the people who organize society; Providence takes its cue from men."

"Are you sure?" asked the Savage. "Are you quite sure that the Edmund in that pneumatic chair hasn't been just as heavily punished as the Edmund who's wounded and bleeding to death? The gods are just. Haven't they used his pleasant vices as an instrument to degrade him?"

"Degrade him from what position? As a happy, hard-working, goods-consuming citizen he's perfect. Of course, if you choose some other standard than ours, then perhaps you might say he was degraded. But you've got to stick to one set of postulates. You can't play Electro-magnetic Golf according to the rules of Centrifugal Bumble-puppy."

"But value dwells not in particular will," said the

Savage. "It holds his estimate and dignity as well wherein 'tis precious of itself as in the prizer."

"Come, come," protested Mustapha Mond, "that's going rather far, isn't it?"

"If you allowed yourselves to think of God, you wouldn't allow yourselves to be degraded by pleasant vices. You'd have a reason for bearing things patiently, for doing things with courage. I've seen it with the Indians."

"I'm sure you have," said Mustapha Mond. "But then we aren't Indians. There isn't any need for a civilized man to bear anything that's seriously unpleasant. And as for doing things — Ford forbid that he should get the idea into his head. It would upset the whole social order if men started doing things on their own."

"What about self-denial, then? If you had a God, you'd have a reason for self-denial."

"But industrial civilization is only possible when there's no self-denial. Self-indulgence up to the very limits imposed by hygiene and economics. Otherwise the wheels stop turning."

"You'd have a reason for chastity!" said the Savage, blushing a little as he spoke the words.

"But chastity means passion, chastity means neurasthenia. And passion and neurasthenia mean instability. And instability means the end of civilization. You can't have a lasting civilization without plenty of pleasant vices."

"But God's the reason for everything noble and fine and heroic. If you had a God . . ."

"My dear young friend," said Mustapha Mond, "civilization has absolutely no need of nobility or heroism. These things are symptoms of political inefficiency. In a properly organized society like ours, nobody has any opportunities for being noble or heroic. Conditions have got to be thoroughly unstable before the occasion can arise. Where there are wars, where there are divided allegiances, where there are temptations to be resisted, objects of love to be fought for or defended — there, obviously, nobility and heroism have some sense. But there aren't any wars nowadays. The greatest care is taken to prevent you from loving any one too much. There's no such thing as a divided allegiance; you're so conditioned that you can't help doing what you ought to do. And what you ought to do is on the whole so pleasant, so many of the natural impulses are allowed free play, that there really aren't any temptations to resist. And if ever, by some unlucky chance, anything unpleasant should somehow happen, why, there's always *soma* to give you a holiday from the facts. And there's always *soma* to calm your anger, to reconcile you to your enemies, to make you patient and long-suffering. In the past you could only accomplish these things by making a great effort and after years of hard moral training. Now, you swallow two or three half-gramme tablets, and there you are. Anybody can be virtuous now. You can carry at least half your mortality about in a bottle. Christianity without tears — that's what *soma* is."

"But the tears are necessary. Don't you remember what Othello said? 'If after every tempest came such calms, may the winds blow till they have wakened death.' There's a story one of the old Indians used to tell us, about the Girl of Mátaski. The young men who wanted to marry her had to do a morning's hoeing in her garden. It seemed easy; but there were flies and mosquitoes, magic ones. Most of the young men simply couldn't stand the biting and stinging. But the one that could — he got the girl."

"Charming! But in civilized countries," said the

Controller, "you can have girls without hoeing for them, and there aren't any flies or mosquitoes to sting you. We got rid of them all centuries ago."

The Savage nodded, frowning. "You got rid of them. Yes, that's just like you. Getting rid of everything unpleasant instead of learning to put up with it. 'Whether 'tis better in the mind to suffer the slings and arrows of outrageous fortune, or to take arms against a sea of troubles and by opposing end them' . . . But you don't do either. Neither suffer nor oppose. You just abolish the slings and arrows. It's too easy."

He was suddenly silent, thinking of his mother. In her room on the thirty-seventh floor, Linda had floated in a sea of singing lights and perfumed caresses — floated away, out of space, out of time, out of the prison of her memories, her habits, her aged and bloated body. And Tomakin, ex-Director of Hatcheries and Conditioning, Tomakin was still on holiday — on holiday from humiliation and pain, in a world where he could not hear those words, that derisive laughter, could not see that hideous face, feel those moist and flabby arms round his neck, in a beautiful world . . .

"What you need," the Savage went on, "is something *with* tears for a change. Nothing costs enough here."

("Twelve and a half million dollars," Henry Foster had protested when the Savage told him that. "Twelve and a half million that's what the new Conditioning Centre cost. Not a cent less.")

"Exposing what is mortal and unsure to all that fortune, death and danger dare, even for an eggshell. Isn't there something in that?" he asked, looking up at Mustapha Mond. "Quite apart from God — though of course God would be a reason for it. Isn't there something in living dangerously?"

"There's a great deal in it," the Controller replied. "Men and women must have their adrenals stimulated from time to time."

"What?" questioned the Savage, uncomprehending.

"It's one of the conditions of perfect health. That's why we've made the V.P.S. treatments compulsory."

"V.P.S.?"

"Violent Passion Surrogate. Regularly once a month. We flood the whole system with adrenin. It's the complete physiological equivalent of fear and rage. All the tonic effects of murdering Desdemona and being murdered by Othello, without any of the inconveniences."

"But I like the inconveniences."

"We don't," said the Controller. "We prefer to do things comfortably."

"But I don't want comfort. I want God, I want poetry, I want real danger, I want freedom, I want goodness. I want sin."

"In fact," said Mustapha Mond, "you're claiming the right to be unhappy."

"All right then," said the Savage defiantly, "I'm claiming the right to be unhappy."

"Not to mention the right to grow old and ugly and impotent; the right to have syphilis and cancer; the right to have too little to eat; the right to be lousy; the right to live in constant apprehension of what may happen to-morrow; the right to catch typhoid; the right to be tortured by unspeakable pains of every kind." There was a long silence.

"I claim them all," said the Savage at last.

Mustapha Mond shrugged his shoulders. "You're welcome," he said.

CHAPTER 18

The door was ajar; they entered.

"John!"

From the bathroom came an unpleasant and characteristic sound.

"Is there anything the matter?" Helmholtz called.

There was no answer. The unpleasant sound was repeated, twice; there was silence. Then, with a click the bathroom door opened and, very pale, the Savage emerged.

"I say," Helmholtz exclaimed solicitously, "you *do* look ill, John!"

"Did you eat something that didn't agree with you?" asked Bernard.

The Savage nodded. "I ate civilization."

"What?"

"It poisoned me; I was defiled. And then," he added, in a lower tone, "I ate my own wickedness."

"Yes, but what exactly? . . . I mean, just now you were . . ."

"Now I am purified," said the Savage. "I drank some mustard and warm water."

The others stared at him in astonishment. "Do you mean to say that you were doing it on purpose?" asked Bernard.

"That's how the Indians always purify themselves." He sat down and, sighing, passed his hand across his forehead. "I shall rest for a few minutes," he said. "I'm rather tired."

"Well, I'm not surprised," said Helmholtz. After a silence, "We've come to say good-bye," he went on in another tone. "We're off to-morrow morning."

"Yes, we're off to-morrow," said Bernard on whose face the Savage remarked a new expression of determined resignation. "And by the way, John," he continued, leaning forward in his chair and laying a hand on the Savage's knee, "I want to say how sorry I am about everything that happened yesterday." He blushed. "How ashamed," he went on, in spite of the unsteadiness of his voice, "how really . . ."

The Savage cut him short and, taking his hand, affectionately pressed it.

"Helmholtz was wonderful to me," Bernard resumed, after a little pause. "If it hadn't been for him, I should . . ."

"Now, now," Helmholtz protested.

There was a silence. In spite of their sadness — because of it, even; for their sadness was the symptom of their love for one another — the three young men were happy.

"I went to see the Controller this morning," said the Savage at last.

"What for?"

"To ask if I mightn't go to the islands with you."

"And what did he say?" asked Helmholtz eagerly.

The Savage shook his head. "He wouldn't let me."

"Why not?"

"He said he wanted to go on with the experiment. But I'm damned," the Savage added, with sudden fury, "I'm damned if I'll go on being experimented with. Not for all the Controllers in the world. I shall go away to-morrow too."

"But where?" the others asked in unison.

The Savage shrugged his shoulders. "Anywhere. I don't care. So long as I can be alone."

From Guildford the down-line followed the Wey valley to Godalming, then, over Milford and Witley, proceeded to Haslemere and on through Petersfield towards Portsmouth. Roughly parallel to it, the upline passed over Worplesden, Tongham, Puttenham, Elstead and Grayshott. Between the Hog's Back and Hindhead there were points where the two lines were not more than six or seven kilometres apart. The distance was too small for careless flyers — particularly at night and when they had taken half a gramme too much. There had been accidents. Serious ones. It had been decided to deflect the upline a few kilometres to the west. Between Grayshott and Tongham four abandoned air-lighthouses marked the course of the old Portsmouth-to-London road. The skies above them were silent and deserted. It was over Selborne, Bordon and Farnham that the helicopters now ceaselessly hummed and roared.

The Savage had chosen as his hermitage the old lighthouse which stood on the crest of the hill between Puttenham and Elstead. The building was of ferro-concrete and in excellent condition — almost too comfortable the Savage had thought when he first explored the place, almost too civilizedly luxurious. He pacified his conscience by promising himself a compensatingly harder self-discipline, purifications the more complete and thorough. His first night in the hermitage was, deliberately, a sleepless one. He spent the hours on his knees praying, now to that Heaven from which the guilty Claudius had begged forgiveness, now in Zuñi to Awonawilona, now to Jesus and Pookong, now to his own guardian animal, the eagle. From time to time he stretched out his arms as though he were on the Cross, and held them thus through long minutes of an ache that gradually increased till it became a tremulous and excruciating agony; held them, in voluntary crucifixion, while he repeated, through clenched teeth (the sweat, meanwhile, pouring down his face), "Oh, forgive me! Oh, make me pure! Oh, help me to be good!" again and again, till he was on the point of fainting from the pain.

When morning came, he felt he had earned the right to inhabit the lighthouse; yet, even though there still *was* glass in most of the windows, even though the view from the platform *was* so fine. For the very reason why he had chosen the lighthouse had become almost instantly a reason for going somewhere else. He had decided to live there because the view was so beautiful, because, from his vantage point, he seemed to be looking out on to the incarnation of a divine being. But who was he to be pampered with the daily and hourly sight of loveliness? Who was he to be living in the visible presence of God? All he deserved to live in was some filthy sty, some blind hole in the ground. Stiff and still aching after his long night of pain, but for that very reason inwardly reassured, he climbed up to the platform of his tower, he looked out over the bright sunrise world which he had regained the right to inhabit. On the north the view was bounded by the long chalk ridge of the Hog's Back, from behind whose eastern extremity rose the towers of the seven sky-scrapers which constituted Guildford. Seeing them, the Savage made a grimace; but he was to become reconciled to them in course of time; for at night they twinkled gaily with geometrical constellations, or else, flood-lighted, pointed their luminous fingers (with a gesture whose significance nobody in England but the Savage now understood) solemnly towards the plumbless mysteries of heaven.

In the valley which separated the Hog's Back from the sandy hill on which the lighthouse stood, Puttenham was a modest little village nine stories high, with silos, a poultry farm, and a small vitamin-D factory. On the other side of the lighthouse, towards the South, the ground fell away in long slopes of heather to a chain of ponds.

Beyond them, above the intervening woods, rose the fourteen-story tower of Elstead. Dim in the hazy English air, Hindhead and Selborne invited the eye into a blue romantic distance. But it was not alone the distance that had attracted the Savage to his lighthouse; the near was as seductive as the far. The woods, the open stretches of heather and yellow gorse, the clumps of Scotch firs, the shining ponds with their over-hanging birch trees, their water lilies, their beds of rushes — these were beautiful and, to an eye accustomed to the aridities of the American desert, astonishing. And then the solitude! Whole days passed during which he never saw a human being. The lighthouse was only a quarter of an hour's flight from the Charing-T Tower; but the hills of Malpais were hardly more deserted than this Surrey heath. The crowds that daily left London, left it only to play Electro-magnetic Golf or Tennis. Puttenham possessed no links; the nearest Riemann-surfaces were at Guildford. Flowers and a land-scape were the only attractions here. And so, as there was no good reason for coming, nobody came. During the first days the Savage lived alone and undisturbed.

Of the money which, on his first arrival, John had received for his personal expenses, most had been spent on his equipment. Before leaving London he had bought four viscose-woollen blankets, rope and string, nails, glue, a few tools, matches (though he intended in due course to make a fire drill), some pots and pans, two dozen packets of seeds, and ten kilogrammes of wheat flour. "No, *not* synthetic starch and cotton-waste flour-substitute," he had insisted. "Even though it is more nourishing." But when it came to pan-glandular biscuits and vitaminized beef-surrogate, he had not been able to resist the shopman's persuasion. Looking at the tins now, he bitterly reproached himself for his weakness. Loathesome civilized stuff! He had made up his mind that he would never eat it, even if he were starving. "That'll teach them," he thought vindictively. It would also teach him.

He counted his money. The little that remained would be enough, he hoped, to tide him over the winter. By next spring, his garden would be producing enough to make him independent of the outside world. Meanwhile, there would always be game. He had seen plenty of rabbits, and there were waterfowl on the ponds. He set to work at once to make a bow and arrows.

There were ash trees near the lighthouse and, for arrow shafts, a whole copse full of beautifully straight hazel saplings. He began by felling a young ash, cut out six feet of unbranched stem, stripped off the bark and, paring by paring, shaved away the white wood, as old Mitsima had taught him, until he had a stave of his own height, stiff at the thickened centre, lively and quick at the slender tips. The work gave him an intense pleasure. After those weeks of idleness in London, with nothing to do, whenever he wanted anything, but to press a switch or turn a handle, it was pure delight to be doing something that demanded skill and patience.

He had almost finished whittling the stave into shape, when he realized with a start that he was singing — *singing!* It was as though, stumbling upon himself from the outside, he had suddenly caught himself out, taken himself flagrantly at fault. Guiltily he blushed. After all, it was not to sing and enjoy himself that he had come here. It was to escape further contamination by the filth of civilized life; it was to be purified and made good; it was actively to make amends. He realized to his dismay that, absorbed in the whittling of his bow, he had forgotten what he had sworn to himself he would constantly remember — poor Linda, and his own murderous unkindness to her, and those loathsome twins, swarming like lice across the mystery of her death, insulting, with their presence, not merely his own grief and repentance, but the very gods themselves. He had sworn to remember, he had sworn unceasingly to make amends. And there was he, sitting happily over his bow-stave, singing, actually singing. . . .

He went indoors, opened the box of mustard, and put some water to boil on the fire.

Half an hour later, three Delta-Minus land-workers from one of the Puttenham Bokanovsky Groups happened to be driving to Elstead and, at the top of the hill, were astonished to see a young man standing outside the abandoned lighthouse stripped to the waist and hitting himself with a whip of knotted cords. His back was horizontally streaked with crimson, and from weal to weal ran thin trickles of blood. The driver of the lorry pulled up at the side of the road and, with his two companions, stared open-mouthed at the extraordinary spectacle. One, two three — they counted the strokes. After the eighth, the young man interrupted his self-punishment to run to the wood's edge and there be violently sick. When he had finished, he picked up the whip and began hitting himself again. Nine, ten, eleven, twelve . . .

"Ford!" whispered the driver. And his twins were of the same opinion.

"Fordey!" they said.

Three days later, like turkey buzzards settling on a corpse, the reporters came.

Dried and hardened over a slow fire of green wood, the bow was ready. The Savage was busy on his arrows. Thirty hazel sticks had been whittled and dried, tipped with sharp nails, carefully nocked. He had made a raid one night on the Puttenham poultry farm, and now had feathers enough to equip a whole armoury. It was at work upon the feathering of his shafts that the first of the reporters found him. Noiseless on his pneumatic shoes, the man came up behind him.

"Good-morning, Mr. Savage," he said. "I am the representative of *The Hourly Radio*."

Startled as though by the bite of a snake, the Savage sprang to his feet, scattering arrows, feathers, glue-pot and brush in all directions.

"I beg your pardon," said the reporter, with genuine compunction. "I had no intention . . ." He touched his hat — the aluminum stove-pipe hat in which he carried his wireless receiver and transmitter. "Excuse my not taking it off," he said. "It's a bit heavy. Well, as I was saying, I am the representative of *The Hourly* . . ."

"What do you want?" asked the Savage, scowling. The reporter returned his most ingratiating smile.

"Well, of course, our readers would be profoundly interested . . ." He put his head on one side, his smile became almost coquettish. "Just a few words from you, Mr. Savage." And rapidly, with a series of ritual gestures, he uncoiled two wires connected to the portable battery buckled round his waist; plugged them simultaneously into the sides of his aluminum hat; touched a spring on the crown — and antennæ shot up into the air; touched another spring on the peak of the brim — and, like a jack-in-the-box, out jumped a microphone and hung there, quivering, six inches in front of his nose; pulled down a pair of receivers over his ears; pressed a switch on the left side of the hat — and from within came a faint waspy buzzing; turned a knob on the right — and the buzzing was interrupted by a stethoscopic wheeze and cackle, by hiccoughs and sudden squeaks. "Hullo," he said to the microphone, "hullo, hullo . . ." A bell suddenly rang inside his hat. "Is that you, Edzel? Primo Mellon speaking. Yes, I've got hold of him. Mr. Savage will now take the microphone and say a few words. Won't you, Mr. Savage?" He looked up at the Savage with another of those winning smiles of his. "Just tell our readers why you came here. What made you leave London (hold on, Edzel!) so very suddenly. And, of course, that whip." (The Savage started. How did they know about the whip?) "We're all crazy to know about the whip. And then something about Civilization. You know the sort of stuff. 'What I think of the Civilized Girl.' Just a few words, a very few . . ."

The Savage obeyed with a disconcerting literalness. Five words he uttered and no more — five words, the same as those he had said to Bernard about the Arch-Community-Songster of Canterbury. *"Háni! Sons éso tse-ná!"* And seizing the reporter by the shoulder, he spun him round (the young man revealed himself invitingly well-covered), aimed and, with all the force and accuracy of a champion foot-and-mouth-baller, delivered a most prodigious kick.

Eight minutes later, a new edition of *The Hourly Radio* was on sale in the streets of London. "HOURLY RADIO REPORTER HAS COCCYX KICKED BY MYSTERY SAVAGE," ran the headlines on the front page. "SENSATION IN SURREY."

"Sensation even in London," thought the reporter when, on his return, he read the words. And a very painful sensation, what was more. He sat down gingerly to his luncheon.

Undeterred by that cautionary bruise on their colleague's coccyx, four other reporters, representing *The New York Times, The Frankfurt Four-Dimensional Continuum, The Fordian Science Monitor,* and *The Delta Mirror,* called that afternoon at the lighthouse and met with receptions of progressively increasing violence.

From a safe distance and still rubbing his buttocks, "Benighted fool!" shouted the man from *The Fordian Science Monitor,* "why don't you take *soma*?"

"Get away!" The Savage shook his fist.

The other retreated a few steps then turned round again. "Evil's an unreality if you take a couple of grammes."

"*Kohakwa iyathtokyai!*" The tone was menacingly derisive.

"Pain's a delusion."

"Oh, is it?" said the Savage and, picking up a thick hazel switch, strode forward.

The man from *The Fordian Science Monitor* made a dash for his helicopter.

After that the Savage was left for a time in peace. A few helicopters came and hovered inquisitively round the tower. He shot an arrow into the importunately nearest of them. It pierced the aluminum floor of the cabin; there was a shrill yell, and the machine went rocketing up into the air with all the acceleration that its super-charger could give it. The others, in future, kept their distance respectfully. Ignoring their tiresome humming (he likened himself in his imagination to one of the suitors of the Maiden of Mátsaki, unmoved and persistent among the winged vermin), the Savage dug at what was to be his garden. After a time the vermin evidently became bored and flew away; for hours at a stretch the sky above his head was empty and, but for the larks, silent.

The weather was breathlessly hot, there was thunder in the air. He had dug all the morning and was resting, stretched out along the floor. And suddenly the thought of Lenina was a real presence, naked and tangible, saying "Sweet!" and "Put your arms round me!" in shoes and socks, perfumed. Impudent strumpet! But oh, oh, her arms round his neck, the lifting of her breasts, her mouth! Eternity was in our lips and eyes. Lenina . . . No, no, no, no! He sprang to his feet and, half naked as he was, ran out of the house. At the edge of the heath stood a clump of hoary juniper bushes. He flung himself against them, he embraced, not the smooth body of his desires, but an armful of green spikes. Sharp, with a thousand points, they pricked him. He tried to think of poor Linda, breathless and dumb, with her clutching hands and the unutterable terror in her eyes. Poor Linda whom he had sworn to remember. But it was still the presence of Lenina that haunted him. Lenina whom he had promised to forget. Even through the stab and sting of the juniper needles, his wincing flesh was aware of her, unescapably real. "Sweet, sweet . . . And if you wanted me too, why didn't you . . ."

The whip was hanging on a nail by the door, ready to hand against the arrival of reporters. In a frenzy the Savage ran back to the house, seized it, whirled it. The knotted cords bit into his flesh.

"Strumpet! Strumpet!" he shouted at every blow as though it were Lenina (and how frantically, without knowing it, he wished it were), white, warm, scented, infamous Lenina that he was flogging thus. "Strumpet!" And then, in a voice of despair, "Oh, Linda, forgive me.

Forgive me, God. I'm bad. I'm wicked. I'm . . . No, no, you strumpet, you strumpet!"

From his carefully constructed hide in the wood three hundred metres away, Darwin Bonaparte, the Feely Corporation's most expert big game photographer had watched the whole proceedings. Patience and skill had been rewarded. He had spent three days sitting inside the bole of an artificial oak tree, three nights crawling on his belly through the heather, hiding microphones in gorse bushes, burying wires in the soft grey sand. Seventy-two hours of profound discomfort. But now the great moment had come — the greatest, Darwin Bonaparte had time to reflect, as he moved among his instruments, the greatest since his taking of the famous all-howling stereoscopic feely of the gorillas' wedding. "Splendid," he said to himself, as the Savage started his astonishing performance. "Splendid!" He kept his telescopic cameras carefully aimed — glued to their moving objective; clapped on a higher power to get a close-up of the frantic and distorted face (admirable!); switched over, for half a minute, to slow motion (an exquisitely comical effect, he promised himself); listened in, meanwhile, to the blows, the groans, the wild and raving words that were being recorded on the sound-track at the edge of his film, tried the effect of a little amplification (yes, that was decidedly better); was delighted to hear, in a momentary lull, the shrill singing of a lark; wished the Savage would turn round so that he could get a good close-up of the blood on his back — and almost instantly (what astonishing luck!) the accommodating fellow did turn round, and he was able to take a perfect close-up.

"Well, that was grand!" he said to himself when it was all over. "Really grand!" He mopped his face. When they had put in the feely effects at the studio, it would be a wonderful film. Almost as good, thought Darwin Bonaparte, as the *Sperm Whale's Love-Life* — and that, by Ford, was saying a good deal!

Twelve days later *The Savage of Surrey* had been released and could be seen, heard and felt in every first-class feely-palace in Western Europe.

The effect of Darwin Bonaparte's film was immediate and enormous. On the afternoon which followed the evening of its release John's rustic solitude was suddenly broken by the arrival overhead of a great swarm of helicopters.

He was digging in his garden — digging, too, in his own mind, laboriously turning up the substance of his thought. Death — and he drove in his spade once, and again, and yet again. And all our yesterdays have lighted fools the way to dusty death. A convincing thunder rumbled through the words. He lifted another spadeful of earth. Why had Linda died? Why had she been allowed to become gradually less than human and at last . . . He shuddered. A good kissing carrion. He planted his foot on his spade and stamped it fiercely into the tough ground. As flies to wanton boys are we to the gods; they kill us for their sport. Thunder again; words that proclaimed themselves true — truer somehow than truth itself. And yet that same Gloucester had called them ever-gentle gods. Besides, thy best of rest is sleep and that thou oft provok'st; yet grossly fear'st thy death which is no more. No more than sleep. Sleep. Perchance to dream. His spade struck against a stone; he stooped to pick it up. For in that sleep of death, what dreams? . . .

A humming overhead had become a roar; and suddenly he was in shadow, there was something between the sun and him. He looked up, startled, from his digging, from his thoughts; looked up in a dazzled bewilderment, his mind still wandering in that other world of truer-than-truth, still focussed on the immensities of death and deity; looked up and saw, close above him, the swarm of hovering machines. Like locusts they came, hung poised, descended all around him on the heather. And from out of the bellies of these giant grasshoppers stepped men in white viscose-flannels, women (for the weather was hot) in acetate-shantung pyjamas or velveteen shorts and sleeveless, half-unzipped singlets — one couple from each. In a few minutes there were dozens of them, standing in a wide circle round the lighthouse, staring, laughing, clicking their cameras, throwing (as to an ape) peanuts, packets of sex-hormone chewing-gum, pan-glandular *petits beurres*. And every moment — for across the Hog's Back the stream of traffic now flowed unceasingly — their numbers increased. As in a nightmare, the dozens became scores, the scores hundreds.

The Savage had retreated towards cover, and now, in the posture of an animal at bay, stood with his back to the wall of the lighthouse, staring from face to face in speechless horror, like a man out of his senses.

From this stupor he was aroused to a more immediate sense of reality by the impact on his cheek of a well-aimed packet of chewing-gum. A shock of startling pain — and he was broad awake, awake and fiercely angry.

"Go away!" he shouted.

The ape had spoken; there was a burst of laughter and hand-clapping. "Good old Savage! Hurrah, hurrah!" And through the babel he heard cries of: "Whip, whip, the whip!"

Acting on the word's suggestion, he seized the bunch of knotted cords from its nail behind the door and shook it at his tormentors.

There was a yell of ironical applause.

Menacingly he advanced towards them. A woman cried out in fear. The line wavered at its most immediately threatened point, then stiffened again, stood firm. The consciousness of being in overwhelming force had given these sightseers a courage which the Savage had not expected of them. Taken aback, he halted and looked round.

"Why don't you leave me alone?" There was an almost plaintive note in his anger.

"Have a few magnesium-salted almonds!" said the man who, if the Savage were to advance, would be the first to be attacked. He held out a packet. "They're really very good, you know," he added, with a rather nervous smile of propitiation. "And the magnesium salts will help to keep you young."

The Savage ignored his offer. "What do you want with me?" he asked, turning from one grinning face to another. "What do you want with me?"

"The whip," answered a hundred voices confusedly. "Do the whipping stunt. Let's see the whipping stunt."

Then, in unison and on a slow, heavy rhythm, "We —want—the—whip," shouted a group at the end of the line. "We—want—the—whip."

Others at once took up the cry, and the phrase was repeated, parrot-fashion, again and again, with an ever-growing volume of sound, until, by the seventh or eighth reiteration, no other word was being spoken. "We—want—the—whip."

They were all crying together; and, intoxicated by the noise, the unanimity, the sense of rhythmical atonement, they might, it seemed, have gone on for hours — almost indefinitely. But at about the twenty-fifth repetition the proceedings were startlingly interrupted.

Yet another helicopter had arrived from across the Hog's Back, hung poised above the crowd, then dropped within a few yards of where the Savage was standing, in the open space between the line of sightseers and the lighthouse. The roar of the air screws momentarily drowned the shouting; then, as the machine touched the ground and the engines were turned off: "We—want—the—whip; we—want—the—whip," broke out again in the same loud, insistent monotone.

The door of the helicopter opened, and out stepped, first a fair and ruddy-faced young man, then, in green velveteen shorts, white shirt, and jockey cap, a young woman.

At the sight of the young woman, the Savage started, recoiled, turned pale.

The young woman stood, smiling at him — an uncertain, imploring, almost abject smile. The seconds passed. Her lips moved, she was saying something; but the sound of her voice was covered by the loud reiterated refrain of the sightseers.

"We—want—the—whip! We—want—the—whip!"

The young woman pressed both hands to her left side, and on that peach-bright, doll-beautiful face of hers appeared a strangely incongruous expression of yearning distress. Her blue eyes seemed to grow larger, brighter; and suddenly two tears rolled down her cheeks. Inaudibly, she spoke again; then, with a quick, impassioned gesture stretched out her arms towards the Savage, stepped forward.

"We—want—the—whip! We—want . . ."

And all of a sudden they had what they wanted.

"Strumpet!" The Savage had rushed at her like a madman. "Fitchew!" Like a madman, he was slashing at her with his whip of small cords.

Terrified, she had turned to flee, had tripped and fallen in the heather. "Henry, Henry!" she shouted. But her ruddy-faced companion had bolted out of harm's way behind the helicopter.

With a whoop of delighted excitement the line broke; there was a convergent stampede towards that magnetic centre of attraction. Pain was a fascinating horror.

"Fry, lechery, fry!" Frenzied, the Savage slashed again.

Hungrily they gathered round, pushing and scrambling like swine about the trough.

"Oh, the flesh!" The Savage ground his teeth. This time it was on his shoulders that the whip descended. "Kill it, kill it!"

Drawn by the fascination of the horror of pain and, from within, impelled by that habit of cooperation, that desire for unanimity and atonement, which their conditioning had so ineradicably implanted in them, they began to mime the frenzy of his gestures, striking at one another as the Savage struck at his own rebellious flesh, or at that plump incarnation of turpitude writhing in the heather at his feet.

"Kill it, kill it, kill it . . ." The Savage went on shouting.

Then suddenly somebody started singing "Orgy-porgy" and, in a moment, they had all caught up the refrain and, singing, had begun to dance. Orgy-porgy, round and round and round, beating one another in six-eight time. Orgy-porgy . . .

It was after midnight when the last of the helicopters took its flight. Stupefied by *soma*, and exhausted by a long-drawn frenzy of sensuality, the Savage lay sleeping in the heather. The sun was already high when he awoke. He lay for a moment, blinking in owlish incomprehension at the light; then suddenly remembered — everything.

"Oh, my God, my God!" He covered his eyes with his hand.

That evening the swarm of helicopters that came buzzing across the Hog's Back was a dark cloud ten kilometres long. The description of last night's orgy of atonement had been in all the papers.

"Savage!" called the first arrivals, as they a-lighted from their machine. "Mr. Savage!"

There was no answer.

The door of the lighthouse was ajar. They pushed it open and walked into a shuttered twilight. Through an archway on the further side of the room they could see the bottom of the staircase that led up to the higher floors. Just under the crown of the arch dangled a pair of feet.

"Mr. Savage!"

Slowly, very slowly, like two unhurried compass needles, the feet turned towards the right; north, north-east, east, south-east, south, south-south-west; then paused, and, after a few seconds, turned as unhurriedly back towards the left. South-south-west, south, south-east, east. . . .

Table of Contents

Related Readings

The Politics of
Stem Cell Research
by Jeffrey P. Kahn, Ph.D., M.P.H.
(June 25, 2001)

The Bush administration is attracting attention for its effort to resolve the question of federal funding for human embryonic stem cell research.

Thinking about whether the research should go forward very much depends on one's view of the status of human embryos and how that ought to be weighed against the promise of stem cell research. So far, the best stem cells seem to come from human embryos, which are destroyed in the process of removing stem cells.

For some, embryonic stem cell research requires the taking of a human life, but for others, it represents the acceptable use of cells from very early stage embryos that would never have developed into a person. The research is considered critical by many scientists and disease advocacy groups, who say it could lead to treatment — or even cures — for conditions like diabetes and Parkinson's. But for others, the promise of stem cell research is outweighed by the moral cost of the source of the cells.

What are the policy options, what are their ethical implications, and can there really be a middle ground?

This debate began in the early 1980s, with a ban on federal funding for research involving either the use of fetal tissue or harm to human embryos. The ban did not make such research illegal, but it prevented the use of federal dollars to support it.

The ban was lifted for funding of fetal tissue research in 1993, when promising approaches were proposed for treatment of Parkinson's disease, but the ban on federal funding for human embryo research remains in effect.

Before the change in administrations, the National Institutes of Health (NIH) requested a legal ruling about whether funding of research involving embryonic stem cells would violate the ban. The ruling was that research on the cells themselves would not violate the ban, so long as federal funding was not used to collect the cells from embryos. The Clinton administration proposed to fund research proposals that adhered to this distinction, though no funding was granted before President Clinton left office.

The fine distinction in the NIH policy created the possibility of a private market for supplying stem cells for publicly funded research. For those who object to the destruction of embryos for stem cell research, this represents an unacceptable end-run around the intent of the original research ban.

In practice, the embryos used in the collection of stem cells were left over from attempts to assist reproduction — donated by couples who used *in vitro* fertilization. There are about 200,000 frozen embryos throughout the world, all awaiting decisions about what should be done with them. The vast majority will either remain frozen indefinitely or be discarded, so proponents of embryonic stem cell research ask, why not allow them to be donated for research purposes? To ban such use would have the effect of exporting stem cell research overseas to countries where it is not illegal — in fact, the United Kingdom has already given approval to such research.

White House policymakers must decide how far to go in allowing stem cell research, or whether to ban funding altogether. One possible compromise is to fund only research using the embryonic stem cell lines that already exist, and refuse funding for research that relies on future destruction of embryos, even if the cells are collected in the private sector. But the administration would still have a problem with "dirty hands" — public monies would be spent on research that required and relied on the destruction of embryos. Limiting research to a few cell lines is less than scientists hope for, but may be all the Bush administration can muster.

Editor's Note: After the writing of this article President Bush in fact decided to allow federal funding for research only if existing embryonic stem cell lines were used.

"Baby, It's You! And You, and You..."
from *Time* Magazine
by Nancy Gibbs et al.
(February 19, 2001)

Renegade scientists say they are ready to start applying the technology of cloning to human beings. Can they really do it, and how scary would that be?

Before we assume that the market for human clones consists mainly of narcissists who think the world deserves more of them or neo-Nazis who dream of cloning Hitler or crackpots and mavericks and mischief makers of all kinds, it is worth taking a tour of the marketplace. We might just meet ourselves there.

Imagine for a moment that your daughter needs a bone-marrow transplant and no one can provide a match; that your wife's early menopause has made her infertile; or that your five-year-old has drowned in a lake and your grief has made it impossible to get your mind around the fact that he is gone forever. Would the news then really be so easy to dismiss that around the world, there are scientists in labs pressing ahead with plans to duplicate a human being, deploying the same technology that allowed Scottish scientists to clone Dolly the sheep four years ago?

All it took was that first headline about the astonishing ewe, and fertility experts began to hear the questions every day. Our two-year-old daughter died in a car crash; we saved a lock of her hair in a baby book. Can you clone her? Why does the law allow people more freedom to destroy fetuses than to create them?

My husband had cancer and is sterile.
Can you help us?

The inquiries are pouring in because some scientists are ever more willing to say yes, perhaps we can. Last month a well-known infertility specialist, Panayiotis Zavos of the University of Kentucky, announced that he and Italian researcher Severino Antinori, the man who almost seven years ago helped a 62-year-old woman give birth using donor eggs, were forming a consortium to produce the first human clone. Researchers in South Korea claim they have already created a cloned human embryo, though they destroyed it rather than implanting it in a surrogate mother to develop. Recent cover stories in *Wired* and the *New York Times Magazine* tracked the efforts of the Raelians, a religious group committed to, among other things, welcoming the first extraterrestrials when they appear. They intend to clone the cells of a dead 10-month-old boy whose devastated parents hope, in effect, to bring him back to life as a newborn. The Raelians say they have the lab and the scientists, and — most important, considering the amount of trial and error involved — they say they have 50 women lined up to act as surrogates to carry a cloned baby to term.

Given what researchers have learned since Dolly, no one thinks the mechanics of cloning are very hard: take a donor egg, suck out the nucleus, and hence the DNA, and fuse it with, say, a skin cell from the human being copied. Then, with the help of an electrical current, the reconstituted cell should begin growing into a genetic duplicate. "It's inevitable that someone will try and someone will succeed," predicts Delores Lamb, an infertility expert at Baylor University. The consensus among biotechnology specialists is that within a few years — some scientists believe a few months — the news will break of the birth of the first human clone.

At that moment, at least two things will happen — one private, one public. The meaning of what it is to be human — which until now has involved, at the very least, the mysterious melding of two different people's DNA — will shift forever, along with our understanding of the relationship between parents and children, means and ends, ends and beginnings. And as a result, the conversation that has occupied scientists and ethicists for years, about how much man should mess with nature when it comes to reproduction, will drop onto every kitchen table, every pulpit, every politician's desk. Our fierce national debate over issues like abortion and euthanasia will seem tame and transparent compared with the questions that human cloning raises.

That has many scientists scared to death. Because even if all these headlines are hype and we are actually far away from seeing the first human clone, the very fact that at this moment, the research is proceeding underground, unaccountable, poses a real threat. The risk lies not just with potential babies born deformed, as many animal clones are; not just with desperate couples and cancer patients and other potential "clients" whose hopes may be raised and hearts broken and life savings wiped out. The immediate risk is that a backlash against renegade science might strike at responsible science as well.

The more scared people are of some of this research, scientists worry, the less likely they are to tolerate any of it. Yet variations on cloning technology are already used in biotechnology labs all across the country. It is these techniques that will allow, among other things, the creation of cloned herds of sheep and cows that produce medicines in their milk. Researchers also hope that one day, the ability to clone adult human cells will make it possible to "grow" new hearts and livers and nerve cells.

But some of the same techniques could also be used to grow a baby. Trying to block one line of research could impede another and so reduce the chances of finding cures for ailments such as Alzheimer's and Parkinson's, cancer and heart disease. Were some shocking break-through in human cloning to cause "an over-compensatory response by legislators," says Rockefeller University cloning expert Tony Perry, "that could be disastrous. At some point, it will potentially cost lives." So we are left with choices and trade-offs and a need to think through whether it is this technology that alarms us or just certain ways of using it.

By day, Randolfe Wicker, 63, runs a lighting shop in New York City. But in his spare time, as spokesman for the Human Cloning Foundation, he is the face of cloning fervor in the U.S. "I took one step in this adventure, and it took over me like quicksand,"says Wicker. He is planning to have some of his skin cells stored for future cloning. "If I'm not cloned before I die, my estate will be set up so that I can be cloned after," he says, admitting, however, that he hasn't found a lawyer willing to help. "It's hard to write a will with all these uncertainties," he concedes. "A lot of lawyers will look at me crazy."

As a gay man, Wicker has long been frustrated that he cannot readily have children of his own; as he gets older, his desire to reproduce grows stronger. He knows that a clone would not be a photocopy of him but talks about the traits the boy might possess: "He will like the color blue, Middle Eastern food and romantic Spanish music that's out of fashion." And then he hints at the heart of his motive. "I can thumb my nose at Mr. Death and say, 'You might get me, but you're not going to get all of me,'" he says. "The special formula that is me will live on into another lifetime. It's a partial triumph over death. I would leave my imprint not in sand but in cement."

This kind of talk makes ethicists conclude that even people who think they know about cloning — let alone the rest of us — don't fully understand its implications. "Cloning," notes ethicist Arthur Caplan of the University of Pennsylvania, "can't make you immortal because clearly the clone is a different person. If I take twins and shoot one of them, it will be faint consolation to the dead one that the other one is still running around, even though they are genetically identical. So the road to immortality is not through cloning."

Still, cloning is the kind of issue so confounding that you envy the purists at either end of the argument. For the Roman Catholic Church, the entire question is one of world view: whether life is a gift of love or just one more industrial product, a little more valuable than most. Those who believe that the soul enters the body at the moment of conception think it is fine for God to make clones; He does it about 4,000 times a day, when a fertilized egg splits into identical twins. But when it comes to massaging a human life, for the scientist to do mechanically what God does naturally is to interfere with His work, and no possible benefit can justify that presumption.

On the other end of the argument are the libertarians who don't like politicians or clerics or ethics boards interfering with what they believe should be purely individual decisions. Reproduction is a most fateful lottery; in their view, cloning allows you to hedge your bet. While grieving parents may be confused about the technology — cloning, even if it works, is not resurrection — their motives are their own business. As for infertile couples, "we are interested in giving people the gift of life," Zavos, the aspiring cloner, told *Time* this week. "Ethics is a wonderful word, but we need to look beyond the ethical issues here. It's not an ethical issue. It's a medical issue. We have a duty here. Some people need this to complete the life cycle, to reproduce."

In the messy middle are the vast majority of people who view the prospect with a vague alarm, an uneasy sense that science is dragging us into dark woods with no paths and no easy way to turn back. Ian Wilmut, the scientist who cloned Dolly but has come out publicly against human cloning, was not trying to help sheep have genetically related children. "He was trying to help farmers produce genetically improved sheep," notes Hastings Center ethicist Erik Parens. "And surely that's how the technology will go with us too." Cloning, Parens says, "is not simply this isolated technique out there that a few deluded folks are going to avail themselves of, whether they think it is a key to immortality or a way to bring someone back from the dead. It's part of a much bigger project. Essentially the big-picture question is, To what extent do we want to go down the path of using reproductive technologies to genetically shape our children?"

At the moment, the American public is plainly not ready to move quickly on cloning. In a *Time/*

CNN poll last week, 90% of respondents thought it was a bad idea to clone human beings. "Cloning right now looks like it's coming to us on a magic carpet, piloted by a cult leader, sold to whoever can afford it," says ethicist Caplan. "That makes people nervous."

And it helps explain why so much of the research is being done secretly. We may learn of the first human clone only months, even years, after he or she is born — if the event hasn't happened already, as some scientists speculate. The team that cloned Dolly waited until she was seven months old to announce her existence. Creating her took 277 tries, and right up until her birth, scientists around the world were saying that cloning a mammal from an adult cell was impossible. "There's a significant gap between what scientists are willing to talk about in public and their private aspirations," says British futurist Patrick Dixon. "The law of genetics is that the work is always significantly further ahead than the news. In the digital world, everything is hyped because there are no moral issues — there is just media excitement. Gene technology creates so many ethical issues that scientists are scared stiff of a public reaction if the end results of their research are known."

Of course, attitudes often change over time. *In-vitro* fertilization was effectively illegal in many states 20 years ago, and the idea of trans- planting a heart was once considered horrifying. Public opinion on cloning will evolve just as it did on these issues, advocates predict. But in the meantime, the crusaders are mostly driven underground. Princeton biologist Lee Silver says fertility specialists have told him that they have no problem with cloning and would be happy to provide it as a service to their clients who could afford it. But these same specialists would never tell inquiring reporters that, Silver says — it's too hot a topic right now. "I think what's happened is that all the mainstream doctors have taken a hands-off approach because of this huge public outcry. But I think what they are hoping is that some fringe group will pioneer it and that it will slowly come into the mainstream and then they will be able to provide it to their patients."

All it will take, some predict, is that first snapshot. "Once you have a picture of a normal baby with 10 fingers and 10 toes, that changes everything," says San Mateo, Calif., attorney and cloning advocate Mark Eibert, who gets inquiries from infertile couples every day. "Once they put a child in front of the cameras, they've won." On the other hand, notes Gregory Pence, a professor of philosophy at the University of Alabama at Birmingham and author of *Who's Afraid of Human Cloning?*, "if the first baby is defective, cloning will be banned for the next 100 years."

"I wouldn't mind being the first person cloned if it were free. I don't mind being a guinea pig," says Doug Dorner, 35. He and his wife Nancy both work in health care. "We're not afraid of technology," he says. Dorner has known since he was 16 that he would never be able to have children the old-fashioned way. A battle with lymphoma left him sterile, so when he and Nancy started thinking of having children, he began following the scientific developments in cloning more closely. The more he read, the more excited he got. "Technology saved my life when I was 16," he says, but at the cost of his fertility. "I think technology should help me have a kid. That's a fair trade."

Talk to the Dorners, and you get a glimpse of choices that most parents can scarcely imagine having to make. Which parent, for instance, would they want to clone? Nancy feels she would be bonded to the child just from carrying him, so why not let the child have Doug's genetic material? Does it bother her to know she would, in effect, be raising her husband as a little boy? "It wouldn't be that different. He already acts like a five-year-old sometimes," she says with a laugh.

How do they imagine raising a cloned child, given the knowledge they would have going in? "I'd know exactly what his basic drives were," says Doug. The boy's dreams and aspirations, however, would be his own, Doug insists. "I used to dream of being a fighter pilot," he recalls, a dream lost when he got cancer. While they are at it, why not clone Doug twice? "Hmm. Two of the same kid," Doug ponders. "We'll cross that bridge when we come to it. But I know we'd never clone our clone to have a second child. Once you start copying something, who knows what the next copies will be like?"

In fact the risks involved with cloning mammals are so great that Wilmut, the premier cloner, calls it "criminally irresponsible" for scientists to be experimenting on humans today. Even after four years of practice with animal cloning, the failure rate is still overwhelming: 98% of embryos never implant or die off during gestation or soon after birth. Animals that survive can be nearly twice as big at birth as is normal, or have extra-large organs or heart trouble or poor immune systems. Dolly's "mother" was six years old when she was cloned. That may explain why Dolly's cells show signs of being older than they actually are — scientists joked that she was really a sheep in lamb's clothing. This deviation raises the possibility that beings created by cloning adults will age abnormally fast.

"We had a cloned sheep born just before Christmas that was clearly not normal," says

Wilmut. "We hoped for a few days it would improve and then, out of kindness, we euthanized it, because it obviously would never be healthy." Wilmut believes "it is almost a certainty" that cloned human children would be born with similar maladies. Of course, we don't euthanize babies. But these kids would probably die very prematurely anyway. Wilmut pauses to consider the genie he has released with Dolly and the hopes he has raised. "It seems such a profound irony," he says, "that in trying to make a copy of a child who has died tragically, one of the most likely outcomes is another dead child."

That does not seem to deter the scientists who work on the Clonaid project run by the Raelian sect. They say they are willing to try to clone a dead child. Though their outfit is easy to mock, they may be even further along than the competition, in part because they have an advantage over other teams. A formidable obstacle to human cloning is that donor eggs are a rare commodity, as are potential surrogate mothers, and the Raelians claim to have a supply of both.

Earlier this month, according to Brigitte Boisselier, Clonaid's scientific director, somewhere in North America, a young woman walked into a Clonaid laboratory whose location is kept secret. Then, in a procedure that has been done thousands of times, a doctor inserted a probe, removed 15 eggs from the woman's ovaries and placed them in a chemical soup. Last week two other Clonaid scientists, according to the group, practiced the delicate art of removing the genetic material from each of the woman's eggs. Within the next few weeks, the Raelian scientific team plans to place another cell next to the enucleated egg.

This second cell, they say, comes from a 10-month-old boy who died during surgery.

The two cells will be hit with an electrical charge, according to the scenario, and will fuse, forming a new hybrid cell that no longer has the genes of the young woman but now has the genes of the dead child. Once the single cell has developed into six to eight cells, the next step is to follow the existing, standard technology of assisted reproduction: gingerly insert the embryo into a woman's womb and hope it implants. Clonaid scientists expect to have implanted the first cloned human embryo in a surrogate mother by next month.

Even if the technology is basic, and even if it appeals to some infertile couples, should grieving parents really be pursuing this route? "It's a sign of our growing despotism over the next generation," argues University of Chicago bioethicist Leon Kass. Cloning introduces the possibility of parents' making choices for their children far more fundamental than whether to give them piano lessons or straighten their teeth. "It's not just that parents will have particular hopes for these children," says Kass. "They will have expectations based on a life that has already been lived. What a thing to do — to carry on the life of a person who has died."

The libertarians are ready with their answers. "I think we're hypercritical about people's reasons for having children," says Pence. "If they want to re-create their dead children, so what?" People have always had self-serving reasons for having children, he argues, whether to ensure there's someone to care for them in their old age or to relive their youth vicariously. Cloning is just another reproductive tool; the fact that it is not a perfect tool, in Pence's view, should not mean it should be outlawed altogether. "We know there are millions of girls who smoke and drink during pregnancy, and we know what the risks to the fetus are, but we don't do anything about it," he notes. "If we're going to regulate cloning, maybe we should regulate that too."

Olga Tomusyak was two weeks shy of her seventh birthday when she fell out of the window of her family's apartment. Her parents could barely speak for a week after she died. "Life is empty without her," says her mother Tanya, a computer programmer in Sydney, Australia. "Other parents we have talked to who have lost children say it will never go away." Olga's parents cremated the child before thinking of the cloning option. All that remains are their memories, some strands of hair and three baby teeth, so they have begun investigating whether the teeth could yield the nuclei to clone her one day.

While it is theoretically possible to extract DNA from the teeth, scientists say it is extremely unlikely.

"You can't expect the new baby will be exactly like her. We know that is not possible," says Tanya. "We think of the clone as her twin or at least a baby who will look like her." The parents would consider the new little girl as much Olga's baby as their own. "Anything that grows from her will remind us of her," says Tanya. Though she and her husband are young enough to have other children, for now, this is the child they want.

Once parents begin to entertain the option of holding on to some part of a child, why would the reverse not be true? "Bill" is a guidance counselor in Southern California, a forty-something expectant father who has been learning everything he can about the process of cloning. But it is not a lost child he is looking to replicate. He is interested in cloning his mother, who is dying of pancreatic cancer. He has talked to her husband, his siblings, everyone except her doctor — and her, for fear that it will make her think they have given up hope on her. He confides, "We might end up making a decision without telling her."

His goal is to extract a tissue specimen from his mother while it's still possible and store it, to await the day when — if — cloning becomes technically safe and socially acceptable. Late last week, as his mother's health weakened, the family began considering bringing up the subject with her because they need her cooperation to take the sample. Meanwhile, Bill has already contacted two labs about tissue storage, one as a backup. "I'm in touch with a couple of different people who might be doing that," he says, adding that both are in the U.S. "It seems like a little bit of an underground movement, you know — people are a little reluctant that if they announce it, they might be targeted, like the abortion clinics."

If Bill's hopes were to materialize and the clone were born, who would that person be? "It wouldn't be my mother but a person who would be very similar to my mother, with certain traits. She has a lot of great traits: compassion and intelligence and looks," he says. And yet, perhaps inevitably, he talks as though this is a way to rewind and replay the life of someone he loves.

"She really didn't have the opportunities we had in the baby-boom generation, because her parents experienced the Depression and the war," he says. "So the feeling is that maybe we could give her some opportunities that she didn't have. It would be sort of like we're taking care of her now. You know how when your parents age and everything shifts, you start taking care of them? Well, this would be an extension of that."

A world in which cloning is commonplace confounds every human relationship, often in ways most potential clients haven't considered. For instance, if a woman gives birth to her own clone, is the child her daughter or her sister? Or, says bioethicist Kass, "let's say the child grows up to be the spitting image of its mother. What impact will that have on the relationship between the father and his child if that child looks exactly like the woman he fell in love with?" Or, he continues, "let's say the parents have a cloned son and then get divorced. How will the mother feel about seeing a copy of the person she hates most in the world every day? Everyone thinks about cloning from the point of view of the parents. No one looks at it from the point of view of the clone."

If infertile couples avoid the complications of choosing which of them to clone and instead look elsewhere for their DNA, what sorts of values govern that choice? Do they pick an uncle because he's musical, a willing neighbor because she's brilliant? Through that door lies the whole unsettling debate about designer babies, fueled already by the commercial sperm banks that promise genius DNA to prospective parents. Sperm banks give you a shot at passing along certain traits; cloning all but assures it.

Whatever the moral quandaries, the one-stop-shopping aspect of cloning is a plus to many gay couples. Lesbians would have the chance to give birth with no male involved at all; one woman could contribute the ovum, the other the DNA. Christine DeShazo and her partner Michele Thomas of Miramar, Fla., have been in touch with Zavos about producing a baby this way. Because they have already been ostracized as homosexuals, they aren't worried about the added social sting that would come with cloning. "Now [people] would say, 'Not only are you a lesbian, you are a cloning lesbian,'" says Thomas. As for potential health problems, "I would love our baby if its hand was attached to its head," she says. DeShazo adds, "If it came out green, I would love it. Our little alien . . ."

Just as women have long been able to have children without a male sexual partner through artificial insemination, men could potentially become dads alone: replace the DNA from a donor egg with one's own and then recruit a surrogate mother to carry the child. Some gay-rights advocates even argue that should sexual preference prove to have a biological basis, and should genetic screening lead to terminations of gay embryos, homosexuals would have an obligation to produce gay children through cloning.

All sorts of people might be attracted to the idea of the ultimate experiment in single parent-hood. Jack Barker, a marketing specialist for a corporate-relocation company in Minneapolis, is 36 and happily unmarried. "I've come to the conclusion that I don't need a partner but can still have a child," he says. "And a clone would be the perfect child to have because I know exactly what I'm getting." He understands that the child would not be a copy of him. "We'd be genetically identical," says Barker. "But he wouldn't be raised by my parents — he'd be raised by me." Cloning, he hopes, might even let him improve on the original: "I have bad allergies and asthma. It would be nice to have a kid like you but with those improvements."

Cloning advocates view the possibilities as a kind of liberation from travails assumed to be part of life: the danger that your baby will be born with a disease that will kill him or her, the risk that you may one day need a replacement organ and die waiting for it, the helplessness you feel when confronted with unbearable loss. The challenge facing cloning pioneers is to make the case convincingly that the technology itself is not immoral, however immorally it could be used.

One obvious way is to point to the broader benefits. Thus cloning proponents like to attach themselves to the whole arena of stem-cell research, the brave new world of inquiry into how the wonderfully pliable cells of seven-day-old embryos behave. Embryonic stem cells eventually turn into every kind of tissue, including brain, muscle, nerve and blood. If scientists could harness their powers, these cells could serve as the body's self-repair kit, providing cures for Parkinson's, diabetes, Alzheimer's and paralysis. Actors Christopher Reeve [1952–2004], paralyzed by a fall from a horse, and Michael J. Fox, who suffers from Parkinson's, are among those who have pushed Congress to overturn the government's restrictions on federal funding of embryonic-stem-cell research.

But if the cloners want to climb on this train in hopes of riding it to a public relations victory, the mainstream scientists want to push them off. Because researchers see the potential benefits of understanding embryonic stem cells as immense, they are intent on avoiding controversy over their use. Being linked with the human-cloning activists is their nightmare. Says Michael West, president of Massachusetts-based Advanced Cell Technology Act, a biotech company that uses cloning technology to develop human medicines: "We're really concerned that if someone goes off and clones a Raelian, there could be an overreaction to this craziness

— especially by regulators and Congress. We're desperately concerned — and it's a bad metaphor — about throwing the baby out with the bath water."

Scientists at ACT are leery of revealing too much about their animal-cloning research, much less their work on human embryos. "What we're doing is the first step toward cloning a human being, but we're not cloning a human being," says West. "The miracle of cloning isn't what people think it is. Cloning allows you to make a genetically identical copy of an animal, yes, but in the eyes of a biologist, the real miracle is seeing a skin cell being put back into the egg cell, taking it back in time to when it was an undifferentiated cell, which then can turn into any cell in the body." Which means that new, pristine tissue could be grown in labs to replace damaged or diseased parts of the body. And since these replacement parts would be produced using skin or other cells from the suffering patient, there would be no risk of rejection. "That means you've solved the age-old problem of transplantation," says West. "It's huge."

So far, the main source of embryonic stem cells is "leftover" embryos from IVF clinics; cloning embryos could provide an almost unlimited source. Progress could come even faster if Congress were to lift the restrictions on federal funding — which might have the added safety benefit of the federal oversight that comes with federal dollars. "We're concerned about George W.'s position and whether he'll let existing guidelines stay in place," says West. "People are begging to work on those cells."

That impulse is enough to put the Roman Catholic Church in full revolt; the Vatican has long condemned any research that involves creating and experimenting with human embryos, the vast majority of which inevitably perish. The church believes that the soul is created at the moment of conception, and that the embryo is worthy of protection. It reportedly took 104 attempts before the first IVF baby, Louise Brown, was born; cloning Dolly took more than twice that. Imagine, say opponents, how many embryos would be lost in the effort to clone a human. This loss is mass murder, says David Byers, director of the National Conference of Catholic Bishops' commission on science and human values. "Each of the embryos is a human being simply by dint of its genetic makeup."

Last week 160 bishops and five cardinals met for three days behind closed doors in Irving, Texas, to wrestle with the issues biotechnology presents. But the cloning debate does not break cleanly even along religious lines. "Rebecca," a thirty-something San Francisco Bay Area resident, spent seven years trying to conceive a child with her husband. Having "been to hell and back" with IVF treatment, Rebecca is now as thoroughly committed to cloning as she is to Christianity. "It's in the Bible — be fruitful and multiply," she says. "People say, 'You're playing God.' But we're not. We're using the raw materials the good Lord gave us. What does the doctor do when the heart has stopped? They have to do direct massage of the heart. You could say the doctor is playing God. But we save a life. With human cloning, we're not so much saving a life as creating a new being by manipulation of the raw materials, DNA, the blueprint for life. You're simply using it in a more creative manner."

A field where emotions run so strong and hope runs so deep is fertile ground for profiteers and charlatans. In her effort to clone her daughter

Olga, Tanya Tomusyak contacted an Australian firm, Southern Cross Genetics, which was founded three years ago by entrepreneur Graeme Sloan to preserve DNA for future cloning. In an e-mail, Sloan told the parents that Olga's teeth would provide more than enough DNA — even though that possibility is remote. "All DNA samples are placed into computer-controlled liquid-nitrogen tanks for long-term storage," he wrote. "The cost of doing a DNA fingerprint and genetic profile and placing the sample into storage would be $2,500. Please note that all of our fees are in U.S. dollars."

When contacted by *Time*, Sloan admitted, "I don't have a scientific background. I'm pure business. I'd be lying if I said I wasn't here to make a dollar out of it. But I would like to see organ cloning become a reality." He was inspired to launch the business, he says, after a young cousin died of leukemia. "There's megadollars involved, and everyone is racing to be the first," he says. As for his own slice of the pie, Sloan says he just sold his firm to a French company, which he refuses to name, and he was heading for Hawaii last week. The Southern Cross factory address turns out to be his mother's house, and his "office" phone is answered by a man claiming to be his brother David — although his mother says she has no son by that name.

The more such peddlers proliferate, the more politicians will be tempted to invoke prohibitions. Four states — California, Louisiana, Michigan and Rhode Island — have already banned human cloning, and this spring Texas may become the fifth. Republican state senator Jane Nelson has introduced a bill in Austin that would impose a fine of as much as $1 million for researchers who use cloning technology to initiate pregnancy in humans. The proposed Texas law would permit embryonic-stem-cell research, but bills proposed in other states were so broadly written that they could have stopped those activities too.

"The short answer to the cloning question," says ethicist Caplan, "is that anybody who clones somebody today should be arrested. It would be barbaric human experimentation. It would be killing fetuses and embryos for no purpose, none, except for curiosity. But if you can't agree that that's wrong to do, and if the media can't agree to condemn rather than gawk, that's a condemnation of us all."

Chapter 3 from
Brave New World Revisited
by Aldous Huxley
(1894-1963)

The shortest and broadest road to the nightmare of Brave New World leads, as I have pointed out, through over-population and the accelerating increase of human numbers — twenty-eight hundred millions today, fifty-five hundred millions by the turn of the century, with most of humanity facing the choice between anarchy and totalitarian control. But the increasing pressure of numbers upon available resources is not the only force propelling us in the direction of totalitarianism. This blind biological enemy of freedom is allied with immensely powerful forces generated by the very advances in technology of which we are most proud. Justifiably proud, it may be added; for these advances are the fruits of genius and persistent hard work, of logic, imagination and self-denial — in a word, of moral and intellectual virtues for which one can feel nothing but admiration. But the Nature of Things is such that nobody in this world ever gets anything for nothing. These amazing and admirable advances have had to be paid for. Indeed, like last year's washing machine, they are still being paid for — and each installment is higher than the last. Many historians, many sociologists and psychologists have written at length, and with deep concern, about the price that Western man has had to pay and will go on paying for technological progress. They point out, for example, that democracy can hardly be expected to flourish in societies where political and economic power is being progressively concentrated and centralized.

But the progress of technology has led and is still leading to just such a concentration and centralization of power. As the machinery of mass production is made more efficient it tends to become more complex and more expensive — and so less available to the enterpriser of limited means. Moreover, mass production cannot work without mass distribution; but mass distribution raises problems which only the largest producers can satisfactorily solve. In a world of mass production and mass distribution the Little Man, with his inadequate stock of working capital, is at a grave disadvantage. In competition with the Big Man, he loses his money and finally his very existence as an independent producer; the Big Man has gobbled him up. As the Little Men disappear, more and more economic power comes to be wielded by fewer and fewer people. Under a dictatorship the Big Business, made possible by advancing technology and the consequent ruin of Little Business, is controlled by the State — that is to say, by a small group of party leaders and the soldiers, policemen and civil servants who carry out their orders. In a capitalist democracy, such as the United States, it is controlled by what Professor C. Wright Mills has called the Power Elite. This Power Elite directly employs several millions of the country's working force in its factories, offices and stores, controls many millions more by lending them the money to buy its products, and, through its ownership of the media of mass communication, influences the thoughts, the feelings and the actions of virtually everybody. To parody the words of Winston Churchill, never have so many been manipulated by so few. We are far indeed from Jefferson's ideal of a genuinely free society composed of a hierarchy of self-governing units

— "the elementary republics of the wards, the county republics, the State republics and the Republic of the Union, forming a gradation of authorities."

We see, then, that modern technology has led to the concentration of economic and political power, and to the development of a society controlled (ruthlessly in the totalitarian states, politely and inconspicuously in the democracies) by Big Business and Big Government. But societies are composed of individuals and are good only insofar as they help individuals to realize their potentialities and to lead a happy and creative life. How have individuals been affected by the techno-logical advances of recent years? Here is the answer to this question given by a philosopher-psychiatrist, Dr. Erich Fromm:

Our contemporary Western society, in spite of its material, intellectual and political progress, is increasingly less conducive to mental health, and tends to undermine the inner security, happiness, reason and the capacity for love in the individual; it tends to turn him into an automaton who pays for his human failure with increasing mental sickness, and with despair hidden under a frantic drive for work and so-called pleasure.

Our "increasing mental sickness" may find expression in neurotic symptoms. These symptoms are conspicuous and extremely distressing. But "let us beware," says Dr. Fromm, "of defining mental hygiene as the prevention of symptoms. Symptoms as such are not our enemy, but our friend; where there are symptoms there is a conflict, and conflict always indicates that the forces of life which strive for integration and happiness are still fighting." The really hopeless victims of mental illness are to be found among those who appear to be most normal.

"Many of them are normal because they are so well adjusted to our mode of existence, because their human voice has been silenced so early in their lives, that they do not even struggle or suffer or develop symptoms as the neurotic does." They are normal not in what may be called the absolute sense of the word; they are normal only in relation to a profoundly abnormal society. Their perfect adjustment to that abnormal society is a measure of their mental sickness. These millions of abnormally normal people, living without fuss in a society to which, if they were fully human beings, they ought not to be adjusted, still cherish "the illusion of individuality," but in fact they have been to a great extent deindividualized. Their conformity is developing into something like uniformity. But "uniformity and freedom are incompatible. Uniformity and mental health are incompatible too. . . . Man is not made to be an automaton, and if he becomes one, the basis for mental health is destroyed."

In the course of evolution nature has gone to endless trouble to see that every individual is unlike every other individual. We reproduce our kind by bringing the father's genes into contact with the mother's. These hereditary factors may be combined in an almost infinite number of ways. Physically and mentally, each one of us is unique. Any culture which, in the interests of efficiency or in the name of some political or religious dogma, seeks to standardize the human individual, commits an outrage against man's biological nature.

Science may be defined as the reduction of multiplicity to unity. It seeks to explain the endlessly diverse phenomena of nature by ignoring the uniqueness of particular events, concentrating on what they have in common and finally abstracting some kind of "law," in terms of which they make sense and can be effectively dealt with. For examples, apples fall from the tree and the moon moves across the sky. People had been observing these facts from time immemorial. With Gertrude Stein they were convinced that an apple is an apple is an apple, whereas the moon is the moon is the moon. It remained for Isaac Newton to perceive what these very dissimilar phenomena had in common, and to formulate a theory of gravitation in terms of which certain aspects of the behavior of apples, of the heavenly bodies and indeed of everything else in the physical universe could be explained and dealt with in terms of a single system of ideas. In the same spirit the artist takes the innumerable diversities and uniquenesses of the outer world and his own imagination and gives them meaning within an orderly system of plastic, literary or musical patterns. The wish to impose order upon confusion, to bring harmony out of dissonance and unity out of multiplicity is a kind of intellectual instinct, a primary and funda-mental urge of the mind. Within the realms of science, art and philosophy the workings of what I may call this "Will to Order" are mainly beneficent. True, the Will to Order has produced many pre-mature syntheses based upon insufficient evidence, many absurd systems of metaphysics and theology, much pedantic mistaking of notions for realities, of symbols and abstractions for the data of immediate experience. But these errors, however regrettable, do not do much harm, at any rate directly — though it sometimes happens that a bad philosophical system may do harm indirectly, by being used as a justification for senseless and inhuman actions. It is in the social sphere, in the realm of politics and economics, that the Will of the Order becomes really dangerous.

Here the theoretical reduction of unmanageable multiplicity to comprehensible unity becomes the practical reduction of human diversity to subhuman uniformity, of freedom to servitude. In politics the equivalent of a fully developed scientific theory or philosophical system is a totalitarian dictatorship. In economics, the equivalent of a beautifully composed work of art is the smoothly running factory in which the workers are perfectly adjusted to the machines. The Will to Order can make tyrants out of those who merely aspire to clear up a mess. The beauty of tidiness is used as a justification for despotism.

Organization is indispensable; for liberty arises and has meaning only within a self-regulating community of freely co-operating individuals. But, though indispensable, organization can also be fatal. Too much organization transforms men and women into automata, suffocates the creative spirit and abolishes the very possibility of freedom. As usual, the only safe course is in the middle, between the extremes of laissez-faire at one end of the scale and of total control at the other.

During the past century the successive advances in technology have been accompanied by corresponding advances in organization. Complicated machinery has had to be matched by complicated social arrangements, designed to work as smoothly and efficiently as the new instruments of production. In order to fit into these organizations, individuals have had to deindividualize themselves, have had to deny their native diversity and conform to a standard pattern, have had to do their best to become automata.

The dehumanizing effects of over-organization are reinforced by the dehumanizing effects of over-population. Industry, as it expands, draws an ever greater proportion of humanity's increasing numbers into large cities. But life in large cities is not conducive to mental health (the highest incidence of schizophrenia, we are told, occurs among the swarming inhabitants of industrial slums); nor does it foster the kind of responsible freedom within small self-governing groups, which is the first condition of a genuine democracy. City life is anonymous and, as it were, abstract. People are related to one another, not as total personalities, but as the embodiments of economic functions or, when they are not at work, as irresponsible seekers of entertainment. Subjected to this kind of life, individuals tend to feel lonely and insignificant. Their existence ceases to have any point or meaning.

Biologically speaking, man is a moderately gregarious, not a completely social animal — a creature more like a wolf, let us say, or an elephant, than like a bee or an ant. In their original form human societies bore no resemblance to the hive or the ant heap; they were merely packs. Civilization is, among other things, the process by which primitive packs are transformed into an analogue, crude and mechanical, of the social insects' organic communities. At the present time the pressures of over-population and technological change are accelerating this process. The termitary has come to seem a realizable and even, in some eyes, a desirable ideal. Needless to say, the ideal will never in fact be realized. A great gulf separates the social insect from the not too gregarious, big-brained mammal; and even though the mammal should do his best to imitate the insect, the gulf would remain. However hard they try, men cannot create a social organism, they can only create an organization. In the process of trying to create an organism they will merely create a totalitarian despotism.

Brave New World presents a fanciful and somewhat ribald picture of a society, in which the attempt to recreate human beings in the likeness of termites has been pushed almost to the limits of the possible. That we are being propelled in the direction of Brave New World is obvious. But no less obvious is the fact that we can, if we so desire, refuse to co-operate with the blind forces that are propelling us. For the moment, however, the wish to resist does not seem to be very strong or widespread. As Mr. William Whyte has shown in his remarkable book, *The Organization Man,* a new Social Ethic is replacing our traditional ethical system — the system in which the individual is primary. The key words in this Social Ethic are "adjustment," "adaptation," "socially orientated behavior," "belongingness," "acquisition of social skills," "team work," "group living," "group loyalty," "group dynamics," "group thinking," "group creativity." Its basic assumption is that the social whole has greater worth and significance than its individual parts, that inborn biological differences should be sacrificed to cultural uniformity, that the rights of the collectivity take precedence over what the eighteenth century called the Rights of Man. According to the Social Ethic, Jesus was completely wrong in asserting that the Sabbath was made for man. On the contrary, man was made for the Sabbath, and must sacrifice his inherited idiosyncrasies and pretend to be the kind of standardized good mixer that organizers of group activity regard as ideal for their purposes. This ideal man is the man who displays "dynamic conformity" (delicious phrase!) and an intense loyalty to the group, an unflagging desire to subordinate himself, to belong. And the ideal man must have an ideal wife, highly gregarious, infinitely adaptable and not merely resigned to the fact that her husband's first loyalty is to the Corporation, but actively loyal on her own account. "He for God only," as Milton said of Adam and Eve, "she for God in him." And in one important respect the wife of the ideal organization man is a good deal worse off than our First Mother. She and Adam were permitted by the Lord to be completely uninhibited in the matter of "youthful dalliance."

> Nor turned, I ween,
> Adam from his fair spouse, nor Eve the rites
> Mysterious of connubial love refused.

Today, according to a writer in the *Harvard Business Review,* the wife of the man who is trying to live up to the ideal proposed by the Social Ethic, "must not demand too much of her husband's time and interest. Because of his single-minded concentration on his job, even his sexual activity must be relegated to a secondary place." The monk makes vows of poverty, obedience and chastity. The organization man is allowed to be rich, but promises obedience ("he accepts authority without resentment, he looks up to his superiors" — *Mussolini ha sempre ragione*) and he must be prepared, for the greater glory of the organization that employs him, to forswear even conjugal love.

It is worth remarking that, in *1984,* the members of the Party are compelled to conform to a sexual ethic of more than Puritan severity. In *Brave New World,* on the other hand, all are permitted to indulge their sexual impulses without let or hindrance. The society described in Orwell's fable is a society permanently at war, and the aim of its rulers is first, of course, to exercise power for its own delightful sake and, second, to keep their subjects in that state of constant tension which a state of constant war demands of those who wage it. By crusading against sexuality the bosses are able to maintain the required tension in their followers and at the same time can satisfy their lust for power in a most gratifying way. The society described in *Brave New World* is a world-state, in which war has been eliminated and where the first aim of the rulers is at all costs to keep their subjects from making trouble. This they achieve by (among other methods) legalizing a degree of sexual freedom (made possible by the abolition of the family) that practically guarantees the Brave New Worlders against any form of destructive (or creative) emotional tension. In *1984* the lust for power is satisfied by inflicting pain; in *Brave New World,* by inflicting a hardly less humiliating pleasure.

The current Social Ethic, it is obvious, is merely a justification after the fact of the less desirable consequences of over-organization. It represents a pathetic attempt to make a virtue of necessity, to extract a positive value from an unpleasant datum. It is a very unrealistic, and therefore very dangerous, system of morality. The social whole, whose value is assumed to be greater than that of its component parts, is not an organism in the sense that a hive or a termitary may be thought of as an organism. It is merely an organization, a piece of social machinery. There can be no value except in relation to life and awareness. An organization is neither conscious nor alive. Its value is instrumental and derivative. It is not good in itself; it is good only to the extent that it promotes the good of the individuals who are the parts of the collective whole. To give organizations precedence over persons is to subordinate ends to means. What happens when ends are subordinated to means was clearly demonstrated by Hitler and Stalin. Under their hideous rule personal ends were subordinated to organizational means by a mixture of violence and propaganda, systematic terror and the systematic manipulation of minds. In the more efficient dictatorships of tomorrow there will probably be much less violence than under Hitler and Stalin. Under their hideous rule personal ends were subordinated to organizational means by a mixture of violence and propaganda, systematic terror and the systematic manipulation of minds. In the more efficient dictatorships of tomorrow there will probably be much less violence than under Hitler and Stalin. The future dictator's subjects will be painlessly regimented by a corps of highly trained social engineers. "The challenge of social engineering in our time," writes an enthusiastic advocate of this new science, "is like the challenge of technical engineering fifty years ago. If the first half of the twentieth century was the era of the technical engineers, the second half may well be the era of the social engineers"— and the twenty-first century, I suppose, will be the era of World Controllers, the scientific caste system and Brave New World. To the question *quis custodiet custodes?* — Who will mount guard over our guardians, who will engineer the engineers? — the answer is a bland denial that they need any supervision. There seems to be a touching belief among certain Ph.D.'s in sociology that Ph.D.'s in sociology will never be corrupted by power. Like Sir Galahad's, their strength is as the strength of ten because their heart is pure — and their heart is pure because they are scientists and have taken six thousand hours of social studies.

Alas, higher education is not necessarily a gaurantee of higher virtue, or higher political wisdom. And to these misgivings on ethical and psychological grounds must be added misgivings of a purely scientific character. Can we accept the theories on which the social engineers base their practice, and in terms of which they justify their manipulations of human beings? For example, Professor Elton Mayo tells us categorically that "man's desire to be continuously associated *in work with his fellows* is a strong, if not the strongest human characteristic." This, I would say, is manifestly untrue. Some people have the kind of desire described by Mayo; others do not. It is a matter of temperament and inherited constitution. Any social organization based upon the assumption that "man" (whoever "man" may be) desires to be continuously associated with his fellows would be, for many individual men and women, a bed of Procrustes. Only by being amputated or stretched upon the rack could they be adjusted to it.

Again, how romantically misleading are the lyrical accounts of the Middle Ages with which many contemporary theorists of social relations adorn their works! "Membership in a guild, manorial estate or village protected medieval man throughout his life and gave him peace and serenity." Protected him from what, we may ask. Certainly not from remorseless bullying at the hands of his superiors. And along with all that "peace and serenity" there was, throughout the Middle Ages, an enormous amount of chronic frustration, acute unhappiness and a passionate resentment against the rigid, hierarchical system that permitted no vertical movement up the social ladder and, for those who were bound to the land, very little horizontal movement in space.

The impersonal forces of over-population and over-organization, and the social engineers who are trying to direct these forces, are pushing us in the direction of a new medieval system. This revival will be made more acceptable than the original by such Brave-New-Worldian amenities as infant conditioning, sleep-teaching and drug-induced euphoria; but, for the majority of men and women, it will still be a kind of servitude.

Subliminal Advertising

Comments on articles compiled by John Leckenby

(Bracketed references at end of each comment refer to sources listed starting on page 308)

THE ORIGINATOR OF THE TERM "SUBLIMINAL ADVERTISING"— JAMES VICARY

Subliminal advertising is a technique of exposing consumers to product pictures, brand names, or other marketing stimuli without the consumers having conscious awareness. Once exposed to a subliminal marketing stimulus, the consumer is believed to decode the information and act upon it without being able to acknowledge a communication stimulus [26].

What is commonly referred to as subliminal advertising has been the focus of a great deal of attention for more than three decades. The term "subthreshold effects," first popularized by Packard in 1957, preceded the popular notion of "subliminal advertising" whose originator is James Vicary. [21]. Perhaps the most widely known claim concerning the power of subliminal advertising was made in 1957 by James Vicary, a market researcher. He claimed that over a six-week period, 45,699 patrons at a movie theater in Fort Lee, New Jersey, were shown two advertising messages, Eat Pop-corn and Drink Coca-Cola, while they watched the film *Picnic*. According to Vicary, a message was flashed for 3/1000 of a second once every five seconds. The duration of the messages was so short that they were never consciously perceived. Despite the fact that the customers were not aware of perceiving the message, Vicary claimed that over the six-week period the sales of popcorn rose 57% and the sales of Coca-Cola rose 18.1%. Vicary's claims are often accepted as established facts. However, Vicary never released a detailed description of his study, and there has never been any independent evidence to support his claims. Also, in an interview with *Advertising Age* in 1962, Vicary stated that the original study was a fabrication. The weight of the evidence suggests that it was indeed a fabrication [13].

THE SECOND WIDESPREAD WORRY ABOUT SUBLIMINAL ADVERTISING—WILSON BRYAN KEY

More recently, Key has claimed that hidden or embedded messages are widespread and effective. In the 1970s, Wilson Bryan Key wrote such books as *Subliminal Seduction and Media Sexploitation* in which he claimed subliminal sexual symbols or objects are often used to entice consumers to buy and use various products and services. One of Key's most famous claims is that the word *sex* was often embedded in products and advertisements. For example, he claimed that the word *sex* was printed on Ritz crackers and was embedded in the ice cubes of the drink shown in a well-known ad for Gilbey's Gin. According to Key, despite the fact that the embedded words are not consciously perceived, they are unconsciously perceived and can elicit sexual arousal, which in turn makes the products more attractive to consumers [13].

EMPIRICAL EVIDENCES OF SUBLIMINAL ADVERTISING

Even though Key's claims have been widely discredited by academicians who have examined marketing applications scientifically, widespread use of the term "subliminal advertising" in connection with a paucity of empirical evidence that subliminal techniques are used by the advertising industry served to increase the level of public awareness of subliminal advertising [21]. Actually, despite the result of the study conducted by Rogers and Seiler that the majority of advertising practitioners denied ever using subliminal techniques [22], according to Rogers and Smith, 74.3% of their subjects were aware of subliminal advertising and 72.2% of respondents who believed advertisers deliberately included subliminal messages (61.5% of subjects) also believed that subliminal advertising was effective [21]. A few empirical evidences that serve to keep the public's fear of subliminal advertising alive are as follows.

The Pepsi Cool Can

In 1990, Pepsi actually withdrew one of its "Cool Can" designs after someone protested that Pepsi was subliminally manipulating people by designing the cans such that when six-packs were stacked at grocery stores, the word SEX would emerge from the seemingly random design. Critics alleged that the red and blue lines on the "Cool Can" design were far from random [27].

The Camel

Tobacco companies have also been the target of accusations of visual embeds. One common alleged embed of sexually suggestive imagery is on the standard pack of Camel cigarettes. Apparently, if you look closely enough at the [front left] leg of the camel on the cigarette pack, you can see an image of a naked man standing tall facing the rear of the camel with a private part showing. [27].

The 'RATS' Ad

In September 2000, two Democratic senators asked the Federal Communications Commission for a review of the Republican National Committee's ad.

It was discovered that if the ad was slowed down, the word "RATS" appeared clearly on the screen in large, white letters superimposed over the words "The Gore Prescription Plan" while an announcer criticized Gore's prescription drug plan. In a fraction of a second, the word disappeared, and the words "BUREAUCRATS DECIDE" showed up in smaller letters. The "RATS" ad ran more than 4,400 times in 33 markets nationwide in two weeks, costing the RNC more than $2,576,600 [28].

THE EFFECTS OF SUBLIMINAL ADVERTISING

Experimental results

The notion of subliminal perception has generated substantial controversy for several decades, both within and outside psychology. Although controversy persists, there seems to be little doubt that observers' responses can be shown to be affected by stimuli they claim not to have seen [16].

The premise of subliminal perception has been that the unconscious mind can receive information presented below the threshold for conscious perception. The result may be attitude and even behavioral change based on information that the individual is not consciously aware of receiving [20]. Some psychology studies have shown the effects of subliminal perceptions on the affective responses, and, in other research, experiments have shown that subliminal stimuli can influence high-level cognitive processes, including preferences for geometric shapes, liking of individuals, personality judgments, and ratings of one's self-concept. In addition, recent investigations suggest that subliminally presented stimuli can influence behavior [4].

However, with the possible exceptions of Hawkins' [6], Cuperfain and Clarke's [3], and

Kilbourne, Painton, and Ridley's [7] studies, the empirical studies directed toward investigating subliminal effects have failed to show conclusive results in an advertising context [24]. Hawkins' finding of increased thirst ratings following subliminal exposure to COKE have been used as empirical evidence that subliminal advertising can directly affect consumption-relevant behavior. However, Beatty and Hawkins, who conducted a replication study of Hawkins' found no significant differences in the mean thirst ratings [2]. In addition, Cuperfain and Clarke's, and Kilbourne, Painton, and Ridley's studies contain so many methodological flaws that they cannot be said to have advanced the case regarding any possible advertising application [16].

More recently, some evidence suggests that subliminal messages may influence affective reactions to marketing stimuli. For example, Aylesworth [and Goldstein] [1] found that sexually suggestive subliminal embeds in an ad significantly increased upbeat feelings and significantly increased negative feeling. However, they said that even though clearly, subliminal embeds have some influence on the audience, it appears to be very subtle and to consist almost entirely of effects on feelings rather than cognitive measures. And they added that the effects on feelings scales are in opposing directions and may cancel each other out, and concluded that traditional ad measures such as recall, attitudes toward advertisements and attitudes toward brands have not been sensitive to the possible effects of subliminal advertising.

The major issue of subliminal advertising is whether consumer exposure to subliminal stimuli can effectively manipulate the behavior of consumers and provide advertisers with a tool to bypass consumers' defenses without their being aware of what is happening. Trappery [26] conducted a meta-analysis to scientifically evaluate whether or not subliminal marketing stimuli are an effective means for influencing consumer choice behavior. After collecting the effect sizes of subliminal stimuli on consumer behavior from 23 studies selected based on a predetermined set of rules, he calculated a total of these 23 effect sizes. The resulting correlation coefficient ($r = 0.0585$) falls between the effect of aspirin on heart attacks (0.03) and the relationship between alcohol abuse and a tour of duty in Vietnam (0.07), leading to the conclusion that subliminal advertising has little influence on the consumer's decision to select between alternatives.

EXPLANATIONS ABOUT THE INEFFECTIVENESS OF SUBLIMINAL ADVERTISING

The original popular fears of subliminal influence are founded on a vague notion that weak and typically sordid stimuli are presented by advertisers at a rate too rapid or in a form too disguised to be detected by even a vigilant observer, and that these stimuli somehow penetrate one's defense. Marketing scholars have tended not to address this notion directly, but rather have discounted subliminal advertising on the grounds the approach will not work in the real world [24].

Moore's arguments

Moore summarized his arguments against subliminal advertising along two lines of reasoning:

1. Subliminal stimuli are usually so weak that they are not perceived by observers, and even if they are, they are usually nullified by other, strong stimuli present at the same time.

2. People are very much in control of their own

overt responses to stimuli, and hence, even if they perceive subliminal stimuli, they can screen out any attempts to effect undesired behavior.

Moore continued the discussion in terms of two possible kinds of subliminal influence which he labeled "strong effects" and "weak effects." "Weak effects" are said to be influences on emotional responses, such as attitudes or wishes, while "strong effects" are considered actual manipulations of buyer behavior. Moore contended that "weak effects" are unlikely because the stimulus energy of a subliminal stimuli are embedded among many others. According to him, it is most improbable that a subliminal stimulus could compete successfully with other supraliminal sources of stimulation. That is why such carefully controlled conditions are necessary for obtaining the effects in the laboratory [16]. He also argued that "strong effects" are improbable because the control that individuals have over their own overt behavior prevents undesired actions [24].

Saegert's arguments

Saegert argued that Silverman's psychodynamic activation theory provided a conceptual basis for how changes in behavior might result from subliminal stimulation. Silverman's theory is derived from the Freudian notion that unconscious wishes can serve to activate feelings within an individual, and these feelings may lead to specific behaviors. An example of one of Silverman's theories is the hypothesis that severe feelings of depression result from the suppression of unconscious aggression wishes which cannot be expressed overtly in a socially desirable manner. According to him, these wishes are susceptible to aggression-arousing stimuli which in turn lead to turning of unconscious aggression against the self, thus activating greater feelings of depression. Silverman offered support for this psychodynamic activation principle through tachistoscopic presentation of subliminal stimuli [24].

However, Saegert said that even though Silverman's theory is useful in outlining a plausible model of subliminal influence, at the same time, especially in an advertising context, it points out the great difficulty that an advertiser would have in developing a practical program to take advantage of subliminal advertising techniques. That is, stimulus conditions Silverman's theory specifies make it highly unlikely that successful use of subliminal messages could be achieved in a promotional context. These include the following: (a) the wish to be heightened by the subliminal stimulus must be unconscious, (b) the message must be subliminal, (c) to be effective, the presented stimulus must precisely match the unconscious wishin psychological meaning. In addition, the advertiser should be careful indeed to assure that the desired responses are expressible in a socially acceptable way [24].

Conclusion

The notion of subliminal perception has generated substantial controversy for several decades, both within and outside psychology. Even though it has not yet been impossible to describe reliable conditions under which *subliminal* effects are likely to occur for at least three reasons: inconsistent use of the term subliminal, lack of adequately precise and standardized processes, and lack of an adequate conception of unconscious processes [20], there seems to be little doubt that observers' responses can be shown to be affected by stimuli they claim not to have seen [16]. In addition, the results of the studies that demonstrated different characteristics that distinguish conscious from unconscious perception provide rather compelling evidence for the importance of unconscious perceptual processes in influencing our reactions to stimuli [12].

However, with a paucity of exceptions, the empirical studies directed toward investigating subliminal effects have failed to show conclusive results in an advertising context [24]. And, with these results, marketing scholars have discounted subliminal advertising on the grounds the approach will not work in the real world [24].

Their first reason to discount the effectiveness of subliminal advertising is a clear difference between subliminal effects found in a laboratory study and the possible real world effects of subliminal advertising. In the lab experiment, subjects are in a controlled environment with their full attention devoted to the messages. However, at home in an actual television viewing situation, by contrast, viewers pay much less attention to, and are much less involved in, the processing of advertisements. Further, there are many sources of distraction surrounding the viewer, which would minimize the likelihood of subliminal processing should a subliminal ad be presented [2]. Another is that influence from weak, subliminal stimuli is likely to pale in comparison to the highly salient and powerful stimuli already competing for the consumers' attention [4]. In addition, despite the fact that there is no convincing empirical evidence showing that subliminal messages affect behavior, which is, of course, the ultimate goal of advertising, practitioners would be unwise to test ethical boundaries of advertising when consciously processed elements of ads can easily be used to accomplish the same goals more effectively [1].

However, despite the overall lack of empirical evidence showing that subliminal advertising may be effective, a large percentage of consumers believe firms use subliminal advertising to enhance sales, and various surveys have demonstrated fairly widespread public acceptance of the notion of subliminal advertising [15]. Several decades have already passed after Vicary and Key claimed the power of subliminal advertising. It is not just to accuse them of giving the advertising industry a bad name till now. We'd better figure out what keeps the public's fear of subliminal manipulation alive. It could be the scientific community that does a poor job of communicating its findings, or it could be media that popularize pseudo-science, or it could be a few unethical practitioners [who] rely on subliminal tactics. Whatever the reason is, advertisers should pay attention to consumer opinions about subliminal advertising because these perceptions, whether true or not, influence their views on advertisements and the industry as a whole.

REFERENCES

[1] Aylesworth, A. B., & Goodstein, R. C. (1999), "Effects of Archetypal Embeds on Feelings: An Indirect Route to Affecting Attitudes, *Journal of Advertising*, 28(3), 73.

[2] Beatty, S. E., & Hawkins, D. I. (1989), "Subliminal Stimulation: Some New Data and Interpretation," *Journal of Advertising*, 18(3), 4-8.

[3] Cuperfain, R., & Clarke, T. K. (1985), "A New Perspective on Subliminal Perception,"*Journal of Advertising*, 14(1), 36-41.

[4] Epley, N., Savitsy, K., & Kachelski, R. A. (1999), "What Every Skeptic Should Know About Subliminal Persuasion," *Skeptical Inquirer*, 23(5), 40-46.

[5] Groeger, J. A. (1984), "Evidence of Unconscious Semantic Processing from a Forced-Error Situation," *British Journal of Psychology*, 75, 305-14.

[6] Hawkins, D. (1970), "The Effects of Subliminal on Drive Level and Brand Preference," *Journal of Marketing Research*, 7(3), 322-6.

[7] Kilbourne, W. E., Painton, S., & Ridley, D. (1985), "The Effect of Sexual Embedding on Responses to Magazine Advertisements," *Journal of Advertising*, 14(2), 48-56.

[8] Kunst-Wilson, W. R., & Zajonc, R. B. (1980), "Affective Discrimination of Stimuli That Cannot Be Recognized," *Science*, 207, 557-8.

[9] Leibniz, G. W. (1981), *New Essays on Human Understandings*, Cambridge, England: Cambridge University Press. (Original works written ca. 1704).

[10] Marcel, A. J. (1980), "Conscious and Preconscious Recognition of Polysemous Words: Locating the Selective Effects of Prior Verbal Context," *Attention and Performance VIII*, Hillside, NJ: Erlbaum, 435-57.

[11] Merikle, P. M. (1992), "Perception Without Awareness: Critical Issues," *American Psychologist*, 47(6), 792-5.

[12] Merikle, P. M., & Daneman, M. (1998), "Psychological Investigation of Unconscious Perception," *Journal of Consciousness Studies*, 5, 5-18.

[13] Merikle, P. M. (2000). *Encyclopedia of Psychology*, Available: http://watarts.uwaterloo.ca/~pmerikle/papers/subliminalperception.html

[14] Moore, T. E. (1982), "Subliminal Advertising: What You See Is What You Get," *Journal of Marketing*, 6 (Spring), 38-47.

[15] Moore, T. E. (1988), "Guest Editorial," *Psychology and Marketing*, 5(4), 291-6.

[16] Moore, T. E. (1988), "The Case Against Subliminal Manipulation," *Psychology and Marketing*, 5(4), 297-316.

[17] Moore, T. E. (1992), "Subliminal Perception: Facts and Fallacies," *Skeptical Inquirer*, 1992 (Spring). Available: http://www.csicop.org/si/9204/subliminal-perception.html

[18] Murphy, S. T., & Zajonc, R. B. (1993), "Affect, Cognition, and Awareness: Affective Priming with Optimal and Suboptimal Stimulus Exposures," *Journal of Personality and Social Psychology*, 64, 723-39.

[19] Neuberg, S. L. (1988), "Behavioral Implications of Information Presented Outside of Conscious Awareness: The Effect of Subliminal Presentation of Trait Information on Behavior in the Prisoner's Dilemma Game," *Social Cognition*, 6, 207-30.

[20] Pratkanis, A. R., & Greenwald, A. G. (1988), "Recent Perspectives on Unconscious Processing: Still No Marketing Applications," *Psychology & Marketing*, 5 (Winter), 337-53.

[21] Rogers, M., & Smith, K. H. (1993), "Public Perception of Subliminal Advertising: Why Practitioners Shouldn't Ignore This Issue," *Journal of Advertising Research*, 33(2), 10.

[22] Rogers, M., & Seiler, C. A. (1994), "The Answer Is No: A National Survey of Advertising Industry Practitioners and Their Clients About Whether They Use Subliminal Advertising," *Journal of Advertising Research*, 34(2), 36.

[23] Rosen, D. L., & Singh, S. N. (1992), "An Investigation of Subliminal Embed Effect on Multiple Measures of Advertising Effectiveness," *Psychology & Marketing*, 9(2), 157-73.

[24] Saegert, J. (1987), "Why Marketing Should Quit Giving Subliminal Advertising the Benefit of the Doubt," *Psychology & Marketing*, 4, 107-20.

[25] Theus, K. T. (1994), "Subliminal Advertising and the Psychology of Processing Unconscious Stimuli: A Review of Research," *Psychology & Marketing*, 11(3), 271-90.

[26] Trappery, C. (1996), "A Meta-Analysis of Consumer Choice and Subliminal Advertising," *Psychology & Marketing*, 13(5), 517-30.

[27] Available at: http://sbed.umn.edu/subliminal/index.html

[28] Available at: http://www.cnn.com/2000/ALLPOLITICS/stories/09/13/bush.ad/index.html

Current Issues About Drug Use

DRUGS AND TERROR: UNDERSTANDING THE LINK AND THE IMPACT ON AMERICA

http://www.theantidrug.com/drugs_terror/
understanding_impact.asp

> *"It's so important for Americans to know that the traffic in drugs finances the work of terror, sustaining terrorists, that terrorists use drug profits to fund their cells to commit acts of murder. If you quit drugs, you join the fight against terror in America."*
>
> — President George W. Bush

There is an undeniable link between acts of terror and illicit drugs. Law enforcement officials around the world have long recognized this close connection, but a changing world and recent events have made this link more relevant in the daily lives of all Americans. The bottom line is simple: terror and drug groups are linked in a mutually-beneficial relationship by money, tactics, geography and politics. Americans must understand that our individual choices about illicit drug use have the power to support or undermine our nation's war on terrorism.

Drugs form an important part of the financial infrastructure of terror networks. Twelve of the 28 terror organizations identified by the U.S. Department of State in October 2001 traffic in drugs. Drug income is the primary source of revenue for many of the more powerful international terrorist groups. The Revolutionary Armed Forces of Colombia (FARC) receives about $300 million from drug sales annually. The United Self Defense Forces of Colombia (AUC) relies on the illegal drug trade for 40-70 percent of its income. Peru's Shining Path is more dependent on drug money than ever before. And the Taliban regime in Afghanistan, which provided safe haven to Osama Bin Laden and his Al Qaeda network, used revenues from opium and heroin to stay in power. In 2000, Afghanistan was responsible for more than 70 percent of the world's opium trade, resulting in significant income to the Taliban.

Drug traffickers and terrorists use similar methods to achieve their criminal ends. Most importantly, they share a common disregard for human life. Many drug trafficking organizations engage in acts that most people would consider terrorist in nature. These include gruesome public killing of innocents, large-scale bombings intended to intimidate government, kidnappings and torture. These organizations prey on young people both to grow their ranks and to keep their illegitimate businesses operating. Money laundering, arms-for-drugs exchanges and use of phony documents are common among terrorist and drug groups.

Drug traffickers and terrorist organizations both attack the underpinnings of legitimate government institutions to achieve their objectives, or enjoy the protection of governments that condone terror or drug trafficking. Drug traffickers and terror groups are both drawn to regions where central government authority is weak. If a terror group already controls a region and has excluded or neutralized legitimate government institutions, drug protection only requires a business deal.

The growing link between terrorists and the drug trade contributes to an increased threat to America. Drug and terrorist organizations are taking advantage of the global economy to expand the scope, scale and reach of their activities and, as a result, their ability to harm American citizens and to damage U.S. interests is dramatically expanding. As state sponsors for their activities become scarce, terrorists are increasingly dependent on drug financing. The combined force of their alliance poses an enhanced threat to regional stability, American national security and the future of our country's youth.

Parents, educators, faith and community leaders recognize that youth drug use is a serious issue in this country, and they work tirelessly to educate children about the dangers of substance abuse. Today there is a new reason to continue this important effort: the illegal drug trade is linked to the support of terror groups across the globe. Buying and using illegal drugs is not a victimless crime — it has negative consequences that can touch the lives of people around the world.

September 11th has brought the complex and horrific reality of terrorism into the lives of all Americans. Many are asking, "How did this happen?" and "What can I do?" The link between terror and drugs is an important part of the puzzle, as is the recognition that individual decisions about using drugs have real-world consequences.

CLUB DRUGS —
COMMUNITY DRUG ALERT BULLETIN
http://www.drugabuse.gov/ClubAlert/ClubdrugAlert.html

Dear Colleague;

In recent years, a number of our Nation's best monitoring mechanisms have detected alarming increases in the popularity of some dangerous substances known collectively as "club drugs." These drugs are often used by young adults at all-night dance parties, such as "raves" or "trances," dance clubs, and bars. But in the past few years, these drugs have been found increasingly in more mainstream settings.

"Club drug" is a vague term that refers to a wide variety of drugs including MDMA (Ecstasy), GHB, Rohypnol, ketamine, methamphetamine, and LSD. Uncertainties about the drug sources, pharmacological agents, chemicals used to manufacture them, and possible contaminants make it difficult to determine toxicity, consequences, and symptoms. However, the information in this bulletin is based on scientifically sound data regarding the use of these drugs.

Data on students reported through the NIDA-sponsored 2003 Monitoring the Future (MTF) study showed declines in use of MDMA and LSD. The use of methamphetamine, Rohypnol, ketamine, and GHB remained unchanged and these drugs continue to present a threat to our communities. NIDA-supported research has shown that use of club drugs can cause serious health problems and, in some cases, even death. Used in combination with alcohol, these drugs can be even more dangerous. In recent years, there has been an increase in reports of club drugs used to commit sexual assaults — yet another reason NIDA is alerting you to these trends. Thus, we are issuing this updated alert to aid communities in their information gathering activities.

What follows is an overview of the scientific data on several of the most prevalent club drugs. Because many of the drug use trends are still emerging, some of the data presented here are preliminary. However, we feel obliged to share what we know now to help you and your community as you anticipate or respond to club drug–related problems. We also will increase our research efforts on the effects of club drugs and will facilitate the development of treatment and prevention strategies targeted to the populations that abuse club drugs.

As new research emerges, NIDA will continue to disseminate findings to you quickly. To this end, we have established a Web site to provide scientific information about club drugs — www.clubdrugs.org. We hope this information will be helpful as you combat drug use in your own community.

Sincerely,

Nora D. Volkow, M.D., Director
The National Institute on Drug Abuse

SOME FACTS ABOUT CLUB DRUGS

Methylenedioxymethamphetamine (MDMA):

Slang or Street Names: *Ecstasy, XTC, X, Adam, Clarity, Lover's Speed*

Chemically, MDMA is similar to the stimulant amphetamine and the hallucinogen mescaline. MDMA can produce both stimulant and mild sensory-altering effects.

- Methylenedioxyamphetamine (MDA), methylenedioxyethylamphetamine (MDEA), and paramethoxyamphetamine (PMA) are chemically similar to MDMA, are sometimes found in ecstasy tablets, and can produce deleterious health effects.

- MDMA is usually taken orally, via a tablet or capsule. Its effects last approximately 3 to 6 hours, though depression, sleep problems, and anxiety have been reported for days to weeks afterwards.

- MDMA can produce a significant increase in heart rate and blood pressure and a sense of alertness similar to that associated with amphetamine use.

- MDMA can cause a marked increase in body temperature (hyperthermia), which may further be exacerbated by hot and crowded conditions characteristic of the rave environment.

Hyperthermia can lead to liver, kidney, and cardiovascular system failure. MDMA can interfere with its own metabolism (breakdown), so repeated use over a short interval of time can lead to especially harmful levels in the body.

▪MDMA users can become dehydrated, prompting increased water consumption. In some cases, this has led to the problem of "water intoxication" or hyponatremia, a potentially fatal condition in which excessive water consumption causes a dramatic decrease in electrolytes. MDMA can affect the hormone that regulates the amount of sodium in the blood, which can also cause hyponatremia.

▪In animal studies, repeated administration of MDMA was found to produce long-lasting, perhaps permanent, damage to the neurons that release serotonin. In humans, chronic use of MDMA has been associated with memory impairment, which may indicate damage to the parts of the brain involved in memory processing.

▪Recent animal studies have shown that binge use of MDMA is toxic to the heart. Health effects observed included arrhythmia, heart muscle damage, and reductions in heart rate and blood pressure. (Initially, MDMA increases heart rate and blood pressure, but following repeated use, this effect is reversed.)

▪Newborn rats exposed to MDMA develop impairments of spatial learning and memory that are seen when the rats become young adults. The newborn stage of rodent brain development is analogous to late third trimester in humans.

▪NIDA's 2003 Monitoring the Future (MTF)

study reported that 2.1 percent of 8th-graders, 3.0 percent of 10th-graders, and 4.5 percent of 12th-graders had used MDMA in the 12 months prior to the survey. This is a decrease from 2001 peak rates of 3.5, 6.2, and 9.2 percent, respectively.

*MDMA abuse has been reported across the country, including most of the 21 areas that are monitored by NIDA's Community Epidemiology Work Group (CEWG), a network of researchers that provide ongoing community-level surveillance of drug abuse. CEWG cities in which MDMA use has been reported include: Chicago, Denver, Miami, Atlanta, New Orleans, San Francisco, Austin, Seattle, Boston, Detroit, New York, St. Louis, Dallas, Baltimore, Los Angeles, Minneapolis/St. Paul, Newark, Philadelphia, and Washington, DC.

Gamma-hydroxybutyrate (GHB)

Slang or Street Names: *Grievous Bodily Harm, G, Liquid Ecstasy, Georgia Home Boy*

GHB can be produced in clear liquid, white powder, tablet, and capsule forms, and it is often used in combination with alcohol, making it even more hazardous. GHB has been increasingly involved in poisonings, overdoses, drug-facilitated sexual assaults (such as "date rapes"), and fatalities. The drug is used predominantly by adolescents and young adults — often when they attend nightclubs and raves — and is prominent in many gay male communities.

■GHB is usually abused either for its intoxicating/sedating/euphoria-inducing properties or for its growth hormone-releasing effects.

■Chemicals that can be converted by the body into GHB include gamma-butyrolactone (GBL) and 1,4- butanediol (BD), which are found in a number of products that are labeled as cleaning agents and are often sold over the Internet and in retail stores.

- GHB is a central nervous system depressant and its intoxicating effects begin 10 to 20 minutes after the drug is taken. The effects typically last up to 4 hours, depending on the dosage. At higher doses, GHB's sedative effects may result in sleep, coma, or death.

- GHB is cleared from the body relatively quickly (in approximately 2 hours). There are no GHB detection tests for use in emergency rooms and many clinicians are unfamiliar with it, so many GHB incidents go undetected.

- In July 2002, the Food and Drug Administration approved the medically supervised use of GHB for the treatment of cataplexy (episodes in which muscles suddenly go limp) associated with narcolepsy.

*CEWG cities in which GHB abuse has been reported include: Detroit, Phoenix, Honolulu, Miami, New York, Atlanta, Minneapolis/St. Paul, Dallas, Seattle, San Francisco, San Diego, New Orleans, Newark, Los Angeles, Baltimore, Boston, and Denver.

Ketamine

Slang or Street Names: *Special K, K, Vitamin K, Cat Valium*

Ketamine is an anesthetic that can be injected, snorted, or smoked. It has been approved for both human and animal use in medical settings since 1970. About 90 percent of the ketamine sold legally today is intended for veterinary use.

- Large doses cause reactions similar to those associated with use of phencyclidine (PCP), such as dream-like states and altered perceptions or hallucinations.

- Ketamine is produced in liquid form or as a white powder that is often snorted or smoked with marijuana or tobacco products. In some cities (Boston, New Orleans, and Minneapolis/St. Paul, for example), ketamine has been reported to be injected intramuscularly.

- Low-dose intoxication from ketamine results in impaired attention, learning ability, and memory.

- At higher doses, ketamine can cause delirium, amnesia, impaired motor function, high blood pressure, depression, and potentially fatal respiratory problems.

*CEWG cities in which ketamine abuse has been reported include: Seattle, Miami, New York, Chicago, Minneapolis/St. Paul, Newark, Boston, Detroit, New Orleans, and San Diego.

Rohypnol

Slang or Street Names: *Roofies, Rophies, Roche, Forget-me Pill*

Rohypnol (flunitrazepam) belongs to the class of drugs known as benzodiazepines (which include Valium, Halcion, Xanax, and Versed). Rohypnol is not approved for prescription use in the United States, although it is used in many countries as a treatment for insomnia, as a sedative, and as a presurgery anesthetic.

- Rohypnol is tasteless and odorless, and it dissolves easily in carbonated beverages. The sedative and toxic effects of Rohypnol are aggravated by concurrent use of alcohol. Even without alcohol, a dose of Rohypnol as small as 1 mg can impair a user for 8 to 12 hours.

- Rohypnol is usually taken orally, although there are reports that it can be ground up and snorted.

- The drug can cause profound "anterograde amnesia"; that is, individuals may not remember events they experienced while under the effects of the drug. Reportedly, it has been used in sexual assaults.

- Other adverse effects associated with Rohypnol include decreased blood pressure, drowsiness, visual disturbances, dizziness, confusion, gastrointestinal disturbances, and urinary retention.

*CEWG areas in which Rohypnol abuse has been reported include: Miami, Houston, and sites along the Texas-Mexico border.

Methamphetamine

Slang or Street Names: *Speed, Ice, Chalk, Meth, Crystal, Crank, Fire, Glass*

Methamphetamine is a toxic, addictive stimulant that affects many areas of the central nervous system. The drug is often made in clandestine laboratories from relatively inexpensive over-the-counter ingredients. It is used by diverse groups, including clubgoers, in some areas of the country. Methamphetamine has been available in western and southwestern regions of the country for several years, but appears to be increasingly available in other regions.

- Methamphetamine can be smoked, snorted, injected, or ingested orally. It is a white, odorless, bitter-tasting crystalline powder that dissolves easily in beverages.

- Methamphetamine is typically sold through networks; not on the street like many other illicit drugs.

- Methamphetamine abuse is associated with serious health consequences, including memory loss, aggression, violence, psychotic behavior, and cardiac and neurological damage.

▪Methamphetamine abusers typically display signs of agitation, excited speech, decreased appetite, and increased physical activity levels.

▪Methamphetamine is neurotoxic. Abusers may suffer significant reductions in dopamine transporters and receptors.

▪Methamphetamine abuse can contribute to higher rates of infectious disease transmission, especially hepatitis and HIV/AIDS.

▪NIDA's 2003 MTF study found that 3.2 percent of 12th-graders, 3.3 percent of 10th-graders, and 2.5 percent of 8th-graders had used methamphetamine within the past year.

*CEWG cities in which methamphetamine abuse has been reported include: San Diego, San Francisco, Phoenix, Atlanta, St. Louis, Denver, Honolulu, Los Angeles, Minneapolis/St. Paul, Philadelphia, Boston, Seattle, and Dallas. Methamphetamine abuse has also been reported in many rural areas of the country.

Lysergic Acid Diethylamide (LSD)

Slang or Street Names: *Acid, Boomers, Yellow Sunshines*

LSD is a hallucinogen, inducing abnormalities in sensory perceptions. The effects of LSD are unpredictable depending on the amount taken, on the surroundings in which the drug is used, and on the user's personality, mood, and expectations.

▪LSD is typically taken by mouth. It is sold in tablet, capsule, and liquid forms, as well as on pieces of blotter paper that have absorbed the drug.

- Typically, an LSD user feels the effects of the drug 30 to 90 minutes after taking it. The physical effects include dilated pupils, elevated body temperature, increased heart rate and blood pressure, sweating, loss of appetite, sleeplessness, dry mouth, and tremors.

- LSD users frequently report numbness, weakness, trembling, and nausea.

- There are two long-term disorders associated with LSD — persistent psychosis and hallucinogen persisting perception disorder (which used to be called "flashbacks").

- NIDA's MTF survey data found that LSD use has decreased significantly among 10th- and 12th-graders over the past few years. In 2003, past year use reached the lowest levels in the history of the survey: 1.3 percent of 8th-graders, 1.7 percent of 10th-graders, and 1.9 percent of 12th-graders reported past year use of LSD.

*CEWG cities in which LSD abuse has been reported include: Boston, Detroit, Seattle, Chicago, Denver, New Orleans, San Francisco, Atlanta, and Phoenix.

---

* Information from NIDA's Community Epidemiology Work Group (CEWG), a network of epidemiologists and researchers from 21 U.S. metropolitan areas who monitor drug use trends.

These publications may be reprinted without permission.

For free publications contact the National Clearinghouse for Alcohol and Drug Information (NCADI) at 1-800-729-6686.

NIDA Community Alert Bulletin on Club Drugs was published in December 1999 and updated May 2004.

Spring Break Study Brings "Startling" Results

Bharath M. Josiam, Ph.D., and George L. Smeaton, Ph.D.

Two American professors worked with an Australian researcher to study the phenomenon of spring break. The researchers termed their findings "startling."

During spring break, more than half a million college students descend upon beach destinations to engage in potentially damaging or even life-threatening behavior that is accepted and even paid for by their parents or other adults," the researchers reported.

This American phenomenon has developed into a monster of momentous proportions. "Extreme behavior such as binge drinking, drug taking and sexual promiscuity are pretty much accepted or, in fact, expected," the researchers note.

Some additional findings, in brief, were as follows:

• 75 percent of college males reported being intoxicated on a daily basis during break; 43.6 percent of females reported the same.

• Nearly half of the males and more than 40 percent of females reported being drunk to the point of vomiting or passing out at least once during break.

• 33 percent of males and 10 percent of females reported being drunk more than once a day.

• 20 percent of males and 3.5 percent of females reported being drunk "continuously" while on break.

- Drugs were abused more during break, with marijuana being the drug of choice.

- Marijuana users were also found to consume more alcohol than non-users.

- Marijuana use was twice as high among fraternity members, and frat membership was also associated with more alcohol consumption.

Most "shocking" was sexual behavior, Josiam and Smeaton reported:

- Males had sex with more new partners during break than during a typical week at home.

- Males in a committed relationship at home were far more likely to have new sexual partners during break than those who had no long-term relationship.

- Few students who had sex during break used condoms consistently, even if a condom was in the room.

- Among women, those with higher alcohol consumption were more likely to have been the victim of sexual aggression.

Smeaton and Josiam agree that more education and an environment that marginalizes rather than glamorizes binge drinking is needed and that more research is called for.

All Summer in a Day
by Ray Bradbury
(1920-   )

---

*No one in the class could remember
a time when there wasn't rain.*

"Ready?"

"Ready."

"Now?"

"Soon."

"Do the scientists really know? Will it happen today, will it?"

"Look, look; see for yourself!"

The children pressed to each other like so many roses, so many weeds, intermixed, peering out for a look at the hidden sun.

It rained.

It had been raining for seven years; thousands upon thousands of days compounded and filled from one end to the other with rain, with the drum and gush of water, with the sweet crystal fall of showers and the concussion of storms so heavy they were tidal waves come over the islands. A thousand forests had been crushed under the rain and grown up a thousand times to be crushed again. And this way of life was forever on the planet Venus, and this was the school room of the children of the rocket men and women who had come to a raining world to set up civilization and live out their lives.

"It's stopping, it's stopping!"

"Yes, yes!"

Margot stood apart from them, from these children who could never remember a time when there wasn't rain and rain and rain. They were all nine years old, and if there had been a day, seven years ago, when the sun came out for an hour and showed its face to the stunned world, they could not recall. Sometimes, at night, she heard them stir, in remembrance, and she knew they were dreaming and remembering gold or a yellow crayon or a coin large enough to buy the world with. She knew that they thought they remembered a warmness, like a blushing in the face, in the body, in the arms and legs and trembling hands. But then they always awoke to the tatting drum, the endless shaking down of clear bead necklaces upon the roof, the walk, the gardens, the forest, and their dreams were gone.

All day yesterday they had read in class about the sun. About how like a lemon it was, and how hot. And they had written small stories or essays or poems about it:

I think the sun is a flower,
That blooms for just one hour.

That was Margot's poem, read in a quiet voice in the still classroom while the rain was falling outside.

"Aw, you didn't write that!" protested one of the boys.

"I did," said Margot. "I *did*."

"William!" said the teacher.

But that was yesterday. Now the rain was slackening, and the children were crushed to the great thick windows.

"Where's teacher?"

"She'll be back."

"She'd better hurry, we'll miss it!"

They turned on themselves, like a feverish wheel, all tumbling spokes.

Margot stood alone. She was a very frail girl who looked as if she had been lost in the rain for years and the rain had washed out the blue from her eyes and the red from her mouth and the yellow from her hair. She was an old photograph dusted from an album, whitened away, and if she spoke at all her voice would be a ghost. Now she stood, separate, staring at the rain and the loud wet world beyond the huge glass.

"What're *you* looking at?" said William.

Margot said nothing.

"Speak when you're spoken to." He gave her a shove. But she did not move; rather, she let herself be moved only by him and nothing else.

They edged away from her, they would not look at her. She felt them go away. And this was because she would play no games with them in the echoing tunnels of the underground city. If they tagged her and ran, she stood blinking after them and did not follow. When the class sang songs about happiness and life and games, her lips barely moved. Only when they sang about the sun and the summer did her lips move as she watched the drenched windows.

And then, of course, the biggest crime of all was that she had come here only five years ago from Earth, and she remembered the sun and the way the sun was and the sky was when she was four in Ohio. And they, they had been on Venus all their lives, and they had been only two years old when last the sun came out and had long since forgotten the color and heat of it and the way that it really was. But Margot remembered.

"It's like a penny," she said once, eyes closed.

"No it's not!" the children cried.

"It's like a fire," she said, "in the stove."

"You're lying, you don't remember!" cried the children.

But she remembered and stood quietly apart from all of them and watched the patterning windows. And once, a month ago, she had refused to shower in the school shower rooms, had clutched her hands to her ears and over her head, screaming the water mustn't touch her head. So after that, dimly, dimly, she sensed it, she was different and they knew her difference and kept away.

There was talk that her father and mother were taking her back to Earth next year; it seemed vital to her that they do so, though it would mean the loss of thousands of dollars to her family. And so, the children hated her for all of these reasons of big and little consequence. They hated her pale snow face, her waiting silence, her thinness, and her possible future.

"Get away!" The boy gave her another push. "What're you waiting for?"

Then, for the first time, she turned and looked at him. And what she was waiting for was in her eyes.

"Well, don't wait around here!" cried the boy savagely. "You won't see nothing!"

Her lips moved.

"Nothing!" he cried. "It was all a joke, wasn't it?" He turned to the other children. "Nothing's happening today. *Is* it?"

They all blinked at him and then, understanding, laughed and shook their heads.
"Nothing, nothing!"

"Oh, but," Margot whispered, her eyes
helpless. "But, this is the day, the scientists predict,
they say, they *know*, the sun . . ."

"All a joke!" said the boy, and seized her
roughly. "Hey, everyone, let's put her in a closet
before teacher comes!"

"No," said Margot, falling back.

They surged about her, caught her up and
bore her, protesting, and then pleading, and
then crying, back into a tunnel, a room, a closet,
where they slammed and locked the door. They
stood looking at the door and saw it tremble from
her beating and throwing herself against it. They
heard her muffled cries. Then, smiling, they turned
and went out and back
down the tunnel, just as the teacher arrived.

"Ready, children?" She glanced at her watch.

"Yes!" said everyone.

"Are we all here?"

"Yes!"

The rain slackened still more.

They crowded to the huge door.

The rain stopped.

It was as if, in the midst of a film, concerning
an avalanche, a tornado, a hurricane, a volcanic
eruption, something had, first, gone wrong with
the sound apparatus, thus muffling and finally
cutting off all noise, all of the blasts and repercus-
sions and thunders, and then, second, ripped
the film from the projector and inserted in its
place a peaceful tropical slide which did not

move or tremor. The world ground to a standstill. The silence was so immense and unbelievable that you felt your ears had been stuffed or you had lost your hearing altogether. The children put their hands to their ears. They stood apart. The door slid back and the smell of the silent, waiting world came in to them.

The sun came out.

It was the color of flaming bronze and it was very large. And the sky around it was a blazing blue tile color. And the jungle burned with sunlight as the children, released from their spell, rushed out, yelling, into the springtime.

"Now don't go too far," called the teacher after them. "You've only two hours, you know. You wouldn't want to get caught out!"

But they were running and turning their faces up to the sky and feeling the sun on their cheeks like a warm iron; they were taking off their jackets and letting the sun burn their arms.

"Oh, it's better than the sun lamps, isn't it?"

"Much, much better!"

They stopped running and stood in the great jungle that covered Venus, that grew and never stopped growing, tumultuously, even as you watched it. It was a nest of octopi, clustering up great arms of flesh-like weed, wavering, flowering in this brief spring. It was the color of rubber and ash, this jungle, from the many years without sun. It was the color of stones and white cheeses and ink, and it was the color of the moon.

The children lay out, laughing, on the jungle mattress, and heard it sigh and squeak under them, resilient and alive. They ran among the trees, they slipped and fell, they pushed each other, they played hide-and-seek and tag, but most of all they squinted at the sun until the tears ran down their faces, they put their hands up to that yellowness and that amazing blueness and they breathed of the fresh, fresh air and listened and listened to the silence which suspended them in a blessed sea of no sound and no motion. They looked at every-thing and savored everything. Then, wildly, like animals escaped from their caves, they ran and

ran in shouting circles. They ran for an hour and did not stop running.

And then —

In the midst of their running— one of the girls wailed.

Everyone stopped.

The girl, standing in the open, held out her hand.

"Oh, look, look," she said, trembling.

They came slowly to look at her opened palm.

In the center of it, cupped and huge, was a single raindrop.

She began to cry, looking at it.

They glanced quietly at the sky.

"Oh. Oh."

A few cold drops fell on their noses and their cheeks and their mouths. The sun faded behind a stir of mist. A wind blew cool around them. They turned and started to walk back toward the underground house, their hands at their sides, their smiles vanishing away.

A boom of thunder startled them and like leaves before a new hurricane, they tumbled upon each other and ran. Lightning struck ten miles away, five miles away, a mile, a half mile. The sky darkened into midnight in a flash.

They stood in the doorway of the underground house for a moment until it was raining
hard. Then they closed the door and heard the
gigantic sound of the rain falling in tons and
avalanches, everywhere and forever.

"Will it be seven more years?"

"Yes. Seven."

Then one of them gave a little cry.

"Margot!"

"What?"

"She's still in the closet where we locked her."

"Margot."

They stood as if someone had driven them,
like so many stakes, into the floor. They looked at
each other and then looked away. They glanced
out at the world that was raining now and raining
and raining steadily. They could not meet each
other's glances. Their faces were solemn and pale.
They looked at their hands and feet, their faces
down.

"Margot."

One of the girls said, "Well . . .?"

No one moved.

"Go on," whispered the girl.

They walked slowly down the hall in the
sound of the cold rain. They turned through the
doorway to the room in the sound of the storm
and thunder, lightning on their faces, blue and
terrible. They walked over to the closet door
slowly and stood by it.

Behind the closed door was only silence.

They unlocked the door, even more slowly,
and let Margot out.

Excerpt from
On Becoming a Person
by Carl R. Rogers (1961)

RELATIONSHIPS CAN BE LIVED ON A REAL BASIS

There is another effect which counseling seems to have on the way our clients experience their family relationships. The client discovers, often to his great surprise, that a relationship can be lived on the basis of the real feelings, rather than on the basis of a defensive pretense. There is a deep and comforting significance to this, as we have already seen in the case of Mrs. M. To discover that feelings of shame and anger and annoyance can be expressed, and that the relationship still survives, is reassuring. To find that one can express tenderness and sensitivity and fearfulness and yet not be betrayed — this is a deeply strengthening thing. It seems that part of the reason this works out constructively is that in therapy the individual learns to recognize and express his feelings *as* his own feelings, not as a fact about another person. Thus, to say to one's spouse "What you are doing is all wrong," is likely to lead only to debate. But to say, "I feel very much annoyed by what you're doing," is to state one fact about the speaker's feelings, a fact which no one can deny. It no longer is an accusation about another, but a feeling which exists in oneself. "You are to blame for my feelings of inadequacy" is a debatable point, but "I feel inadequate when you do thus and so" simply contributes a real fact about the relationship.

But it is not only at the verbal level that it operates. The person who accepts his own feelings within himself, finds that a relationship can be lived on the basis of these real feelings. Let me illustrate this with a series of excerpts from the recorded interviews with Mrs. S.

Mrs. S. lived with her ten year old daughter and her seventy year old mother, who dominated the household by her "poor health." Mrs. S. was controlled by her mother, and unable to control her daughter, Carol. She felt resentful of her mother, but could not express this, because "I have felt guilty all my life. I grew up feeling guilty because everything that I did I felt was a . . . in some way affecting my mother's health. . . . In fact, a few years ago, it came to the point where I was having dreams at night about . . . shaking my mother and . . . I'd . . . I got the feeling that I just wanted to push her out of the way.
And . . . I can understand how Carol might feel. She doesn't dare . . . and neither do I."

Mrs. S. knows that most people think she would be much better off if she left her mother, but she cannot. "I know that if I do leave her, that I couldn't possibly be happy, I'd be so worried about her. And I'd feel so badly about leaving a poor old lady alone."

As she complains about the extent to which she is dominated and controlled, she begins to see the part she is playing, a cowardly part. "I feel that my hands are tied. Perhaps I'm at fault . . . more than mother is. In fact I know I am, but I've sort of become a coward where mother's concerned. I'll do anything to avoid one of the scenes that she puts on about little things."

As she understands herself better she comes to an inward conclusion to try to live in the relationship according to what she believes is right, rather than in terms of her mother's wishes. She reports this at the beginning of an interview. "Well, I've made a stupendous discovery, that perhaps it's been my fault entirely in over-compensating to mother . . . in other words, spoiling her. So I made up my mind like I do every morning, but I think this time it's gonna work, that I would try to . . . oh, to be calm and quiet, and . . . if she does go into one of her spells, to just more or less ignore it as you would a child who throws a tantrum just to get attention. So I tried it. And she got angry over some little thing. And she jumped up from the table and went into her room. Well, I didn't rush in and say, oh, I'm sorry, and beg her to come back, and I simply just ignored it. So in a few minutes, why, she came back and sat down and was a little sulky but she was over it. So I'm going to try that for a while and. . . ."

Mrs. S. realizes clearly that the basis for her new behavior is that she has come genuinely to accept her own feelings toward her mother. She says, "Well, why not face it? You see, I've been feeling so horrible, and thinking what a horrible person I was to resent my mother. Well, let's just say, okay, I resent her; and I'm sorry; but let's face it and I'll try to make the best of it."

As she accepts herself more she becomes much more able to meet some of her own needs as well as those of her mother. "There's a lot of things that I've wanted to do for years and that I'm just going to start to do. Now, mother can be alone till ten o'clock at night there. She has a telephone by her bed and . . . if a fire starts or something, there are neighbors, or if she becomes ill . . . so I'm going to take some night courses through the public schools you know, and I'm going to do a lot of things that I've wanted to do all my life, and have sort of been a martyr in staying home resenting it . . . that I had to, and thinking, oh, well, and not doing it. Well, I'm going to now. And I think after the first time I go, she'll be all right."

Her new found feelings are soon put to a test in the relationship with her mother. "My mother had a very severe heart attack the other day and I said, well, you'd better go to the hospital and . . . and you certainly need hospitalization; and I whipped her down to the doctor, and the doctor said her heart was fine and she oughta get out and have a little fun. So she's going to visit a friend for a week and see the shows and have a good time. So . . . actually when it came down to getting ready to go to the hospital, how cruel I am to her by contradicting her in front of Carol and all that sort of thing, why, then she backed down and when she was faced with the fact that she . . . and her heart's just as strong as a bull's, why, she thought she might as well use it to have some fun with. So that's fine. Working out fine."

Up to this point it might seem as though the relationship had improved for Mrs. S., but not for her mother. There is, however, another side to the picture. Somewhat later Mrs. S. says "I still am very, very sorry for mother. I would hate to be like she is. And another thing, you know, I just got to the point where I just hated mother; I couldn't stand to touch her, or . . . I mean . . . brush against her or something. I don't mean, just for the moment, while I was angry or anything. But . . . I've also found myself, oh, feeling a little affectionate toward her; two or three times I've gone in without even thinking, kissed her good night, and I used to just holler from the front door.

And . . . I've been feeling kindlier toward her; that resentment that I've had is going, along with the hold that she had over me, you see. So . . . that, I noticed that yesterday when I was helping her get ready and so forth; I fixed her hair and there was the longest time I couldn't stand to touch her; and I was doing her hair in pin curls and so forth; and I . . . it suddenly came to me, well, now this doesn't bother me a bit; in fact it's kind of fun."

These excerpts seem to me to portray a pattern of change in family relationships which is very familiar to us. Mrs. S. feels, though she hardly dares admit it even to herself, resentful of her mother and as though she had no rights of her own. It seems as though nothing but difficulty could result from letting these feelings exist openly in the relationship. Yet as she tentatively permits them to enter the situation she finds herself acting with more assurance, more integrity. The relationship improves rather than deteriorates. Most surprising of all, when the relationship is lived on the basis of the real feelings, she finds that resentment and hate are not the only feelings she has toward her mother. Fondness, affection and enjoyment are also feelings which enter the relationship. It seems clear that there may be moments of discord, dislike, and anger between the two. But there will also be respect and understanding and liking. They seem to have learned what many other clients have also learned, that a relationship does not have to be lived on a basis of pretense, but can be lived on the basis of the fluctuating variety of feelings which actually exist.

It may seem, from the illustrations I have chosen, that it is only negative feelings which are difficult to express or live. This is far from true.

Mr. K., a young professional man, found it fully as difficult to discover the positive feelings which lay beneath his façade, as the negative. A brief excerpt will indicate the changed quality of his relationship with his three-year-old daughter.

He says, "The thing that I was thinking about as I rode down here was — how differently I see our little girl — I was playing with her this morning — and — I we just, ah, well — why is it so hard for me to get words out now? This was a really wonderful experience — very warm, and it was a happy and pleasant thing, and it seems that I saw and felt her so close to me. Here's what I think is significant — before, I could talk about Judy. I could say positive things about her and funny little things she'd do and just talk about her as though I were and felt like a real happy father, but there was some unreal quality . . . as though I was just saying these things because I *should* be feeling this stuff and this is the way a father *should* talk about his daughter but somehow this wasn't really true because I did have these negative and mixed up feelings about her. Now I do think she is the most wonderful kid in the world."

T: "Before, you felt as though "I *should* be a happy father' — this morning you *are* a happy father. . . ."

"It certainly felt that way this morning. She just rolled around on the bed . . . and then she asked me if I wanted to go to sleep again and I said okay and then she said well, I'll go get my blankets . . . and then she told me a story . . . about three stories in one . . . all jumbled up and . . . it just felt like *this* is what I *really* want . . . I *want* to have this experience. It felt that I was . . . I felt grown up, I guess. I felt that I was a man . . .

now this sounds strange, but it did feel as though I was a grownup responsible loving father, who was big enough, and serious enough, and also happy enough to be the father of this child. Whereas before I did feel weak and maybe almost undeserving, ineligible to be that important, because it is a very important thing to be a father."

He has found it possible to accept positive feelings toward himself as a good father, and to fully accept this warm love for his little girl. He no longer has to pretend he loves her, fearful that some different feeling may be lurking underneath.

I think it will not surprise you that shortly after this he told how he could be much more free in expressing anger and annoyance at his little daughter, also. He is learning that the feelings which exist are good enough to live by. They do not have to be coated with a veneer.

IMPROVEMENT IN TWO-WAY COMMUNICATION

Experience in therapy seems to bring about another change in the way our clients live in their family relationships. They learn something about how to initiate and maintain real two-way communication. To understand another person's thoughts and feelings thoroughly, with the meanings they have for him, and to be thoroughly understood by this other person in return — this is one of the most rewarding of human experiences, and all too rare. Individuals who have come to us for therapy often report their pleasure in discovering that such genuine communication is possible with members of their own families.

In part this seems to be due, quite directly, to their experience of communication with the counselor. It is such a relief, such a blessed relaxation of defenses, to find oneself understood, that the individual wishes to create this atmosphere for others. To find, in the therapeutic relationship that one's most awful thoughts, one's most bizarre and abnormal feelings, one's most ridiculous dreams and hopes, one's most evil behaviors, can all be understood by another, is a tremendously releasing experience. One begins to see it as a resource he could extend to others.

But there appears to be an even more fundamental reason why these clients can understand members of their families. When we are living behind a façade, when we are trying to act in ways that are not in accord with our feelings, then we dare not listen freely to another. We must always have our guard up, lest he pierce the pretense of our façade. But when a client is living in the way I have been describing, when he tends to express his real feelings in the situation in which they occur, when his family relationships are lived on the basis of the feelings which actually exist, then he is no longer defensive and he can really listen to, and understand, another member of his family. He can let himself see how life appears to this other person.

Something of what I am saying may be illustrated from the experience of Mrs. S., the woman quoted in the preceding section. In a followup contact after the conclusion of her interviews, Mrs. S. was asked to give some of her own reactions to her experience. She says, "I didn't feel at first that it was counseling. You know? I thought, well, I'm just talking, but . . . by giving it a little thought, I realize that it is counseling and of the very best kind, because I've had advice, and excellent advice from doctors and family and friends and . . . it's never worked. And I think in

order to reach people, you can't put up barriers
and things of that sort, because then you don't
get the true reaction. . . . But I've given it a great
deal of thought and I'm sort of working it with
Carol a little bit now (laughing) or trying to, you
know. And . . . grandma says to her, how can
you be so mean to your poor sick old grandmother, you know. And I just know how Carol
feels. She just wants to hit her because she's so
terrible! But I sort of haven't been saying too
much to Carol or trying to guide her. But I've
been trying to draw her out . . . let her feel that
I'm with her and behind her, no matter what
she does. And let her tell me how she feels,
and her little reactions to things, and it's working
out fine. She has told me, oh, grandma's been
old and sick for so long, mother. And I said, yes.
And I don't condemn her nor do I praise her,
and so she is, just in this short time beginning to
. . . oh, get little things off her mind and . . .
without my probing or trying to . . . so it's sort
of working on her. And it seems to be working
on mother a little bit too."

I think we may say of Mrs. S. that having
accepted her own feelings, and having been
more willing to express them and to live in them,
she now finds more willingness on her own part
to understand her daughter and her mother,
and to feel empathically their own reactions to life.
She is sufficiently free of defensiveness to be able
to listen in an accepting manner, and to sense the
way life feels to them. This kind of development
seems characteristic of the change which occurs
in the family life of our clients.

WILLINGNESS FOR ANOTHER TO BE SEPARATE

There is one final tendency which we have
noticed and which I would like to describe.

It is quite noticeable that our clients tend in the direction of permitting each member of the family to have his own feelings and to be a separate person. This may seem a strange statement, but it is actually a most radical step. Many of us are perhaps unaware of the tremendous pressure we tend to put on our wives, our husbands, our children, to have the same feelings we do. It is often as though we said, "If you want me to love you, then you must have the same feelings I do. If I feel your behavior is bad, you must feel so too. If I feel a certain goal is desirable, you must feels so too." Now the tendency which we see in our clients is the opposite of this. There is a willingness for the other person to have different feelings, different values, different goals. In short, there is a willingness for him to be a separate person.

It is my belief that this tendency develops as the person discovers that he can trust his own feelings and reactions — that his own deep impulses are not destructive or catastrophic, and that he himself need not be guarded, but can meet life on a real basis. As he thus learns that he can trust himself, with his own uniqueness, he becomes more able to trust his wife, or his child, and to accept the unique feelings and values which exist in this other person.

Something of what I mean is contained in letters from a woman and her husband. They are friends of mine and had obtained a copy of a book I had written because they were interested in what I was doing. But the effect of the book seemed to be similar to therapy. The wife wrote me and included in her letter a paragraph giving her reactions. "Lest you think that we are completely frivolous, we have been reading

Client-Centered Therapy. I have almost finished it. Most of the usual things you say about books don't apply, at least for me. In fact it was pretty close to a counseling experience. It set me to thinking about some of the unsatisfactory relationships in our family, particularly my attitude toward Phillip (her 14-year-old son). I realized that I hadn't shown him any real love for a long time, because I was so resentful of his apparent indifference in trying to measure up to any of the standards that I have always thought were important. Since I have stopped taking most of the responsi-bility for his goals, and have responded to him as a person, as I always have to Nancy, for instance, it is surprising what changes have appeared in his attitudes. Not earth-shaking — but a heart-warming beginning. We no longer heckle him about his school work, and the other day he volunteered that he had gotten an S — satisfactory grade — on a math exam. The first time this year."

A few months later I heard from her husband. "You wouldn't recognize Phil. . . . While he is hardly garrulous, he is not nearly the sphinx that he was, and he is doing much better in school, although we do not expect him to be graduated cum laude. You should take a great deal of credit for his improvement, because he began to blossom when I finally began to trust him to be himself, and ceased trying to mold him into the glorified image of his father at a similar age. Oh to undo our past errors!"

This concept of trusting the individual to be himself has come to have a great deal of meaning to me. I sometimes fantasize about what it would mean if a child were treated in this fashion from the first. Suppose a child were permitted to have his own feelings — suppose he never had to disown his feelings in order to be loved. Suppose his parents were free to have and express their own unique feelings, which often would be different from his, and often different between themselves. I like to think of all the meanings that such an experience would have. It would mean that the child would grow up respecting himself as a unique person. It would mean that even when his behavior had to be thwarted, he could retain open "ownership" of his feelings. It would mean that his behavior would be a realistic balance, taking into account his own feelings and the known and open feelings of others. He would, I believe, be a responsible and self-directing individual, who would never need to conceal his feelings from himself, who would never need to live behind a façade. He would be relatively free of the maladjustments which cripple so many of us.

THE GENERAL PICTURE

If I have been able correctly to discern the trends in the experience of our clients, then client-centered therapy seems to have a number of implications for family life. Let me attempt to restate these in somewhat more general form.

It appears that an individual finds it satisfying in the long run to express any strong or persistent emotional attitudes in the situation in which they arise, to the person with whom they are concerned, and to the depth to which they exist. This is more satisfying than refusing to admit that such feelings exist, or permitting them to pile up to an explosive degree, or directing them toward some situation other than the one in which they arose.

It seems that the individual discovers that it is more satisfying in the long run to live a given family relationship on the basis of the real interpersonal feelings which exist, rather than living the relationship on the basis of a pretense. A part of this discovery is that the fear that the relationship will be destroyed if the true feelings are admitted, is usually unfounded, particularly when the feelings are expressed as belonging to oneself, not as stating something about the other person.

Our clients find that as they express themselves more freely, as the surface character of the relationship matches more closely the fluctuating attitudes which underlie it, they can lay aside some of their defenses and truly listen to the other person. Often for the first time they begin to understand how the other person feels, and why he feels that way. This mutual understanding begins to pervade the interpersonal interaction.

Finally, there is an increasing willingness for the other person to be himself. As I am more willing to be myself, I find I am more ready to permit you to be yourself, with all that that implies. This means that the family circle tends in the direction of becoming a number of separate and unique persons with individual goals and values, but bound together by the real feelings — positive and negative — which exist between them, and by the satisfying bond of mutual understanding of at least a portion of each other's private worlds.

It is in these ways, I believe, that a therapy which results in the individual becoming more fully and more deeply himself, results also in his finding greater satisfaction in realistic family relationships, which likewise promote the same end — that of facilitating each member of the family in the process of discovering, and becoming, himself.

Harrison Bergeron
by Kurt Vonnegut, Jr.
(1922-2007)

The year was 2081, and everybody was finally equal. They weren't only equal before God and the law. They were equal every which way. Nobody was smarter than anybody else. Nobody was better looking than anybody else. Nobody was stronger or quicker than anybody else. All this equality was due to the 211th, 212th, and 213th Amendments to the Constitution, and to the unceasing vigilance of agents of the United States Handicapper General.

Some things about living still weren't quite right, though. April, for instance, still drove people crazy by not being springtime. And it was in that clammy month that the H-G men took George and Hazel Bergeron's fourteen-year-old son, Harrison, away.

It was tragic, all right, but George and Hazel couldn't think about it very hard. Hazel had a perfectly average intelligence, which meant she couldn't think about anything except in short bursts. And George, while his intelligence was way above normal, had a little mental handicap radio in his ear. He was required by law to wear it at all times. It was tuned to a government transmitter. Every twenty seconds or so, the transmitter would send out some sharp noise to keep people like George from taking unfair advantage of their brains.

George and Hazel were watching television. There were tears on Hazel's cheeks, and she'd forgotten for the moment what they were about.

On the television screen were ballerinas.

A buzzer sounded in George's head. His

thoughts fled in panic, like bandits from a burglar alarm.

"That was a real pretty dance, that dance they just did," said Hazel.

"Huh?" said George.

"That dance — it was nice," said Hazel.

"Yup," said George. He tried to think a little about the ballerinas. They weren't really very good — no better than anybody else would have been, anyway. They were burdened with sashweights and bags of birdshot, and their faces were masked, so that no one, seeing a free and graceful gesture or a pretty face, would feel like something the cat drug in. George was toying with the vague notion that maybe dancers shouldn't be handicapped. But he didn't get very far with it before another noise in his ear radio scattered his thoughts.

George winced. So did two out of the eight ballerinas.

Hazel saw him wince. Having no mental handicap herself, she had to ask George what the latest sound had been.

"Sounded like somebody hitting a milk bottle with a ball peen hammer," said George.

"I'd think it would be real interesting, hearing all the different sounds," said Hazel, a little envious. "All the things they think up."

"Um," said George.

"Only, if I was Handicapper General, you know what I would do?" said Hazel. Hazel, as a matter of fact, bore a strong resemblance to the Handicapper General, a woman named Diana Moon Glampers. "If I was Diana Moon Glampers," said Hazel, "I'd have chimes on Sunday — just chimes. Kind of in honor of religion."

"I could think, if it was just chimes," said George.

"Well — maybe make 'em real loud," said Hazel. "I think I'd make a good Handicapper General."

"Good as anybody else," said George.

"Who knows better'n I do what normal is?" said Hazel.

"Right," said George. He began to think glimmeringly about his abnormal son who was now in jail, about Harrison, but a twenty-one gun salute in his head stopped that.

"Boy!" said Hazel, "that was a doozy, wasn't it?"

It was such a doozy that George was white and trembling, and tears stood on the rims of his red eyes. Two of the eight ballerinas that had collapsed to the studio floor, were holding their temples.

"All of a sudden you look so tired," said Hazel. "Why don't you stretch out on the sofa, so's you can rest your handicap bag on the pillows, honeybunch." She was referring to the forty-seven pounds of birdshot in a canvas bag, which was padlocked around George's neck. "Go on and rest the bag for a little while," she said. "I don't care if you're not equal to me for a while."

George weighed the bag with his hands. "I don't mind it," he said. "I don't notice it any more. It's just a part of me."

"You been so tired lately — kind of wore out," said Hazel. "If there was just some way we could make a little hole in the bottom of the bag, and just take out a few of them lead balls. Just a few."

"Two years in prison and two thousand dollars fine for every ball I took out," said George. "I don't call that a bargain."

"If you could just take a few out when you came home from work," said Hazel. "I mean —

you don't compete with anybody around here. You just set around."

"If I tried to get away with it," said George, "then other people'd get away with it — and pretty soon we'd be right back to the dark ages again, with everybody competing against everybody else. You wouldn't like that, would you?"

"I'd hate it," said Hazel.

"There you are," said George. "The minute people start cheating on laws, what do you think happens to society?"

If Hazel hadn't been able to come up with an answer to this question, George couldn't have supplied one. A siren was going off in his head.

"Reckon it'd fall all apart," said Hazel.

"What would?" said George blankly.

"Society," said Hazel uncertainly. "Wasn't that what you just said?"

"Who knows?" said George.

The television program was suddenly interrupted for a news bulletin. It wasn't clear at first as to what the bulletin was about, since the announcer, like all announcers, had a serious speech impediment. For about half a minute, and in a state of high excitement, the announcer tried to say, "Ladies and Gentlemen —"

He finally gave up, handed the bulletin to a ballerina to read.

"That's all right —" Hazel said of the announcer, "he tried. That's the big thing. He tried to do the best he could with what God gave him. He should get a nice raise for trying so hard."

"Ladies and Gentlemen —" said the ballerina, reading the bulletin. She must have been extraordinarily beautiful, because the mask she wore was hideous. And it was easy to see that she was the strongest and most graceful of all the dancers, for her handicap bags were as big as those worn by two-hundred pound men.

And she had to apologize at once for her voice, which was a very unfair voice for a woman to use. Her voice was a warm, luminous, timeless melody. "Excuse me —" she said, and she began again, making her voice absolutely uncompetitive.

"Harrison Bergeron, age fourteen," she said in a grackle squawk, "has just escaped from jail, where he was held on suspicion of plotting to overthrow the government. He is a genius and an athlete, is under-handicapped, and should be regarded as extremely dangerous."

A police photograph of Harrison Bergeron was flashed on the screen — upside down, then sideways, upside down again, then right side up. The picture showed the full length of Harrison against a background calibrated in feet and inches. He was exactly seven feet tall.

The rest of Harrison's appearance was Halloween and hardware. Nobody had ever born heavier handicaps. He had outgrown hindrances faster than the H-G men could think them up. Instead of a little ear radio for a mental handicap, he wore a tremendous pair of earphones, and spectacles with thick wavy lenses. The spectacles were intended to make him not only half blind, but to give him whanging headaches besides.

Scrap metal was hung all over him. Ordinarily there was a certain symmetry, a military neatness to the handicaps issued to strong people, but Harrison looked like a walking junkyard. In the race of life, Harrison carried three hundred pounds.

And to offset his good looks, the H-G men required that he wear at all times a red rubber ball for a nose, keep his eyebrows shaved off, and cover his even white teeth with black caps at snaggle-tooth random.

"If you see this boy," said the ballerina, "do not — I repeat, do not — try to reason with him."

There was the shriek of a door being torn from its hinges.

Screams and barking cries of consternation came from the television set. The photograph of Harrison Bergeron on the screen jumped again and again, as though dancing to the tune of an earthquake.

George Bergeron correctly identified the earthquake, and well he might have — for many was the time his own home had danced to the same crashing tune. "My God —" said George, "that must be Harrison!"

The realization was blasted from his mind instantly by the sound of an automobile collision in his head.

When George could open his eyes again, the photograph of Harrison was gone. A living, breathing Harrison filled the screen.

Clanking, clownish, and huge, Harrison stood in the center of the studio. The knob of the uprooted studio door was still in his hand. Ballerinas, technicians, musicians, and announcers cowered on their knees before him, expecting to die.

"I am the Emperor!" cried Harrison. "Do you hear? I am the Emperor! Everybody must do what I say at once!" He stamped his foot and the studio shook.

"Even as I stand here —" he bellowed, "crippled, hobbled, sickened — I am a greater ruler than any man who ever lived! Now watch me become what I *can* become!"

Harrison tore the straps of his handicap harness like wet tissue paper, tore straps guaranteed to support five thousand pounds.

Harrison's scrap-iron handicaps crashed to the floor.

Harrison thrust his thumbs under the bar of the padlock that secured his head harness. The bar snapped like celery. Harrison smashed his headphones and spectacles against the wall.

He flung away his rubber-ball nose, revealed a man that would have awed Thor, the god of thunder.

"I shall now select my Empress!" he said, looking down on the cowering people. "Let the first woman who dares rise to her feet claim her mate and her throne!"

A moment passed, and then a ballerina arose, swaying like a willow.

Harrison plucked the mental handicap from her ear, snapped off her physical handicaps with marvelous delicacy. Last of all he removed her mask.

She was blindingly beautiful.

"Now —" said Harrison, taking her hand, "shall we show the people the meaning of the word dance? Music!" he commanded.

The musicians scrambled back into their chairs, and Harrison stripped them of their handicaps, too. "Play your best," he told them, "and I'll make you barons and dukes and earls."

The music began. It was normal at first —
cheap, silly, false. But Harrison snatched two
musicians from their chairs, waved them like
batons as he sang the music as he wanted it
played. He slammed them back into their chairs.

The music began again and was much
improved.

Harrison and his Empress merely listened
to the music for a while — listened gravely,
as though synchronizing their heartbeats with it.

They shifted their weights to their toes.

Harrison placed his big hands on the girl's
tiny waist, letting her sense the weightlessness
that would soon be hers.

And then, in an explosion of joy and grace,
into the air they sprang!

Not only were the laws of the land abandoned, but the law of gravity and the laws of
motion as well.

They reeled, whirled, swiveled, flounced,
capered, gamboled, and spun.

They leaped like deer on the moon.

The studio ceiling was thirty feet high,
but each leap brought the dancers nearer to it.

It became their obvious intention to kiss the
ceiling.

They kissed it.

And then, neutralizing gravity with love and
pure will, they remained suspended in air inches
below the ceiling, and they kissed each other for
a long, long time.

It was then that Diana Moon Glampers,
the Handicapper General, came into the studio
with a double-barreled ten-gauge shotgun.

She fired twice, and the Emperor and the Empress were dead before they hit the floor.

Diana Moon Gampers loaded the gun again. She aimed it at the musicians and told them they had ten seconds to get their handicaps back on.

It was then that the Bergerons' television tube burned out.

Hazel turned to comment about the blackout to George. But George had gone out into the kitchen for a can of beer.

George came back in with the beer, paused while a handicap signal shook him up. And then he sat down again. "You been crying?" he said to Hazel.

"Yup," she said.

"What about?" he said.

"I forget," she said. "Something real sad on television."

"What was it?" he said.

"It's all kind of mixed up in my mind," said Hazel.

"Forget sad things," said George.

"I always do," said Hazel.

"That's my girl," said George. He winced. There was the sound of a rivetting gun in his head.

"Gee — I could tell that one was a doozy," said Hazel.

"You can say that again," said George.

"Gee —" said Hazel, "I could tell that one was a doozy."

Excerpt from
On Death and Dying
by Elisabeth Kübler-Ross, M.D.
(1926-2004)

COPING WITH THE REALITY OF TERMINAL ILLNESS IN THE FAMILY

Family members undergo different stages of adjustment similar to the ones described for our patients. At first many of them cannot believe that it is true. They may deny the fact that there is such an illness in the family or "shop around" from doctor to doctor in the vain hope of hearing that this was the wrong diagnosis. They may seek help and reassurance (that it is all not true) from fortune-tellers and faith healers. They may arrange for expensive trips to famous clinics and physicians and only gradually face up to the reality which may change their life so drastically. Greatly dependent on the patient's attitude, awareness, and ability to communicate, the family then undergoes certain changes. If they are able to share their common concerns, they can take care of important matters early and under less pressure of time and emotions. If each one tries to keep a secret from the other, they will keep an artificial barrier between them which will make it difficult for any preparatory grief for the patient or his family. The end result will be much more dramatic than for those who can talk and cry together at times.

Just as the patient goes through a stage of anger, the immediate family will experience the same emotional reaction. They will be angry alternately with the doctor who examined the patient first and did not come forth with the diagnosis and the doctor who confronted them with the sad reality. They may project their rage to the hospital personnel who never care enough, no matter how efficient the care is in reality. There is a great deal of envy in this reaction, as family members often feel cheated at not being able or allowed to be with the patient and to care for him. There is also much guilt and a wish to make up for missed past opportunities. The more we can help the relative to express these emotions before the death of a loved one, the more comfortable the family member will be.

When anger, resentment, and guilt can be worked through, the family will then go through a phase of preparatory grief, just as the dying person does. The more this grief can be expressed before death, the less unbearable it becomes afterward. We often hear relatives say proudly of themselves that they always tried to keep a smiling face when confronted with the patient, until one day they just could not keep the façade any longer. Little do they realize that genuine emotions on the part of a member of the family are much easier to take than a make-believe mask which the patient can see through anyway and which means to him a disguise rather than a sharing of a sad situation.

If members of a family can share these emotions together, they will gradually face the reality of impending separation and come to an acceptance of it together. The most heartbreaking time, perhaps, for the family is the final phase, when the patient is slowly detaching himself from his world including his family. They do not understand that a dying man who has found peace and acceptance in his death will have to separate himself, step by step, from his environment, including his most loved ones. How could he ever be ready to die if he continued to hold onto the meaningful relationships of which a

man has so many? When the patient asks to be
visited only by a few more friends, then by his
children and finally only by his wife, it should be
understood that that is the way of separating
himself gradually. It is often misinterpreted by
the immediate family as a rejection, and we
have met several husbands and wives who have
reacted dramatically to this normal and healthy
detachment. I think we can be of greatest service
to them if we help them understand that only
patients who have worked through their dying are
able to detach themselves slowly and peacefully in
this manner. It should be a source of comfort and
solace to them and not one of grief and resentment.
It is during this time that the family needs the
most support, the patient perhaps the least. I do
not mean to imply by this that the patient should
then be left alone. We should always be available, but a patient who has reached this stage
of acceptance and decathexis usually requires
little in terms of interpersonal relationship. If the
meaning of this detachment is not explained
to the family, problems can arise as described
in the case of Mrs. W. (Chapter VII).

The most tragic death is perhaps — aside
from the very young — the death of the very old
when we look at it from the point of view of
the family. Whether the generations have lived
together or separately, each generation has a
need and a right to live their own lives, to have
their own privacy, their own needs fulfilled appropriate to their generation. The old folks have out-
lived their usefulness in terms of our economic
system and have earned, on the other hand, a
right to live out their lives in dignity and peace.
As long as they are healthy in body and mind
and self-supporting, this may all be quite possible.
We have seen many old men and women,

however, who have become disabled physically or emotionally and who require a tremendous sum of money for a dignified maintenance at a level their family desires for them. The family is then often confronted with a difficult decision, namely, to mobilize all available money, including loans and savings for their own retirement, in order to afford such final care. The tragedy of these old people is perhaps that the amount of money and often financial sacrifice does not involve any improvement of the condition but is a mere maintenance at a minimal level of existence. If medical complications occur, the expenses are manifold and the family often wishes for a quick and painless death, but rarely expresses that wish openly. That such wishes bring about feelings of guilt is obvious.

I am reminded of an old woman who had been hospitalized for several weeks and required extensive and expensive nursing care in a private hospital. Everybody expected her to die soon, but day after day she remained in an unchanged condition. Her daughter was torn between sending her to a nursing home or keeping her in the hospital, where she apparently wanted to stay. Her son-in-law was angry at her for having used up their life savings and had innumerable arguments with his wife, who felt too guilty to take her out of the hospital. When I visited the old woman she looked frightened and weary. I asked her simply what she was so afraid of. She looked at me and finally expressed what she had been unable to communicate before, because she herself realized how unrealistic her fears were. She was afraid of "being eaten up alive by the worms." While I was catching my breath and tried to understand the real meaning of this statement, her daughter blurted out, "If that's what's keeping you

from dying, we can burn you," by which she
naturally meant that a cremation would
prevent her from having any contact with earth-
worms. All her suppressed anger was in this
statement. I sat with the old woman alone for
a while. We talked calmly about her life-long
phobias and her fear of death which was
presented in this fear of worms, as if she would
be aware of them after her death. She felt greatly
relieved for having expressed it and had nothing
but understanding for her daughter's anger.
I encouraged her to share some of these
feelings with her daughter, so that the latter
might not have to feel so bad about her outburst.

When I met the daughter outside the
room I told her of her mother's understanding,
and they finally got together to talk about their
concerns, ending up by making arrangements
for the funeral, a cremation. Instead of sitting
silently in anger, they communicated and
consoled each other. The mother died the next
day. If I had not seen the peaceful look on her
face during her last day, I might have worried
that this outburst of anger might have killed her.

Another aspect that is often not taken into
account is what kind of fatal illness the patient
has. There are certain expectations of cancer, just
as there are certain pictures associated with heart
disease. The former is often viewed as a lingering,
pain-producing illness while the latter can strike
suddenly, painless but final. I think there is a
great deal of difference if a loved one dies slowly
with much time available for preparatory grief
on both sides, compared to the feared phone call,
"It happened, it's all over." It is easier to talk to a
cancer patient about death and dying than it is

with a cardiac patient, who arouses concerns in us that we might frighten him and thus provoke a coronary, i.e., his death. The relatives of a cancer patient are therefore more amenable to discussing the expected end than the family of someone with heart disease, when the end can come any moment and a discussion may provoke it, at least in the opinion of many members of families whom we have spoken with.

I remember a mother of a young man in Colorado who did not allow her son to take any exercise, not even the most minimal kind, in spite of the contrary advice on the part of his doctors. In conversations this mother would often make statements like "if he does too much he will drop dead on me," as if she expected a hostile act on the part of her son to be committed against her. She was totally unaware of her own hostility even after sharing with us some of her resentment for having "such a weak son," whom she very often associated with her ineffective and unsuccessful husband. It took months of careful, patient listening to this mother before she was able to express some of her own destructive wishes toward her child. She rationalized these by the fact that he was the cause of her limited social and professional life, thus rendering her as ineffective as she regarded her husband to be. These are complicated family situations, in which a sick member of the family is rendered more incapable of functioning because of the relative's conflicts. If we can learn to respond to such family members with compassion and understanding rather than judgment and criticism, we also help the patient bear his handicap with more ease and dignity.

The following example of Mr. P. demonstrates the difficulties that can occur for the patient when he is ready to separate himself but the family is unable to accept the reality, thus contributing to the patient's conflicts. Our goal should always be to help the patient and his family face the crisis together in order to achieve acceptance of this final reality simultaneously.

Mr. P. was a man in his mid-fifties who looked about fifteen years older than his age. The doctors felt that he had only a poor chance to respond to " and marasmus, but mainly because of his lack of "fighting spirit." Mr. P. had his stomach removed because of cancer five years prior to this hospitalization. At first he accepted his illness quite well and was full of hope. As he grew weaker and thinner, he became increasingly depressed until the time of his readmission, when a chest X-ray revealed metastatic tumors in his lungs. The patient had not been informed of the biopsy result when I saw him. The question was raised as to the advisability of possible radiation or surgery for a man in his weak condition. Our interview proceeded in two sessions. The first visit served the purpose of introducing myself and of telling him that I was available should he wish to talk about the seriousness of his illness and the problems that this might cause. A telephone interrupted us and I left the room, asking him to think about it. I also informed him about the time of my next visit.

When I saw him the next day, Mr. P. put his arm out in welcome and signaled to the chair as an invitation to sit down. In spite of many interruptions by a change of infusion bottles, distribution of medication, and routine pulse and blood pressure measurements, we sat for over an hour. Mr. P. had sensed that he would be allowed to "open his shades" as he called it. There was no defensiveness, no evasiveness in his accounts. He was a man whose hours seemed to count, who had no precious time to lose, and who seemed to be eager to share his concerns and regrets with someone who could listen.

The day before, he made the statement, "I want to sleep, sleep, sleep, and not wake up." Today he repeated the same thing, but added the word "but." I looked at him questioningly and he proceeded to tell me with a weak soft voice that his wife had come to visit him. She was convinced that he would make it. She expected him home to take care of the garden and the flowers. She also reminded him of his promise to retire soon, to move to Arizona perhaps, to have a few more good years. . . .

He talked with much warmth and affection about his daughter, twenty-one years old, who came to visit him on a leave from college, and who was shocked to see him in this condition. He mentioned all these things, as if he was to be blamed for disappointing his family, for not living up to their expectations.

I mentioned that to him and he nodded. He talked about all the regrets he had. He spent the first years of his marriage accumulating material goods for his family, trying to "make them a good home," and by doing so spent most of his time away from home and family. After the occurrence of cancer he spared every moment to be with them, but by then, it seemed to be too late. His daughter was away at school and had her own friends. When she was small and needed and wanted him, he was too busy making money.

Talking about his present condition he said, "Sleep is the only relief. Every moment of awakening is anguish, pure anguish. There is no relief.

I am thinking in envy of two men I saw executed. I sat right in front of the first man. I felt nothing. Now, I think, he was a lucky guy. He deserved to die. He had no anguish, it was fast and painless. Here I lie in bed, every hour, every day is agony."

Mr. P. was not so much concerned about pain and physical discomfort as he was tortured by regrets for not being able to fulfill his family's expectations, for being "a failure." He was tortured by his tremendous need to "let go and sleep, sleep, sleep" and the continuous flow of expectations from his environment. "The nurses come in and say I have to eat or I get too weak, the doctors come in and tell me about the new treatment they started, and expect me to be happy about it; my wife comes and tells me about the work I am supposed to do when I get out of here, and my daughter just looks at me and says 'You have to get well'— how can a man die in peace this way?"

For a brief moment he smiled and said, "I will take this treatment and go home once more. I will return to work the next day and make a bit more money. My insurance will pay for my daughter's education anyway, but she still needs a father for a while. But you know and I know, I just cannot do it. Maybe they have to learn to face it. It would make dying so much easier!"

Mr. P. showed as well as Mrs. W. (in Chapter VII) how difficult it is for patients to face impending and anticipated death when the family is not ready to "let go" and implicitly or explicitly prevents them from separating themselves from the involvements here on earth. Mrs. W.'s husband just stood at her bedside, reminding her of their happy marriage which should not end and pleading with the doctors to do everything humanly possible to prevent her from dying. Mr. P.'s wife reminded him of unfulfilled promises and undone tasks, thus communicating the same needs to him, namely, to have him around for many more years to come. I cannot say that both these partners used denial. Both of them knew the reality of the condition of their spouses. Yet both, because of their own needs, looked away from this reality. They faced it when talking with other people but denied it in front of the patients. And it was the patients who needed to hear that they too were aware of the seriousness of their condition and were able to accept this reality. Without this knowledge "every moment of awakening is pure anguish," in Mr. P.'s words. Our interview ended with the expression of hope that the important people in his environment would learn to face the reality of his dying rather than expressing hope for a prolonging of his life.

This man was ready to separate himself from this world. He was ready to enter the final stage when the end is more promising or there is not enough strength left to live. One might argue whether an all-out medical effort is appropriate in such circumstances. With enough infusions and transfusions, vitamins, energizers, and anti-depressant medication, with psychotherapy and symptomatic treatment, many such patients may be given an additional "lease on life." I have heard more curses than words of appreciation for the gained time, and I repeat my conviction that a patient has a right to die in peace and dignity. He should not be used to fulfill our own needs when his own wishes are in opposition to ours. I am referring to patients who have a physical illness but who are sane and capable enough to make decisions for themselves. Their wishes and opinions should be respected, they should be listened to and consulted. If the patient's wishes are contrary to our beliefs or convictions, we should express this conflict openly and leave the decisions up to the patient in respect to further interventions or treatments. In the many terminally ill patients I have so far interviewed, I have not seen any irrational behavior or unacceptable requests, and this includes the two psychotic women earlier described, who followed through with their treatment, one of them in spite of her otherwise almost complete denial of her illness.

THE FAMILY AFTER DEATH HAS OCCURRED

Once the patient dies, I find it cruel and inappropriate to speak of the love of God. When we lose someone, especially when we have had little if any time to prepare ourselves, we are enraged, angry, in despair; we should be allowed to express these feelings. The family members are often left alone as soon as they have given consent for autopsy. Bitter, angry, or just numb, they walk through the corridors of the hospital, unable often to face the brutal reality. The first few days may be filled with busy-work, with arrangements and visiting relatives. The void and emptiness is felt after the funeral, after the departure of the relatives. It is at this time that family members feel most grateful to have someone to talk to, especially if it is someone who had recent contact with the deceased and who can share anecdotes of some good moments towards the end of the deceased's life. This helps the relative over the shock and the initial grief and prepares him for a gradual acceptance.

Many relatives are preoccupied by memories and ruminate in fantasies, often even talk to the deceased as if he was still alive. They not only isolate themselves from the living but make it harder for themselves to face the reality of the person's death. For some, however, this is the only way they can cope with the loss, and it would be cruel indeed to ridicule them or to confront them daily with the unacceptable reality. It would be more helpful to understand this need and to help them separate themselves by taking them out of their isolation gradually. I have seen this behavior mainly in young widows who had lost their husbands at an early age and were rather unprepared. It may be more frequently encountered in the days of war where death of a young person occurs elsewhere, though I believe a war always makes relatives more aware of the possibility of no return. They are therefore more prepared for that death than, for example, for the unexpected death of a young man through a rapidly progressing illness.

A last word should be mentioned about the children. They are often the forgotten ones. Not so much that nobody cares; the opposite is often true. But few people feel comfortable talking to a child about death. Young children have different concepts of death, and they have to be taken into consideration in order to talk to them and to under- stand their communications. Up to the age of three a child is concerned only about separation, later followed by the fear of mutilation. It is at this age that the small child begins to mobilize, to take his first trips out "into the world," the sidewalk trips by tricycle. It is in this environment that he may see the first beloved pet run over by a car or a beautiful bird torn apart by a cat. This is what mutilation means to him, since it is the age when he is concerned about the integrity of his body and is threatened by anything that can destroy it.

Also, death, as outlined in Chapter I, is not a permanent fact for the three-to-five-year-old. It is as temporary as burying a flower bulb into the soil in the fall to have it come up again the following spring.

After the age of five death is often regarded as a man, a bogey-man who comes to take people away; it is still attributed to an outward intervention.

Around the age of nine to ten the realistic conception begins to show, namely, death as a permanent biological process.

Children will react differently to the death of a parent, from a silent withdrawal and isolation to a wild loud mourning which attracts attention and thus a replacement of a loved and needed object. Since children cannot yet differentiate between the wish and the deed (as outlined in Chapter I), they may feel a great deal of remorse and guilt. They will feel responsible for having killed the parents and thus fear a gruesome punishment in retribution. They may, on the other hand, take the separation relatively calmly and utter such statements as "She will come back for the spring vacation" or secretly put an apple out for her — in order to assure that she has enough to eat for the temporary trip. If adults, who are upset already during this period, do not understand such children and reprimand or correct them, the children may hold inside their own way of grieving — which is often a root for later emotional disturbance.

With an adolescent, however, things are not much different than with an adult. Naturally adolescence is in itself a difficult time and added loss of a parent is often too much for such a youngster to endure. They should be listened to and allowed to ventilate their feelings, whether they be guilt, anger or plain sadness.

RESOLUTION OF GRIEF AND ANGER

What I am saying again here is, let the relative talk, cry, or scream if necessary. Let them share and ventilate, but be available. The relative has a long time of mourning ahead of him, when the problems for the dead are solved. He needs help and assistance from the confirmation of a so-called bad diagnosis until months after the death of a member of the family.

By help I naturally do not assume that this has to be professional counseling of any form; most people neither need nor can afford this. But they need a human being, a friend, doctor, nurse, or chaplain — it matters little. The social worker may be the most meaningful one, if she has helped with arrangements for a nursing home and if the family wishes to talk more about their mother in that particular set-up, which may have been a source of guilt feelings for not having kept her at home. Such families have at times visited other old folks in the same nursing home and continued their task of caring for someone, perhaps as a partial denial, perhaps just to do good for all the missed opportunities with Grandma. No matter what the underlying reason we should try to understand their needs and to help relatives direct these needs constructively to diminish guilt, shame, or fear of retribution. The most meaningful help that we can give any relative, child or adult, is to share his feelings before the event of death and to allow him to work through his feelings, whether they are rational or irrational.

If we tolerate their anger, whether it is directed at us, at the deceased, or at God, we are helping them take a great step towards acceptance without guilt. If we blame them for daring to ventilate such socially poorly tolerated thoughts, we are blameworthy for prolonging their grief, shame, and guilt which often results in physical and emotional ill health.

"The Eye of the Beholder":
Episode 42 from *The Twilight Zone*
by Rod Serling
(November 11, 1960)

EPISODE SUMMARY

Suspended in time and space for a moment, your introduction to Miss Janet Tyler, who lives in a very private world of darkness, a universe whose dimensions are the size, thickness, length of a swath of bandages that cover her face. In a moment we'll go back into this room and also in a moment we'll look under those bandages, keeping in mind, of course, that we're not to be surprised by what we see, because this isn't just a hospital, and this patient 307 is not just a woman. This happens to be the Twilight Zone, and Miss Janet Tyler, with you, is about to enter it.

A woman is lying in a hospital bed with her face bandaged up. The nurse comes into her room with some sleeping medicine. The woman takes the opportunity to ask the nurse about how the day was since she obviously wasn't able to tell. Then she asks when they will take the bandages off. The nurse tells her the bandages won't come off until they can decide if they can fix her face. It's a pretty bad face according to the woman. Ever since she was a little girl people have been turning away from her in horror. She doesn't want to be beautiful. She just wants people not to scream when they see her. The nurse promises that they might take off the bandages tomorrow, or the next day. The nurse leaves to smoke a cigarette at the reception table. There, she and another nurse discuss the poor fate of patient 307, Janet Tyler. Dr. Bernardi stops by to look after Miss Tyler. He promises to remove the bandages soon.

This is Janet's eleventh visit to the hospital in an attempt to fix her face. She has not responded previously to any of the proven techniques. Her case is also not correctable by plastic surgery. The doctor, however, is hopeful that the latest treatment may have worked. Eleven is the mandatory number of experiments. After eleven visits, they are not permitted to help out any further. The doctor tries to explain how they have gone to great lengths to help her fit into society. Janet wants to go outside and sit in the garden to feel the air and to feel normal. She breaks down and starts crying. The doctor explains about the special area where people "of her kind" have been congregated. Janet claims it's nothing more than a ghetto designed for freaks. Janet goes on a tirade about how the state is not God and it shouldn't have the power to segregate out those that are not normal. Her breakdown progresses as she pleads for the doctor to remove the bandages.

A couple of nurses arrive to help out with the situation. Dr. Bernardi makes the call to remove the bandages. Later, he is relaxing in his office smoking a cigarette when Janet's nurse stops by. She correctly perceives that Bernardi has become personally involved in Tyler's case. The doctor says that he has looked beyond Janet's face and has discovered who she really is. According to him, people like her should be allowed to be different. The nurse reminds him that he's speaking of treason. Later that night, the leader is on the television speaking of glorious conformity. While he's lecturing, Dr. Bernardi is taking off Miss Tyler's bandages. He explains the procedure to her, and he also tells her that if she becomes emotional he will have to put her under sedation. Janet agrees, and the doctor starts to remove the bandages, layer by layer. At the last stage he asks her if she wants a mirror, but she nervously declines.

The last of the bandages are removed, right after the doctor reminds Miss Tyler that she can still live a long life among people of her own kind if the treatment failed. Apparently the treatment has been a failure because the nurses recoil in horror and the doctor proclaims, "No change, no change at all!" Janet Tyler raises her head and is revealed to be a beautiful blonde. She panics and tries to run away. Then the faces of everybody else are revealed: misshaped mouths, pig-like noses, and very large bumps over the eyes. Janet breaks free and runs down the hospital corridors until finally stopping when she runs into a room with another freak: Walter Smith. Mr. Smith is in charge of the village that Miss Tyler will be going to. Walter reassures Janet that it doesn't matter what they look like, because beauty is in the eye of the beholder. Together, they walk out of the hospital hand-in-hand. . . .

Now the questions that come to mind: where is this place and when is it, what kind of world where ugliness is the norm and beauty the deviation from that norm? You want an answer? The answer is, it doesn't make any difference. Because the old saying happens to be true. Beauty is in the eye of the beholder, in this year or a hundred years hence, on this planet or wherever there is human life, perhaps out amongst the stars. Beauty is in the eye of the beholder. Lesson to be learned in the Twilight Zone.

JANET TYLER: Nurse?

THE NURSE: Time for your sleeping medicine, honey.

JANET TYLER: Is it night already?

THE NURSE: It's nine-thirty.

JANET TYLER: What about the day?

THE NURSE: Well, what about it?

JANET TYLER: Well, was it a beautiful day? Was it warm? Was the sun up?

THE NURSE: Oh, it was kind of warm.

JANET TYLER: Yes, and clouds? Were there clouds in the sky?

THE NURSE: I suppose there were. I never was much for staring up at the sky.

JANET TYLER: No? I used to like to look at the clouds a lot. If you stare at them long enough, they become things. You know what I mean? People, ships, anything you want, really.

THE NURSE: It's time to take your temperature now.

JANET TYLER: Oh, please, one more thing, Nurse.

THE NURSE: Well?

JANET TYLER: When will they take the bandages off? How long, Nurse?

THE NURSE: Until they decide whether or not they can fix your face.

JANET TYLER: I guess it's pretty bad, isn't it?

THE NURSE: I've seen worse.

JANET TYLER: Well, yes, but it's pretty bad, isn't it? Oh, I know it's pretty bad. Ever since I can remember, ever since I was a little girl, people have turned away when they looked at me. Funny, the very first thing I can remember is another little child screaming when she looked at me. Oh, I never really wanted to be beautiful, you know? I mean, I never wanted to look like a painting. I never even wanted to be loved, really. I just wanted people not to scream when they looked at me. When, Nurse? When, when, when will they take the bandages off?

Episode 42 from The Twilight Zone   **373**

THE NURSE: Maybe tomorrow. Maybe the
next day. You've been waiting so long now.
It doesn't really make much difference whether
it's two weeks or days now. Does it?

THE NURSE: Doctor Bernardi? Evening report on
patient 307. No temperature change. Resting
comfortably.

DR. BERNARDI: Thank you, Nurse. I'll be down later.

THE RECEPTIONIST: Ever see her face, 307?

THE NURSE: Indeed I have. If it were mine, I'd
bury myself in a grave someplace. Poor thing.
Some people want to live no matter what.
Cigarette?

THE NURSE: Blood pressure and temperature are
normal, Doctor. There's been no change.

DR. BERNARDI: All right. Come back around
eleven o'clock, Nurse. Give her the usual
sedative then.

THE NURSE: All right, Doctor.

DR. BERNARDI: Well, it's warm this evening,
Miss Tyler.

JANET TYLER: Yes? I thought it was but I couldn't
be sure.

DR. BERNARDI: Well, it's very warm. You can take
my word for that. We'll have those bandages
off you very soon. I expect you're pretty uncomfortable.

JANET TYLER: Well, I'm used to bandages on my
face.

DR. BERNARDI: I have no doubt. This is your ninth
visit here. It is the ninth?

JANET TYLER: The eleventh. You know, sometimes I think I've lived my whole life inside of a dark cave with walls of gauze, and the wind that blows in through the mouth of the cave smells of ether and disinfectant. But there's a kind of a comfort living inside this cave. Wonderfully private. Nobody can ever see me. It's hopeless, isn't it, Doctor? I'll never look any differently.

DR. BERNARDI: Well, that's hard to say. Up to now, you haven't responded to the shots or the medications, any of the proven techniques. Frankly, you've stumped us, Miss Tyler. Nothing we've done so far has made any difference at all. However, we're very hopeful for what this last treatment may have accomplished. There's no telling, of course, until we get the bandages off. I'm sorry your case is not one that we could have handled with plastic surgery, but your bone structure, flesh type, many factors prohibit the surgical approach. Your eleventh visit.

JANET TYLER: No more after this, are there, Doctor? No more tries?

DR. BERNARDI: Eleven is the mandatory number of experiments. We're not permitted to do any more after eleven.

JANET TYLER: Now what, Doctor?

DR. BERNARDI: Well, you're kind of jumping the gun, aren't you, Miss Tyler? You may very well have responded to these last injections. There's no way of telling until we get the bandages off.

JANET TYLER: And if I haven't responded? Then what?

DR. BERNARDI: Then there are alternatives.

JANET TYLER: Like?

DR. BERNARDI: Don't you know?

JANET TYLER: Yes, I know.

DR. BERNARDI: You realize, of course, Miss Tyler, why these rules are in effect. Each of us is afforded as much opportunity as possible to fit in with society. In your case, think of the time and money and the effort expended to make you look . . .

JANET TYLER: Look like what, Doctor?

DR. BERNARDI: Normal, the way you'd like to look.

JANET TYLER: Doctor? Doctor, may I walk outside? Please, may I? May I just go and sit in the garden? Just for a little while? Just, just to feel the air? Just to smell the flowers? Just, just to make believe I am normal? If I sit out there in the darkness, then the whole world is dark, and I'm more a part of it like that. Not just one grotesque, ugly woman with a bandage on her face, with a special darkness all her own. I want to belong. I want to be like everybody. Please, Doctor. Please help me.

DR. BERNARDI: There are many others who share your misfortune. People who look much as you do. One of the alternatives, just in the event that this last treatment is not successful, is simply to allow you to move into a special area in which people of your kind have been congregated.

JANET TYLER: People of my kind congregated? You mean segregated! You mean imprisoned, don't you, Doctor? You're talking about a ghetto, aren't you? A ghetto designed for freaks!

DR. BERNARDI: Miss Tyler! Now, the state is not unsympathetic. Your presence here in this hospital is proof of that. It's doing all it can for you. But you're not being rational, Miss Tyler. Now you know you can't expect to live any kind of a life among normal people.

JANET TYLER: I could try. I could wear a mask
  or this bandage. I wouldn't bother anybody.
  I'd just go my own way. I'd get a job, any job.
  Who are you people anyway? What is
  this State? Who makes all these rules and
  conditions and statutes that people who are
  different have to stay away from the people
  who are normal? The State isn't God, Doctor.

DR. BERNARDI: Miss Tyler, please.

JANET TYLER: The State is not God! It hasn't the
  right to penalize somebody for an accident of
  birth! It hasn't the right to make ugliness a
  crime!

DR. BERNARDI: Miss Tyler! Miss Tyler, stop this
  immediately!

JANET TYLER: I feel the night out there. I feel the
  air. I can smell the flowers. Oh, please, please,
  take this off me. Please. Please take this off me.
  Please take this off me. Oh, please, take this off
  me! Take it off me! Take it off me! Help! Somebody help me! Help! No, no, no, no, let me go.
  Let me go. Please, please, let me go. Let me go,
  please. Oh, please. Please, let me go. Please,
  please, let me go.

DR. BERNARDI: All right, then I will take the
  bandages off you. Get the anesthetist.

THE NURSE: Yes, Doctor.

THE NURSE: You look tired, Doctor.

DR. BERNARDI: Do I? Well, I hadn't thought about
  it. I suppose I am.

THE NURSE: You've been under a great deal of
  tension. I know how much it means to you,
  this case in 307.

DR. BERNARDI: Well, you try to be impersonal
  about these things. You do everything

medically possible, everything humanly possible, and then in the end you cross your fingers and you hope for a miracle. And, you know, once in a while a miracle does happen. Just often enough to let you know that you're not wrong or foolish to hope for one.

THE NURSE: You're destroying yourself this way. Forgive me, but you mustn't let yourself get personally involved here.

DR. BERNARDI: I know. You think I haven't told myself that? You see, Nurse, I've looked underneath those bandages.

THE NURSE: So have I. It's horrible.

DR. BERNARDI: No, I mean deeper than that. Deeper than that pitiful, twisted lump of flesh. Deeper even than that misshapen skeletal mask. I've seen that woman's real face, Nurse. The face of her real self. It's a good face. It's a human face.

THE NURSE: I understand. But I must confess. It's easier for me to think of her as human when her face is covered up.

DR. BERNARDI: But why? Why must we feel that way, Nurse? What is the dimensional difference between beauty and something repellent? Is it skin deep? No, less than that! Why, Nurse? Why shouldn't people be allowed to be different? Why?

THE NURSE: Doctor, be careful! What you're talking
. . .

DR. BERNARDI: I know . . . treason.

THE NURSE: Oh, this case has upset your balance, your sense of values.

DR. BERNARDI: Well, I suppose. Don't be concerned, Nurse. I'll be all right once the bandages are off. Once I know one way or the other.

THE RECEPTIONIST: Leader's speaking tonight. He goes on in just a few minutes.

(Pushes a button and TV screen appears)

THE ANNOUNCER: And now, ladies and gentlemen, our Leader.

THE LEADER: Good evening, ladies and gentlemen. Tonight, I shall talk to you about glorious conformity, about the delight and the ultimate pleasure of our unified society.

DR. BERNARDI: Now, I have to ask you once again, Miss Tyler, and I must insist that you promise you'll remain rational. No tantrums. No temperament. No violence. You understand? Now, I'll tell you precisely what I'm going to do. I'm going to cut the bandages a section at a time, then I'm going to unwrap the bandages very gradually. The process has to be slow so that your eyes can become accustomed to the light. As you know, these injections may have had some effect on your vision.

JANET TYLER: I understand.

DR. BERNARDI: So now, as I unwrap, I want you to keep your eyes open and I want you to describe to me the various shadings of light as you perceive it.

JANET TYLER: All right.

DR. BERNARDI: Now, if you make any movement or if you start getting emotional on us, Miss Tyler, I'm going to have to have the nurses hold you down and have the anesthetist put you under sedation. You understand?

JANET TYLER: I promise I won't.

DR. BERNARDI: All right, then.

DR. BERNARDI: Do you see any light now, Miss Tyler?

JANET TYLER: Oh, just a little. It looks gray.

DR. BERNARDI: All right, now. Just be very quiet.

DR. BERNARDI: Now, Miss Tyler?

JANET TYLER: Oh, it's much brighter.

DR. BERNARDI: Good, good. Look up toward the light.

DR. BERNARDI: How about now, Miss Tyler?

JANET TYLER: Oh, yes. It's very bright.

DR. BERNARDI: Good, good, now.

DR. BERNARDI: I'm at the last layer of bandages, Miss Tyler.

JANET TYLER: Oh, I can just see you. I can just distinguish your outline vaguely but I can just see you.

DR. BERNARDI: Good. All right, Miss Tyler, I'm going to remove the last of the bandages now. Would you like a mirror?

JANET TYLER: No. No, thank you. No mirror.

DR. BERNARDI: All right, then. I want you to remember this, please. Miss Tyler, are you listening?

JANET TYLER: Yes, I'm listening.

DR. BERNARDI: Now, we have done all we could do. If we've been successful, well and good, there are no problems. But if, on the other hand, this final treatment has not achieved the desired result, please remember, Miss Tyler, that you can still live a long and fruitful life among people of your own kind. As soon as we discover the results, we'll either release you, or . . .

JANET TYLER: Doctor?

DR. BERNARDI: Yes?

JANET TYLER: If I'm still terribly ugly, well, is there any other alternative? Could I please be put away?

DR. BERNARDI: Well, under certain circumstances, Miss Tyler, the State does provide for the extermination of undesirables. However, there are many factors to be considered in the decision. Under the present circumstances, I doubt very much whether we would be permitted to do anything but transfer you to a communal group of people with your disability.

JANET TYLER: You'll make me go then?

DR. BERNARDI: That probably'd be the case. Now remain very quiet. Keep your eyes open. All right, Miss Tyler. Here comes the last of it. I wish you every good luck.

DR. BERNARDI: No change! No change at all!

DR. BERNARDI: I was afraid of this. Turn on the light. Needle, please.

DR. BERNARDI: Stop that patient! Stop her!

THE LEADER: We know now that there must be a single purpose! A single norm! A single approach! A single entity of peoples! A single virtue! A single morality! A single frame of reference! A single philosophy of government! We must cut out all that is different like a cancerous growth! It is essential in this society that we not only have a norm, but that we conform to that norm! Differences weaken us! Variations destroy us! An incredible permissiveness to deviation from this norm is what has ended nations and brought them to their knees! Conformity we must worship and hold sacred! Conformity is the key to survival!

DR. BERNARDI: Miss Tyler? Miss Tyler, don't be afraid. He's only a representative from the group you're going to live with. Now, oddly enough, you've come right to him. Now, come on now. Don't be afraid. He's not going to hurt you. He won't hurt you. It's all right. It's all right, Miss Tyler. Now, this is Mr. Smith. Mr. Walter Smith. Mr. Smith is in charge of the village group in the north. He'll take you there tonight. It's the only way now.

WALTER SMITH: Miss Tyler, we have a lovely village and wonderful people. I think you're going to like it where I'm going to take you. You'll be with your own kind. And in a little while, oh, you'll be amazed how little a while, you'll feel a sense of great belonging. You'll feel a sense of being loved. And you will be loved, Miss Tyler. Miss Tyler, would you get your things now? You can leave anytime.

JANET TYLER: Mr. Smith?

WALTER SMITH: Yes?

JANET TYLER: Why do we have to look like this?

WALTER SMITH: I don't know, Miss Tyler. I really don't know. But you know something?

It doesn't matter. There's an old saying.
A very, very old saying. Beauty is in the eye
of the beholder. When we leave here, when
we go to the village, try to think of that,
Miss Tyler. Say it over and over to yourself.
Beauty is in the eye of the beholder. Come on
now. We'll get your things and we'll leave.

DR. BERNARDI: Goodbye, Miss Tyler.

"A Red, Red Rose"
by Robert Burns
(1759-1796)

O, my luve is like a red, red rose,
    That's newly sprung in June.
O, my luve is like the melodie,
    That's sweetly play'd in tune.

As fair art thou, my bonie lass,
    So deep in luve am I,
And I will luve thee still, my dear,
    Till a' the seas gang dry.

Till a' the seas gang dry, my dear,
    And the rocks melt wi' the sun!
And I will luve thee still, my dear,
    While the sands o' life shall run.

And fare thee weel, my only luve,
    And fare thee weel a while!
And I will come again, my luve,
    Tho' it were ten thousand mile!

"To My Dear and Loving Husband"
by Anne Bradstreet
(1612-1672)

If ever two were one, then surely we.
If ever man were lov'd byt wife, then thee;
If ever wife was happy in a man,
Compare me ye women if you can.
I prize thy love more than whole Mines of gold,
Or all the riches that the East doth hold.
My love is such that Rivers cannot quench,
Nor ought but love from thee, give recompence.
Thy love is such I can no way repay,
The heavens reward thee manifold I pray.
Then while we live, in love lets so persever,
That when we live no more, we may live ever.

Song: "How Many Times Do I Love Thee, Dear?"
by Thomas Lovell Beddoes
(1803-1849)

How many times do I love thee, dear?
    Tell me how many thoughts there be
        In the atmosphere
        Of a new-fall'n year,
Whose white and sable hours appear
    The latest flake of Eternity —
So many times do I love thee, dear.

How many times do I love again?
    Tell me how many beads there are
            In a silver chain
        Of evening rain,
Unraveled from the tumbling main,
    And the reading the eye of a yellow star —
So many times do I love again.

"How Do I Love Thee?"
by Elizabeth Barrett Browning
(1806-1861)

How do I love thee? Let me count the ways.

I love thee to the depth and bredth and height

My soul can reach, when feeling out of sight

For the ends of Being and ideal Grace.

I love thee to the level of everyday's

Most quiet need, by sun and candle-light.

I love thee freely, as men strive for Right;

I love thee purely, as they turn from Praise.

I love thee with the passion put to use

In my old griefs, and with my childhood's faith.

I love thee with a love I seemed to lose

With my lost saints, — I love thee with the breath,

Smiles, tears, of all my life! — and, if God choose,

I shall but love thee better after death.

"Where Do Babies Come From?"
from *The N.Y. Times Magazine*
by Sara Corbett
(June 16, 2002)

Outside Phnom Penh, along a road running west to Cambodia's more rural provinces, sits an orphanage. It was built on a defunct rice paddy and caters exclusively to Americans wishing to adopt children. To get there, would-be parents travel from the city in air-conditioned cars with hired Cambodian drivers, passing windowless garment factories and the shanty settlements that have grown up to house thousands of workers. They pass legless land-mine victims begging for money and old women wheeling carts of coconuts in the stultifying sun.

Finally, they turn down a narrow washboard lane, which runs through a village and past a small Buddhist wat, or temple. Occasionally, the rice farmers look up from their work to watch the cars as they rise like apparitions from the dust — white faces peering expectantly from the back seats — and then disappear again, headed toward the orphanage. The moment is one of mutual disorientation.

Until recently, the cars seemed always to come — sometimes once a week but increasingly more like once a day, as greater numbers of Americans arrived from half a world away, their bags stuffed with Baby Gap clothing and Whoozit toys, their hearts piloted by no more than a passport photo of a Cambodian child sent months earlier. If the United States is seen as the world's great exporter — of culture, of goods, of ideology — then this must count as an unlikely pilgrim's route.

At the end of the road, there are roughly 150 children housed at a place called the Asian Orphan Association, a collection of aluminum-roofed buildings sparsely shaded by coconut palms. They eat mainly rice porridge and sleep on straw mats spread across the floor, tended by nannies fanning themselves languidly in the humid air. Mosquitoes float in clouds. The infants fill two rooms the size of a convention hall, sprawled in bamboo baby baskets that hang from the ceiling, floating like human pendants above a gleaming tile floor. Nearby, a group of 5- and 6-year-olds dressed in Green Bay Packers jerseys and cotton jumpers sit raptly before a Khmer soap opera playing on a small television set.

But whereas the children were once leaving, whereas adoptive parents used to show up for the sweet awkwardness of having a baby placed in their arms for the first time, the adoptions have now stopped. This orphanage, along with 15 others that work with American adoption agencies, has become the focus of a U.S. investigation of adoption practices in Cambodia, one that questions whether adoption has morphed from an altruistic pursuit into a highly lucrative industry. If the U.S. government worries that these children have become commodities in a twisted free market, adoptive parents tend to view them as needy orphans robbed of the opportunity for a better life.

Harder, perhaps, to know are the hearts of the Cambodian people. Decades of political upheaval — including the dictator Pol Pot's genocide of three million Cambodians in the mid-70's — have left the country crippled by epidemic levels of AIDS and tuberculosis and mired in poverty that is virtually unimaginable to an American mind. Meanwhile, fertility rates are among the highest in Southeast Asia. There are Cambodians who will crowd a baby stroller pushed by American parents and stroke the cheek of the adopted child inside, lending tacit approval. "Lucky baby," they will say in Khmer, "Lucky baby." There are others who pointedly avert their gaze.

In the village near the orphanage, the faces of the rice farmers betray nothing, glancing up as they do when another car heads back down the dusty road toward Phnom Penh. For a Cambodian living on less than a dollar a day, there is no conjuring an orphan's journey from straw mat and daily porridge to a lovingly painted nursery and organic squash dished up in suburban Boston. And for the Americans sitting in the back seat, holding a child who has arrived in their laps with virtually no history, no hint of parentage nor of what fate or ill circumstance may have brought him or her to this unlikely moment, for these new parents the child is its own mystery.

Visiting Cambodia earlier this spring, I met a newly adopted baby named Rachel Chronister. She was an ethereal-looking 8-month-old with charcoal eyes and wisps of dark hair and was, at the time, living in a high-rise apartment in Phnom Penh with her adoptive American parents, Christina and Ben Chronister, and their two biological children, ages 5 and 6. The Chronisters started the adoption process last summer, were matched with Rachel in October and were told by their adoption agency that she would be living with them in their Seattle-area home by Christmastime.

But in the fall, consular offices at the U.S. Embassy began flagging what they considered to be fraudulent documents coming from several orphanages, including the Asian Orphan Association, where Rachel was living. Consequently, the issuing of visas to U.S.-bound orphans ground nearly to a halt. On Dec. 21, James Ziglar, commissioner of the Immigration and Naturalization Service, formally suspended new visa processing for adopted children in Cambodia, citing suspicions that they were being bought or stolen from their parents and put into orphanages with false paperwork in order to feed the growing American demand for babies. "Documents didn't match up; signatures were forged," says Bill Strassberger, an I.N.S. spokesman. "The paperwork would say babies had been abandoned in a certain village, and then an investigation would show that no baby had been abandoned in that place for years."

This marks the first time the U.S. government has stopped processing orphan visas in a foreign country, apparently because it seemed unlikely the Cambodian government would take action. While Cambodia, which began allowing foreign adoption in 1989, is now cooperating with the investigation, the country previously had done little to combat child trafficking.

When the United States announced its moratorium, Christina and Ben Chronister were one of an estimated 400 families caught with adoptions in midprocess. And as the U.S government pledged to conduct a "special humanitarian initiative," sending a task force consisting of American and Cambodian officials to each orphanage in order to review pending cases individually, the Chronisters and a handful of other eager parents had flown to Phnom Penh to wait. The Cambodian government had already sent them an official "adoption decree," which allowed them legally to pick up their children, but without I.N.S. approval they could not bring them home. When I first encountered the Chronisters in March, they had been in Cambodia for several weeks and were growing increasingly impatient for news that Rachel's case had been cleared. "All we want," Christina said dolefully, sitting by the apartment building's small pool one afternoon, "is to bring our family home."

For Christina, who had grown up with two adopted Asian-American sisters, Rachel's adoption felt like a natural way to complete the family. She and Ben originally sought to adopt a child from China, but learning that it would take more than a year, they turned instead to Cambodia. Over the last several years, Cambodia's popularity with Americans looking to adopt has sky-rocketed. According to the U.S. State Department, applications leapt from 249 in 1998 to about 100 a month in the summer of 2001. The growth mirrors a larger boom in international adoptions, and the increase in Cambodia most likely has to do with the fact that parents adopting there normally have a child in their arms within three to six months of completing their agency paper-work — a boon compared with the 12 or more months parents spend waiting for most foreign and state-side adoptions to be completed.

Kent M. Wiedemann, who until last month was the U.S. ambassador to Cambodia, says that the growing interest in Cambodian adoptions has resulted in new orphanages built expressly to keep the parade of Americans happy and that, more worryingly, these orphanages are filled with children who seem custom-ordered to suit American tastes. In the words of one aid worker, it is the "cute and cuddlies" who drive the adoption business, meaning the children who are healthy, young and preferably female. While there are no statistics on the age and sex of children sent to the United States, agency workers say that parents request girls over boys by a margin of four to one and that the demand for infants is great.

Our adoptive preferences have not been lost on aspiring capitalists. Two years ago, when an American nonprofit group, the Sharing Foundation, opened a state-of-the-art orphanage called Roteang not far from Phnom Penh, the entrepreneurs emerged from the woodwork. "Cambodians would come to the gate and say, 'Baby girl . . . $200,'" says Nancy Hendrie, a pediatrician from Boston and the foundation's director. She is quick to add that once orphanage employees turned down these initial offers, the baby sellers stopped coming. "But someone, obviously, had given them the impression that Americans pay for babies," she says.

Americans do indeed pay to adopt babies, but the money train is expected to stop short of rewarding birth parents or anyone who might profit from delivering a baby to an orphanage. Instead, adoptive parents pay agencies anywhere from $13,000 to $20,000. The agencies then contract with people known as "adoption facilitators" who work on the ground in Cambodia handling everything from finding children to pushing adoption paperwork through the requisite government ministries, passing out a commonly acknowledged bundle of bribes along the way. According to agency directors, a facilitator's fee can account for up to $9,000 of an adoption's total expense — money that is wired directly into a facilitator's private bank account or delivered in cash by adopting parents upon their arrival in Cambodia. How this money is used is indeterminate: some portion covers orphanage overhead, some offsets the facilitator's expenses and much of it, I.N.S. investigators say, is raw profit.

According to one of Cambodia's largest human rights organizations, the League for the Defense and Promotion of Human Rights (Licadho), the moneymaking potential in foreign adoptions is so great that it has inspired a network of unofficial "recruiters" who scour neighborhoods in search of young children, often prying birth mothers with lies or false promises in addition to cash in order to get them to turn over their children. Licadho alleges that the recruiters are paid off by facilitators or orphanage directors, who then bribe low-level government officials to create phony paperwork that can be submitted for adoption processing. Along the way, a child is in effect, laundered — moved into an orphanage with no true record of his or her birth-place or parents, rendering the child untraceable. "If a birth mother goes looking for her child," says Naly Pilorge, the deputy director of Licadho, "he or she is practically impossible to find."

Christina Chronister has heard Licadho's claims and says she believes they are exaggerated. She is quick to defend the Asian Orphan Association and its director, an affable Cambodian man named Serey Puth, who facilitated Rachel's adoption and whose orphanage work, says Chronister, is motivated by love for children. One muggy morning this spring, she and I went to visit Puth, 43, who speaks fluent English and in addition to over-seeing the orphanage operates a successful import operation in Phnom Penh. Puth is one of seven adoption facilitators working in Cambodia — three of them are American women; the rest are Cambodian men — and by most accounts, they are a highly competitive lot. While some, like Puth, maintain their own orphanages, others contract with state-run or private facilities to place children with adoptive parents.

As facilitators go, Puth was in the enviable position of having a host of especially adoptable children at his disposal. According to a chart in the office, girls outnumbered boys 95 to 62, and the majority of the orphanage's children were under a year old. Twenty-eight of the 157 children already had adoptive parents waiting for them in the States. Christina Chronister had come primarily to take photos of these children, which she planned to e-mail back to a group of waiting parents she met through online groups concerned with Cambo- dian adoption. It was hard not to be moved by the sight of her, a hazel-eyed, ponytailed woman of 30, making her way through the orphanage's caver-nous rooms, snapping photographs. "Your mommy loves you," she would say, bending to touch a baby's shoulder. Sometimes, she would wrap her arms around a child and squeeze tightly, as if to administer a transcontinental dose of love.

A few of the orphanage's children had obvious disabilities — there was a 1-year-old girl with a head tumor; a boy with a cleft palate — but their overall health bore stark contrast to the images I would take away from my visit a few days later to the Nutrition Center, a large orphanage in central Phnom Penh. There, I would see babies with bodies whittled so thin by AIDS that they hardly resembled babies, as well as entire rooms filled with 7- and 8-year-old children whose palsied limbs and vacant expressions bespoke a bleak future. Touring Puth's orphanage was a decidedly less provocative expe-rience, one more tailored to the feel-good part of adoption in which we might congratulate ourselves for giving a child a better life without the burden of feeling guilty about more needy children being left behind.

Licadho claims that in order to maintain the appearance of propriety, some orphanages will keep a respectable number of older and disabled children while maintaining what Nancy Hendrie calls a "side stash" of infants elsewhere —

including in houses that also operate as store-fronts for purchasing children. Last September, under pressure from Licadho, the police in Phnom Penh raided two such houses after being tipped-off by a Cambodian woman who claimed she had sold her two children. Police officers discovered 10 babies and two older children there and took four adults into custody under suspicion of child trafficking. Two of the children were promptly hospitalized.

The following day, Serey Puth produced documents stating that the 12 children were registered at his orphanage and that he had been paying for their care. While human rights workers say they believe the houses were merely way stations for children who had been bought from birth parents and would soon be placed for adoption through orphanages, Puth insists the opposite. He had brought the children from the orphanage to one of the houses, he says, believing it to be a medical clinic. (He did admit to me, however, that he wasn't sure whether the woman running the clinic was in fact a doctor.) Early this year, charges against the four people connected to the houses were dropped after several key witnesses suddenly — and suspiciously, say embassy officials — recanted their testimony. Puth himself was not charged. He denies any wrongdoing. "I have never paid for a child," he says.

When I went looking for the house Puth had called a clinic, I found it padlocked and shuttered. It was located on a garbage-strewn dirt avenue in one of the city's poorer corners, a section of the Tuol Kok district known as Construction Area 2. Inside the house next door, a round-faced woman sat on a hammock, nursing her year-old son. Speaking through a translator, she said that the supposed clinic had operated for about a year leading up to the raid, run by a Cambodian woman and a nanny, and had been filled with small children. She seemed genuinely concerned. And her characterization was consistent with police reports regarding the raid. "Mothers brought them here to sell," she said. "They were very poor. A boy was $150; a girl was $180." (In Cambodia, the dollar is the currency of choice in any big-ticket transaction.) Periodically, a man came and took the children away, to a place she called a "child center." She declined to give her name, saying she feared for her safety. "This is a very bad business," the woman said finally. "They lie to people, and tell them if they give their children away, they will get money from abroad."

The act of adoption is, at its best, one motivated by equal parts compassion and need. Historically, Americans have adopted children left parentless by war: 8,000 Japanese and European orphans were adopted in the late 1940's; thousands more came from Korea a decade later. Since then, adoption agencies have launched programs everywhere from Azerbaijan to Sierra Leone. According to the State Department figures, the number of international adoptions in the last decade has doubled, with a record 19,237 children granted orphan visas last year.

Domestic adoptions still outnumber international ones, but that margin appears to be quickly closing. Like Cambodia, the United States has no shortage of adoptable children: it is just that most of them are over the age of 5 and living in foster care. There is also the little-discussed issue of race: white infants make up the minority of available children but are also the most requested. In addition, the growing movement toward "open adoption" in this country allows for varying degrees of information and contact between birth parents and adoptive parents. This, coupled with the specter of several high-profile court cases in which biological parents have successfully reclaimed their children after years of separation, can intimidate potential adopters. "I was terrified of hooking up with a birth mother who would change her mind, even if there was only a small chance of it happening," says an Oregon mother, describing her decision to adopt from Cambodia instead of domestically.

In this respect, international adoption appears to be more straightforward and decidedly more anonymous, though the situation in Cambodia and other countries suggests that adoption, in any setting, is irrefutably complicated. "People go overseas to adopt because there's no legal risk regarding birth parents," says Samuel C. Totaro, a Pennsylvania attorney specializing in adoption. "Those parents' legal rights have been all but terminated."

Every year, thousands of international adoptions are conducted legitimately, though the possibilities for exploitation always exist. As prospective parents spell out their wishes and adoption agencies work to meet them, the quest to find the youngest children and the quickest turnaround often leads to less-developed countries, where regulations surrounding adoption tend to be loose and the amount of money involved can be dazzlingly influential. A team of U.S. government researchers reported last year that "almost every discussion we had of adoption in Romania involved the use of commercial terms, terms such as 'auction' and 'market' and 'price.' " (The Romanian government has since suspended adoptions.) Similar problems exist in Guatemala, and in the last few years, child-smuggling rings geared toward adoption have been broken up everywhere from Vietnam to Cyprus to Mexico.

Mary Lib Mooney, director of the National Association of Ethical Adoption Professionals, blames the large number of U.S. agencies using freelance facilitators, who operate on commission, rather than salaried staff members to locate adoptable children in foreign countries for the cycle of corruption. "They go to these countries, and they hire any Tom, Dick or Harry," she says. "Whether it's the trash man or a schoolteacher, they hire whoever can get the most babies for them. It's money, money, money."

The agencies I spoke with claimed to do their best to check out the facilitators' backgrounds, but they admitted that hard information can be difficult to come by. Wide Horizons for Children, an agency that makes 500 adoption placements a year, has used Serey Puth as its facilitator for about a year, paying him $6,900 for each child placed. And while the agency divorced itself from another facilitator working in the Republic of Georgia because of questionable ethics, it remains supportive of Puth. "I'm not a detective," says Vicki Peterson, executive director of Wide Horizons. "Until I see some real evidence that he's involved in a way that's inappropriate, I'm not in a position to feel that we shouldn't be working with him." Anne Polasko, who runs the Asia program for a Maryland agency called Adoptions Together, traveled to Cambodia in December to establish a program there, but she "didn't have a good feeling" about the facilitator she had planned to hire. "It really is hard to know who you're dealing with over there," Polasko says.

In Cambodia, there is no centralized registry for births and deaths. Record-keeping is done at the village level, if at all, and children do not generally receive birth certificates unless they are being considered for adoption. Because of a complex set of statutes in U.S. immigration law, children who are abandoned — as opposed to delivered to an orphanage by their parents — tend to have an easier time meeting requirements for an orphan visa. By the time an application reaches the U.S. Embassy for processing, a child's birth history more often than not has been entirely erased.

According to her documents, the Chronisters' little girl, Rachel, had spent the first part of her life named Suorsdey Rath. (Soursdey loosely translates to "hello." Rath, the Khmer word for "ward of the state," appears in many adopted children's names.) She arrived at the orphanage when she was about 5 days old. On the morning Christina and I visited, Serey Puth pulled Rachel's dossier from the drawer of a shiny file cabinet where he keeps the orphans' records. It was, as most orphanage files are, only a few pages long, containing a brief medical history and a single sheet written in Khmer, saying that she was born on June 26, 2001, and had been abandoned on July 1 in a village called Cheng Meng. There was a request for the orphanage "to kindly accept" the baby, signed by the village chief and notarized. Upon her arrival at the or-phanage, Rath had been issued a birth certificate. With no information to work with, Puth says that he guessed at the infant's birth date. In the spaces provided for the names of her birth mother and father, he had written in "Unknown." After a mandatory 90-day waiting period, he alerted an adoption agency that she had become available. Twelve days after that, Soursdey Rath was offered to the Chronisters.

For Christina, our meeting with Puth was a chance to fill in some of the informational holes in her daughter's documents. "Who named her?" she asked.

"The village chief," Puth said.

"Where is this village?"

"Oh, maybe two kilometers from here."

When I asked for directions to the village, Puth insisted on coming along. Soon, we were sitting in the two-room concrete home belonging to the chief of the rice-farming village. He was a heavy-lidded, Buddha-bellied man named Phon Phorn, who greeted us stoically after we woke him from a midday nap. Any time a pedestrian or motor-bike passed down the single-lane dirt track that served as the village's thoroughfare, Phorn leaned forward in his chair like a watchful troll. As chief of Meng Cheng, a community of 182 families, he served primarily as arbiter in local land disputes. Speaking through a translator and with Serey Puth listening carefully from a nearby seat, Phorn told us that he had been finding two or three abandoned babies a month, sometimes more. He shook his head sadly. "There are a lot of country people working in the garment factories," he said. "Unmarried women get pregnant, and they are afraid to go home to their villages. Maybe they know this is a safe place to leave the children."

If birth parents knew Phorn's village as a friendly place to abandon infants, then word curiously seemed to have spread, following the U.S. adoption suspension, that the Asian Orphan Association was no longer accepting children. Cheng Meng's last orphan, Phorn said, was abandoned early last July. All things being accurate, that orphan would have been Suorsdey Rath, the Chronisters' daughter. The news caused Christina to sit up in her seat, realizing that Phorn remembered the girl, that this unexpressive village chief offered a gossamer line into the clouds of her daughter's past.

"Why did you name her Soursdey?" she asked.

The chief allowed himself a smile. "It's a happy name," he said.

"Where did you find her?"

He would show us.

And so it was that we ended up on a dusty corner of red earth where Cheng Meng's two roads bisect and where the village office, a pitch-roofed building with a community water pump, sits behind barbed wire. Phorn gestured to a patch of ground littered with palm husks next to a wooden fence post, a few feet from the intersection. *"Here,"* he said. *"This is where they leave the babies."* He added that the infants are usually left early in the morning and that he hears their cries from his office, about 30 yards away. When I asked if he has caught a glimpse of a person or a car, or if a parent ever simply brings the child to his door, his answer was unequivocal: "Never."

It seemed possible that Phorn had been coached on this answer. Serey Puth also claims that in three years of running one of the area's largest orphanages, he has never met an infant's birth parent. Given that the U.S. investigation is centered on possible monetary transactions between birth parents and adoption facilitators or their associates, the safest answer may be to deny any interactions with birth parents whatsoever. Licadho suspects that a good number of the orphanage's children never passed through Cheng Meng at all, but rather came from other sources. A village chief, the group suggests, might be paid to provide paperwork stating that he discovered an infant abandoned in his village. (I.N.S. investigators claim, for example, that Phon Phorn's wife told them there hadn't been an infant found there in years.)

Nancy Hendrie, the American doctor who oversees the Roteang orphanage, says that desperate birth parents are seldom anonymous, that fathers or relatives routinely deliver children directly to her orphanage or give them to its staff nannies when they are visiting their home villages. The Roteang orphanage, she claims, has records on the birth parents of all but one of its 77 children, though it submits the requisite "abandonment" documents to the U.S. and Cambodian governments in order to get adoptions approved. While she regrets the duplicity, Hendrie scoffs at Puth's assertion that the majority of his orphanage's children are found in Cheng Meng and another neighboring village. "Cambodian people are not heartless," she says. "They don't leave newborn children lying by the side of the road."

At the fence post, Christina Chronister spent a long moment staring at the desolate corner as the sun beat down on the dry rice fields around her. She took a few pictures of the spot for Rachel's scrapbook, then put the camera away and squinted again at the ground. Had her daughter been left there last July, the height of the rainy season, approximately 5 days old and, as Phorn recalled, wrapped in a piece of cloth? It seemed impossibly possible. Who knew what the circumstances were? What American could even begin to imagine?

I asked Christina what she would tell Rachel someday about the invisible birth parents and the village fence post. She said: "I'll tell her everything I know. I'll tell her it was a quiet corner close to a good orphanage. Somebody cared enough to bring her here." She looked around one last time before beginning to walk away. "I see it as an act of love."

Not long after my visit to the fence post, I spent some time with a 3-year-old girl named Narak Den, a moon-faced child with silky cropped hair and attentive brown eyes. She was born in 1999 and lived with her mother and younger brother in a densely populated settlement west of Phnom Penh until she was 2 — at which point her mother, who was hungry, pregnant again and having trouble affording rent, decided to sell her. Den's mother had heard about a place, a medical clinic of sorts in the Toul Kok district of Phnom Penh, where you could take a child, and so that's what she did. She was given $50 and promised another $100 in a week.

I was told this story by the child's 51-year-old aunt, Narin Keo, one humid evening this spring as we sat cross-legged in her two-room, tin-roofed shack on the outskirts of Phnom Penh. The day's last light was fading, and so we talked in the gathering darkness, surrounded by Keo's own three children and her elderly mother. On the floor, several emaciated kittens pranced playfully in and out of a small basket. The 3-year-old, Den, sat quietly by her aunt's feet, dressed in purple shorts and a shirt with puppy dogs.

"When she told me she sold her baby," Keo said through a translator, "I could not do anything but cry." She added that she persuaded her younger sister to reveal the child's whereabouts by threatening her with a stick. And when she implored her sister to return the money in exchange for Den, who had been gone two days at that point, her sister confessed that she had already spent half of it. Keo, who is divorced and unemployed, then borrowed 100,000 Cambodian riel (about $50) from a neighbor, agreeing to pay 25 percent interest monthly.

It was Keo's 22-year-old daughter, a garment worker named Marida Kong, who followed the mother's directions to an unmarked clinic in Construction Area 12 — a place she would later recognize in the newspapers as the site of the September police raid — and asked for the child back. She brought a police officer with her for good measure and was nonetheless met with reluctance by the man and woman who appeared to be running the clinic. "They told me that this baby was bought for adoption for foreigners," Kong said that night. "They showed me a file written in English." When Kong persisted, the couple finally relented. Kong says that she paid $50, and Den was returned to her, wearing a yellow paper bracelet that indicated she was scheduled to be moved from the clinic the next day.

Den now lives with her aunt, grandmother and cousins, the six of them supported by Kong's garment-factory wages of between $40 and $70 a month, depending on how much work is available. The family struggles with the never-diminishing high-interest loan it took to remove Den from the Toul Kok clinic. Last year, Den's mother moved to the countryside, but not before she sold Den's brother, a year-old boy, to the same clinic. Keo explained that apologetically, saying they had no money to go looking for him. "I tried to stop her," she said. "We don't know where the baby boy has gone."

According to Keo, her sister was told that when her son was adopted, his new parents would send money from abroad. Since then, the mother has heard no news.

I had a number of conversations with families like Keo's who said they had sold, or been approached to sell, their children. One woman, Bopha Meas, claimed that several years ago an American facilitator named Lauryn Galindo offered to place her three children in an orphanage. She suggested that Meas could not possibly care for them on her own and showed her a picture of a well-fed American couple holding a Cambodian baby — proof, it would seem, of some better alternative. According to Meas, Galindo said she would give her $700, an offer Meas declined. Galindo, who has facilitated more than 400 Cambodian adoptions, acknowledged meeting with Meas but denied offering to buy the children. "There's absolutely no truth to that allegation," she said.

Another woman wept on the phone from her home in a rural province, begging me — through a translator — to find her 5-year-old son, Rasme Hang, who she had relinquished in exchange for $100 when he was 8 months old, having been told that he would go to the United States and that the adoptive parents would send photos. "I want to know he's O.K.," she said.

Finally, there was Chanthea Chea, a 31-year-old sturdily built woman whose hair hung in a ponytail down her back. Her husband divorced her last year when she was six months pregnant. Three days after her baby son was born in June, she was approached by a neighbor. He said, "Ah sister, if you have problems feeding your child because he has no father, I think you should send him to an orphanage where they raise children," she recalled. Chea, who was exhausted and hungry after birth and could not continue her job farming mushrooms, said that she would think about it. The following day, the man resurfaced with two women who claimed to represent an aid organization helping women and children.

Chea allowed her neighbor and the two women to take her infant son for a medical exam with the promise that they would return with him in an hour or two. But the boy never came back. Instead, Chea said that her neighbor took her to a house in Construction Area 12, near the clinic that was later raided. The two supposed aid workers pushed her to sign papers, relinquishing her son. "I asked them where my child was, and they said they already sent him to the orphanage," Chea said. After sitting at a table for two hours, feeling hopeless, Chea agreed to turn over her son to an unnamed orphanage with the understanding that she could visit him there once a week. There was no talk, she said, of adoption. The women gave her an $80 "donation" and told her she would receive an additional $30 a month as she recovered from the birth.

That night, Chea had a change of heart. "I went back to my house," she told me. "I could not sleep. I was weeping. In the morning, I brought the money back, but they said in order to get my child back I must pay $160. That night I lit a joss stick and candle and prayed for my child to come back to me." Chea said that she returned to the clinic several times over the next month, asking to see her son, but each time was turned away. At one point, Chea said she was given a passport-size photo of her son to assure her of his well-being.

When news of the police raid broke in early September, Chea sought the help of Licadho, the human rights group. The boy turned up in the custody of an organization run by an adoption facilitator named Sea Visoth, who, like Puth, works with American agencies. (Visoth could not be reached for comment.) Chea took the case to court, and after she accurately described her son's birthmarks to a judge in November, the boy was returned to her. "I was separated from my child for almost four months," she told me. "When I met him again, I almost couldn't breathe." Meanwhile, three people — Chea's neighbor, and the two women who paid her for the child, one of whom, according to the court officials, is Sea Visoth's wife — have been charged with human trafficking but have yet to be prosecuted. Sea Visoth was not charged.

Not long after Chea's court date, the U.S. Embassy produced an identical copy of the boy's passport photo, which had been included in an adoption application. The paperwork — signed by the director of a state-run orphanage in a rural province far from where Chea had relinquished her son — claimed the boy's name was Borin Rath and that he had been "abandoned and picked up by a kind person" before being dropped off at the orphanage on June 15. According to the embassy, Borin Rath had been matched with a couple in Maryland and his adoption was in the "final stages" of processing. Chea said she has since given the boy a name of her own — Sak Kada — meaning "strong spirit and good luck." Embassy officials say the family in Maryland has been matched with another child.

Adoptive American parents like to call attention to the paradoxes of their situation, especially in the increasingly complex skein of reproductive politics. "The government's holding up my adoption because maybe somebody gave the birth mother $25?" asked Janice Corkery, an Atlanta woman who was in Phnom Penh adopting

Cambodian twins. "I did in-vitro and paid someone for her eggs! Isn't that baby-buying?" Others make the point that privately arranged adoptions in the United States often require adoptive parents to pay a birth mother's medical and living expenses — up to tens of thousands of dollars — during and after pregnancy. In a country like Cambodia, where thousands of children die of malnutrition or disease each year and even more children fuel a booming sex trade, there are those who question the harm in giving a birth parent some money so that she can properly look after the rest of her family.

Yet the experience of someone like Chanthea Chea, whose poverty and relative powerlessness appear to have been aptly exploited, seems to offer a cautionary tale about what happens when first-world money flows into the third-world adoption. Narin Keo, the aunt who went into debt to buy back her sister's child, says her sister was unduly influenced by the offer of money. "If no money was involved," she said, "she wouldn't have given up her babies." As far as she was concerned, the promise of a better life in the United States should not eclipse love, even when staying in Cambodia means inevitable hardship. "I understand they have food over there, but I would not feel calm if I could not see my niece," Keo said. Finally, she reiterated her disgust for what her sister had done — and possibly for the impression it created about Cambodian women and their children. "Being a mother is important," she said that night as I took leave of the small, unlighted shack she shared with her family. She gestured to the half-starved kittens, now curled in the shadows next to their mother. "Even an animal," Keo said, "takes care of its children."

When is an orphan no longer an orphan? Christina Chronister says she feels that Suorsdey

Rath became her daughter in October, when an adoption agency employee e-mailed the child's name and photo in what is commonly called a "referral." From that day on, Chronister says, it became painful to imagine the girl sitting parentless in an orphanage.

While the Chronisters went to Phnom Penh, other waiting adoptive families have had little choice but to maintain their vigils at home, photos of Cambodian children stuck uselessly to the refrigerator. In the eyes of the U.S. government, however, an agency referral has virtually no meaning: a child is not formally adopted until both the Cambodian and the U.S. governments have signed off on the process. This kind of appraisal infuriates prospective parents, who accuse the I.N.S. and the U.S. Embassy of viewing their situation heartlessly. In recent months, families waiting to adopt from Cambodia have engaged in a passionate letter-writing campaign to Congress. They have picketed the I.N.S. building in Washington, toting posters that bear the plaintive faces of orphanage children, emblazoned with slogans like "The Only Family That Wants Me Is in the U.S."

Few seem willing to consider the government's assertion that some of these children may have been bought or that birth parents could have been intentionally misled. At the very least, many insist that shady practices are sporadic rather than systemic and that a shutdown of adoption is unwarranted. Most remain convinced that their particular agencies, facilitators and orphanages are not suspect. Adoption agencies appear even less capable of self-examination. I talked to a number of agency representatives who extolled their own virtues while happily smearing their competitors with off-the-record tales of underhanded behavior, particularly on the part of rival agencies' facilitators. "For my money, there's not an entirely reliable facilitator out there," Ambassador Kent Wiedemann says. "We don't trust any of them."

All this leaves adoptive parents in a particularly tough spot, often consumed by their wish for a child and left with spotty information not just about the people and process involved but also about the child they have chosen to adopt. Last spring, a woman named Dale Edmonds traveled to Phnom Penh to pick up two siblings — an 18-month-old boy and a 6-year-old girl — she was adopting using the services of an American facilitator named Harriet Brener-Sam. Once home, Edmonds, a native of New Zealand living in Singapore, learned enough Khmer to converse with her adopted daughter. Her daughter claimed to be 11 years old and not 6. She also said that she and her brother had been born with names different from those given to Edmonds and had been instructed not to discuss their history. More alarmingly, Edmonds says Brener-Sam told her that her children's birth mother was living in Phnom Penh. Edmonds returned with her children to Cambodia late in the fall and was able to locate their mother and another sister.

Edmonds will not discuss the birth mother's circumstances, saying it would violate her children's privacy, but she says that the birth family was repeatedly denied access to the children during their eight-month stay in an orphanage. The birth mother did not object to the siblings' move to Singapore, and Edmonds and her husband have now, at the mother's request, adopted her other daughter. What matters most, Edmonds says, is that her Cambodian-born children were stripped of their names and histories and essentially hidden from their birth family. "I wanted to think our adoption was ethical," she says. "It hurt bitterly to have those beliefs challenged." (Harriet Brener-Sam declined to comment on Edmonds's account.)

Other parents say they will wait for the I.N.S. to produce credible proof before accepting the U.S. government's allegations. "The only way I would ever return Isaac is if his birth mother came forward and could prove he was hers," said Dawn Smith, an Indiana mother who spent three months in Phnom Penh before being cleared to take her son home in May. She pointed out that since the United States suspended adoptions, Cambodian birth parents have not exactly lined up to reclaim their children. "Even if the government proves these children were trafficked," Smith said, "they're still going to sit in orphanages."

And life in a third-world orphanage can be demonstrably cruel. A Missouri couple who received an agency referral in September stood by from a distance of 12,000 miles as their 10-month-old adoptive daughter struggled with pneumonia. A boy destined for Ohio came down with malaria, and just before Christmas, an infant named Tia, who had been matched with a family in Florida since October, died at her Phnom Penh orphanage.

In the meantime, since the December shut-down, the I.N.S. has cleared 141 children for adoption. But it is proceeding with a criminal investigation that could involve charges against citizens of both Cambodia and the United States, though the agency will not discuss its progress. Strassberger, the I.N.S. spokesman, concedes that it is difficult to conclusively establish that a child has been trafficked, given the poor record-keeping and endemic corruption in Cambodia.

"We know that something is not right, but because we can't prove it in U.S. courts under the U.S. system of justice, we have no choice but to approve [an application] and allow the child to come in as an orphan," he says.

As a result, the United States plans to continue its moratorium on new adoptions until the Cambodian government passes legislation intended to eliminate child trafficking. Until it does, hundreds of legitimately parentless children will collect in orphanages around Cambodia, growing older without a family.

This thought keeps Christina Chronister up at night, despite the fact that Rachel's adoption was cleared by I.N.S. in late April. The family flew home immediately and was greeted by a group of friends at the airport in Seattle. But Christina still spends hours corresponding with fellow adoptive parents, many of whom continue to hope for I.N.S. approval. The children at the orphanage at the end of the dusty road, she says, live quietly at the back of her mind. There is Piseth, a chubby 3-year-old who tumbled around the toddler area. There is Chan Thol, a little girl not much older than Rachel, whose adoptive family waits in Missouri, and Saran, a sad-eyed 7-year-old boy who once he turns 8 will no longer be eligible for adoption under Cambodian law. Rachel herself will celebrate her first birthday with a big party at the end of this month, a happy baby surrounded by her American family in a comfortable suburb, the mysteries of her past remaining just that.

"The Packaged Soul?" from
The Hidden Persuaders
by Vance Packard (1914-1996)

*Truly here is the "custom-made" man of today —
ready to help build a new and greater era in the
annals of diesel engineering.*

—Diesel Power

The disturbing Orwellian configurations of the
world toward which the persuaders seem to be
nudging us — even if unwittingly — can be
seen most clearly in some of their bolder, more
imaginative efforts. . . .

In early 1956 a retired advertising man named
John G. Schneider (formerly with Fuller, Smith and
Ross, Kenyon and Eckhardt, and other ad agencies)
wrote a satirical novel called *The Golden Kazzo,*
which projected to the 1960 Presidential election
the trends in political merchandising that had
already become clear. By 1960 the ad men from
Madison Avenue had taken over completely.
Schneider explained this was the culmination
of the trend started in 1952 when ad men
entered the very top policy-making councils of
both parties, when "for the first time" candidates
became "merchandise," political campaigns became
"sales-promotion jobs," and the electorate was
a "market."

By 1960 the Presidency is just another product
to peddle through tried-and-true merchandising
strategies. Speeches are banned as too dull for
citizens accustomed to TV to take. (Even the
five-minute quickies of 1956 had become unen-
durable.) Instead the candidate is given a walk-on
or centerpiece type of treatment in "spectaculars"
carefully designed to drive home a big point.

(Remember the election-eve pageant of 1956 where "little people" reported to President Eisenhower on why they liked him?)

The 1960 contest, as projected by Schneider, boiled down to a gigantic struggle between two giant ad agencies, one called Reade and Bratton for the Republicans and one simply called B.S.& J. for the Democrats. When one of the two candidates, Henry Clay Adams, timidly suggests he ought to make a foreign-policy speech on the crisis in the atomic age his account executive Blade Reade gives him a real lecture. "Look," he said, "if you want to impress the longhairs, intellectuals, and Columbia students, do it on your own time, not on my TV time. Consider your market, man! . . . Your market is forty, fifty million slobs sitting at home catching your stuff on TV and radio. Are those slobs worried about the atomic age! Nuts. They're worried about next Friday's grocery bill." Several of the merchandising journals gave Mr. Schneider's book a careful review, and none that I saw expressed shock or pain at his implications.

So much for fictional projections into the future. Some of the real-life situations that are being heralded as trends are perhaps more astonishing or disconcerting, as you choose.

A vast development of homes going up at Miramar, Florida, is being called the world's most perfect community by its backers. *Tide,* the merchandisers' journal, admonished America's merchandisers to pay attention to this trail-blazing development as it might be "tomorrow's marketing target." The journal said of Miramar: "Its immediate success . . . has a particular signifi-cance for marketers, for the trend to 'packaged' homes in 'packaged' communities may indicate where and how tomorrow's consumer will live. . . ." Its founder, youthful Robert W. Gordon, advises me Miramar has become "a bustling little community" and is well on its way to offering a "completely integrated community" for four thousand families.

What does it mean to buy a "packaged" home in a "packaged" community? For many (but apparently not all) of the Miramar families it means they simply had to bring their suitcases, nothing more. No fuss with moving vans, or shopping for food, or waiting for your new neighbors to make friendly overtures. The homes are completely furnished, even down to linens, china, silver, and a refrigerator full of food. And you pay for it all, even the refrigerator full of food, on the installment plan.

Perhaps the most novel and portentous service available at Miramar — and all for the one packaged price — is that it may also package your social life for you. As Mr. Gordon put it: "Anyone can move into one of the homes with nothing but their personal possessions, and start living as a part of the community five minutes later." Where else could you be playing bridge with your new neighbors the same night you move in! In short, friendship is being merchandised along with real estate, all in one glossy package. *Tide* described this aspect of its town of tomorrow in these words: "To make Miramar as homey and congenial as possible, the builders have established what might be called 'regimented recreation.' As soon as a family moves in the lady of the house will get an invitation to join any number of activities ranging from bridge games to literary teas. Her husband will be introduced, by Miramar, to local groups interested in anything from fish breeding to water skiing."

In the trends toward other-mindedness, group living, and consumption-mindedness as spelled out by Dr. Riesman [in *The Lonely Crowd*], Miramar may represent something of an ultimate for modern man.

Another sort of projection, a projection of the trend toward the "social engineering" of our lives in industry, can be seen perhaps in a remarkable trade school in Los Angeles. It has been turning out students according to a blueprint and in effect certifies its graduates to be cooperative candidates for industry. This institution, National Schools, which is on South Figueroa Street, trains diesel mechanics, electricians, electrical technologists, machinists, auto repairmen and mechanics, radio and TV mechanics, etc. (Established 1905.)

I first came across this breeding ground for the man of tomorrow in an article admiringly titled "Custom-made Men" in *Diesel Power*. The article faced another on "lubrication elements" and appeared in the early days of the depth approach to personnel training. The diesel journal was plainly awed by the exciting potentialities of social engineering, and said that while miraculous advances had been made in the technical field, "one vital branch of engineering has been, until recently, woefully neglected — the science of human engineering." It went on to be explicit: "Human engineering, as we refer to it here, is the science of molding and adjusting the attitude of industrial personnel. By this process a worker's mechanical ability and know-how will be balanced by equal skill in the art of demonstrating a co-operative attitude toward his job, employer, and fellow employees."

The newest trend, it went on to explain, is to develop in the worker this co-operative outlook prior to his actual employment, while he is receiving his training, when "he is most receptive to this new approach." National Schools in Los Angeles, it said, has been a unique laboratory in developing many phases of human engineering. It followed the progress of the graduate as he went out into industry and checked not only on the technical skills he showed but on "his attitude toward his work and associates." These findings were compared with a transcript of his school work. By such analysis plus surveying employers on the traits they desire in employees, National Schools, it said, has been able "to develop the ideal blue print for determining the type of personnel industry needs." National students, it stated, were taught basic concepts of human behavior, and "special emphasis is placed on the clear-cut discussion and study of every subject that will tend to give the student a better under-standing of capital-labor co-operation. To this end . . . representative authorities in the diesel industry have been made associate faculty members at National Schools — where they lecture."Truly, it exulted, here was the "custom-made" man ready to help build a greater tomorrow for diesel engineering!

The kind of tomorrow we may be tending toward in the merchandising of products may be exemplified by the use of depth probing on little girls to discover their vulnerability to advertising messages. No one, literally no one, evidently is to be spared from the all-seeing, Big Brotherish eye of the motivational analyst if a merchandising opportunity seems to beckon. The case I am about to relate may seem extreme today — but will it tomorrow?

This case in point, involving a Chicago ad agency's depth probing on behalf of a leading home-permanent preparation, was proudly described by the agency's president in a speech to an advertising conference at the University of Michigan. He cited it in detail, with slides, to illustrate his theme: "How Motivation Studies May Be Used by Creative People to Improve Advertising."

The problem was how to break through women's resistance to giving home permanents to their little girls. Many felt the home permanent ought to wait until high-school age, "along with lipstick and dating." (Some mothers, I've found in my own probing, also suspect home permanents are bad for the hair of little girls and have some moral pangs about it.) At any rate, the agency found, by depth interviewing mothers, that they needed "reassurance" before most of them would feel easy about giving home permanents to their little ones. The agency set out, by depth probing little girls, to find a basis for offering such reassurance. It hoped to find that little girls actually "need" curly hair, and to that end devised a series of projective tests, which were presented to the little girls as "games." When the little girls were shown a carefully devised projective picture of a little girl at a window they reportedly read into the picture the fact that she was "lonely because her straight hair made her unattractive and unwanted." When they were given projective sentence-completion tests they allegedly equated pretty hair with being happy and straight hair with "bad, unloved things."

The agency president summed up the findings of the probing of both mothers (their own early childhood yearnings) and daughters by stating: "We could see, despite the mothers' superficial doubts about home permanents for children, the mothers had a very strong underlying wish for curly-haired little girls." (This is not too hard to believe in view of the fact that hair-preparation merchandisers have been hammering away to condition American females to the wavy-hair-makes-you-lovely themes for decades.)

A seven-and-a-half-pound volume of data detailing all the probings was turned over to the agency's "creative" people and a series of "creative workshops" was held with "a leading authority in the field of child psychology" conducting the discussions. This authority apparently needed to reassure some of the creative people themselves about the project because the authority stated: "Some of you may react, as many older women do, and say, 'How awful to give a child a permanent,' and never stop to think that what they are really saying is, 'How awful to make a girl attractive and make her have respect for herself.'"

The child psychologist analyzed each piece of copy, layout, and TV story board for its psychological validity to make sure it would "ring true to parents." One upshot of all this consulting was a TV commercial designed to help a mother subconsciously recognize "her child's questions, 'Will I be beautiful or ugly, loved or unloved?' because they are her own childhood wishes, too."

Another possible view of tomorrow may be seen in the search to find ways to make us less troublesome and complaining while staying in hospitals. Dr. Dichter undertook this exploration, and his findings were reported in detail in a series of articles in *The Modern Hospital*. The study was undertaken because of the constant complaints of patients about food, bills, routine, boredom, nurses. They were generally irritable, and hospitals that tried to remove the complaints by changing routines, diets, etc., seemed to get nowhere.

So the depth probing of patients began. One fifty-year-old woman recalled her shame at being chided by a hospital aide for calling out for her mother several times during the night. Probers found that patients in hospitals were often filled with infantile insecurities. They weren't just scared of dying but scared because they were helpless like a child. And they began acting like children. Dr. Dichter reported that his most significant finding "deals with the regression of the patient to a child's irrationality. . . . Over and over in each of the interviews, in one form or another, there echoed the basic cry, 'I'm frightened. . . .'" He said the grownup's regression to a child's helplessness and dependence and his search for symbolic assurance were clear. In searching for this symbolic assurance the patient begins seeing the doctor as father and the nurse as mother.

What should the hospitals do with all these adult-children? The answer was obvious. Treat them like children, apply to grownups the same techniques they had been applying in the children's wards to make the children feel loved and secure. For one thing there mustn't be any signs of dissension between doctor and nurse because it would remind the patients of their childhood fears when mother and father quarreled.

Eventually — say by A.D. 2000 — perhaps all this depth manipulation of the psychological variety will seem amusingly old-fashioned. By then perhaps the biophysicists will take over with "biocontrol," which is depth persuasion carried to its ultimate. Biocontrol is the new science of controlling mental processes, emotional reactions, and sense perceptions by bioelectrical signals.

The National Electronics Conference meeting in Chicago in 1956 heard electrical engineer Curtiss R. Schafer, of the Norden-Ketay Corporation, explore the startling possibilities of biocontrol. As he envisioned it, electronics could take over the control of unruly humans. This could save the indoctrinators and thought controllers a lot of fuss and bother. He made it sound relatively simple.

Planes, missiles, and machine tools already are guided by electronics, and the human brain — being essentially a digital computer — can be, too. Already, through biocontrol, scientists have changed people's sense of balance. And they have made animals with full bellies feel hunger, and made them feel fearful when they have nothing to fear. *Time* magazine quoted him as explaining:

The ultimate achievement of biocontrol may be the control of man himself. . . . The controlled subjects would never be permitted to think as individuals. A few months after birth, a surgeon would equip each child with a socket mounted under the scalp and electrodes reaching selected areas of brain tissue. . . . The child's sensory perceptions and muscular activity could be either modified or completely controlled by bioelectric signals radiating from state-controlled transmitters.

He added the reassuring thought that the electrodes "cause no discomfort."

I am sure that the psycho-persuaders of today would be appalled at the prospect of such indignity being committed on man. They are mostly decent, likable people, products of our relentlessly progressive era. Most of them want to control us just a little bit, in order to sell us some product we may find useful or disseminate with us a viewpoint that may be entirely worthy.

But when you are manipulating, where do you stop? Who is to fix the point at which manipulative attempts become socially undesirable?

Films of Related Interest

Alfie   Lewis Gilbert 1966
Promiscuity, corrupted relationships.

Artificial Intelligence: AI   Steven Spielberg 2001
Futuristic Pinocchio story of a robotic "mecha" boy who develops a
never-ending love for his human mother and longs for her affection
after she abandons him when her son, who was cryogenically
frozen, is cured of disease.

Blade Runner   Ridley Scott 1982
Science fiction tale of machine slaves escaping man's control.

Boys from Brazil   Franklin Schaffner 1978
Cloning boys for Nazi purposes.

Carnal Knowledge   Mike Nichols 1971
Promiscuity, shallow relationships.

Fear and Loathing in Las Vegas   Terry Gilliam 1998
Two individuals use drugs heavily as they search for a way to obtain
the American Dream.

Forbidden Planet   Fred M. Wilcox 1956
Starship crew investigates a futuristic planet once inhabited by an
advanced race. Psychological dynamics of the subconscious,
advance of technology, use of control to maintain stability, and
conflicting sexual emotions are explored.

The Great Santini   Lewis John Carlino 1979
Family relationships, lack of affection.

The Island   Michael Bay 2005
Human clones contained in a utopian society escape after revealing
a sinister plan and learn of their true existence – they are to be used
as replacement parts and organs for their original counterparts.

Logan's Run   Michael Anderson 1976
Futuristic society.

Minority Report   Steven Spielberg 2002
Submission of individualism and privacy to government in exchange
for safety, scientific advances resulting in brain mapping, bioethical
questions, hedonism and youth

Requiem for a Dream   Darren Aronofsky 2000
Four ambitious individuals' lives are shattered by addiction as they
use drugs to escape reality.

Sixth Day   Roger Spottiswoode 2000
Cloning, control of individual's life.

Soylent Green   Richard Fleischer 1973
Overpopulation, lack of food, corruption.

Total Recall   Paul Verhoeven 1990
Mind control, ability to alter reality.

V for Vendetta   James McTeigue 2005
Set in a futuristic totalitarian Great Britain, a masked vigilante uses
terrorist tactics to fight an oppressive government, and revolt against
tyranny.

Zardoz   John Boorman 1973
Castes of intellectuals, savages, killers keeping order.

Web Pages of Related Interest

http://www.poleshift.org/sublim
Subliminal advertising techniques with links to books, related websites about advertising, and subliminal suggestions to persuade consumers to buy a specific item or vote for a person

http://www.streetdrugs.org
Website with educational information for parents, teachers, students, law enforcement officers, health professionals, or anyone interested in learning about the dangers of illegal drugs; includes an alphabetical drug index, and other related topics and links

http://www.humancloning.org/
Homepage of the Human Cloning Foundation (HCF), an organization dedicated to the promotion of human cloning and other forms of biotechnology; includes essays on the benefits of cloning and various links as to why cloning should be practiced

http://www.cloninginformation.org/
Americans to Ban Cloning (ABC) coalition's website, which provides information on why human cloning could be a potential threat to mankind, leading to the commercialization of human life and control of human beings; includes links to the latest news on cloning, commentaries on issues surrounding cloning, and ways to contact Congress

http://www.genengnews.com
Website of on-line publication *Genetic Engineering News (GEN)*, first in the field of biotechnology to cover industrial biotechnology, biopharmaceutical, agricultural, chemical, enzyme, and environmental markets from applied research through commercialization; source for news on biotechnology, bioregulation, bioprocess, bioresearch and technology transfer; each issue includes BioProcess Tutorials, New Products, Wall Street Biobeat, Clinical Trials Update, Collaborations and Agreements, University Gene Beat, People, Calendar and Biotechnology on the World Wide Web; links to publishers in the field of biotechnology, conferences, industry news, biomolecular technologies, environmental monitoring and access control, laboratory equipment, bioinformatics software for genomic research and drug discovery

http://www.overpopulation.org/
Tracking of world population, significance, environmental impact, religious implications, lobbying women's issues, educational materials, teenage pregnancy, family planning to prevent abortion, overconsumption, migration and brain drain, urbanization, human impact, smart growth, economics, philosophies, aging populations, forum for opinions

Books of Related Interest

1984 George Orwell 1949
Grim future through mind control. Everbind# 524934

Beyond the Big Talk:
Every Parent's Guide to Raising Sexually Healthy Teens –
from Middle School to College Debra W. Haffner 2001
Peer pressure, dating and parties, alcohol and drugs,
sexual harassment, abstinence. Everbind# 045178

Beyond This Horizon Robert Heinlein 1981
Genetic engineering, utopia. Everbind# 435613

A Clockwork Orange Anthony Burgess 1965
Satire on the inhumanity of man, futuristic culture, aversion therapy,
brainwashing. Everbind# 312836

Erewhon Samuel Butler 1970
Demagoguery takes the place of common sense and reason,
a world through which Butler was satirizing organized religion,
sentimental notions of familial sanctity, and the complacency
of the Victorian middle class. Everbind# 430571

Fahrenheit 451 Ray Bradbury 1953
A dystopia where books are burned to control and maintain social
stability; censorship, totalitarian government, conformity, futurism.
Everbind# 342968

The House of the Scorpion Nancy Farmer 2002
Explores the moral and ethical aspects of cloning;
corrupt drug empire, greedy individuals. Everbind# 852231

Jurassic Park Michael Crichton 1990
Genetic engineering breakthrough leads to a method for recovering
and cloning dinosaur DNA. Technology advances quicker than
human knowledge. Everbind# 370775

The People's Tycoon:
Henry Ford and the American Century Steven Watts 2005
Explores the many facets of Henry Ford's life and personality,
his achievements and controversies. Everbind# 707225

Sex and Sensibility: The Thinking Parent's Guide to
Talking Sense About Sex Deborah M. Roffman 2000
Five core parenting skills: affirming children's emerging sexuality;
providing accurate sexual information; demonstrating the
connection between values and action; setting safe
and healthy limits; and providing constant
and effective anticipatory guidance. Everbind# 205206

Silent Spring Rachel Carson 1962
Warning of pesticides affecting birds
and future food supply. Everbind# 249060

The Wasteland and Other Poems T.S. Eliot 1922
Sterility of life, lack of meaningful relationships. Everbind# 526848

We Yevgeny Zamyatin 1993
The future inspired by actual totalitarian repression
in the Soviet Union. Everbind# 633132

When Bad Things
Happen to Good People Harold Kushner 1983
Power of faith to sustain oneself in hardship
and the grief of death. Everbind# 034728